Also by Jason Sheehan

Cooking Dirty: A Story of Life, Sex, Love and Death in the Kitchen

A PRIVATE LITTLE WAR

BY JASON SHEEHAN

47N⬤RTH

Published by 47North
P.O. Box 400818
Las Vegas, NV 89140

ISBN-10: 1611098947
ISBN-13: 9781611098945

LCCN: 2013936767

For my father, Mike Sheehan, who taught me to love stories and spaceships and the future, and my son, Maddox, for whom I hope to do the same someday.

A PRIVATE LITTLE WAR

ACTIVE DUTY ROSTER:

Priority to Chief of Ops, Chief of Comms,
All Sqdrn Commanders, Carpenter 7 Ep, TAG 14-447
Report Key: 100B4RC5-AA001-C7EP0365
Tracking Number: 14-447aaa
Attack Code: None
Originator Group: FBLE
Updated By Group: FALSE
SigAct: Disperse

NAME	POSIT
Acevedo, Simon P.	Flt. Mechanic
Anquiano, Edison M.	Chief Medical Off.
Ballinger, Patrice M.	Ordinance Spec.
Berthold, Louis H.	Airman
Bishop, Lori R.	Comms
Carter, Kevin H.	Captain, 2 Sqdrn
Czerwinska, Alicja	Flt. Nurse
Derosiers, Bryce L.	Engineer, Elec.
Diaz, Daniel C.	Airman
Forsyth, Noemi R.	Engineer, Comms
Galambos, Soma	Crew, Ground
Gottlieb, Roger R.	Crew Lead, Ground
Habib, Emanuel A.	Flt. Mechanic
Halstrom, William J.	Senior Airman
Hardman, Emile H.	Airman
Harper, Shun L.	Comms
Hawker, Jackson M.	Flt. Lt., 2 Sqdrn
Hill, Thomas J.	Airman
Jordaan, Deviser S.	Engineer, Flt.
Khoury, Stephen A.	Machinist
Komatsu, Miu L.	Lead Engineer
Lambert, Rudolph W.	Crew, Ground
Lucas, Eden H.	Corp. Comms Off.
Marsh, Chloe D.	Engineer, Flt.

McCudden, James L.	Comms
McElroy, William R.	Flt. Mechanic
McRae, Juan R.	Lead Machinist
Meleuire, Stavros F.	Crew, Ground
Moller, Eric A.	Lead Engineer
O'Day, Ernst R.	Airman
Pan, Sheng W.	Crew, Ground
Petty, Maxwell B.	Armorer
Prinzi, Theodore R.	Flt. Commander
Rice, David M.	Airman
Riviera, Raoul M.	Crew, Ground
Roberts, John C.	Quartermaster
Rockwell, Castor S.	Crew, Ground
Ross, Morris V.	Airman
Serdikov, Victoria G.	Lead Mechanic
Solvay, Mikke B.	Comms
Stork, George R.	Airman
Tanner, Yoshi P.	Comms
Teague, Fennimore A.	Captain, 3 Sqdrn
Vaughn, Porter M.	Flt. Lt., 1 Sqdrn
Voss, Charles A.	Flt. Lt., 3 Sqdrn
Williams, John S.	Flt. Nurse
Willis, Diane R.	Lead Comms
Wolfe, Albert X.	Airman

NOTE: *Engineer team (Derosiers, Forsyth, Jordaan, Khoury, Komatsu, Marsh, McRae, Moller) will* **ExFil** *at 90/365 Zulu, via Cavalier (orders incl.). Material support is Request-As-Needed via Cavalier until 90/365. Contract termination at 365/365 Zulu unless otherwise ordered.* **Mission ExFil** *at 365/365 via available transport (orders TK).*

PART 1
THESE ARE THE GOOD TIMES

"When I was a young man, I carried my pack

And I lived the free life of a rover.

From the Murray's green basin to the dusty outback,

I waltzed my matilda all over.

Then in 1915, my country said, 'Son,

It's time to stop rambling 'cuz there's work to be done.'

So they gave me a tin hat and they gave me a gun

And they sent me away to the war."

"And the Band Played Waltzing Matilda," Eric Bogle, 1972

IT WAS A BAD TIME. Everything was cold and sometimes everything was wet. When the wet and cold came together, everything would freeze and tent canvas would become like boards and breath would fog the air, laddering upward from mouths like curses given corporeal form. The ammunition, if not carefully kept, would green and foul and jam up the guns so that the men started stealing hammers from the machine shop, passing them around hand to hand until, one day, there were no more hammers in the machine shop and Ted had to order everyone to give them back.

"All of them," he said. "Now."

And so the men came up with the hammers—from their flight bags, from their pockets, or tucked beneath the seats of their machines. Every other man or so had stolen a hammer, and every other man or so gave his hammer back.

Kevin Carter did not give his hammer back. He stood with the other men as half slunk away to fetch back the hammers that they'd used to bang the shit out of their guns' breeches when the shitty, greened ammo fouled their smooth operation. He stared after those who had to walk the flight line looking for their machines and watched those who rummaged through their kits for the tools, and when Ted looked him in the eyes, Kevin folded his arms across his chest and met Ted's gaze with guiltless, frozen calm.

Of course he'd stolen a hammer. He'd been one of the first. But he'd be damned if he was going to give it back just because Ted had *asked*. Besides, it was in his machine in the longhouse and, at the moment, it'd seemed like a long way to walk.

Danny Diaz was dead. Mikke Solvay had drank himself useless and been sent home. Rog Gottlieb had gotten sick and was extracted in a coma that was next door to death. John Williams had been crippled with both legs shattered below the knee. None of the trip alarms worked. They were electronic—tiny little screamers, no bigger than a baby's fist—and the cold and the wet fucked with their internal whatevers so that they failed as fast as they were deployed to the perimeters of the field. Also, they were all supposed to be connected together by lengths of hair-fine wire, but the indigs—the friendly indigs—knew about the wire and so stole every yard of it the minute it was laid. No one could figure what they did with it, but that didn't stop them from stealing it. No one could figure what they did with dead batteries either, or buttons clipped off uniforms or shell casings, but they stole those, too.

The contact fuses in the bombs corroded. The cords that held the tents up would grow a white fur that looked like frost but wasn't. Shortly after, they'd snap, and a tent would come down or sag like a drunk punched in the stomach and, for ten minutes or an hour, the men would all have something to laugh about. Especially if it happened in the middle of the night or in the rain. And even though no one was dying (or anyway, no one who mattered), it was a bad time for the war. Everyone thought so. And it made a lot of the men sick just thinking about it. They were fighting the weather as much as they were fighting the enemy and, slowly, they were losing. They all knew that something was going to have to change, and soon. There was just that kind of feeling in the air.

| | | | | | | | | | | |

Two nights ago, the company had gotten word that Connelly's 4th had moved into position across the river. They'd been turned back at the bridge, again near Riverbend, but had finally made their crossing at a heretofore undiscovered ford two miles downriver and were digging in by dawn. They were exhausted, but nearly at full strength due, in large part, to the overwhelming cowardice of Connelly himself. He was afraid of the dark, was the word. Doubly afraid of fighting in it. Triply afraid of dying in it. It was rumored that the downriver ford was found accidentally by some of his pikemen who'd stumbled onto it while retreating.

It was dark so, obviously, the company's planes couldn't fly.

| | | | | | | | | | | | |

The next night, Durba's riflemen were put in place to secure the ford. On paper, they were the First Indigenous Rifle Company—the First IRC, attached as the fifth company, supernumerary to Connelly's four-company native battalion of foot-sloggers and local militia—but called themselves just Durba's Rifles or, sometimes, the Left Hand of God, because Antoinne Durba (who'd claimed on many raving, red-faced occasions as a drunken guest at the Flyboy encampment, to once have been a missionary before finding another calling more suited to his disposition) was a man of vociferous, if rather selective, Christian faith. He seemed only to like those bits of scripture where God, in his infinite wisdom, was smiting something or someone, and had a disturbing tendency to insert his own name into these verses in place of the Almighty, referring to himself always in the third person—Durba smasheth this, Durba fucketh that all up and back again.

As a stand-in for the Lord Jesus was Durba's only daughter, Marie, who'd once been his first sergeant and second-in-command. What made this proxy arrangement disconcerting (even more so than Durba's own self-promotion within the spiritual hierarchy) was the fact that Marie had been killed more than six months ago—pierced through by a cavalryman's lance on the Sispetain moors during a disastrous attempt by Connelly's indigs to hold the last of the region's high ground against an onslaught by overwhelming numbers of someone else's. Marie'd been in the dirt now for some time, but that never stopped Durba from speaking of her as though she'd just gone 'round the other side of some tree for a piss. It got to a point where it began to bother some of the pilots and, one night, Carter asked him if he, Durba, still thought Marie sang the Lord's praises so prettily with half a foot of native hardwood through her lungs.

"All souls live eternally in the light of God's righteous fury," said Durba.

"That count for the monkeys, too?" Carter asked.

"The natives here are abominations in his eyes," said Durba. "Heathens who worship trees and clouds."

"Well, if Marie loved Jesus and is dead and the monkeys pray to sticks and dirt but are still alive, whose fucking god does the math say is winning?"

At that point, the theological discussion devolved into punching, and the two of them had to be pulled apart and hustled out opposite doors. It was Fennimore Teague, Carter's friend, who'd dragged him outside, shoved him backward, and held him off with one hand flat on Carter's chest while Carter spit part of a broken tooth into the dirt.

"Baby, that was somewhat less than hospitable," Fenn said, smiling while watching Carter close. "What do we say? No talking about politics, sex, or religion at the dinner table."

Carter said that Durba had started it. That all he'd done was ask a question. That everyone was just as tired of hearing about Durba's dead cunt of a daughter as he was and that no amount of *talking* was going to bring her back.

"Talking is what the man has left, Kev," Fenn said. "To keep her close. Though I grant you, at this point, odds on her resurrection are running very long indeed."

They laughed. What else was there to do? Everyone knew Durba was too sensitive. Eventually, Carter apologized and showed Durba the tooth he'd broken and showed him how he could spit whiskey through the hole like a sniper. The war went on and on.

Durba took position across the ford without firing a shot, though it was again rumored that Connelly, in a panic, had nearly ordered his 4th company to retreat once more when he'd heard the riflemen moving up in the night behind him.

The men—the pilots—laughed about this. "Connelly . . . ," said Tommy Hill. "Fought every battle he ever saw walking backward." They shook their heads, rattled their drinks, and said Connelly's name over and over again the way one might speak of a younger brother or favorite pet, forever mixed up in something complicated beyond their years or wit.

"Connelly . . . Going to outlive us all."

"Connelly . . . Fucking Connelly."

"Connelly . . . ," said Albert Wolfe. "That man is going to chickenshit himself right through this war. Afraid of the dark. Whoever heard of such a thing?"

Again, it was dark, so the planes couldn't fly.

2

WHEN TED PRINZI SLEPT, HE DREAMED OF SLEEPING. Of clean white sheets and clean white spaces. Of cool plastic curves, aquiline cambers that existed nowhere in nature, and the competence of institutional design. He dreamed of a space among a thousand spaces. A million. More. And of a deprivation of the senses as pure as summer sunlight filtered through a sheet.

It wasn't a lot, but it was his: Ted Prinzi's clean and aired-out place. Dry, warm, bright, and completely artificial. Manufactured. In the moments before sleep would come to him—if he was having difficulty letting it overtake him—he would imagine this room. Furnish it. Add small fillips of detail, shave down a curve here, soften the glow of a hidden light there. It was no place that he knew, but it was close to several. A station berth he'd kept for some time once. Acceleration stasis aboard the *Swift*. Any one of a half-dozen hospital rooms, each as sterile and generic as a uniform.

He dreamed of nothing but interstices: The moment of slipping, for the first time, between those stiff, cool, white sheets, toenails hissing against the cloth. The moment of waking to a white purity of artificial light and artificial heat and artificial air, all so perfect and formless and affectless that it was itself like a kind of blind, deaf and brainless dispossession of the senses. Nothing ever happened in his dreams. Nothing ever had to. It was enough to be warm and clean and bathed in light, to reach out and touch a soft, plastic curve and know that it had never been any natural or dirt-bound thing.

Ted was sleeping when Diane came for him. Asleep and dreaming of cool whiteness in his tent that smelled of must and mold and smoke, under canvas the color of rot, of sickness, on his straight iron cot that squeaked when he moved, beneath piles of blankets that scratched like steel wool and stank of sweat, skin, hair, breath, feet and him.

She must've knocked on the wood frame of the door, but Ted hadn't heard her. She must've called his name. She was polite like that, if politeness was the right word.

When Ted swam up out of whiteness, she was standing over him, reaching out a hand that she drew back quickly when she saw his eyes pop open, terror-bright. She pulled the hand back and held it pressed between her small, boyish breasts, cupped by her other hand as if Ted had bitten her.

"Call for you," she said.

"What?"

"Call."

Ted was wearing his jumpsuit. Two pairs of socks. He dug his hands into a pocket of warmth beneath the curve of his back and closed his eyes again. He could hear voices outside, the buzz of engines. It was day, barely, and still the cold chewed at his face, smelling vaguely of ammonia.

"Ted."

"Don't, Diane," Ted said. He thought that maybe he could recapture the dream if he tried. He could feel the wisps of it still trailing through his mind.

"The call . . ."

"Get Eddie. Take it yourself. I don't care."

"It's the company."

Ted coughed. He squeezed his eyes tighter shut, until whiteness exploded behind his lids, willing himself to sleep, ordering himself to dream. "Who else would it be?"

"No, I mean the *company* company. Direct from the offices."

Ted opened his eyes. The engine sounds were cycling, getting louder and softer. There was shouting.

"Personal for you," she said.

"Get out."

"But—"

"Go. I'll be there in one minute."

It took him less. As soon as Diane left, Ted hurled himself out of bed and to his feet, splashed icy water on his face from a pan that was capped with a thin skin of ice that he'd had to crack with a fist. He pulled on a clean uniform shirt, pants that he pressed carefully every night between gun cases, his boots and belt and sidearm. He scratched furiously at his scalp, took three seconds to clear his lungs (hands balled into fists, knuckles digging into his knees as he bent double), then squared himself behind the closed door of his tent before charging out into the graying dawn like a man who knew what was going on.

|| | | | | | | | | | |

The smell of fuel was thick, like breathing soup, and the air felt wet and greasy against his skin. The sky was old iron, socked in with close-hung clouds that seemed near enough to touch, to comb through with his fingers like an ashen pudding. A sodden ceiling forever crashing in toward the earth.

The atmosphere here was strange. The light, diffuse and irrational; making dawns the color of a bruise, of sickness, of toothaches or misery. Ted had seen men cowering beneath it, crouched under a gangrene sky and looking out as though haunted. Possessed by a cold, unquantifiable fear that something was just wrong and getting wronger by the hour, here in this place where even the light was cruel.

Ted coughed again, stamping out across the dirt in the direction of the comms tent, and saw a mess of activity out by the longhouse across the stubble field—men and machines in a tumult. The mess and chaos of a war that, sometimes, refused to be fought by anyone.

Ted had been on Carpenter 7 Epsilon for two years. Ted, his men, his machines, the tents, Diane, the FTL relay, all of it. Two years spent trying to complete a mission that should've taken a week or a month. A year on the outside.

Carpenter 7 Epsilon (known locally as Iaxo) was a footnote. The mission was a double-hush, back-burner project long-tailed into the Flyboy Inc. corporate Annual Operations Plan for eight quarters running but sick now with blown deadlines and cost overruns. Ted had been there when it was new—a fresh idea so ripe that his bosses had been wiping drool off their chins when they'd discovered it. So exciting that they couldn't stand up too fast without snapping their dicks off at the root. In two years, there'd been successes, but not enough of them. There'd been too many mystifying failures.

And now it'd gone sour and Ted had been waiting for this call for most of a year—a hint from a friend, a former compatriot, from someone in the organization who'd been told to carefully, quietly, *gently* warn Ted Prinzi that bad news was coming fast and that he'd be wise to prepare for it. Nothing official, of course. Just a nod in the direction of calamity, which was the way things were done in the back channels of the company he'd spent most of his life working for.

Inside the comms tent it was warm—proscribed machinery bleeding heat as a consequence of information. Diane was guarding the FTL relay with crossed arms and a set jaw that radiated menace. The other controllers ignored her with a fixity that was reflexive. She was at the end of another night shift and wasn't ever a terribly pleasant woman at the beginning of one.

Ted made for the relay. When Diane didn't move aside quite quickly enough, Ted pushed her without really thinking about it. Not roughly, but still. When he moved to sit down, Diane felt the place where Ted's palm had cupped her shoulder, trailing her fingertips across it as though hunting for the dissipating warmth of his touch.

Ted didn't notice that either. He had eyes only for the technology. The screens were all live, but there was no picture, no telepresence. A zillion dollars in technology, and they were using it like two tin cans and a string hundreds of light-years long. He sat, put the phones on his head, coughed into his fist, and closed his eyes.

"This is Op Chief, Carpenter 7 Epsilon, TAG 14-447 actual. Go ahead."

|||||||||||||

He'd guessed the call would come from Garros, deputy chief of external ops, based out of London, Earth—the ancestral Flyboy headquarters. Ted knew Garros a little and thought that the courtesy would not be completely unusual coming from his mouth. In the dark, he'd imagined the conversation a hundred different ways.

Or maybe it would be Jackson Chaudhary, the assistant deputy. That would be insulting, but not devastatingly so. Ted had decided long ago not to let it show in his voice if it was Chaudhary who made the call; that a courtesy was a courtesy even if it was delivered in a discourteous fashion. He would act the professional, bite his tongue, and remember to call Chaudhary sir no matter how much it pained him.

Tallis Marks, who managed operational security, would be bad, as would anyone in his department. If the call came from the security department, it would be a flag—a warning that meant arrests were imminent, or worse—and it would be expected that he would know that. To act appropriately no matter how deep the blood got.

Slava, Oliver, Victor Wes, that fat fuck Apostol who'd breadcrumbed his way into the CFO's seat after Hinrik's third stroke. It could be any of them. Loewenhardt, even, though that was probably expecting too much. Better that it wasn't Loewenhardt, but Ted knew that so long as the call—the warning call, the one to inform him personally that the *official* bad news would be coming at some later date—came from someone above the line and inside the London headquarters, someone of management level or above, assistant to a deputy or higher, everything would be okay. It would be bad, but not, so to speak, fatally so. He'd won wars for his company. Bled for them. He'd spent so long in Indian country that he'd grown feathers—which was something he said now about himself because it was something that Garros had said to him once, years ago, when introducing him to a prospective client. *Prinzi, come here. Gavril, this is Ted Prinzi, one of our battle captains. Where are you just in from, Ted? Doesn't matter. Gavril, this man has spent so long in Indian country he's growing feathers. I can't even keep track of the fights he's won . . .*

"Commander Prinzi?" said the disembodied voice on the other end of the relay. Ted didn't recognize it. He mentally checked Garros off the list. Chaudhary. Marks. Loewenhardt, of course. Also Slava, Oliver, Wes and Apostol, Ballard, Coley, Ma, Archer. Ted ran down the Flyboy org chart in his head. He racked his brain to come up with another name. Someone else. Someone who'd maybe been promoted since he'd left. Someone new.

"Who is this?" Ted asked.

| | | | | | | | | | | |

Diane watched as Ted seemed to receive an invisible punch in the chest. He folded, put the points of his elbows on the table in front of him, and sunk his head down until he was gripping the back of his own neck with strong hands. She could see the rise and fall of his shoulders as he breathed. Panic breaths. Sharp and shallow like silent laughter. She could hear only one side of the conversation, but she was worried that she'd woken him for no good reason even though she had orders to fetch him for any call originating from the home office, at any hour. Standing orders, given to her almost a year ago and refreshed with maddening frequency anytime it crossed Ted's mind to do so.

Ted said, "You're a clerk in the accounting department . . . "

Ted said, "Oh, I'm sorry. *Assistant* clerk. How long you been working for the company, son?"

Ted said, "Two weeks?"

Ted said, "That must be really exciting for you . . . "

Ted said, "I'm ready. What's the message?"

Diane figured she was going to be yelled at. This was obviously just some bit of paperwork or some small detail that plainly didn't rise to the level of involving the commander. *Stupid,* she said to herself and bit down on the inside of her cheek until the pain became sharp and clarifying. *Stupid, stupid, stupid.*

But when Ted disconnected a few seconds later, he said nothing. He stood, straightened his uniform, looked briefly around the room, then turned and strode purposefully toward the door without saying a word. When he walked out, a blast of cold air whipped in and, briefly, Diane luxuriated in it, feeling like she'd dodged a bullet that had come almost close enough for her to hear.

IN THE MORNING, word had come down that they would fly in the early afternoon.

"Reconnaissance, they reckon," Charlie'd said, and that was his idea of a joke. The pilots laughed because there was nothing else worth laughing at. The coffee was terrible and most of them were still hungover from the night before. Then Charlie threw up in the dirt next to the officers' table in the mess tent they'd pitched two years ago and called the Flyboy O Club, and everyone laughed at that, too.

They pulled the planes out, the pilots pitching in to help drag them into position, and they argued over who was going where and what plane needed what and when. The morning light, the false dawn, was strange and silvery and got into everyone's heads, making tempers short and sharp. Charlie Voss and Lefty Berthold got into it outside the big sliding doors of the longhouse and almost went after each other, but a couple of the mechanics pulled them apart at the last minute.

Kevin Carter, captain of two squadron, was sitting on the lower wing of his biplane, forearms resting on his knees while he hummed some snatch of nonsense to himself. Fennimore Teague, captain of number three, stood near him, leaning back against the stiff, doped skin of the fuselage, watching the excitement with a careful eye. Charlie was in his squadron, Lefty in Carter's. Neither man could be spared if one or the other got in a lucky punch.

"Lefty's a prick; you know that," Fenn said.

Carter looked up and watched the two men shoving each other—their faces twisted in sudden rage over nothing. He couldn't hear what they were shouting at each other over the burr and cough of engines starting up, choking out, burning through idle fuel, but he knew that it didn't matter. There was nothing of consequence anywhere on this planet; therefore the argument couldn't be about anything of substance. About air. About breath. About blood. Plenty to go around.

"Your Charlie is no better," Carter said.

"He is, though," Fenn replied. "Much."

Carter considered that a moment. "Yeah, you're right," he conceded. "He is. But I think Lefty could take him."

"Really?"

"Really."

"What can you bet?"

Carter thought for a second. "Whole jar of peanut butter. What do you got?"

"My virgin sister's cherry."

Somewhere an engine caught and coughed to life. Carter sniffed. "Those are high stakes."

"Not when I know I'm going to win."

Carter watched Charlie Voss take a wild swing at Lefty and miss by a country mile. Both men were being held back now by three or four other men, and neither of them seemed to be trying too hard to break free. "If I'm not mistaken, I believe you said your sister was forty and had two kids."

"Yup. And you don't have any whole jar of peanut butter."

"You've also said you didn't have a sister."

"And I don't much like peanut butter anyway."

Carter chuckled and eased himself to his feet. He was in all his gear. Had slept in most of it like the filthy, careless barbarian that he half wanted to be. They watched as the scrap broke up of its own heat—the offended parties spinning off across the cold field like atoms being split—and then Fenn looked away. When he saw Ted come banging out of the comms tent with his eyes fixed on some distant horizon, making straight for the evacuated tent line, Fenn tracked him with squinted eyes, like he was watching an enemy coming down high out of the sun.

"That's bad news walking, right there," Fenn said.

Carter glanced in Ted's direction, then stretched. His back was killing him and, as far as he knew, Ted Prinzi was never anything but bad news—sometimes walking, sometimes not. He just wanted to get up in the air and kill something.

Time passed. By afternoon, a damp fog had settled in the lowlands and rain was expected—so, obviously, the planes couldn't fly.

| | | | | | | | | | | | |

The rain held off. Ugly gray-black clouds massed in wet clots on the horizon but then hung there as if dithering about approaching any closer to the pilots' obvious magnificence. To pass the time, they played indig baseball—a game that'd been invented by one of the men (no one remembered who) and involved more than the usual number of bats and balls, more than the usual amount of punching the opposing team.

The pilots played on one side. The other was made up of a dozen or so of the camp followers—big, hairy, slumping indigs who'd been pulled off whatever odd jobs they were doing and drafted into playing whether they wanted to or not. They cringed a lot, muffed bare-handed catches of the men's line drives, looked wide-eyed and terrified every time one of the pilots went streaking out into the bush to tackle one of them. They clapped their hands and bowed whenever the pilots laughed at them for their ineptitude at a game they didn't understand and were being forced to play by men they understood even less.

Being neighborly, the pilots would always help the indigs back to their feet, give them a couple of hard punches in the arm or chest that appeared (maybe) brotherly because the hitting was always attended by a flinty smile. Then there would be more clapping, more bowing, some amount of the indig language that none of the men understood but imagined to mean *Good play!* or *Wasn't that fun?* even if it was far more likely that it meant something closer to *Why are you doing this?* or *Please don't hit me again.*

At one point, Jack Hawker, who was pitching for both sides, laid a nice, fat, slow ball across the plate for George Stork, who hit it like it had said something nasty about his mother. The ball climbed into the smothering sky, zipping along as pretty as anything, and seemed destined for home-run distance.

But then it suddenly faltered as though it'd hit thick air, seemed to hang a moment, and fell short of the distant tree line. One of the indigs went scrambling for it, put a hand on it, and loped into the base path between second and third, meaning to tag Stork out. But Stork was already running and he didn't slow—just lowered his shoulder and plowed straight into the monkey like a truck. Both of them went down in the pounded dirt. Both of them got up again and even from the sidelines, the company men could hear the indig shouting. They could see it waving its arms around. Stork waved his arms, too. The indig hissed at him and bared sharp teeth. Stork calmly reached down, drew his sidearm, and shot the indig through the face.

"Well, shit," said Carter, who'd gone out to join Jack on the mound. "Guess that's game then."

"Trouble with your indig," said Jack Hawker, Carter's squadron leader from number two, in his languid, roughneck accent, "is that he don't understand basic sportsmanship."

"Trouble with the indigs," countered Stork as he walked back toward home plate, brushing dirt and grass from his pants and smudging a bit of blood from his knuckles, "is that they don't understand baseball."

| | | | | | | | | | | | |

They went up in the late afternoon. The fog had burned off, the rain never materialized, and the men were bored, so they rolled their planes out of the longhouse again, splashed some fuel into them, and went out hunting. Sightseeing, they called it. Reconnaissance in force. Carter took two squadron out into badland, and they managed to maintain formation until they crossed the twisting snake of the river that was just called the River because there was no need to name it anything else.

After that, each plane just sort of wandered off on its own, spinning and looping and buzzing the tops of the alien trees because there was nothing else to do.

On the radio, David Rice was telling a long and convoluted story about his last deployment as a naval aviator, on garrison duty, flying off one of the big colonial carriers.

"It was orbit work," he was saying. "BMF Ashland, over Balantyne. You ever been on one of the big boats, you know it's dull as fuck, right?"

Carter had done some carrier duty, though not as a naval. BMF, that stood for *Big Motherfucker*. Capital-plus. Command element for an entire battle group. A ship that'd been assembled in orbit and would never, ever know gravity.

"Right, Davey," he said. "Dull as fuck. Roger that."

"So we fly ten hours, down for twenty. And down for twenty, that's rough, right? Nothing to do. Like liberty every day, but it gets dull."

"As fuck," said Carter.

"Right . . ."

Davey had a friend who was a bad garrison soldier. Always in trouble. Threatening MPs, getting in fights, whatever. Spent more time under restraint than in his fighter.

"So his big thing was making rain, right? He'd get into the hangar bay, up in the lift gantries, and he'd bring, like, five gallons of water with him. Drink the water while he was up there. Just drink and drink. And then he'd spend hours pissing down on the MP posts from, what? Three hundred feet up or whatever. But the thing is, with the drive thrust, corriolis, the weird gravity, he'd have to know how to aim it just right—standing up there on the cats with his dick in his hand and—"

"Got one!"

The call-in from Jack Hawker on the all-hands channel interrupted Davey's story.

"Two squadron flight, I have a target."

"The hell you do," said Carter. "Illuminate and hold for confirm."

Carter strained against the belts, trying to look everywhere at once because, really, he hadn't been keeping close track of where his planes were. He hung an arm out over the cockpit rail and banged a gloved hand on the biplane's skin in annoyance.

After a few seconds he saw the bright point of white light from a hand-fired magnesium signal flare and knew where Jack was, so he tuned his radio to the flight address channel and called everyone in.

"Two squadron, rally on that flare."

Come to find, Jack really had spotted something: an armed indig supply column moving in the shade, foot-slogging along the edge of a stand of fat, bushy trees way off in the middle of Indian country. Carter dutifully called it in. At altitude, it was impossible to tell whose indigs they were. Could've been friendly, supplies coming in for Connelly or Durba, scouts, outriders, anything. Could've been decidedly unfriendly, too. They all looked the same, even up close, but there were maps, supposedly. Schedules. The controllers sometimes knew right from left.

The call came in from comms: "No friendlies reported. Guns are free."

Carter addressed the squadron: "Tallyho, motherfuckers. Get some."

And they did, swarming around the area and then dropping like stones from the sky on short strafing runs, hitting the line from both ends with machine guns like museum-grade antiques so the monkeys wouldn't know which way to run, making them dance.

When the indigs on the ground finally got their shit together, they abandoned their carts and their packs and whatever else they'd been hauling and hustled back into the trees, so Carter ordered those pilots so equipped to switch to cannons. They shredded the trees for a while— splitting the stumpy trunks like balsa and blowing the ever-loving shit out of the flora. And when that had less of an effect than he'd hoped, he ordered the squadron to switch to incendiary ammunition in hopes of lighting the stand of trees on fire and smoking the little fuckers out into the open.

The planes flew around for a time crazily, like gnats disturbed in the fading sun, while the pilots strained to pop the covers on their guns, unbreech their belts of standard AP, dig out the red-tip ammo from boxes secured by shock cords and stashed under or behind seats, then reload with control sticks pinned between their knees and their wings waggling like a bunch of spastics.

Somewhere to their west, three squadron was chasing heffalumps— the native equivalent of a water buffalo, but about the size of an elephant and with glossy black skin like oil floating on water. It would sometimes take an entire belt of ammo to bring one down, screaming and kicking up the earth. And even in the cold they rotted and stank. First squadron had taken up a blocking position near the water, hoping for stragglers panicked by all the fire and flying, but they were unlucky and went home early, blue-balled and angrier and more bored than they'd been before climbing into their planes.

Down on the ground, the indigs had come to the edge of the trees again to see what was happening. They'd formed a line, and when the planes started to dive again, they loosed flights of arrows and stones.

Slings and arrows, Carter thought. *Actual slings and fucking arrows . . .* It never ceased to amaze him how persistent the dumb monkeys could be. How stupidly brave and tenacious like the clap.

In any event, firing on the planes made them bad indigs (no matter what they'd been before Carter's squadron had opened up on them, they were bad *now*), so in recognition of their foolhardy monkey courage and dedication to this dumb game of war, two squadron dove and dove and killed every single one of them.

When it got too dark to play, the pilots came home and retired themselves to the field house or mess where, by lantern light, they commenced (or continued) drinking, watched movies that they'd all seen a hundred times, played cards. The camp was under radiation blackout—part of the terms of operating in this place—so there were no soft calls home to sweethearts with weeping, declarations of love, or apology for terrors committed, witnessed, or cheered; no mail, no news, no stealing of entertainment from the distant ether. Iaxo was a war without cliché, it sometimes seemed to them, and it annoyed everyone to no end.

For a time, Captain Carter chose to linger among the boys, playing a few hands of poker in the mess with cards gone soft from passing through so many fingers. At one point, he saw Vic and Willy McElroy come in, laughing over some private joke. Vic was the mission's chief mechanic on Iaxo. Willy was one of the ground crew who did double duty on the lathe and stamping press when he wasn't walking planes around.

They'd been in the machine shop together, were blacked to the elbows and smudged about the face with engine oil and grease. Carter looked and Vic was there, standing in her rumpled jumpsuit and tattered leathers, smiling, eyes the color of new leaves, black hair tied back and spilling over her collar. He looked again and she was gone, having ducked out a different door, her brief passage leaving a burn on Carter's retinas like his gaze passing across the hot light of a distant sun. Willy, too, stood confused as if wondering where she'd gone. Shrugging, he went to scrub up. Carter stood and made for his tent, consciously choosing a different door than Vic.

"Fastest disengage I've seen in a year," he heard someone behind him say as he stepped out, then a cloudburst of laughter.

THE NIGHT PASSED AND THEN IT WAS DAY. Carter was off the roster, so he slept mostly, woke, flipped through an electronic copy of Rickenbacker's book. He was looking for the good parts, the killing parts, as he thumbed through the page tabs out of habit, eyes gliding across the words like grease until there were no more and then switching to a manual on air-to-ground combat maneuvers, nicely illustrated. He told himself that he wasn't going to get out of his bed all day, but then he did because there was no reason to stay in it. Less reason to get up, but he was bored and, somewhere, he smelled the greasy smell of hot food cooking. Meat.

It wasn't food. The camp indigs were seeing to the mortal remains of the one that Stork had killed. They were burning him in some ooga-booga ceremony up on a hill, and the smell blowing down across the field was like hot fat and barbecue, which immediately made Carter lose his appetite. He went looking for a drink instead, and found one. Then another. Planes went up and planes came down. He saw Fenn moving between the flight line and the tents, walking like his gear weighed a wet ton, but only because he thought no one was looking. The camp indigs rattled around the rutted paths between tents in ones and twos, not seeming to be doing anything useful, not talking, just shuffling across the land like hairy ghosts, stinking like wet carpets and touching tent pegs, marking posts and the metal of generator bodies with their twitching fingers. Everything was sodden and cold, and Carter felt like he was rotting from the outside in.

|||||||||||||

Ted spent the day down on the flight line making a nuisance of himself— tapping the fuel tanks and counting bullets and bombs and guns and trigger fingers. He asked for maintenance reports, then refused to read them—slapping the folded sheafs of hard copy against his leg and walking around each plane individually, running his fingers over joints and plucking at stays like guitar strings, opening engine compartments, and looking for signs of wear that he wouldn't have recognized had they been labeled. When he was done, Vic, Willy McElroy, and Manny had to go over everything again just to make sure Ted hadn't fucked anything up with his fussing.

In the back rooms of the mess, Ted counted the scant supplies remaining while Johnny Roberts, the quartermaster, cook, and part-time mechanic who everyone called Johnny All-Around, watched over his shoulder and tried not to act nervous. Ted scratched down numbers on a fold of paper he kept pulling out of his pocket and then putting back in. He counted beans and he counted bags of egg powder. He sniffed at the purified water tanks. He counted rolls of shit-paper. Nothing seemed to please him. It'd been a long time since they'd last been resupplied, and they were short on just about everything, which, if nothing else, made the counting go quicker.

Around lunchtime, Ted drank instant coffee in the mess and no one came to his table to join him. Something in him burned, slow and smoky, and the smell was enough to make people change their path when they got close to him. For amusement, Ted counted tent poles and panels of canvas. He counted mugs and plates and silverware. The silverware reminded him of the hammers, and he made a note on his piece of paper to go back and count the hammers again—to see if any were still missing.

Mostly, Ted counted time: days and hours; minutes like pebbles held in the palm; seconds like grains of sand. The call he'd gotten was eating at him. He'd tried to place a couple more of his own in the time since—quietly, in the slack hours, pretending that the maddening lack of connection was precisely what he'd expected, for the benefit of anyone who might be taking notice. The calls were like smoke signals in the night. Either the other Indians were all looking in the wrong direction, or they were willfully ignoring him. Privately, he suspected that it was the latter. Was almost sure of it.

After lunch, he stepped outside. The abos were up on Signal Hill—the only rise of land in the area, a pimple on an otherwise flat plain—and they were burning something. They stood clustered in a tight circle around the fire and when Ted squinted, he thought he could see them swaying together.

"Kumbay-fucking-ya," he said out loud. He'd heard that George Stork had shot one of the friendlies in an argument and figured that this was the logical conclusion of that probably unwise action. He counted the abos and that was simple: the normal number, less one.

Ted knew that today, tonight, maybe tomorrow, another call would come. An official call, laying out the bad news in the simplest terms, the most mechanical of language. It wouldn't come to him, but he'd hear of it. These were the ways things worked. The call would come and then he would know exactly how fucked they were. Right now, he could only guess. An educated guess, but still. If someone were to stop him right now and ask him, *Hey, Ted. How fucked are we?* he could say several things.

He could say, *We are somewhat fucked, I think.*

He could say, *We're pretty well fucked.*

He could say, *We are not fucked at all. Nothing is fucked here.*

He could say, *We are so fucked you don't even know.*

All of those things would be equally true. All of them would be equally untrue.

When he'd gotten his call, the message had been only this: The accounting division at the London office needed an updated roster of all active-duty employees currently involved in the Carpenter 7 operation. This was to include all combat personnel, all operational and support personnel, all outside contractors and civilians under recurring payment arrangements, and all management-level employees. Those who were dead or rotated out-of-theater were not to be included in this list. This was not a personnel roster, but a duty roster, understood?

Understood.   .

Upon receipt of this updated roster, all pay and benefits occurring from employment by Flyboy Inc. would be suspended, pending executive review, understood?

Understood.

"Are you sure?" the assistant clerk on the other end of the line had asked him.

"Are you fucking questioning my hearing?" Ted had asked. "Are you saying I can't fucking understand what you're telling me without it being spelled out?"

"No, I mean it says here that I'm supposed to ask if you're sure you understand."

"It says that."

"Uh-huh."

Ted had sighed. "I understand. Just tell them that I understand."

In the time since that call, Ted had *not* organized a roster. He had not included all combat personnel, all operational and support personnel, all outside contractors and civilians under recurring payment arrangements, and all management-level employees. He had not made a list and would not be submitting it to the accounting division. Instead, he counted tent poles and gallons of clean water and rolls of shit-paper. The counting he was doing was purely for his own edification. He had to know where things stood. He felt that he needed to get a handle on things—on the *situation,* as it were—and to know with some specificity how many bullets, how many beans, how many grains of rice and dead abos and days and hours and minutes there were, just so he could know. It was important, or at least felt that way. Also, he couldn't think of anything else to do.

| | | | | | | | | | | | |

The night was the night. Then there was the day. Carter's roster position came up and he flew. He and Fenn talked about girls and then they talked about weapons delivery packages and then they talked about a movie that neither of them could completely remember, but they told the story of it to each other until they realized they were each talking about a different movie and decided that their version, with the two movies mashed together, was better than either of the original stories had been. When Fenn went up to fly his patrol, he killed three horses (or what passed for horses here) and two indigs and a cart, but that was only a fraction of what his squadron had killed in total. Carter killed nothing. Some days are lucky and some are not.

Then it was night again. No one flew at night. Carter and Fenn went to find some amusement among their mates but ended up disappointed. In his tent, on the soft edge of sleep and dreaming of sleep, Ted counted seconds because there were no sheep in this godforsaken place. When he got to ten thousand, he started over again at one.

And this was the way the days accumulated, like wet stones dropped into a pail. Eventually, it would become full. Eventually, it would overspill.

THIS WAS LATER. A day, maybe two. Sometimes it got hard to keep track.

In his tent, Ted sat on the edge of his cot like a windup mannequin mostly run down. He sagged in every way a man could—his shoulders sloped and his head hanging like a weight between them, arms dangling like dead limbs on a lightning-struck tree, feet scraping at the wood flooring, spine bowed.

He was exhausted. His lamps were all extinguished. In the dark, every edge of the simple geometry of his quarters shone silver: a bed frame, desk, chair back and stacked gun cases, metal shelves. There was a gentle loveliness to the collected starlight, the diffuse moonglow filtering through a scrim of clouds. It was an enchanting hour. But Ted saw none of it because he sat with his eyes closed, breathing slowly and carefully to keep from coughing while tracing in his mind the white plastic bow of a hospital bed rail he'd once gripped until his knuckles were as pale as it was. Pretty thing. Perfect. He'd had a long night already. Something in him knew that it wasn't over yet.

The supply drop, when it'd come, had been a surprise even to him. He'd been in the mess with the pilots for a time, jaw working, words coming out. Then he'd been in the machine shop where McElroy had been hunched before the lathe, slowly turning out the axle bore of a fourteen-inch wheel hub in order to make it fit the larger post of a Spad mounting. They'd chatted briefly, he and McElroy. Ted had seen him before with Vic, the chief mechanic—the two of them goofing around like kids, laughing. There'd been some kind of edge there, though. Ted had seen it. A lingering like weak magnetism, and Ted had been concerned.

"So," he'd said. "Vic, huh?"

McElroy had nodded his head. He still had his goggles on. It was impossible to see his eyes. "She's good. Great mechanic, 'specially with these old machines."

"Right." Ted had nodded. "Right . . . You fucking her?"

Willy had whitened. Ted had seen it in his jaw and along the back of his neck. He'd stood up from the bench.

"Just asking, son."

McElroy's mouth had been a bloodless line. He still had the wheel hub in his hand, and it'd looked to Ted like he might brain him with it. Throw it maybe. He was a small man, but his blood was up.

"Man to man," Ted said.

"No."

"No, you're not fucking her?"

"No, I ain't interested in your man-to-man."

"Then just answer the question."

"No."

"No, you won't answer?"

"No, I'm not . . . *fucking* her. She's my friend. I have a wife. Back home."

"Back home," Ted repeated.

"Yes."

"Far from home, boy. Just a question."

"And I answered it."

"Hmm."

And that had been that. Personnel issues always bothered Ted. They were not his strong suit. But he was saved from having to pursue this particular issue any further by Eddie Lucas, a company lawyer and lord of the tight-beam relay; a man in regular, high-level contact with London and sent in to do boonie time as mission manager and corporate communications liaison. He'd found Ted in the machine shop with Willy McElroy, walking straight into the middle of their conversation at the point where it'd petered out into a lopsided staring contest.

"Commander," Eddie had said. "A minute of your time?"

Ted had been convinced enough that Willy McElroy wasn't lying to him (not telling the truth, necessarily, but not lying either), so had nodded and turned away. He agreed to follow Eddie back to comms at his request and, going out the door, Ted had heard McElroy finally throw that wheel hub he'd been holding—the clatter of it going into the side of a toolbox with some force was unmistakable—so he supposed he had Eddie to thank for that. Another minute and it might've been his head.

| | | | | | | | | | | | | |

Outside, Eddie had hurried—trotting as though afflicted with a wicked case of the shits and a long way from comfort. Ted hadn't bothered trying to keep up until, in the air above them, he'd heard the dull, thudding booms of frantic deceleration. Of a ship making orbital translation with no notion of sticking around. The sound was like hitting a hollow plastic bucket with a hammer, only vast and echoing and distant in a way that only those who live in the sky might understand. And when Ted looked up, he saw the comet's tail arc of something hot and fast carving its way through the upper strata.

"Supply!" Eddie had called out from the door of the comms tent, pointing skyward, then gesturing for Ted to come inside.

"What?" Ted had yelled back. They'd gotten their last supply drop months ago, dead on the schedule detailed in the corporate ops plan, and weren't due for a re-up for some weeks yet, at right about the time they would run out of everything altogether, which was also precisely according to plan. Forced austerity was a foundational tenet of the company, worshipped like a psalm by its distant bookkeepers. Do more with less. The alternative: Die.

Now Ted broke into a jog, one eye on the sky—looking for the black-among-blackness of the insertion containers, the floating ghosts of tear-away drag chutes—and felt something in his belly twist up like cold fingers curling into a fist. *This is it,* he'd thought. *This is when it all goes bad.*

When he reached the door, Eddie was holding it for him. "We aren't scheduled for another supply drop, Eddie," Ted said. "Why wasn't I told?"

"I was going to ask you the same thing, Commander. I thought maybe you were keeping something from me."

And Ted had known then for sure—the true knowledge of distant powers deciding his fate from very far away. He'd shrugged because, really, there was nothing else to do. The two of them, Eddie and Ted, stood in the doorway of the comms tent looking up silently into the nothingness of the night, the gleaming fire trail of the smuggler's ship already just a purple stain in their eyes, fading like a memory, like a scar in fast-forward. They gawped like primitives waiting on lightning, on forces beyond their reckoning. He'd been too high, Ted had decided. If Eddie was right, if this really was an unscheduled resupply coming in hot, the pilot would have to loop out over the distant ocean, come back again to make his drop. That would take some time. Ted fought down the urge to crouch, to buckle under the weight of night and the unknown and go to ground like he was under fire. He shook off the instinct to run, kept his mouth clamped shut and slapped a hand onto the back of his own neck to keep the hairs down. It'd been Eddie who'd finally broken the strange, quiet hoodoo of the moment.

"I also have some new orders from corporate that I don't quite understand and was hoping you might offer your . . . wisdom."

Ted lowered his gaze, leveling it at Eddie like a gun. In the hesitation between *your* and *wisdom,* there would've been just enough space for Ted to have punched Eddie in the mouth.

Thinking about it later, sitting alone in his tent, Ted kind of wished he had.

In the comms tent, Eddie Lucas had shown Ted the new orders that had come in by burst transmission less than six hours prior, heavily fortified by encryption and translate-at-station code. Eddie had done the laborious work of number, letter, and phrase substitution by hand, hunched over his burn-before-capture code books back in his own private quarters, behind a locked door and under a pin light as if there were spies everywhere. As if the monkeys could've even read a billboard announcing all vile intentions of the company and its people here on Iaxo.

Eddie had inserted the breaks. He'd printed a clean copy to puzzle over when, in final draft, the message had been so clotted with jargon, abbreviation, and nomenclature that he'd been unsure of what, precisely, he was being told to do (or not do) by calculating bosses a billion miles away.

But when he'd shoved the clean sheet under the commander's nose, it'd taken Ted thirty seconds to read the orders twice. To him, the language was music, his native tongue. He'd understood the content of the orders before the end of the first line.

| | | | | | | | | | | |

FINAL ORDERS:
Priority to Chief of Ops, Chief of Comms, Carpenter 7 Ep, TAG 14-447
Report Key: 310B4FC4-AA127-C7EP2365
Tracking Number: None
Attack Code: None
Originator Group: UNKNOWN
Updated by Group: FALSE
SigAct: CCIR Order

1) Please stand by for **DIVERT SUPPLY OP** by HALO delivery, your LKL, this 2400, +/- 12 hrs local. Inbound CLP as per request this 212/365, London, Earth. Scheduled CLP op of 50/365 next has been scrubbed. REPEAT: op 50/365 next **HAS BEEN SCRUBBED** per XO, London, Earth.
2) **DO NOT RETRANSMIT**. Operation Carpenter &c. is under comms/

radiation blackout 48 hrs from time of receipt, this message. Duration unknown.

3) Operation Carpenter &c. is under executive blackout upon receipt, this message, **immediate**. Duration unknown.

4) **NEW ORDERS**: Super orders of this 300/365, operation Carpenter &c. is **ZERO ENGAGE** upon receipt, this message, immediate. Duration IAW local command. Operation Carpenter &c. is **outside compromised**, source unknown ATT. Operation Carpenter &c. now **ASG/JOG IAW local command**. Duration unknown.

5) Retrieval is **NONCOMMIT**, ATT. Duration unknown.

6) SigAct 24 hrs, this message, +/- 24 hrs, for final FCOM, London, Earth. Release pending. No retry. REPEAT: **NO RETRY**.

SPEC ORDERS to follow. OP CONFIRM to follow. Further SigAct by **NONCONFIRM XO**, dts to follow.

|||||||||||||

"I have some questions," Eddie had said when he was sure Ted was finished reading.

Ted sniffed. "You have a copy for me?" he'd asked. He tapped the single sheet with a fingertip. "This was marked CCIR—Commander's Critical Information Requirements. That means you should have a second copy for me."

Eddie produced one, neatly folded in thirds, from inside his jacket and handed it over. Then he repeated himself. "I have some questions."

Ted had straightened up. He'd carefully slipped the copy into one of his own pockets and then smoothed the fabric over it with the palm of one hand. "Corporate is going to be calling you tomorrow," he said. "Ask your questions then. It'll be your last chance."

And then Ted had walked out. There were things he needed to do. He had to go to the field house, organize a party to unload the drop when it landed. He had a request outstanding from Antoinne Durba for air support, so would have to go to the longhouse and have a plane rolled out and readied for a night mission. He would have to tear through the drop, find flares (which they'd been out of, save for a few pistol-fired signal flares, for weeks), get them pulled and hung in a hurry.

Most of the rest of the camp was still or already awake, gathered either in the mess or in the field house—trying to stay warm, rubbing their hands and slapping their own arms, dancing around in the cold, drinking. It was becoming a party. Another stage of the party that'd been going on for as long as they'd been here. Somewhere in the dark, the boys were shouting at one another, running around like savages. In the dirt by the mess, Charlie Voss from three squadron, Raoul, the mechanic, and the armorer, Max, were playing chickenshit with a thumb-sized piece of explosive compound taken from a bomb head and an indistinct length of fusing wire hidden under a helmet. The game was to light the fuse and have everyone start with their hand on the helmet. First one to jerk his hand away—to turn, run for cover, panic in the face of possible grievous injury—was chickenshit and mocked roundly by his braver, stupider companions. In the end, everyone lost more than they won.

At the field house, Ted had sat alone in a corner with his copy of the final orders but did not open them. He ran his thumbnail along the creases that Eddie had put in the paper, turning the single, folded sheet over and over in his hands. Between it and the call he'd gotten, he knew exactly what was happening: They were being lost. Forgotten. No more pay, no more supplies, no more communications. The shipment currently on its way in had likely been freightered months ago and was now being dumped on them early to clear it off the corporate books. Their final pay would be banked somewhere so the lawyers could claim that the mission had been officially terminated at any point in the past three or four months—whatever was required if they were ever called to testify.

Ted felt a sick giggle rising up in him but swallowed it. Bit it off and held it behind the palisade of his teeth. He was an employee. A contractor. Mercenary. There were rules governing nearly everything he was supposed to do under circumstances both bizarre and mundane but very little in the handbook to cover this sort of eventuality. This sudden removal of the parental gaze of his distant bosses. His hands were shaking on the table. He smoothed the paper in front of him again—petting it like a cat. He chewed his lip. He knew what was happening *now*, but he was very unclear on what he was supposed to do next. There were no rules for this. No procedure. He was, as they say, in the dark.

At a certain point, Lefty Berthold from two squadron had ambled over, stood swaying, close to Ted with a drink in his hand, and asked him what he was playing with.

"Love letter, Commander?"

"Something like that," Ted had said.

"It's been some time since anyone here got any mail. Must feel nice."

For a moment, Ted thought Lefty was being sincere, but when he looked up at him, he saw a vacant, dumb smile on the man's face. Berthold was an idiot and a pig. Ted hated him more than a little and only loved him as much as he loved the most generic of his men—as he imagined a father must a child who is a complete and endearing disappointment. He tolerated him the precise distance that blood required.

"Go fuck with someone else, Lefty," he'd said. "I'm in no mood."

Eventually, Ted had stood. He'd spent twenty minutes or more watching men come and go. He had accounted for nearly all of the pilots, so had asked, "Where's Captain Carter?" and the men in the field house had all shrugged, looked away. Ted had stared at them, or tried to. "Lugs," he'd said. "Drunk goddamn mothers." His eyes had been bright. He spit a little when he talked and no one would meet his eye. "There's work to do. None of you go anywhere."

Ted had walked out the door. He would send Captain Carter to fly tonight. This was his plan. Carter was not among the revelers, not in the mess or the field house or running around in the cold and dark. Ted knew this because he'd counted. He imagined that Carter was at home, tucked up warm in bed and sleeping like a good soldier. That was the best he could hope for—that Carter wasn't drunk or sick or out of his head. All he needed was one man.

Outside, Ted had found Fennimore Teague staring daggers at the retreating back of Billy, who was headed out for the flight line with Morris Ross in tow.

"Captain," he'd said.

"Commander."

"What's this all about? You look in a stabbing kind of mood."

Fenn had shaken his head. "Nonsense is all. Billy's going up."

"He does that." Ted had briefly considered having Billy run the flares but had thought better of it. Billy, he thought, wouldn't go. Billy, he thought, would just tell him to fuck off to his face, requiring a reaction from Ted that would end in bad feelings, disciplinary action, worse. Billy was a great pilot, the best of the night fliers, but had, at some point, slipped beyond the point where he took orders easily. With another option available, Billy wasn't worth the trouble. "You seen your boy Carter?"

"Yes," said Fenn, but nothing more.

"Not drinking with the boys."

"No."

"There a problem?"

Fenn had paused, turned his head with a strange, slow deliberation, and looked Ted up and down. "That seems a strange question. I don't know how to answer it."

Ted shook his head. "Nothing," he said. "Forget it. Look, I need someone to fly. Someone sober, who's not going to shit himself or crash his fucking machine. Durba called in movement to his front last night, in the hills. Same thing tonight. Monkey noises, trees going down, whatever. There's something going on, and he wants an illumination mission run so he can stop it before someone has a bad morning."

"Illumination seems in short supply here, Commander." Fenn smiled like someone had stuck fishhooks in his cheeks and pulled—a false, dead thing.

"Was going to do it with signal flares, but now we've got something better. Supply is coming in. And we need friends at the front."

"Tonight?"

"An hour, maybe less. It's inbound right now."

"That's unexpected."

"Not completely."

"Largesse from our corporate masters. Presents from on high . . . "

"Something like that."

"Gifts from wise men."

"Just love hearing yourself talk, don't you, Captain."

"It's Christmas, Commander. I'm getting in the spirit."

Ted straightened up, jerking back just a little from Fenn and eyeing him carefully, trying to ferret out the lie in him. "It is not."

"Is," said Fenn. "Back home. I just enjoy the irony is all."

"Well . . ."

Ted had found himself at a momentary loss for words. He cursed. That explained the twenty-four-hour delay in the confirmation of the final orders, he supposed. The junior accountant on the phone. Beside him, Fenn was humming something. It was "God Rest Ye Merry Gentlemen," and Ted had to turn away for a second to stop from laughing, more bubbles of sick mirth rising in him and tasting of rot and vomit.

"Look," he said, after recovering himself. "I have to be at comms. Someone needs to fly. Someone else needs to run the off-loading. Which guy do you want to be?"

Fenn had clucked his tongue, tilted his head just so. "Cruel," he said. "Very, very cruel." He was one of those people who had total control over his face. An actor's control. A high-functioning sociopath's. He was handsome and knew it, had cutting blue eyes and wheat-straw hair like an overgrown boy with an ancient, cunning old man inside pulling his strings. He used the planes and angles of his face like a second language, with a deliberation that made a person feel like there was always a joke being told that he didn't quite understand and that was, maybe, being told at his expense.

Ted saw none of this, though. Never had. "Just the way of things," he said. "So which is it going to be?"

"Kevin's at home, in the tent. Sleeping, I think. Alone."

"Wise choice," Ted had said. "Everyone's staying put back at the house until the load comes in. Round them up, oversee the off-loading. I'll have someone get Carter's plane ready."

"Vic is around somewhere," Fenn had said. "I'm sure she'd be happy to do it." There'd been a coldness in his voice that, again, completely failed to impress Ted.

He'd gone to wake Carter.

It was dark. Carter was asleep and, like a child, dreaming of soaring without a plane. Of flying, which he loved, and of a place that wasn't this place, which he hated in many lusciously complicated, well-chewed-over ways.

In his sleep Carter didn't hear Ted Prinzi come through the door. He didn't hear Ted approach his cot and, for just a moment, stand and watch him sleeping with a careful eye. He didn't see Ted tighten down his lips as though doing difficult math in his head, looking around at the cramped, despicable shadows of looming filth and clutter in the tent, or square his shoulders or squint down at him in the dark. It wasn't until Ted cleared his throat wetly and began to speak that Carter was jerked suddenly out into rude, unwelcome consciousness.

"On your feet, pilot. Time to earn a paycheck."

Carter stirred, throwing an arm across his face and screwing himself deeper down into the coarse blankets.

"You drunk, Carter?" Ted barked, though he knew full well that Carter was not. He lashed out with a foot and kicked one of the legs of Carter's cot in a way that he felt was comradely but really wasn't at all. "Liquid rations for dinner again, yeah?"

Carter opened his eyes. He saw Ted standing over his cot with a blackout lantern in his hand, playing its shuttered beam across his face. "Go fuck yourself, Ted," he said.

"Orders, pilot. Orders is orders."

"It's dark. We don't fly in the dark."

Ted chuckled damply, a sound like mud cliffs giving way to gravity. Carter knew he'd had a trench cough for months that he couldn't quite shake.

"We do tonight, sweetheart," he said. "Illumination mission. The indigs want some light to kill each other by. You drew the short straw."

Carter sat up with a grunt, rubbed at his eyes, coughed, scratched himself. *Fucking lice,* he thought. "I didn't draw any straw, Ted. I was sleeping, in case you didn't notice."

"I know that, pilot. That's why I drew for you." From the breast pocket of his uniform blouse, Ted took two cigarettes—manufactured, filter-tip cigarettes from a private stash—and put them both in his mouth, lighting them over the smoke-blackened chimney of the lantern. He reached down and stuck one between Carter's lips like he was planting a stake.

Ted said, "See what you get for not staying up and drinking with your mates?" And even though Ted had meant it as a good thing, it made Carter want to punch him straight in his gin blossoms, but he didn't. He took a drag instead and felt himself grow light-headed, sinking back into his thin pillow and stinking blankets.

Ted drew back the lantern and grinned hugely, face lit in harsh angles, head round like a Halloween pumpkin with wet, sucking lips opening like a wound and pulling back into a graveyard smile. The man had teeth like ivory headstones, not one of them his.

"On the flight deck in ten, Carter," he said, then closed the shutter on the lantern with a tinny snap. Everything went dark again. There was just the red tip of Ted's cigarette, glowing from the middle of his face. Then the sound of the door opening. Then the sound of it closing again.

| | | | | | | | | | | |

Outside the tent, Ted took a breath. Then another. He'd counted: One pilot, sober. His chest rattled and hurt from the cold air, but it felt good to be clear of the stinking closeness and claustrophobia of Carter's quarters. He wanted to wash and looked longingly off in the direction of the shower tent, but there wasn't time. With a grunt of disgust, he threw away the cigarette he'd lit and closed his eyes, pinching the bridge of his nose between two fingers as if trying to stave off a headache that was far away yet but coming at a gallop.

Two years, he'd been on Iaxo. Nearly. It'd been seven hundred days, give or take a few hours, as measured by London, Earth. Fewer here, where a day and a night took thirty-one hours and some number of minutes annoying enough that no one bothered counting them. Seven hundred days, each counted and duly logged, marking nothing but an inexplicable and, ultimately, unforgivable failure.

His men were falling apart. Almost all of them. He'd chosen Carter to fly because Carter was the only pilot sleeping, one of the few not drunk or crazed or liable to lose it in the long reach of the night. And if, right now, Kevin Carter was the best of them, Ted knew how poorly that spoke of their situation in general, because Carter had the black cross on him and everyone knew it. Everyone except maybe Carter.

He gave off the pall of death wherever he went, throwing it off like an infection so that Ted had seen other pilots refuse to sit in chairs that Carter had recently vacated or drink from bottles that he had touched. But after seven hundred days here, everyone was coming apart at the seams. Everyone was losing their stuffing.

And now this. He'd spoken to London—been passed down through the ranks to some junior clerk in the accounting department stuck working over Christmas, who'd unknowingly told him that they were being lost here, laid off. He'd received confirmation of that same thing through channels, the lethality of it buried in jargon, clotted with acronym, but none of that making it any less of a death sentence. He touched the pocket with the letter in it. He imagined it like a bullet, slowly crawling its way toward his heart. All of their hearts. Ted knew something that none of the rest of the men did. Not even Eddie. A secret that, for the time being, he would carry alone.

Fucked once again by time—stuck hundreds of light-years from home with a handful of men, a few antique airplanes, a certain number of bombs and hammers and shit-paper and beans and a supply drop coming that he alone now knew was going to be the last one, ever.

Ted had no politics. No philosophy beyond the sure knowledge that seeing the hammer coming down reduced all of life's complications to the simplest equation: Survive or don't. Twenty years of corporate war had taught him many lessons, but this was the one he'd taken most to heart. This was what he believed. Or what he believed that he believed, anyhow. He'd seen the hammer, so what did he have to do next? And when that was done, what came after?

There was noise coming from the infield. Raised voices, the sound of boots on cold ground, and the hiss and pop of hot metal cooling in the darkness. The drop was in. A bull's-eye delivery right into the infield by a jock flying so high that, this time, Ted hadn't even heard the engines. With the new supplies, his accounting was going to be all inaccurate. Fucked by largesse, not want—which was a new experience for him, to be sure, but it left things in no less of an erroneous state. He'd have to start over, do it again tomorrow or the next day. Count everything again. *That* was what he could do next. Not so he could know how bad things were now, but how bad they were going to become. He thought about going to supervise the unloading but didn't. He'd given orders. They would be followed, more or less.

He'd gone to his own tent instead. Distracted, looking back over his shoulder as he walked, he'd stepped on something that'd squished underfoot. He'd lit a match, crouched down to see what it was, and discovered it was a slug, big enough that his size-ten waffle-tread had split it in half with part sticking out one side of his instep, stalk eyes still wriggling, and part sticking out the other.

It'd infuriated him, this slug. What was it doing here? It was nighttime. How could it see? And it was cold—the ground frozen—so where was it going? The slug should not have been there. It made no sense. And this, he'd thought, was how it went. It wasn't ever the big things that got you; it was the little ones. It was walking along in the night on frozen ground and stepping on a slug as long as your forearm: The plain irrationality of this place. That was what drove you crazy.

He'd shaken out the match and stabbed the smoking stub of wood down into the head half of the slug. He'd watched it squirm and writhe on the ground while his breath hissed between clenched teeth.

Welcome to the fucking war.

CARTER GOT UP. He got dressed. There was a process, an unfolding of one's self from the calm of sleep into war, and the first hundred or so times he'd done this, it had been precisely as affecting and heavy as it was supposed to be. He'd really *felt* it, in his belly, balls, and his fingertips—a tingling like powerful magic. Now, it was only a drag.

He put on the catheter and strapped the piss bag to his thigh. The planes they flew here could stay up for twenty hours if needed, and everyone pissed themselves on night missions.

Dog collar next, right against the skin. The clasp in the back could be tricky if a man was drunk or scared enough that his hands shook. Carter's hands did not shake. He wasn't yet awake enough to be scared and wasn't drunk either because he'd chosen to turn in early tonight—to sleep only because all other options were equally tedious and at least while sleeping there was the chance that he might dream about girls. *Stupid me,* he thought to himself as his fingers unerringly found the catches and latched them against the prickling stubble on the back of his neck. *Stupid, stupid me.*

The collar read a pilot's biologicals, controlled the emergency gear—the pump full of oxygenated blood clotting factors, the Protenolol injector (synthetic adrenaline, hell in a very small vial). There'd been a briefing before they'd left for Iaxo where all the equipment had been explained. A small room aboard the *Junholdt*, sour with the smell of antifungal spray and plastics kept too long in a closed space.

Instructing them had been a small and pretty young man with crazy eyes who spoke so fast that Carter had wondered whether he was paid a bonus for the number of words he could say in a minute. When he'd gotten to explaining the dog collar and emergency gear, he'd taken out a laser pointer and stabbed it randomly at the air. A kid playing pirate with a make-believe sword. Everywhere the dot of light touched, he would shout out, "Wound! Wound! Kill! Wound!"

The pilots started twitching away from the bead of red light, started ducking and weaving, dancing where they stood because there were no chairs in which to sit and no room to run. But this only encouraged the young man, and he started yelling, "Bang! Bangbangbang!" until some of the pilots started to protest. How was it fair that this little boy with his laser was getting to kill them where they stood? To say who was wounded and who was dead? From the back of the room Carter had watched it all with a smile on his face, knowing that if the kid at the front of the room wasn't careful, he was going to get himself killed for real.

"Not fair?" the boy had asked, voice still quick, words spilling out of him like water from a split hose, but suddenly serious. "Not fair. A machine gun isn't fair. Flak isn't fair. It doesn't discriminate or play favorites. But if you wear your gear—all of it, every time you go up— you'll live. Simple as that. Everything else will die, you'll live, and the company won't have to pay out death benefits to your next of kin, which we hate to do. The emergency gear will save you. When you pray, pray to Harold Bolstrood, understand?" The kid had thrown his hands into the air, palms up, eyes turned toward the heaven of the *Junholdt*'s smooth steel ceiling. "Say, 'Harold, save me,' and it will be done."

There'd been a moment of quiet, then, "Who the fuck is Harold Bolstrood?" someone had asked. Carter thought it might've been Tommy Hill, but he was never sure.

And the kid, the young man with the crazy eyes and the laser pointer, had cocked his head like a dog hearing its own name. His fine, thin eyebrows had knitted together, and he'd looked, for a silent instant, so sad that he might cry.

"That's me," he'd said. "I invented this. Didn't you know?"

No one wore the pump. No one wore the injector. There was no flak on Iaxo. There were no machine guns other than the ones they'd brought with them. And the emergency gear was bulky and annoying and clumsy and rubbed painful sores onto the arm, so everyone had lost theirs or tossed them into a box somewhere and forgotten all about them, but they still wore the collars because the collars also contained the throat mike for the radio and looked pretty cool besides.

Next came the jumpsuit—bespoke spidersilk of private manufacture, guaranteed to stop most any solid projectile. The pilots wore them like skin, with nothing beneath. Like everyone else's, Carter's jumpsuit smelled terrible.

Thermal knickers, black. Boots to follow, also black, knee-high, fur-lined, comfortable for about five minutes but warm forever. Jacket the same way—long and black, heavy leather with silver buttons and buckles and a high collar. It was all very nice and functional, warm in the cold sky, occasionally bulletproof, but favored mostly because the flight rig made anyone who wore it look wicked, cruel, and indestructible.

Gloves and goggles. A silk scarf—pure china-white and kept immaculately clean as a matter of pride even if nothing else was. Most paid the indigs to do that. Give them a couple of beads or bottlecaps and they'd do most anything. Laundry, fetch and carry, haul the trash, whatever. Carter was no different. He tucked the gloves into his belt and wound the scarf around his throat, leaving its tails flapping over his shoulder, fussing with them vainly until they lay just so.

Each pilot had been issued a helmet. Carter used his to hold warm water when he shaved (which was not often). No one ever actually wore them. Again, a matter of style. Hard to look so dashing and devil-may-care behind a quarter inch of bulletproof mirrored Lexan.

Hard to look so good with a bullet hole in the face, too, but that wasn't much of a concern to the pilots. For the most part, the only bullets fired in anger were theirs. In the two years that the company had been on Iaxo, more men had been put on the sick rolls for cock-rot, cirrhosis, and misadventure (read: cracked their heads falling drunk over a tent peg) than had been injured in the line of duty. More by far.

C'est la guerre.

Once dressed, Carter had little choice but to fly, but he knew that ten minutes was ten minutes in Ted's mind only. A mere suggestion of hurry. And to obey, he thought, would only encourage the man, stroke the armature of ego that kept him upright and stiff, and make him think people listened when he spoke. There was no reason to foster that kind of illusion.

Fenn had been kind, considerate, and thoughtless enough to leave a half-full bottle of the local pop-skull sitting in the dirt next to his cot, so Carter requisitioned it as a spoil of war, eased himself down onto the edge of his bed, and drank it. Near the door, Cat (something less than Carter's pet, something more than just another ugly local rodent) lay curled into a ball on its pile of rags. Silently, Carter raised the bottle in a toast to the sleeping, monstrous thing. *To survival,* he thought, *at any cost.* And then Carter drank. He did not rush. Neither did he linger. There was work to do, but he'd be damned if he was going to do it sober.

| | | | | | | | | | | | |

Back in his own tent, Ted felt each breath like taking in a weight and exhaling only half of it. Steam rose like smoke. His mouth tasted of tar and too long between brushing. He regretted fiercely those few drags he'd taken off that cigarette while standing in Carter's squalid quarters, but it'd been necessary. He'd wanted to bring the man a present—an apology of sorts for slights that Carter couldn't possibly have understood—and a cigarette had seemed the least obviously cajoling. The least fraught. Ted had lit one for himself simply because it'd felt wrong to do otherwise. Appearances mattered, Ted knew. Especially when one had very little else.

He'd taken out the orders from corporate again and laid them on his desk, straightening the folded page until it was square with the corners, the edge, nudging it with his fingertips until it was perfectly aligned.

Ted thought of the coast. Gray water, sick with foam. Cities that looked to have been built from mud by giant idiot children and then abandoned halfway through. The Arkhis Mountains like sharp teeth in an angry mouth. Hills 201, 204, 218a and b, the central highlands—names on corporate maps that were all less terrible for their banality, for the refusal to call them after the awful things that'd been done there when he and his pilots had flown low and dropped fire from the sky.

The Sispetain moors. The bloody fucking moors, and the river valley below them. The city they called Riverbend, then here—the lowlands, a flood plain that never flooded. Ted drummed his fingers on the folded orders. He'd made a tour, for sure. He'd seen some things. They all had. And now it was done. Or would be soon.

They'd dropped, initially, not far from those cities on the coast—the sprawling mud and stone trading centers and maritime capitals everyone knew were the keys to final victory on Iaxo even if no one really knew what they were called. Two years ago, seven hundred days ago—one more than that now, maybe—they'd come down, bearing in like a dart on that first day, and they'd been able to see nothing. Strapped down inside the troop compartment of their dropship, sitting so close they'd almost been on one another's laps, breathing the warm, recycled air and shaking like a hundred individual earthquakes. Their view of Iaxo had been better from orbit, and from orbit it hadn't been very good. But anything was better than trying to stare through steel.

Morale had been an issue. These men, they'd never worked together before. Most of them had never met before finding themselves crammed into the dropship with all their personal gear, survival gear, jump-out kits, whatever. Some 52.2 kilograms per man, about 115 pounds. No one had known whether or not they'd have to fight their way off the dropship—leaping, guns blazing, onto alien soil: the classic hot landing. When Ted had asked, corporate had said no. Corporate had assured Ted: "Quiet as a civilian drop. You're not going to be fighting your way off anything."

But then on the day—the first day, while the men had been sitting through briefings in cold storerooms on how to use the gear bestowed upon them by the company, how to fly planes that no one had flown in centuries—Ted had found fourteen rifles to distribute among the members of the Carpenter 7 mission. Fourteen Hiland-model assault rifles, older than he was, plus clips, cleaning kits, and fourteen thousand rounds of ammunition waiting, crated, unmarked, and sitting on the deck plates of the transport *Junholdt* beside the dropship's ramp. This, Ted had thought, was very strange. Either it was expected to be a hot

LZ or it wasn't. If it was, then why would the company allocate only fourteen rifles instead of one for every man? And if it wasn't, why offer any at all?

Ted had decided that corporate was either lying or stupid or ignorant or maybe all three. He'd shaken his head at the ridiculousness of it all. These had been days when delusion and corporate absurdity had still been funny, not fatal. Ted had a sense of humor then. Or thought he had.

When everyone had lined up to load, he'd assigned the unexpected equipment poverty-style: a loaded rifle to one man, extra ammo to the one going out the door behind him. If the man with the gun should die, the one behind him would pick it up and carry the fight forward. He'd told everyone it was just for safety's sake, hooked his thumbs in his belt, puffed out his chest, and said, "Just in case, yeah? Company's just looking out for our tender asses. But this is going to be quiet as a civilian drop. You're not going to be fighting your way off anything."

And then they'd all buckled in and fallen from the sky like a meteor, from the belly of the *Junholdt* to the soft earth below. Eight minutes of free fall, then atmosphere interface, then forty-four minutes of translation between sky and ground. Ted had kept his eyes open, watching. He'd watched the drop master, who spent the entire fall, up until the last three minutes, reading a tattered paper book with no cover, one arm looped through a standing strap, just like he was riding the train. He watched the men. Eddie Lucas, he remembered, had thrown up an amazing number of times. A few of the men talked, or tried to. Most of the pilots slept.

Arriving on a new planet, *any* new planet, is like being born again. Everything is new. Nothing has a name. For lack of anything better or more productive to do, you ascribe malice or creeping evil to the stupidest of things: that rock, this plant. It's the same everywhere. Everyone does it. After his first half-dozen landings for Flyboy, Ted was never able to look at a baby the same way again, knowing for a stone fact that from the moment they come into the world, they are full of hate and formless terror.

Carpenter, though, was different. Iaxo was different.

Aboard ship, the lights in the troop compartment had gone red for the final sixty seconds of cushioned descent. Ted had rallied everyone up to their feet, organized them. The drop master was standing by the ramp, shouting: "Everyone up! Everyone off! Quick-quick! There ain't no round-trip tickets here!" And Ted had wondered what movie he was living in that'd put those words in his mouth.

The drop master had counted down the final thirty seconds on his hands, holding up three fingers, then two, then counting down from ten—his mouth forming words but no sound coming out. Nerves, Ted remembered. His nerves had been terrible. A weight pressing on his chest so heavy that his legs had gone numb and he'd felt sweat prickling the backs of his ears.

They touched down with a jerk. The assault ramp boomed open, fell to the strange earth, and they all went charging out with a whoop—rifles first, ammo bearers behind, all gushing out of the ass-end of the ship in a single spasm of violence.

And then they'd faltered. All of them. The first men out wound down and stood, finally, stunned, with the rest of the mission all running up their heels.

It'd been like charging into a fairy tale. A sun-dappled glen. Tall grasses unbowing after having been pushed flat by the wash of the dropship's turbines. Wildflowers in purples, golds, and blues, and mountains rising in the middle distance, still young and jagged. Closer, a tree line. Primordial, but sunlit and almost impossibly lovely where it formed a thick bower over the course of a river running over pebbles and flat stones.

That, Ted sometimes thought, was where it'd all gone wrong: in that first, blinking instant. They'd been infected, the lot of them. They'd breathed in, taken the sweet, honey-touched summer perfume of Iaxo into their lungs, and been lost. Like some cosmic joke, in two years here there'd never been another day so lovely. Not another hour.

The drop master had shouted everyone clear of the ramp, running them like sheep out of a pen. When they'd heard the bangs of the restraining bolts letting go and the rumble of the cargo containers rolling down the ramps, many of the men had winced. There was something defiling about the harsh noise, metals grinding on metals, and the plasticky smell of lubricating oil. Ted had wondered whether those were the loudest sounds that had ever been heard here. In the moment, it'd felt like maybe they were.

Ted had taken all the rifles away, trying not to look sheepish about it. He'd wanted to give a speech—some kind of warning, a note of caution to temper the sudden infatuation he saw in too many eyes—but couldn't find the words. Two of the pilots were chasing butterflies, scampering across the field like children and swatting at them with their hands.

So day one, they'd had a party instead. Drinks all around. Without even unpacking, they'd blown down some trees with shaped charges made from unscrewed bomb heads and fusing wire, doused them with kerosene and lit them on fire. They'd mixed ethanol from the medical supplies with bottled water and orange drink powder and poured it into tin cups and pretended they were roughing it while the leaping fires turned midnight to noon for a hundred yards in every direction. They'd posted no security. The rifles had been mounded up in a stack, unfired. They hadn't even uncrated the sidearms. It was a lark. A picnic. That'd been a good night, Ted recalled. Nothing yet had gone wrong. He'd laughed a lot. Slapped the backs of his young murderers. Pissed into the embers of the fire when it'd burned low. They slept as though they'd just invaded Eden and found it lacking snakes.

But everything since then had been falling back—retreat disguised as strategic maneuvering. They'd been given (*granted*, like it was a gift to be handed down) that one day to acclimate and then a heavy lifter had come down, unannounced, from parking orbit—spinning down through the rapidly graying atmosphere like some nightmare insect, steel legs twitching and undulating along the empty curve of its belly. It'd put a hump on all their lightweight gear, waited ten minutes for everyone to load into another cramped troop compartment—jammed in among the huge containers of aviation fuel, construction supplies, and proscribed electronics—then moved them from the wrong side of the mountains, across the moors, across a river, onto a backwater lowland plain and over the somewhat-abbreviated horizon from two walled cities, much smaller than the cities on the coast, that seemed to be the focal points of aggression in the area. Ted had gotten on the blower and asked what the fuck was going on—why they were being moved so far away from the good fight and stuck out in the boonies.

"Orders, sir," said the pilot of the lifter. "Just doing what I'm told. I suggest you shut up and enjoy the ride, sir."

Eight days to dig in. They'd cut airstrips in historical formation—a lopsided triangle mown into the tough, alien grasses, flattened by earthmovers from Cavalier Mechanics. Cavalier was another mercenary company, a military contractor that specialized in moving things and wrecking things and building other things in their place. They'd been contracted by the company prior to arrival and paid by Eddie Lucas, Flyboy Inc.'s Man on Iaxo, out of a private stock of hard currency he held. Paper money was worthless. Promissory notes were worse. But Fast Eddie paid in gold—everyone's favorite color.

After that, vital structures had gone up. Machinery had gone in. Tent lines had been pegged out. The *Junholdt* was long gone and they were cut off—ninety days at least until their next supply drop and the first possible ride out if, for some reason, everything went terribly wrong. It'd taken two days for their own mechanics and flight engineers to assemble the first half-dozen planes once the longhouse was bolted together and raised. One afternoon for test flights. One crash. No injuries.

On the tenth day, Connelly (who actually worked for Eastbourne Services Group, Proxima, though it was tough to tell) had presented himself at the nascent airfield, along with Antoinne Durba and Marie, two of his other company commanders, and a handful of his indigenous officers. Connelly had been decked out in native drag: armored skirt, necklaces of chicken bones, breastplate like the seat of a wicker chair. He had a long beard that he wore tied off like links of sausage, a drooping mustache the color of rust, and had his head mostly shaved. Gone bamboo, totally, and Ted had laughed right at him, not caring a damn who he was.

Durba wore the wreck of a military uniform, patched and tattered. Marie had been lovely, tall and narrow, with long hair blowing out behind her in a breeze, one blind eye whitened like milk, and an old scar that cupped the sharp plane of one cheekbone.

That day was the first time that Ted had seen one of the natives up close. They were tall, dirty, lumpy, furred with something that wasn't really fur but more like the frayed ends of an old rug, matted and overlapping, in colors from ashy gray to shit brown. Their faces appeared dumb and slow and thick, more delicately hairy, with large, heavy heads like slugs of iron pushed down into their sloping shoulders and small eyes set too far apart. Their backs curved oddly, making them appear always hunched, though, at the time, Ted had mistaken this for the exhaustion of the march. In the cups of their shoulders, the points of their elbows, the wings of their tilted hips, you could see the rubbed, bare skin beneath the fur—or not skin, exactly, but something like scales. Plates. The hair all grew from the loose edges of these, and it made Ted think of something he knew: that fingernails were really made of hair, all stuck together.

After that, he couldn't think of anything but that they were talking monsters covered in shredding fingernails. When one of them (a lieutenant, Connelly had said, without the slightest hint of humor) extended a hand for an awkward shake (a thing which, it was plain, was a learned response, uncommon and unfamiliar), Ted had to force himself to take the offered appendage. Three fingers and a thumb, all of them too long. When he'd touched it, the thing's hand was so hot it made him ache. For a day afterward, his fingers smelled like he'd been scratching an old dog—the stink of the aliens warm and soupy and thick.

There'd been other officers there. A representative from Applied Outcomes, another from Cavalier, another from Palas Risk Management. It'd been arranged, he was made to understand—a friendly welcome to the neighborhood by those already doing business there and a dignified exchange of radio frequencies and call signs. Something about it made Ted think of John Company middle managers standing deep in the bush in their mildewed broadcloth suits and pith helmets, trading business cards gone limp in the wet, heavy air.

Like a good manager, Ted had memorized names and faces. He'd shaken hands and mouthed meaningless words about cooperation and mutual concern, showed his guests to a flattened patch of grass in the infield where, eventually, the field house would rise, and then excused himself as quickly as he could, sniffing his fingers as he went. It didn't escape his notice that most of the other professionals shied away from Connelly and his officers, his natives. That they seemed to walk on different earth and breathe different air.

The tight-beam FTL relay had gone live late that same night, and while the commanders and liaisons from all the local merc companies slept rough in the weed-choked infield, Ted had his first conversation with Flyboy corporate, received his standing orders and, come morning, had politely kicked all the other contractors off his field with the explanation that any further combined ops would be planned through the Flyboy Inc. strategic services department. There was a number, a coordinate set. Ted had handed it around as a form of good-bye.

Most of the men had shrugged. Veterans, they knew how corporate wars were fought and understood the clean, distant appeal of office chairs, whiteboards, boardroom politics and proper hierarchies of command. No one ever died of paperwork.

Back in his tent, Ted flicked a corner of the orders on his desk with a clean, trimmed fingernail.

On that morning two years ago, while the other men were gathering up their things and their escorts, Connelly had tried to protest. Standing his ground with his aliens behind him, he'd tried to explain something that Ted wasn't hearing—so new yet to this place that he hadn't grown the necessary ears.

"I have my orders, gentlemen," he'd said, and showed them, as they say, the door.

That had been the first of his serious mistakes. Ted understood that now. But corporate math at the time had predicted completion and cleanup of the Iaxo contract, with minimal to no casualties, at one year, Zulu time. They were here to put down an insurrection, to exploit the ancient enmities of an indigenous, tribal society to aid in the securing of 110 million acres of mixed terrain, and to kill the hell out of one group of natives (called the Lassateirra faction, though Ted didn't know whether that was what they called themselves or what they were *being* called by those who prepared the paperwork) so that other, different kinds of mercenaries and widow-makers (lawyers, mostly, like Eddie) could follow on after them and negotiate with the other, surviving group (called the Akaveen Ctirad), who were apparently less hostile to the notion of handing over vast swaths of their land to developers who would settle it, clear-cut it, mine it raw, and just generally ass-rape the fuck out of it because Iaxo was a vaguely Earthlike planet and while such things weren't exactly rare, they were still extraordinarily valuable. Too valuable to leave to a bunch of fingernail monsters, that was for sure. A bunch of walking rag rugs with pointed sticks and body odor.

Considering all their advantages—their ten-century technological leap on the locals, the logistical support of a distant and powerful private military company, and negotiated aid from several other similar outfits already on the ground—a year had seemed a reasonable strategic assessment to Ted at the time. Even if his planes were museum replicas of Spads and Sopwith Camels being flown by men more accustomed to vacuum fighters and modern strike aircraft, he had the only air force for a million miles in any direction. Flyboy was going to make out well. Ted would collect a nice paycheck and bonus for making a quick and clean job of this place. A clock had been started, with a scheduled pickup in 8,760 hours, as measured in London, Earth, where the company kept their home office.

Ted had set a clock of his own and had placed it proudly on the bedside table in his tent. It'd been the last thing he'd done before going to bed that night, putting 8,500 hours and change on the display and setting it to count down. He'd felt good about things. Strong.

The two walled cities that straddled the river had been taken in short order, soon after Flyboy's arrival in the area, and everything had looked good. The fighting had been almost comically one-sided and, on the ground, the pilots amused themselves with impressions of the combat formations of the enemy—every one of them involving turning one's back and running as fast as possible away. On the night that Riverbend had been taken, the local mercs—the foot-sloggers and tin-hats, leading their companies of Akaveen indigs—had celebrated and accidentally burned half of it to the ground. Ted's pilots had seen the smoke and flames from the air, thought it a counterattack, and nearly bombed the whole lot of them. Everyone had a good laugh about it the next morning, but walking the new front—boots scuffing broken cobblestones, pacing the smashed reaches of the walls along the river that had been breached by Flyboy bombs, and stepping over shattered, burnt bodies that already smelled worse in death than they had in life—Ted had seen many of the victorious merc infantry commanders down by the water scrubbing blood and hair off their body armor and greatcoats, so had always wondered how accidental that fire had really been.

The war had moved up to the high moors—the Sispetain moors, in the language of the fingernail monsters. After almost a year, just when

Ted's clock had been tickling zero, it'd advanced over the foothills until the backside of the mountains they'd seen on insertion had been in sight. His pilots had flown and fought and performed beautifully—all early timidity or anxiousness gone. It was a job and they were the men to do it. Orders came in. Orders were executed. Everyone ate steaks for dinner, sucked fire, and shit high explosives. In that first year, Ted lost three men, but not one of them to combat. There'd been a mechanic who'd had an accident (a plane had fallen on him). Another—Gottlieb, was that his name?—had caught some kind of weird infection that'd taken him down in a day and left him comatose and on a permanent antibiotic drip. And one of the controllers had drank himself half to death and just plain lost his shit. All three had been extracted by the company. All three had been alive when they'd left and probably still were today. It was strange, but Ted couldn't remember any of them. Not really. Maybe it was because none of them were pilots. Ted's pilots had been inviolate. Untouchable.

Sitting in his tent in the dark, with his eyes closed, his lamps extinguished, Ted thought hard about the men who'd been shipped home. One of them might've been called William, he thought. Or Williams. He just wasn't sure.

A year. They'd been on track to almost making the deadline. Coming really close. Within weeks, Ted remembered thinking at the time, and had made similar promises to corporate—speaking through cutouts, to men who reported to other men who reported to other men.

The moors, where they rose and brushed against the feet of the mountains, were the last big part of the map that'd needed to be pacified before pushing on to the cities of the coast with no enemies left at their backs. The thinking was that with one last push—a combined operation utilizing all available forces in the area—the enemy could be broken there, out in the open, in the fields where the slaughter would be extraordinary.

And that was the way things had been going right up until they'd inexplicably turned and gone the other. Marie had died on the moors. Connelly lost more of his indigs than could be counted. Twenty human officers had gone out one night from the Palas FOB with a thousand native troops on a quick march to a collapsing flank position and just disappeared—none of them ever seen again. Skirmishers from Applied Outcomes would report armies massing, and by the time main body troops could be brought to position, the armies would've vanished and it would be nothing but ambush after ambush for miles of hard walking.

Native troops defected in the night, abandoning their lines, then leading the enemy back through the holes they'd created by their absence; leading them unerringly and silently to the bodies of their sleeping friends who would only wake when the blades were going into their skulls, at a weak point in the bone structure between the eyes. Wherever the Akaveen lines of advance were weakest, the path most narrow, Lassateirra indigs would seem to rise from the ugly ground to smash through the ranks. They came from behind, from below, from God only knew where. More than one human officer, stepping out a pace into the dark for a piss or a breath free of the stink of his own native troops, would be found, five minutes or an hour later, with his throat cut, his own dick in his mouth, and when engineers from Cavalier would try to build earthworks of loam and sod, they'd find the earth already choked with bones no matter where they dug. What had been a fight against a few became a war against thousands, tens of thousands, until no square foot of the high moors felt safe that wasn't actively burning or already stacked with the dead.

Things got spooky. Sispetain became like a curse word, something that no one wanted to say out loud. Pieces of it took on an almost animate malice and so were given names. Diller's Cut, the Gap, Cadillac Ridge, the Rockpile—all marks on the corporate maps, renamed by the men who killed and died there because their original, alien names were too long or ridiculous or unpronounceable.

Even the ground seemed angry and would open like a mouth in places for no good reason and swallow men whole. In the aftermath, no one had been exactly sure how it'd happened—the losing. The math had all been so solid. On paper, everyone involved should've already been at home, drinking whiskey and polishing their medals.

There was a saying, coined by men supposedly much smarter than Ted Prinzi, which said that every war looked perfect on paper but that true leadership was knowing what to do when your war moved off paper, out of the boardroom, and down into the mud. That was what Connelly had said to him on that night they'd first met, after the exchange of pleasantries, before Ted had kicked everyone out.

"Look," he'd said. "You have your orders."

"I have my orders."

"But I have to tell you this, Commander. There's this saying. Not mine, but I like it. And it says that while wars might be *planned* on paper, they are all fought down in the mud. Do you know this saying?"

"Not my war."

"What?"

"Not. My. War," Ted had repeated slowly, and jerked a thumb up into the air. "I don't fight in the mud."

Connelly had shaken his head. "You're not understanding me. What I mean is, everything looks very nice on paper, but those papers were not written on Iaxo. This place . . . I don't want to worry you or anything. I'm not trying to . . ." He'd struggled for just the right words, pressing his tongue against his teeth and grunting something that might have been alien talk and might've just been frustration. "You're going to die here thinking like that. Leadership, this saying says, is knowing what to do when your war moves off the paper and down into the mud. And we are *all* here now. In the mud."

"Not me, friend," Ted had said. "That's why God invented airplanes."

In his tent, Ted laid his hand flat over the folded paper on his table. He opened his eyes and watched his own hand, as if not entirely sure what it was going to do. Whether it was going to crumple the orders, leave them, open them.

People said all sorts of things about Connelly. Bad things. Some of them probably true. Ted said lots of bad things about Connelly, too. He'd called the man every name there was. Held him up in his own head like an avatar—the embodiment of the thing he did not ever want to become.

The clock on Ted's bedside table now read -8,041 hours. He thought about resetting it to zero, starting a new kind of countdown, but didn't have the energy. He was so tired.

Thinking back, Ted wished he knew who'd made up that saying in the first place, about the papers and the mud. He wanted to find the man who'd first said that and kill him right fucking dead.

| | | | | | | | | | | | |

Carter had left the tent and Cat behind and drank his bottle walking now. He listened to the night sounds: the rustle of tent canvas moving in the frigid breeze, the scrape and jingle of hoodoo charms hung around the neck of an indig sentry pacing his watch, footsteps crunching in the frozen grass, and the snort of a native post horse, the animal hitched and asleep on all six of its feet.

Everything on Iaxo except the indigs had too many feet by some multiple of two. It was another reason why Carter didn't like it here. Not a big one, but a reason. He took a swallow from the bottle and spit between his teeth.

It was cold. Even in all his gear, it was cold. What he wanted was another cigarette, but there were none. He'd smoked the last of his allotment weeks ago, had won a few more gambling, then smoked those, too. The indigs all smoked stubby pipes filled with a thick, mossy black flora cut with wood shavings for flavor. It made them weird if they smoked enough of it. Weirder than normal. And lit, the mixture smelled like cedar and tasted of burning hair. Carter had tried it, of course. Everyone had. It did nothing but make him sick.

Ted apparently had a stash of cigarettes, and Carter considered trying to find them, steal them, blame it on the natives. He contented himself by stoking the inner furnace with another pull from Fenn's bottle instead and turning up his collar around his ears. He thought about how much of a man's life is determined by what terrible things he chooses not to do.

He walked south through darkness, making for the dim glow of the mess and the close-cut grass of the airfield, stepping finally off the quarter line and onto the clipped fringe of A strip. He crossed at a run out of habit, reflexively glancing skyward and listening for the grumble of a descending engine cycling down. There were lights burning in the longhouse. In the infield, generators were chugging. Once he was clear of the strip and onto the opposite apron, he slowed again, childishly kicking his toes at the frozen ground with each step, stalling as best he could while still, technically, making his way to where his presence was required.

| | | | | | | | | | | |

On the field, Fenn was organizing the unloading of the drop as best as such a thing could be organized. He'd made sure no one had been crushed by the containers coming in, had stood amid the close-pressed mass of men while they'd watched the big boxes steaming, throwing off residual heat and warming them like an invisible fire. When they were cool enough to be cracked, he'd prepared an expedition to the machine shop to fetch generators and lights and pry bars and mallets—making sure that the men were supplied with enough drink to make it there and back safely. They had, but it'd taken them almost a half hour to stagger a couple hundred yards and come back again. And they'd lost at least two men in the process who wouldn't be found again until morning because war was hell even in the quietest of moments.

Back in the field house, the boys had all been drinking party liquor made from dried alien fruit and antifreeze, boiled, condensed, and dripped through gas mask filters. Before Carter had left them to go and try to sleep, before Ted had come and screwed up all the fun, they'd been playing poker under the spectral glow of a halo lamp, betting with corks and shell casings or gambling away their days off and roster positions. Vic had been there for a minute. Tommy Hill and Lefty from Carter's squadron. Ernie O'Day from Fenn's 3rd. Billy Stitches and Morris Ross and Wolfe and Stork and Johnny and some of the mechanics and ground crew as well. Everyone was having trouble sleeping these days. No one liked the mornings, but the nights were becoming unbearable.

Fenn had been talking to someone and so had missed most of Carter's departure, catching only the end of it, which had involved an overturned chair and hard words and the men all jeering him as he'd left—laughing and making jokes about missing his beauty sleep. Someone had bounced a cork off the back of Carter's head. More laughter. Carter'd given the lot of them the one-finger salute, pushed through the door, and made for his tent without saying a word to Fenn.

This was the way the men spent their days and their nights—in jest and sinning and leisure, secretly half hoping for something, *anything,* bad to happen to someone else just so the rest of them would have something to talk about for a while that wasn't the boredom, the shitty weather, their lice, misery or home. It was cheap and it was awful, but it made the time go. And as they all well knew, when there wasn't drink or poker or laughing or games or just simply staring up at the sky and pretending they weren't calculating the distance back to more friendly suns, there was always the slaughter.

It hadn't been an hour later that Ted had come in, counting heads, gathering up his work crew to break down the drop, and looking for someone to fly. Fenn had argued with Billy because Billy wanted to go night flying and wasn't a man who took kindly to being told no anymore. Then he'd sold out Carter to Ted in exchange for staying safe on the ground himself. All things considered, it hadn't been his best night. But one had to take these things philosophically. Although he'd certainly done much worse in the past year, Santa Claus had come regardless. The man's standards for who was naughty and who was nice must really be slipping, Fenn thought, and he wondered how much more killing he would've had to do to tip the scales.

When the search party had come back with the gear for opening the containers, Fenn had done little more than aim them in the proper direction and let them have at it. It was Christmas, after all. That'd been true. And the way he looked at it, every bastard among them—every killer, every defiler, every eye-shooter and psychopath and machine-gun artist—ought to have something to open on Christmas morning.

There were accidents, of course. Arguments. One fistfight. Most of the men were too drunk to walk more than a dozen paces without falling down. The holidays could be difficult, Fenn knew. When no one was looking, he tucked away some of the supplies for himself—loading boxes and packages onto a bomb sledge and dragging it to the mess tent, where he hid everything poorly but well enough to fool a bunch of drunks and mental cases. When he came back, it was to uproarious laughter and men literally doubled over. In among the cases of food and bullets and medical supplies and whatever else, the boys had uncovered a brand-new ice machine. Of all the things . . .

Fenn had caught sight of Carter walking then, kicking his toes at the frozen dirt and making for his plane. He'd raised a hand to wave, but Carter hadn't seen him. He'd called out—meaning to tell him about the ice machine because Fenn knew Carter would appreciate the absurdity of it—but Carter hadn't heard him. Lost in his own world, that man. Fenn shook his head and turned back to the task at hand which, just then, involved loading up another sledge full of commandeered supplies for his tentmate.

Vic had called Carter's plane out of the longhouse when she'd been told to do so. She'd loaded it, muscling the gun truck over the uneven ground herself because it was cold and doing something was warmer than doing nothing. She'd topped up its tank and given it a once-around check, then rubbed a spot on the spine of its tail assembly because there was something about the join of the machines right there that felt like touching a living body, like feeling the regular points of vertebrae pushing up against taut skin. And there was something about touching it right there in order to make sure the machine came home whole.

She was not superstitious. She didn't believe in animism or luck or anything of the sort. She liked machines because she liked rules, order, and the simple interactions of parts made to fit, and she believed in numbers—gear ratios and screw speeds and torque and cylinder synchronization—because numbers were the language of machines. She believed in touching this spot on the planes because, to date, no machine that she'd touched in such a way had ever not come home. This wasn't superstition. This was math.

Vic rubbed the spot with her bare fingertips, feeling them bump over the swelling ribs of the plane through doped cloth and lacquer, and closed her eyes.

"Come home," she said to the machine.

That was part of the ritual, too.

Carter found his ride waiting, primed and topped up, on the taxiway at the friendly end of A strip. He'd done a quick once-around, touching her hard skin and the wire stays between her wings, kicking the tires. He'd shuffled, half dreaming still of hot coffee and cigarettes and imagining in the cold and quiet that he could hear alien leaves falling from alien trees onto alien soil. They blazed up here into russet autumn colors, the leaves. Same as they did at home. Everything turned yellow, red, and gold, and Carter had known dangerous, painfully blissful moments where he'd almost been able to forget where he was except for one variety of tree with leaves that turned pale blue as if suffocating in the cold and that never failed to ruin the view.

He hated those fucking trees.

He'd tossed the bottle out into the grass and pulled himself into the cockpit. He'd buckled in, smeared a thumb's worth of astringent-smelling grease onto his nose and cheeks and the shells of his ears to keep them from freezing in the cold, then blah-blah-blah'd his way through clearances. In the infield, generator-driven lights were burning, but he didn't know why. There were more bodies moving around than should've normally been up and about at this hour.

It didn't matter. With a finger, he teased the engine to life and let it warm a minute in the dark. He closed his eyes. The vibration of his machine tuned high and rumbling was like love, he thought. Like drifting off to sleep with one's whole body pressed against the beating, blood-thrumming heart of a monster. The power of it was intoxicating. More so in this place where any power at all was overwhelming.

The chatter of the radio in his ear startled him. His orders, approach radials, altitude, target information, radio frequencies. Dull. He pulled his gloves on. The green flags came out. He throttled his plane gently forward—bouncing over the uneven ground, struggling to keep her between the pin lights that stuttered to life and lined the runway while one of the ground crew stumbled backward, leading him. Lambert, he thought. Or maybe the other one.

The flags came down. His guide loped out of the way and fell down in the dark. Carter advanced the throttle to the first catch. As the ground began to run away beneath him, he gave the plane more juice, shoving hard at the power handle to open her up and listening to the tone of the engine grow from that throaty rumble into a glorious howl. When, together, they lifted clear of dirt and gravity, it was like being born all over again.

And then there was no sound at all but the roar of the air streaming past him and a distant, droning hum from forward; there was nothing to see in the perfect dark of night flying through the primeval world but the phosphorescent dials of his wet gauges and the dimly glowing iconography of the flight computer rudely hacked into the wood-and-plastic instrument panel.

| | | | | | | | | | | |

Because he was looking for it, Fenn saw Carter's plane lift and vanish like a mote into the darkness. He'd tucked away a nice load of pilfered treats for his friend and, provided Carter didn't die, would surprise him with them when he came back home again.

| | | | | | | | | | | |

Because she was waiting for it, Vic heard the clattering buzz and grumble of Carter's liftoff. She gauged the relative health of the machine by the spectrum of noises it made as it passed by her, took to the air, and faded into distant silence. It was a good machine. Strong. Well maintained. She loved it for all its best qualities, even if they were few and simple and archaic, and she forgave it its grosser incompetencies because it couldn't help being what it was. She was in the machine shop and decided she would wait for it to come home to her before going to bed. Just to make sure nothing bad happened to it in the night. Just for the comfort of seeing it alive and safe one more time.

She ran scarred fingers permanently blacked with grease through her dark hair and dug the hard heels of her palms into her eyes, sighing out a breath that steamed in the cold. A couple hours, she thought. If everything went smoothly. Maybe less. She could wait.

| | | | | | | | | | | |

Because he was listening for it, Ted heard the cough and sputter of an engine catching down on the flight line. He listened to it settle into a growl that climbed the octaves into a keening buzz, then floated up and away into the night. In the dark, he checked the luminescent dial of his watch. Thirty minutes, a little less. Not good, considering he'd asked it to be done in ten, but not terrible either. Not insubordinate. Carter had gone, which was something. Knowing what he knew, there was a part of Ted that was surprised. He thought that maybe if it'd been him, he wouldn't have. He would've said *Fuck you* to himself, rolled over, gone back to bed, and tried to wake up later with some kind of enthusiasm for this war.

Now he stood up, straightened his uniform, cleared his throat and spit into one corner of his tent. Tiredness had left him feeling hollow and light, like he was drifting standing still, but he needed to be at comms. When he went out the door of his tent, he left the final orders from corporate sitting on the edge of his desk, still unopened, but didn't make it ten steps before he came rushing back, crashing through his own door, to slap them off the wood, paw through his drawers for a lighter, and then hold them over the bright flame until they caught. He held the paper until the flames ate their way to his hand, close enough to blacken his fingertips. He held it as long as he could, until the pain made him suck a breath in through his teeth, then threw the final corner up into the air—watching it drift and burn and transmute itself into black smoke and nothingness.

When it was done, he nodded his head once and sat back down again, sucking on his burned fingers like a child. If anyone at comms needed him, they could come find him. He was the goddamn commander, after all. No need for him to be everywhere at once.

CARTER'S PLANE WAS CALLED ROADRUNNER AND IT WAS HIS BABY, his best girl, queen of Iaxo's maddeningly not-quite-earthly sky. She was done up in mottled gray, black, and white night-fighter camo with laughing skulls and swords and flaming spades painted slapdash onto her doped skin of fire-retardant cloth. Childish, but severe. The natural result of drink and paint and too much time on his hands.

She was a mutt, a Sopwith fighter with a little Spad blood dirtying up her clean lines—short in the nose like a Pup with a Camel's forward-leaning wings, but boxy in the tail after the fashion of the elder Spads, modeled on the best notions of those primordial aeronautics hobbyists (Blériot and Saulnier; Béchereau; Herbert Smith; the Italian, Rosatelli; Camm and Fokker) who'd invented the idea of killing from the air cen-turies ago; with a few improvements in weight and airframe dreamed up by the generations of flight engineers who became heir to all that wicked knowledge.

When Carter chose, she could be the fastest thing in the sky—which was to say faster than the few birds that lived here, the bugs, and the clouds shushing icily above him, which were the only competition. Only now, he did not want her to be fast. Now, they—Roadrunner and he—were moving as slowly as any unnatural creature of the air

might while still *remaining* a creature of the air and not suddenly choking out, stalling, and becoming a creature as one with the cold, hard, and
distant ground. He could feel her moving from good air to bad, could
feel the slide of lift along her control surfaces. He could feel her bucking and struggling as they chugged along because she was a machine
that wanted to fly, to climb; that wanted never to descend into the drab
oppression of gravity. And on that one point, Roadrunner and her pilot
were in absolute agreement. Neither had ever done so well with their
gear on the ground as they did in the air.

Roadrunner's instrumentation was archaic. There was a compass (ori-
ented for a different polar environment), dial altimeter, pitch-and-roll
bubble, fuel stick, airspeed indicator, engine RPM and pressure and
temperature gauges. Here, on this world, it was high-line voodoo. And
the onboard computers were both more and less impressive for being
less simple, more contained, and worlds stupider.

The computers were never in complete agreement with the plane's
more elemental mechanisms. Always a difference of opinion. The digital gauges showed a redundant, simplified, and three-color view of the
world; a child's vision, all bright triangles and wavy lines and bold numbers. Between Carter's legs, the idiot lights showed green: fuel, oil pressure, engine temp, hydraulics, prop speed. In the center of his panel, a
computerized map showed hieroglyph landmarks, blinking navigational
aids, distances from this and to that. But it spoke to something in the
distance between the world Carter had known and the world in which
he now found himself that he understood less about how Roadrunner's
analog altimeter knew his distance from the ground or the wet compass
knew the way home than he did about the workings of the FTL drive
on the container ship that'd brought him to the Carpenter system or
the hydrazine thrust belts on the dropship that'd deposited him on Iaxo.

Because the company and its men couldn't use satellite position-
ing (what they were doing on Iaxo was clandestine at its most polite,
but mostly just plain criminal, so the satellites themselves—even the
very small ones—were too conspicuous in orbit around a planet full of
natives who still thought God made the lightning), and because radar
was right out, they were forced to rely on dead reckoning, surface track,
and radio triangulation against preset navigational markers. All of which

was for shit when the difference between flying and crashing was measured in feet and inches, not miles.

So Carter, like his mates, carried a programmable stopwatch instead, accurate to one-hundredth of a second, a handheld UV/thermal spotting scope with a pulse range finder, and a map—pen on paper—made by Billy Stitches from first squadron. Carter had his flash-taped to his thigh and, at night, flew the way a submariner once piloted: trusting his life to the inarguable tick of the clock. Billy, he trusted. The watch, the scope and the map were all he truly believed in—his trinity. For lack of any more solid theological footing, he put his faith in Billy Stitches and, thus far, Billy had never let him down.

It didn't mean he felt any safer, flying blind into the endless dark. And it certainly didn't mean he didn't pilot with a horrible, sick feeling that, at any moment, he was going to crash prop-first into an odd copse of hard alien trees, stick there like a dart, and burn. Night missions, he would always fly with the sour taste of anxious vomit in the back of his throat, squeezing and straining the eyes right out of his head looking for death oncoming at a hundred miles an hour, and then land again, hours and hours later, with a relief like waking alive from a bad dream of falling and a headache that only drink, sleep, or decapitation would cure.

He hated flying at night.

| | | | | | | | | | | |

It surprised Carter when he found Billy Stitches and Morris Ross up in the middle of the night. Billy was out night-flying for fun in a two-seat spotter (a rebuilt Bristol fighter, actually, with a jumped-up rotary V-8 turboprop salvaged from one of the two wrecks the company had so far suffered). Billy was sitting in the gunner's chair, peeking downward, backward, and sideward through UV light amps while Morris flew, sketching terrain details and shouting directions in Morris's ear. Carter had Billy on the radio periodically, making jokes, keeping him amused while he zigged and zagged his way along a broken, preset course to the ford. Carter asked Billy how he could work on his maps at night. Billy told him to shut up before Carter jinxed him. Even with night vision and a moon and a half playing tag through breaks in the clotted clouds, the world below was nothing more than the *suggestion* of a world to Carter. Touches of silver here and there, gilt flourishes, a sense of undulating life, and somewhere off his left wing, the river catching reflections and shattering them against its banks. They had names, those moons. Carter didn't know them.

Much as he disliked it, there were moments when even he felt this world deserved a poet. It had, in instants, a kind of unspoiled beauty that Carter imagined Earth once might've before the earth became home to humans and all their clutter. In the light, Iaxo was occasionally fantastical, something out of a fairy tale. In the night, it was intermittently magic.

Still, it was an easier place to hate than to love. Hating was more useful, too. And for all Carter knew, Iaxo might've already had a poet. Might've had scores of them. And he felt that if he and his friends or others like his friends didn't kill them all, perhaps someday some indig would say something lovely about this place. It was their home, after all. Carter and his kind were just visiting.

Billy called in, saying Morris had gotten him lost.

"How would you know?" asked Carter.

"It's all Zen, son," Billy said. "The maps, the flying. The whole deal. Your problem is you are under the illusion that you actually exist." His laughter grated like iron filings in Carter's teeth.

Billy Stitches was called Billy Stitches because his face looked like a medical school cadaver's face—a practice face on which young and untalented knife artists had attempted to hone their skills. Billy's scars were burn scars, surgery scars, the fleshy archaeological record of meatball reconstruction in a field hospital somewhere back when he was a colonial pilot flying supersonic fighter-bombers and killing for the cause. Alternate version: Billy Stitches was called Billy Stitches because his scars were his pride, earned during a crash-and-burn on some distant hell where everything ate everything and the only safe place for those made of meat was high aloft—dropping jellied fire and chemical defoliant onto alien landscapes that looked like something out of a deep pharmaceutical nightmare.

He'd been flying for a different company at the time, trying to tame this frontier backwater for the pioneer families already on their way. And when he'd gone in, he'd shattered the face shield of his helmet and been force-fed some of the bigger, more jagged pieces.

Eight days he'd survived in the jungle, waiting for rescue. His wounds had rotted, become home to bugs and flies and centipedes, and his hot, sweet blood had driven even the trees into a starving frenzy. Billy was eaten, a little bit at a time, by every living thing in the jungle and would often say that what he was left with when the recovery team finally found him were only those parts that even nature had found undigestible.

| | | | | | | | | | | |

Carter said, "So long as the payroll department is under that same illusion, I think I'll be okay, Billy. Meanwhile, I now have considerably less faith in your maps, knowing you do them blind in the middle of the night."

"Got to trust me, boy. I do this all the damn time. For kicks. Go out in the day with Morris blindfolded for practice!"

"You're going to get yourself dead," Carter told him. Billy laughed again.

"No one pretty as me is going to die in a place as nasty as this, friend."

"You know what they call that, Billy?" Carter asked. "They call that irony."

Billy'd left his radio open and was yelling at Morris. "Morris! *Morris!* Where the hell are we?" Static. "Like hell! If that's where we are, then what's that mountain doing there?" Static. "You're lost, Morris. Admit it, bud. Climb out to fourteen thou and get yourself found again 'fore I slap your head." Static. "Carter? It'll only be irony if I actually end up dead. Till that happens, it's just boyish enthusiasm." Static. "West, Morris! That's a left turn. Where the hell are you going?" Static. "Carter? I'm out, son. If I don't come home, tell the boys it was all Morris's fault and tell your friend Teague to kiss my ragged ass . . ." Laughter, high and giggling, distorted by interference and distance into a manic cackle.

Laughter, then static.

Then just static and nothing else.

| | | | | | | | | | | |

The third version of the story was that Billy'd done it all to himself one night with a trench knife or a piece of broken glass. He'd made eleven tours with the company, seen eleven different worlds. He'd been a Ted before Ted was Ted.

And then he'd just cracked one day. Gone around the bend. The company had retired him, demoted him, sent him to therapy, to a rest home, for some miraculous psychological cure or to take the waters. He'd come back a different man—an artist and an armchair philosopher and happy in some deeply incorruptible way. When he smiled, it looked like he was dying.

"So which story is it, Billy?" the pilots would occasionally ask.

The third one.

No, the first.

The second.

"Does it matter?"

"Come on, Billy. Which one is it?"

"They all are."

Iaxo, of course, was his first mission back. Those scars were still so fresh that he cried in the night from the pain of them. That was the version that Carter chose to believe, which, Carter thought, maybe said more about him than it did about Billy.

| | | | | | | | | | | |

Carter clacked his radio and switched to the control channel, called in his position, clicked the stopwatch and marked himself on Billy's map as a mile and a quarter short of where the flight computer claimed he was. With his goggles pushed up, the rushing air whipped tears from the corners of his eyes, atomizing them off the tips of his ears, frozen despite the liberal application of grease. In the open cockpit, he had to hunch behind the windscreen to hear. When the call-back from the comms tent came, it confirmed that he had calculated correctly and that the computer had not, reading him short by a mile and change. Pinning the stick between his knees, he made corrections and, thirty seconds outside the drop zone, dug the spotting scope out of his jacket and tried to get a fix on the lines.

The river ran southeasterly at this point. Durba's rifles were supposed to be dug in along the bank on the friendly side with Connelly's 4th in a reactionary position a quarter mile downriver on the unfriendly bank. Carter's orders were to move in support of Durba, illuminating a cross, two miles by two miles, starting at a point a quarter mile forward of Durba's position and immediately to Connelly's left, because it was thought that somewhere in that area were a bunch of scheming indigs meaning to make a nuisance of themselves come morning. Durba wanted to catch them napping, give them a good scare to the tune of a few minutes' concentrated rifle fire, and chase them off before they got any fancy ideas about trying to take back the ford.

The ford had become important because, other than the bridge, it was the only reasonable river crossing between the fortified towns of Riverbend to the north and Southbend to the south. Obviously, these were the visitors' names for these places. The natives called them something else, but no one much cared what. Gurgle and Mumble, Burble and Babble—something wet and dreadful and altogether alien. The bridge—itself just a pile of rocks and sticks stacked somewhat higher than the water at full flow—was solidly held now by the other side, as were the two towns and everything east of the river.

These had been the lines for months now, ever since the fight had forced everyone off the moors and high ground to the east and back across the river in battles that would've made Napoleon weep. Indig infantry and cavalry on their ridiculous six-legged horses had arranged into lines that'd stretched for miles, all wheeling and clashing while the company and its pilots bombed and machine-gunned them with virtual impunity. For weeks, the fighting had gone on. In some places, the stony sod of the moors had drank up so much indig blood that it turned to brackish mud deep enough to mire horses and suck down cart wheels to the hub. Carter remembered doing barrel rolls over Diller's Cut as the forward lines being maintained by Palas collapsed for the last time, his guns chattering until they jammed, bomb garlands empty. He could close his eyes and still see entire wings of fighters diving like hawks to break columns of reinforcements pouring in from invisible strongholds in the foothills when things had gone from bad to worse.

The loss of life, among the indigs, anyway, had been phenomenal, unbelievable, enormous—the kind of war a man dreams about at his most perverse and fervent. A sweaty, sickening kind of bloodlust; fathomless like dying of thirst on the ocean. Though since none of that incredible loss had been among the company's pilots, they'd all found it great fun and talked of it like a vacation that'd come just in the nick of time.

Connelly, though, had suffered on the moors. Durba had suffered, losing his daughter toward the end of things when, almost impossibly, losing had become a foregone conclusion, then an actual reality. There were other contractors working on Iaxo prior to the Sispetain campaign, and they'd all suffered, too, Carter knew. Ambushes, desertions, human officers being murdered by their own native troops. And once the opposition had gotten themselves organized and started throwing thousands of bodies into the grinder—cavalry charges crashing against fortified machine-gun positions, Lassateirra infantry with iron knives and spears appearing out of nowhere, behind previously secure lines, to rush sleeping encampments of Akaveen and their human officers or moving columns of troops, slaughtering everything in sight, stealing everything they could grab, then vanishing—the fronts had all collapsed. It became a retreat. Then a rout. And everyone down in the mud and the blood and the filth had suffered save the princes of the air with their exclusive contract and flying machines.

But ever since then, the company's men on Iaxo had done what they could to help the mudfoot mercenaries fighting on their side. It was guilt, a little bit. Ted's, predominantly. Some of it was wanting to present a unified front to the indigs on both sides just in case one of these days their gravy train went all to shit.

It was widely assumed that Connelly the Coward, in command of his own fourth company, would retreat as soon as he saw the flares or heard the rifles tuning up. From the position he held, though, his avenues of escape were limited. He couldn't cross back over the river where he was, and moving upriver toward the ford would only bring him closer to the fighting, so everyone knew he wouldn't do that. His only choices would be to hold fast, head farther southeast down the bank or forward, deeper into unfriendly territory. No matter what he did, the friendlies on the ground would either come out equal by morning or have bought a whole new swath of land owing to Connelly's dependable nighttime skittishness. Durba would then be free to cross the ford himself, move downriver to take Connelly's old position (or reinforce him if he'd held). Come the dawn, five hundred indig foot soldiers under native command would move up to secure the rear.

It was a simple plan, elegant and tactically sound in that so much of tactics has to do not with the ordering of men to do what you want them to do but with knowing what they'll do all on account of their own recklessness, stupidity, or fright, and then adapting to the inevitable. Carter had received his specific orders in-flight, by radio—one of the controllers reading to him from pages written by somebody else. On paper, it'd seemed brilliant.

Durba had a field radio. The way things were supposed to go, he would call in as soon as he heard Roadrunner overhead, light up a UV strobe to mark the front of his own lines, then act as forward observer, spotting for Carter on his run. Meanwhile, Carter would buzz over pretty as can be at three hundred feet, drop a dozen impact-trigger parachute flares, split-loop west, lay out another line to finish the cross, then say good-bye and go home for a hot breakfast and a nap, content in the knowledge that, thanks to his hard work, one fine lot of alien critters whom he'd never met and didn't care a damn for would have the opportunity to slaughter some other lot about whom he cared even less in the middle of the night rather than having to wait a few hours for the sun to rise. Good for them, Carter figured. Luck and all. He'd sleep soundly no matter what. He mostly did.

So now he followed the river in with one eye on the stopwatch, the other glued to the optic of the spotter's scope. He was counting down the seconds, maintaining a steady crawl speed, waiting on Durba's call. His night vision was blown because of the scope, the light amps, the burr of swirling ultraviolet. The tree cover along the banks was too dense for him to see anything worthwhile. On UV, it was a soft, quiet kaleidoscope of green and tangles. And on thermal, Iaxo was a bad disco—all blobby reds and blues and oranges and blacks mixing and separating like oils on a plate. For love or money, he couldn't pick out the nice clean entrenched line that Durba ought to have had laid out—one hundred native rifles plus a seven-man off-world command element, their combined body heat like a snake of fire crawling against the cold indigo nothing of the ground—and instead saw only a jumbled, seething mess of heat signatures smoldering so crazily out of proportion that, for a moment, he thought the scope had gone tits-up on him.

At twenty seconds out, Durba should've been able to hear Roadrunner coming. A biplane is not a quiet machine. In this place where a tree falling is cacophonous and men walking can be the loudest noise in the forest, a nine-cylinder rotary whines and clatters and roars like a cam stripping off the pivot of the world. Carter touched gloved fingers to the map on his thigh. He felt something in his chest squirm.

Fifteen seconds. Ten. Carter ought to have been right on top of them, but still nothing. In the freezing cold, the back of his neck began to sweat. Not a peep from the radio. Strange.

Walking blind in one's own dark bedroom, there are only two sensations: perfect confidence and absolute panic. Nothing between. And one bleeds into the other so quickly. One second, you know, vaguely or precisely, just where you are and where everything is in relation to you. The next, everything comes unstuck. One wrong step, one chair out of place, and one loses one's self completely so that all of a midnight comes crashing down in a terror of unfixedness. This was what Carter was feeling—the sickly slide into sudden dread and disorientation.

Five seconds out. This was as good as overshooting and would already require a long climb out and a new approach. So much for the element of surprise, Carter thought. At which point he was completely surprised by the sudden squawk of the radio crackling to life. The voice on the other end, though, rather than having the laconic drawl of Tony Fong, Durba's Earthside Chinese-Texan radioman and occasional guest at the Flyboy O Club, was speaking indig—a language Carter had always thought contained far too many hisses and consonants and sounded like a wet cat being beaten with an abacus. He spoke a dozen words of it, most of them obscene. The indig on the other end of the radio wasn't using any of those, just hissing and clattering, clicking away. Carter fumbled with the handset and the stick. Roadrunner fought to roll over on him because she was not a machine that took inattention cheerfully. He tried to focus on the details, straightening out one thing at a time.

Carter was having a fracture experience—a moment of unconscious denial of the obvious owing to a lack of belief in the potentiality of change. A quick sum: Take one hundred rifles in the hands of one hundred native infantrymen, add seven mercenary officers well versed in the intricacies of commanding indigenous forces and one dark night on foreign shores. Subtract one radio contact. What is left?

Disaster. With Durba himself, a first sergeant, three lieutenants (one of whom owed Carter money), a medic, and Tony Fong all on the ground, all human and all English-speakers, that meant that either one large catastrophe or seven individual and highly unlikely catastrophes must have occurred in order to leave an indig holding the radio. But Carter simply could not imagine any event or series of events that would've seen all seven of these men incapacitated at the critical moment. Because while the other side was fighting with bows and arrows, pointy sticks, and rocks, Antoinne Durba had goddamn *rifles*. Granted, they weren't anything fancy. One hundred reproduction Martini-Henry, lever-action 11 mm long rifles and three museum-piece compressor-driven light machine guns. But still: rifles. *Ask the American Indians what kind of difference a few white men with boom sticks had made in their lives,* he thought.

Carter's mind raced. He was breathing heavy. He fiddled with the radio dials. Put a knee into the bottom of the flight computer, hoping to jog its microchips into making this all better.

Fracture experience. All evidence to the contrary, his first thought was that Tony must've been out having a piss or something. Meanwhile, all around him people were silently moving the furniture in his darkened bedroom. Everything was about to change.

Carter passed clear over what should've been Durba's position, clicked the stopwatch, slammed the throttle forward and laid Roadrunner over into a steep, spiraling climb. On the other end of the radio, the indig voice was still chittering away. Tough to tell when those fellows were in a panic, Carter knew. Everything they said sounded like a death rattle. But he heard no gunfire in the background, no sounds of distress. Was the indig in his ear begging, crying, praying for him to smite down his enemies from the sky? A bored, disconnected, and indifferent god, Carter switched his radio back over to the command frequency, pointed his prop toward the clouds, and let the altimeter spin.

He called in: "Control, this is Roadrunner. Radio check, copy?"

"Copy Roadrunner. This is air control. Hold one."

A woman's voice. Carter knew her but couldn't quite remember her name. Donna? He wasn't accustomed to dealing with the night shift.

"Donna?" he asked.

"Diane, Carter."

Shit. Of course, Diane. Short, froggish, used to go around with the men for a bit, Carter recalled, then didn't. At which point she'd taken over the tent on night shift to keep away from the pilots entirely.

He keyed the channel again. "Sorry, Diane. I've got a problem here. Can't raise Durba."

Diane mumbled something cruel about males in general.

"Repeat that, control. Didn't quite catch it."

"Hold position, Carter. And shut up for a minute while we get you sorted out. Monitor this channel. Control out."

He climbed to five thousand feet, leveled out, and circled.

And circled some more.

Billy's channel was closed. Hopefully, he clicked over to what should've been Durba's, but the indig on the other end was still carrying on. Back to control, then, and silence as he eased the throttle and fuel mix down near stall and started box-waltzing the area, laying out mile-long trails broken by ninety-degree left breaks. It was at this point—exactly far too late—that Carter thought to himself how it might've been a good idea to have made at least a passing attempt at learning the language of the animals for whom he'd been fighting these past months. Something more than the curse words anyhow. It wasn't like he hadn't had the time.

He locked the stick between his knees and stretched, his back popping all in a line like a zipper. He yawned, dug the scope out of his jacket again, shed altitude until he was cruising a thousand feet off the deck, and took another look around. The forest below remained the same sea of blobby color cut through by the squirming black snake of the river. The UV light amps turned everything shimmering silver tarnished with electric verdigris. In the dark, at altitude, an ocean and a forest looked the same. Both dull. Carter closed his eyes, talked just to hear himself speaking.

"Control, this is Roadrunner. What am I doing here, Diane?"

"Flying 'round in circles, looks like. Just keep it up. And keep an eye out for anything unusual."

"Unusual like how?"

"Unusual like unusual, Roadrunner. I don't know. Do you see anything unusual right now?"

"It's nighttime. It's dark."

"Which means you have nothing to report, so clear the channel."

"Diane, what happened to Antoinne?"

Ted was up when Tanner, one of the other flight controllers, knocked on the door of his tent. Unable to rest and sick with a knot of worry that felt like a stone in his throat, Ted had gotten into the gun cases between which he normally pressed his shirts and trousers and had begun pulling out files and papers, maps, supply logs and repair records. He needed to make some kind of plan. On his table, the clock mocked him with every negative number. He'd removed his sidearm and put it away in a drawer.

Ted got up and jerked open the door. Tanner stood with a hint of attention still in him. He was young, so recently out of service (which one, Ted couldn't recall) that the tatters of discipline still clung to him like the rags of a uniform he couldn't quite completely remove.

"At ease, Tanner," Ted said. "It's the middle of the night. Why are you bothering me?"

"Diane told me to come get you," he said, swallowing the "sir" only with visible difficulty.

"She have a reason?"

"Something wrong with Captain Carter's mission, I think."

Ted closed his eyes, sucking a deep breath through his nose. He suppressed the urge to cough, so choked instead, strangling on the shit in his lungs.

"She said she needs you now."

"About face," Ted croaked.

"What?"

"Turn the fuck around!"

Tanner did, and Ted doubled over—half coughing, half vomiting in the dirt outside his tent with his shoulder pressed into the frame of the door. He did it quickly, coughed again, then stood, shot the cuff on his jacket, wiped the back of his mouth with his shirtsleeve, straightened his jacket, and told Tanner to turn back around.

"Let's go," he said. "Tell me the problem while we walk."

| | | | | | | | | | | |

Carter just happened to be looking over the side of the plane—out past the forward edge of the lower wing—when the world ended. He was squinting down into the big black nothing below him, comparing it in his head to the big black nothings in front of him and to either side, trying to make it resolve into some kind of answer by force of exasperated will alone when, quite unexpectedly, it did.

For just an instant, as the first bright blooms of the explosions flared blindingly below him, Carter thought that somehow he had done this: that his hatred of this place and its people had suddenly been made impossibly manifest in scourging fire from his eyes. He watched, dumbstruck and gawping like a yokel, frantically touching hands to all of his controls, wondering, in a panic, if he'd accidentally triggered a bomb drop even though he wasn't carrying bombs and none of the planes here were capable of carrying anything large enough to look like Alfred Nobel's wrath from a mile up.

And then, suddenly, Carter's fracture experience—last vestige of the peace of the ignorant and all-powerful—is ripped from him, carried away on the rising energy of the shock wave that lifts them up, the man and his plane, and carries them briefly free of gravity and airflow and elevator control; lifting them as if on top of a bubble, expanding the sky around them into a torrent of disturbed molecules that, if they had a color, would be like the halo around an angel's head. A shade of preternatural grace and fury.

Together, they billow straight upward, then are dropped like something vile. Carter stomps and throttles Roadrunner into a wide, falling inside bank and flies straight into the collapsing bubble of a second wave that swats them toward the ground with the weight of atmospheres righting themselves. Air cascades onto them like a waterfall, rushing down to fill the pressure void. Carter doesn't even realize he is yelling until he splits back east, comes out of the mess, and feels the control surfaces find some traction.

He levels out into a choppy glide. His throat hurts. His mouth is dry as bone. Ducking behind the windscreen, he pulls his goggles down, says a brief thanks to the man who invented the condom catheter, and then pants like a dog until he gets his breath back.

The radio squawks. Carter'd never closed the channel. Diane was probably deaf now, he thinks. Maybe it served her right.

The flight computer is out, screen black and cold as a dead eye, and Carter is lost, bubble altimeter holding at eight hundred feet, compass nosing east-nor'east. His stopwatch rattles around somewhere by his feet and the radio is clacking now—*squelch, squelch, squelch*. Distress sign. Diane asking if he is dead or dying or knocked brainless or what.

But Carter just breathes, holds the stick in fingers gone numb with shock, keeps his feet away from the pedals because his legs are shaking so badly. He looks out at the night. All around him, the peace of darkness has returned. It is like nothing ever happened at all.

In the comms tent, Diane cranes her neck and looks toward the door. "Did someone go to get the commander?" she asks. "Because we need him in here. Now."

Artillery.

From above, the explosions unfold like flowers—crimson and sharp at the center, then fluffing outward to pale yellow, gray, then black. They blossom, open, then collapse back in on themselves as the laws of physics, momentarily brutalized, reassert themselves. Flames die, waves calm, vacuums are filled, shock stills, and gravity pulls all that dust and debris and death back down to the ground where it belongs. It's fast, yet still appears to happen all in one long, slow motion. This is the difference between bombs and high-explosive artillery shells. Bombs are quick all through. They flare and are gone. Exploding shells, though, do that strange trick of seeming slow. That's how one can tell the difference. See it enough and it's a hard thing to forget.

Carter had seen it enough. Not here. Elsewhere. Other jobs in other places. He'd been caught once in a similar pressure wave, flying low over the trench and bunker lines on a planet called Feldike way out on the rim. Gravity was different there, harder and heavier, the atmosphere thick and poison. The company'd been flying for the cause then, too— Marxist revolt among the miners who'd decided that they deserved a piece of all the money being burned and cut and melted from the planet's guts. Maybe not *entirely* Marxist, actually, but that didn't matter. Those miners could pay up front, would pay an additional fortune when they won. And they were grateful for the help. Until the arrival of the flying circus (sixteen Flyboy squadrons, plus nearly five hundred command, control, and support personnel) the battles on Feldike had been fought mostly with the mining equipment—enormous rolling ore mills the size of an office block, tunneling machines like nightmare millipedes as long and large as bloated, rock-muddled skyscrapers laid on their sides. The machines could take a phenomenal amount of punishment but carried tools able to dish out phenomenal damage: massive stone grinders, lasers meant for cutting rock, jackhammers and rock drills, atomics. On the ground, they fought in environment suits, loader bodies, whatever was available—men like ants scaling the sides of the massive machines and planting demolition charges meant for blowing tunnel mouths, always going for the track linkages, articulated joints, the heat sinks or pilot's compartments that sat behind six-inch-thick bubbles of shatterproof diamondoid but could be popped like a zit by a determined enemy.

The company's arrival had changed the dynamics of the war. The machines still in the hands of management were slow, large targets and could be pummeled from afar by sheaf rockets, laser-guided smart munitions, and bombs meant for cracking mountains. Up close, they could be eviscerated by chain guns firing deuterium-tipped rounds, six thousand per minute, or thermite rockets. They could be crippled by high explosives and then killed by the miners who swarmed over them. On nights off, camped out in the top floors of seized company offices, the pilots would stand with their noses pressed against the diamond glass, watching the distant action like a fireworks show. The best entertainment in town.

The planes they'd flown there had been strange tractor/jet mutants, sucking in the poison atmosphere from a scoop in the nose, accelerating it through the length of the dart-like body and then spitting it out the back end as turbine thrust. They were slow, flew with all the elegance of a brick, fell from the toxic sky like killed birds almost every day from wear and corrosion and just plain orneriness. They'd been custom engineered for the environment just like the biplanes they flew now had been for Iaxo, but Feldike's was an environment that was hostile to everything. There was no native life there. Just humans who'd come for the stones.

The mining company had been almost beaten, had resorted to desperation tactics to dislodge the miners, when Carter'd had his accident. They'd begun employing the magnetic accelerators, once used to fling things into orbit, like primitive mortars, dialing the charge way down and throwing all kinds of things into them, blind-firing in the direction of the trench lines that had, at that point, been dug within fifty miles of the corporate headquarters and port facilities. One thing the miners were very good at was digging. The war was going to be over within a week.

It was a mining charge that'd erupted below Carter's jet on Feldike. Smallish. A couple of kilotons, maybe. Enough to rip a fifty-meter crater in the terrible earth and pop Carter's jet up like a cork, knock it clean into a flip—nose over jet and ass over teakettle. The vacuum caused the turbine to sputter and fail. It'd refused to restart, and Carter had hit the switch, punching out just five hundred feet above the surface, briefly riding a hydrogen peroxide charge clear of the tumbling jet body, then watching the barrage as he descended, sealed cockpit hanging below three drag chutes and heading to ground fast. The explosions then had looked the same as the explosions on Iaxo—weird, slo-mo blooms making umbrellas rather than mushrooms in the heavy gravity but unfolding with the same peculiar indolence.

He'd fallen hard, finally, right in the path of one of the advancing ore mills. The treads rose a hundred feet high, clanking iron links rumbling like the end of the world. Around him, the explosions were still going off, blasting black gashes in the red-brown stone and dirt—the jerry-rigged mortar operators having found their range. He'd been rescued in plenty of time by a recovery team flying a heavy lifter, but he would never forget the image of those treads grinding down on him, his own hands pressed to the cockpit glass, staring past them at the mill pilot in his bubble, the two of them watching each other, waiting to see what would happen next.

EVEN IN HIS PANIC, Carter'd been able to count the explosions blossoming below him on Iaxo. There'd been four of them, walking in a line. And then four more, oblique to him, off his right wing, opening outward and upward and, at a distance—too far away to hurt him—really rather beautiful. Down on the ground, he knew, it would seem like something different entirely.

He poked a shaky finger at the radio, clacking it twice, and adjusted his headset and collar. "Control, this is Roadrunner. Do you copy?"

"Roadrunner, this is control. We copy." Diane still, her professional voice unfazed, even by the screaming. "What is your status?"

"I'm five-by-five. Just shook up, but still in flight and on-target. My flight electronics are out. Can you see where I am?"

"We're trying to reboot you from here, Roadrunner, but I've got you smooth and level at ten-two-five off the deck, heading thirty-eight degrees east by double north, west of target six-point-five miles, closing angle." A pause. "Also, biologicals show you pissed yourself. Nice going there, hotshot."

Bloom of shame in Carter's cheeks not at all unlike the bloom of artillery shells in the distance. "You want to come up here and try flying for me, Diane?" *Everyone pisses themselves on night missions,* Carter thought. *Everyone.* "Jesus Christ, like I need this from some dumb—"

Diane interrupted. "Roadrunner, control. Hold for the commander. Diane out."

Historically speaking, hearing Ted's voice almost never meant one was about to receive good news. All the pilots knew this, discussed it at length sometimes when there was nothing else worth talking about. Bearer of shit and ill tidings was Ted Prinzi. Like Fenn had said, bad news walking.

"Carter?"

"Ted. What the f—"

"Stand down, Captain."

"Artillery, Ted."

"You've got one of Billy's maps with you, Carter, yeah?"

"Did you hear me?"

"Map, Carter. Have one?"

"Artillery."

"Map, Captain."

"Artillery, goddammit. Artillery!"

"Map."

Carter took a breath. "Yeah, map. Why?"

"Good. There's a series of hills then, should be on your nose almost. North-nor'east of the ford a few thousand yards, dead west twenty-two miles from Southbend. Elevation near two hundred ten, ranging about four miles. See it?"

With his flight electronics out, there was no light to see by, so Carter had to fish a mini flashlight out of his jacket one-handed. When he found it, he stuck it in his mouth, then checked the map taped to his thigh, tracing Ted's directions with his finger and finding the hills—the first line of them rising just beyond the reach of the forested bank of the river.

"Got it," he said, keeping the place with his finger, free hand juggling the stick, and speaking around the light held in his teeth. "Why?"

"Because we think the natives have just discovered artillery."

"Didn't I just tell you that?"

"No, I'm telling *you*, Captain. Right now. It's nothing fancy, we don't think."

"Nothing fancy," Carter repeated.

"That's what we think."

"We? Who else you got in there with you, Ted? *I'm* telling you right now. Durba's position was just hit by artillery fire. Saw it myself."

"Right," Ted continued, and it suddenly occurred to Carter that Ted was working off some kind of honcho-in-crisis script, something issued by corporate, kept in a locked drawer in a yellow folder, *To be opened in the event of . . .* Or maybe it was just in his head; a thing he'd practiced, that he'd been cooking up for months.

"As I said, we don't think it's anything fancy. Field cannon and the like. Simple howitzers. But that's a rather precocious leap, technologically speaking, from bows and fucking arrows, don't you think?"

A script. He'd rehearsed it, alone at night in his one-man commander's tent, standing balls-out naked in front of a full-length mirror and standing in his uniform. Cleaning his fake teeth in the morning, mumbling snatches of it into the cold air. Lying in his bed at night, straight as a board, mouthing it like talking dirty to a lover in the dark. Sound tough, make hard jokes, be confident, be strong, act like a man, like the worst actor of all time.

"Carter, don't you think?"

"Yes, Ted. I do," Carter said. *You crazy fucker,* he didn't say. *No fucking bullshit indig monkey suddenly smacked two rocks together and invented what happened down there,* he didn't say. "Though I bet Durba found it more shocking than you do."

"Right," Ted said, cleared his throat into the mike—an incredibly annoying habit—and moved on to page two. "We don't know how many there are, but—"

"Four," Carter interrupted. "There are four. I'm watching them hit the ford right now. Just watched."

"Four . . . Well, that's not very many now, is it?"

Carter wanted to bomb Ted in his tent. Terrified, he wanted very badly to kill something, and his mouth tasted sour. He spit out the flashlight instead, its steel body trailing a string of his spittle.

"Anyway, Carter, it looks like someone out there is trying to level the playing field a bit, and the last goddamn thing we want around here is a level playing field. Bad for business. Bad for you, bad for me. Bad for the company. Means we might have to work for a living instead of getting drunk and just flying around. No fun. That line of hills is your new illumination area, got it?"

He imagined that to the indigs on the ground, for whom anything more technologically advanced than a catapult was astonishing and something like a cigarette lighter inspired pure fucking awe and wonderment, an artillery barrage by one gun would've been enough to scare them out of their gourds. Four had probably been something like the end of the world. He didn't bother speculating to Ted, though. In Carter's experience, Ted was unimpressed by things like the feelings of people who were not Ted.

"Carter?"

"Illumination," he parroted.

"Carter. That hill. On the map. That's your area of operation. Illumination run."

"Illuminating for what?"

"For the bombers. Just gotta find the little rinky-dink fuckers first, yeah? So find them, pilot. And light 'em up."

Without thinking, Carter had brought the plane around again, boxing the compass until he'd come into line with the new target almost by feel. He coughed. His right leg was shaking like it had its own battery. "You want to tell me what's going on, Ted?"

"What?"

"What's, like, going on here. I don't know, just tell me . . ." The explosion, the shock, the pretty lights—they'd knocked something loose in Carter. Through clenched teeth he said, "Tell me what's this done. What's happening."

Even Carter knew he was making very little sense, but the stick was alive in his hand. His feet were working the pedals.

"Going on? Since when is 'going on' any of your goddamn business, pilot? Ending this—that's your business. Go end it." Whistle of feedback, muffled chatter of voices in the tent, then Ted again. "You're on the clock, pilot. Go fly."

"Roger that." Carter pawed at his face with his free hand, dragging fingers down the rough stubble on his cheeks and pressing them into the frozen skin along his jaw.

"Flare the area, try to sort out where those guns are at, then remain on target as air spotter for the rest of the flight. They're on the field now, wheels up in sixty seconds or I'll murder the bunch of them. They should be at your A.O. in less than fifteen. Copy?"

"Copy that, control. Where's Antoinne?"

There was another pause. Ted never had good news.

"We think Durba got his cork popped, Carter. No contact. None expected."

"His boys?"

"The same."

"One of them owed me fifty bucks."

A pause. "Call it a loss and soldier on."

That was one of Ted's favorite phrases. One of the pilots (Carter thought it might've been Lefty Berthold) had once tried to make a list of Ted-isms. It hadn't gone anywhere. Too long. But it'd been a season for lists, for failed attempts at imposing order on the disorderly, of controlling even something so simple as a piece of paper. Everyone had one somewhere.

"Now get there and let's blow some shit up."

On the ground, the engines were warming. Dawn was a couple of hours off yet, so generators and lamps were being hauled around, moved from the infield where they'd been lighting the drop to the field where they illuminated men bent double with their fingers down their throats, frantically trying to vomit their way to sobriety. Planes were being wheeled out onto the strips in a jumble, wingtips tangling, gun trucks being overturned in the black slashes of deep shadow. Max rode a cart full of live bombs like a pony at the fair, whooping the whole way.

Fenn had ducked out of the excitement the minute he'd seen Ted hurrying for the comms tent in the darkness, dogging the heels of some slinking flight controller. Reason enough to make himself scarce. Just playing the odds. He sat on the edge of his bed in his lightless tent now, breath steaming as he stared at the door while pilots tumbled, half-dressed, into their cockpits, pounded the foam-padded cockpit rails while their heads spun, and circled their hands in the air as they shouted to be cleared, to let slip the chains like dogs a-hunting so they could get out there and drop their loads before their hangovers came on and crippled the whole puke-smelling lot of them.

Diane could see them through the netted windows in the control tent and watched while she mouthed commands into the microphone; speaking to ground control, to the pilots, to the mechanics now doing duty as mules—pushing and shoving planes into lift order and hauling to them their consignments of death. Diane sniffed. She loved the smell of the exhaust on the cold air, of the aviation fuel slopped onto the ground by clumsy hands. She loved the smell of the machines warming, and the hot ones returning whole after a flight.

Ten minutes ago, Ted had come roaring into the comms tent like a devil, demanding information from everyone and shouting at the machinery. Diane had felt her pulse quicken. She'd explained the situation in terse, clipped terms: Roadrunner in the air, missed radio contact, explosions, a frantic call-in from Durba's position ten minutes before Carter had arrived on target, then the screaming. Ted had gotten on one of the other radio sets and started making calls. To Connelly, maybe. Or someone else. Numbers that only he had, working with his head down and his eyes closed and sweat standing out on his head like beads of oil even in the cold. He'd reached out from nowhere, his hand like a snake striking, and grabbed Tanner by the belt without looking, dragged him close, bent him down, talked into his ear, and then sent him on his way with a shove. Tanner hit the door at a run, making for the longhouse like he was being chased. Ted coolly moved onto the next call, then the next. Diane had watched him. And when he was done, he'd gotten up and taken her radio to talk to Carter. When he was done with that, he'd gone to the door to stand and watch.

Diane watched, too, as she gave the first clearance to taxi, to lift. She was the one who controlled these boys, these machines. It was she who sent them off to kill, who guided them to their targets and then talked them home again. She watched the plumes of smoke—white against the darkness—belching from exhaust pipes as the pilots goosed their planes forward, their ridiculous scarves giving a white flutter.

She watched the white steam of Ted Prinzi's breath as he stood in the doorway watching the planes rumble down the runway, his hands clenched into furious little fists while his entire body trembled from rage. When he'd turned from the mike while talking with Carter, he'd asked her, "The fuck is wrong with him? He's not making any sense. Check his biologicals again. Is he damaged?"

Not hurt, *damaged*. Like he was just another part of the machine. And Diane had hissed at Ted through her teeth for being that way until it'd occurred to her that Ted was correct. Of course Carter was hurt. That was obvious. He'd almost died. He'd just seen something terrible. He'd been screaming like a child waking from a nightmare and had been so scared that he would've pissed in his pants but for twenty-five cents' worth of rubber and a plastic bag. *Of course* he was hurt. But the important question was, was he damaged? Was he incapable of performing or too broken to fly? Was he so rattled that he'd begun to fall apart? Ted was asking for a woman's opinion, maybe. Probably because he had none of his own.

And she'd said no. He wasn't damaged. Diane had heard plenty of men scream in her time. She'd heard them die. And she knew that those who didn't almost always came back. They were tough machines. Resilient. She sent them off to kill and loved them when they came home whole—the smell of them, the strength, the power of the machine.

"Get him to the fucking target," Ted had said. "We don't have time for him to turn into a girl."

| | | | | | | | | | | |

The artillery struck again and again. Over the ford, Carter found his bearings and took Roadrunner up to five thousand feet in a long, lazy spiral. He loosened his belts enough to scrape his fingers around on the floor until he found his stopwatch, then marked the time, clicked a couple of buttons and, hunching himself into the seat, ducking his head below the screen, and folding his shoulders in against the cold, settled in to wait.

THE SOPWITH CAMEL was never an easy plane with which to do nothing. It wasn't the easiest plane with which to do anything, but doing nothing came unnaturally to it and seemed to bring out every quirk and idiosyncrasy of its nature.

In its day, its first youth, the plane (with its puny Clerget nine-cylinder rotary and radically nose-heavy construction) was not a great climber. It was murder in a dive. Smooth and level flying was tricky. Because of its weight distribution and the torque of its engine, it wanted always to pull right, to roll over like a dog that wouldn't stop doing its favorite trick. Taking off and landing were not its strong suits. Among the pilots who first got to know her, the Camel was known as a trainee killer, taking the lives of many before they'd completed their first flight, before they'd even gotten off the ground. And like an angry pet not quite tamed, the Camel would often maim or kill those who'd come to know her well out of pure, almost animal cussedness.

But to a careful, respectful, and conscientious pilot, there was no machine in the world so fine as the Sopwith F.1. Because of her touchy and unbalanced state, she could out-turn to the right any plane twice, outrun most, out-dive all, out-loop any but the most mad, and out-maneuver anything in the sky in a straight-up fight. In the dawning moments of the twentieth century, she could throw more weight of lead farther and faster than any predator yet devised, and like some dark, panting, and live thing, seemed to grow faster, neater, and more savagely beautiful whenever there was blood in the air. The Camel was the plane that killed the Red Baron, April 21, 1918. It was the Camel that brought down the most enemy planes during the course of that war: 1,293, not counting Richtofen. Highest scoring ace of that war: Donald MacLaren with fifty-four kills. His plane? The bloody Camel.

This was the litany. Carter knew it as well as anyone. He and the other pilots, they'd read the books. They'd committed the facts to memory. The Fokker D.VII sometimes caught fire from running too hot and exploded. The Nieuport's wings could tear off in a dive.

Like bad gene expressions, some of these foibles and intricacies of operation had been carried forward across the centuries. Titanium framing members, modern electronics, laser-milled engine components, high-octane aviation fuel—despite all this, Roadrunner was still more Camel than not: tricky, complex, cruel. But along with her eccentricities, so, too, had she been reborn with all the predatory heat and killing want that'd once been the original Camel's pride. So now, in the icy skies above an alien world hundreds of light-years and centuries distant from the aeries and workshops where she'd been originally conceived, Kevin Carter was left to wrestle with his Camel as she pitched and bucked, growling in frustration as he walked her back and forth and back and forth across the black stretch of night.

Hunched, half-frozen in his seat, he keyed the radio again. "Control, Roadrunner. Time to target for the rest of the wing?"

Twelve minutes, he was told. Then nine, then eight.

"Six minutes, Roadrunner. Two minutes less than when you asked me two minutes ago."

His fingers felt frozen inside his gloves; his face ached. To stay warm, he would duck lower, sit on his hands, breathe into them, and then press them to his cheeks or cup them over his ears. None of this worked. He remembered a joke that had run through the camp for a week or two in the depths of last winter's cold, started inadvertently by Ted. When they'd shipped out for Iaxo, hidden in among their supplies had been four dozen little lozenges of smooth stainless steel—the kind of things that looked like they'd belonged in a surgery. No one had known what they were for the longest time, until someone had figured out that they were actually catalytic hand warmers. Just pour in a drop of fuel, light an internal wick, then cap the thing, and it would give off a steady warmth for twelve hours. The pilots, of course, went nuts for them. They'd keep them in their pockets, shove them inside their gloves, drop one down the front of their knickers so that it rested under their balls, between the cloth and their armor. For two weeks, maybe three, no one complained of the cold.

Then they started to fail. The wicks burnt out. The fuel reservoirs began to leak. When they were down to two or three working units, the men who held them were like the camp's millionaires—lucky beyond all reasonable measure. And when the last one finally gave out and someone asked Ted what they were supposed to do now that they had no way to stay warm in the air, Ted had said, "Think warm thoughts."

Think warm thoughts.

They'd laughed and laughed until they'd realized how unfunny it really was.

There were good reasons why the company flew planes into combat on Iaxo that'd last seen action over the walls of Malaga. First, a biplane was a simple machine. Discounting its engine and guns, it had only about two dozen moving parts. Rudder, flaps, the stick, throttle linkage, interrupter gear, some simple hydraulics. Nothing more. They could be assembled in the field with the most rudimentary tools and maintained with a minimum of effort. In comparison, a modern transatmospheric fighter/bomber had twenty-two moving parts that made up its cockpit latch. Even the earliest twentieth- and twenty-first-century air superiority fighters consisted of thousands of parts, hundreds of interlinked systems, bonded construction airframes. The failure of one little piece meant the machine was grounded. Useless until the part was repaired or replaced. But one of the company's planes on Iaxo? A man could beat on one for an hour with a lead pipe, shoot it full of holes, then light half of it on fire, and the odds would be good that it'd still fly. Sneeze on a modern vacuum fighter and it would be in the shop a week.

Second, a biplane was cheap. The necessary components for building, arming, and outfitting a replica Fokker D.VII or Sopwith Camel could be had for about the same price as one lightly used cruise missile. Wood, titanium, rubber, linen, machine parts—none of that was even illegal. It was cheap as sand. The pieces could be fabricated anywhere, then shipped and assembled like a toy model somewhere else by three monkeys with a torque wrench. The engine was generally the only piece that was difficult to come by since, in an age of orbital-velocity scramjets and LOx-burners, high-range valence motors, and FTL drives no bigger than the average skyscraper, it could be somewhat tricky finding someone with the proper archaic expertise and talking them into scratch-building a 400-horsepower petro-rotary. Tricky, but far from impossible. Some people had the strangest affection for antiques.

|||||||||||||

"Control, Roadrunner."

Diane, exasperated: "Five minutes, Roadrunner."

|||||||||||||

Third, prior to the arrival of Flyboy and their old-timey flying machines on Iaxo, air superiority could've been had by a child with a kite. The ramping up of technology was a function of technology itself: Least application of force was often the most effective application of force—a motto that Flyboy Inc. had both lived and profited by for a century. Fourth, it was fun. Most of the time it was fun. For the pilots, Iaxo had all the excitement of being in a real war with all the danger of a carnival midway.

Carter felt as though he'd been up for days and nights already. In reality, it'd only been an hour and a little, all told. Night flying tore him up, a certain knot of muscles in his back always bunched like a fist, waiting for the surprising crash and bang—flying blind into the side of a mountain. There was a joke: What's the last thing that goes through a pilot's mind in the instant of a crash? The tail of his plane.

His flight computer had twinkled briefly to life a minute ago before dying again with a terrible groaning sound. The cockpit was dark. He'd taped his pocket flashlight to the panel just so he could see his instruments and gauges and was struggling through lazy, slow circles now at ten thousand feet, wallowing like a drunken bumblebee. He thought to himself how none of the constellations here was right. There was no North Star or Big Dipper or Orion and his dog. He could forget sometimes how many things about Iaxo pissed him off, but never for very long. That was just one more.

||||||||||||

"Diane?"

"Carter, just don't."

||||||||||||

There was still another reason why Flyboy had chosen the technological apex of 1918 as its model for combat operations on Iaxo rather than, say, just wiping the natives off the face of their planet with thermobaric bombs and orbital kinetic weapons. As always, there was the Colonial Council.

As was generally the case with fun things, what the company was doing on Iaxo was completely illegal. It was wrong, morally and ethically, and completely against the law as dictated by the council, which stated that bringing advanced technologies to the savages (even advanced technologies that were centuries old by the reckoning of those bringing them) was a big no-no. Chewing gum and transistor radios would get a man tossed in the pokey for twenty years. Getting the poor boondock aliens hooked on Coca-Cola and setting up a fried-chicken franchise? That was worse. And once one strapped on a gun and started picking sides? They called that something like treason, and it would get a man shipped out fast for some fetid hole somewhere for a lifetime of hard labor if he was lucky. Executed if he was not.

But then, a man had to be caught first. A man (or a company) had to be found, prosecuted, proven guilty beyond doubt. And in the end, there were a lot of planets out there in the great, wide whatever and not so many people around who cared too much about what went on anywhere but on their own.

So the Colonial Council—underfunded, undermanned, universally disliked and overly fond of sticking its bureaucratic nose in other people's business—was out there trying to keep watch over the million little flyspeck nothings in the sky; trying to make sure that companies like Flyboy, Cavalier, Eastbourne, and men like Carter, Ted, Durba, and Connelly didn't go around botching up developing cultures with their ray guns, litter, and bad habits.

But as dim and bumbling and near-sighted as the council was generally assumed to be, though, it did have at its disposal the whole of the navy and fifty-six divisions of Colonial Marines who, for the most part, just sat around waiting for an excuse to kill things. That was no small threat. And so, everyone simply tried to avoid the attention of the council and its muscle because they were the law and the law was best avoided whenever possible.

At its most basic, what this came down to was not drawing attention to one's self. To anyone else, moving a couple dozen replicas of antique engines, some titanium, canvas, computers, simple machinery, and a few old guns (disassembled, of course) through customs and shipping security in the belly of a two-hundred-million-ton freighter looked a lot like taking out the trash. Who was going to look at a broken-down copy of a Spandau machine gun or the ribbing assembly of a Morane pusher and think it was anything but a bunch of crap someone forgot to unload a thousand years ago? No one, that's who. Which was, more or less, the Flyboy business plan on Iaxo. To anyone else, the company's best gear looked like garbage. But to the indigs? Pure fucking magic.

These were all good reasons, Carter knew. They made sense. They'd been discussed, turned over, discussed again, endlessly, by the pilots and the crews. It went on and on: an argument perennially favored among those forced by penury, circumstance, and politics back into the avionic stone age, when the zenith of killing technology was a man with a gun riding a 140-horsepower engine through the sky.

All the good reasons in the world didn't make it any less cold, though. And for the time he spent hanging there in the frigid dark, fighting with an aircraft that didn't want to be doing nothing, Carter dreamed of a vacuum suit, a closed cockpit, the relative comfort of sterile, modern warfare. He rolled over and felt the weight of his body straining against the restraints, tilted his head to look down on the world below him, and spit at it out of spite.

| | | | | | | | | | | |

"Roadrunner, control. Four minutes actual."

It was Diane again. Carter righted himself. She was using her professional voice once more, sounding sulky to Carter's ear. He thought maybe Ted had lit into her, but he doubted it. Ted didn't have much to do with the girls on the mission. Fraternization and all that, or so he would occasionally claim. Among the pilots, speculation had run rampant for a time, until it got dull. The boss's sexual predilections—whether he preferred the ladies or the fellas, the boots and leather or maybe the whip—became gross sooner rather than later. And Carter'd always assumed the man was simply asexual, assembled by the company out of spare parts without any manly tackle at all. A command-eunuch. It would explain a lot.

"Make your run at two minutes, then remain on station for fire control, Roadrunner," Diane continued. "Use channel four to talk to wing command, this channel ground. Ted's on two to coordinate. Out."

Carter put his stopwatch on countdown and began spiraling toward the deck, circling out on drift and rudder, his thumb on the fuel cutoff, manually choking the engine, starving it of fuel. The sudden quiet was eerie, but also comforting—a strange tranquility after all the night's action. At two minutes, he would make his run, coming down onto the target in a silent, dead dive in hopes of surprising the indigs or whoever else was down there, not giving them time to run before the bombers came in.

At seven thousand feet he caught a swirling updraft and rode it while he checked the hills through his scope. The targets were easy to pick out now on the bald terrain—a distended yellow blob on a blue-green rise, hot gun barrels throwing out heat like crazy. Another circle, wind rushing along the cowlings, and at five thousand feet the blob separated into four separate heat signatures, tightly grouped, twenty feet between them.

Carter clicked the radio, switched over to the wing frequency. "Bomber night flight, this is Roadrunner, copy?"

"Kevin? This is flight command."

"Evening, Charlie." Carter wondered what Fenn, rightful captain of three squadron, must've had on poor Charlie to shunt off on him a night run that, by all rights, ought to have been his. "Figured you'd be sleeping."

"Passed out apparently doesn't count," said Charlie. "No rest for the wicked, you know. But how's things with you? Ted told us you saw something scary in the dark that needed blowing up?"

"Artillery. Four tubes on the hill. I'm ready to light 'em up."

"Taking fire?"

"What? No. Why? You know something I don't?"

"No, uh . . ." Charlie coughed into the radio, and Carter flinched away at the booming sound of it. "Not at all. Not a lot of time for a briefing before we lifted. Don't really . . ."

"Charlie?"

"Tonight just seems to be the night for new things, doesn't it?"

Understatement, to be sure. Carter took one more fast look through the scope and fixed the target point in his head. "How far out are you, Charlie?"

There was a sound like growling on the other end of the radio, then Charlie cursing under his breath. "One minute and change, Roadrunner. Approaching east-northeast at ten thousand and falling. What's the target elevation?"

"Two hundred and ten off the deck. A little less maybe. I'll leave the porch light on for you. Commencing illumination run. Roadrunner out."

Things happen very quickly now.

Carter banks out into an elongated turn, a flat, inside loop done slow and graceful, then brings the nose back around and on target for a long glide in toward the guns' right flank. The ride is bumpy, his speed having dropped off to almost nothing. But now there is no wind. There is no cold. The stick rattles in his hand. His flares are parachute sabots, heavy and pointed like lawn darts, dropped by hand. He's carrying two dozen attached like shotgun shells in loops hanging from either side of the cockpit. They'll drop straight like bombs, hitting the ground where a contact trigger will detonate a charge that will fire a parachute flare straight up. Less trouble with drift that way. They can easily punch straight through tree cover. Longer time-over-target.

Carter eyeballs the target in the dark. There's nothing there, but he feels now as though he can sense the weight of the guns in some middle distance, their psychic signature. They are close. Engine still off, he bleeds away the last of his airspeed, then noses down into a blind, dead-stick dive toward the nonspecific blackness of the ground. He feels no fear, no apprehension. There is nothing but the hum of blood in his ears, the delicate vibration of air slipping over control surfaces and humming through the wire wing stays. Watching the altimeter spin backward, at eleven hundred feet he eases into the stick, drawing it back toward him slowly until he can feel the nose starting to come up, the elevators bite. Then he takes his thumb off the fuel line.

The engine jumps to life with a shuddering kick. It spits and roars like a Saturday matinee movie monster, howling across the sky, and Carter feels pressed back into his seat by a giant, invisible hand. In an original Camel, this would've ripped the wings clean off. Killed him, killed the machine. But the future is wonderful. He imagines treetops bending in Roadrunner's slipstream.

Carter begins his drop, jerking flares out of their loops and throwing them hard so they'll clear the forward edge of the bottom wing. He can't see anything, the wing obscuring his view. There is the sense of sudden light bursting behind him. Ghostly shadows flicker on his instrument panel.

Inaccurate, but effective—the lights of the first flares will allow him to spot more precisely on his second run. With six flares out, he pushes the throttle forward, lays his machine over into a tight, right turn, and checks his aim.

Too high and too short. He'd come in upslope and the parachutes are drifting higher. He rolls out, combat reflexes making him jink and dodge even when there is no fire, no danger, no need. He lays on more throttle and the machine responds, seeming to leap out ahead of him, to leave him dragging along behind as if stretched on a massive rubber band. Pulling Roadrunner around again to the same attack line, he lays a new stick fifty feet low to give the bombers a bracketed target.

Below him, the ground is suddenly alive with light and shadow, the weird, ghostly parachutes drifting across the hill like spirits, burning magnesium flares so white that they turn everything photo-negative and leave purple smudges on Carter's vision.

He circles out again and climbs, hanging for a minute at the apogee, turning over so he can look up at his handiwork on the ground. There are two staggered, more or less parallel lines of unnatural light punctuating the dark like ellipses; a thought, incomplete and drifting to pointlessness in the air. And somewhere between them, the artillery.

He rolls back over to true, then calls Charlie.

"Bomber flight, time to target?"

"Thirty seconds, Carter. I can see the lights."

"Target is bracketed. I'm making one more drop."

"Make it a fast one."

He takes one quick peek through the scope, magnification only, and can see the position plainly. The guns are squat, big-bore, dug in. It seems to Carter like he could reach out past the lens of the scope and shove his entire fist into their barrels. Tiny little indigs scramble around in a panic, trying to unchock the wheels of their toy cannons, running after the drifting flares and batting their hands as if trying to chase them away. The flares have them lit up good. Carter is happy. But he knows that Charlie and his flight are going to come in high and not have a chance to spot for themselves. He puts his nose down and goes back in one last time to give the boys a bull's-eye.

He drops down low and slow, six hundred feet off the deck, then five, then four. His plane chugs and bucks and tries not to fall. Forty-five, maybe fifty miles an hour and he is tickling the bumblebee limit—that point at which it appears impossible that he can still maintain flight. Three hundred feet. He eases the stick down farther.

The ground crawls by below him, and he watches it unroll—leaning, with his chest pressed against the padded lip of the cockpit, straining against the belts. He can count individual trees clustered at the base of the bald hill, can see the sharp-edged shadows cast by the drifting flares. And then, all of a sudden, the artillery position. He pulls a single flare, holds it, waits, then plants it dead in the middle of them.

Then the throttle, the stick. More throttle until it is all the way open, until he is climbing for the cold and distant stars, engine pulling, roaring joyously, carrying him up and away.

"Charlie, Roadrunner. Copy?"

"Gotcha, Kevin. Go ahead."

"I'm clear. Come in south by five west and drop between the lines. The single flare is bull's-eye, bracket two hundred north-south, copy?"

"Copy that, and much obliged. This is bomber night-flight coming around to south by five west at five thousand feet, run commencing. Flight out."

"Roger that. Let 'er eat. Roadrunner out."

Below and behind him, the explosions are so small that he doesn't even feel them.

THE BOMBERS HIT THE TARGET BEAUTIFULLY, hand-dropping ten-pound fragmentation devices packed with titanium fléchettes around a core of 8-oxy trinitrotoluene. Six bombs per plane, four planes in the wing. By the time they were done, the remains of the artillery position could've been packaged up nicely in several hundred leakproof sandwich bags.

Carter stuck around just long enough to make sure that nothing taller than a foot high was still standing under the ghost-light of the flares, then joined the slow procession of Airco-bodies turning for home. They flew straight. With each bomber sixty pounds lighter after the drop, they were circling home plate within thirty minutes. Generators out, lights on, wheels down—like landing half in a dream already.

Drinks and debrief, short as always. *Get some? Got some.* Big talk around the halo lamps, but none of it about the enemy, about weapons. A deliberate, studious avoidance. Too soon, and maybe to talk about such a thing would make it too real. Ernie O'Day had fumbled a bomb and dropped it into his own cockpit, but it hadn't gone off. Drunk's luck, they all said. Charlie had landed his plane and stepped out crusted in frozen vomit just starting to run. This made Carter think of an old story he'd heard about pilots from the war that'd given birth to the machines they flew now—how they'd used castor oil as a lubricant in their engines and how the pilots, after sitting in the seat, shrouded in clouds of the stuff being blown back into their faces, would suffer from chronic diarrhea from inhaling it, licking it off their lips, whatever. The scarves they wore were originally for wiping the oil from their goggles, for wrapping around their faces to keep their mouths clear, but that never worked—and many of them would find themselves at ten and fifteen thousand feet, sitting on frozen bricks of their own watery shit, knowing that their prize for surviving would only be descending again into lower altitudes and kinder temperatures where it would all start to melt.

Morris and Billy Stitches had found their way home safe, and Billy was laying fiercely into Morris, laughingly, in the way of brothers who love each other and cover it over with beatings and insults, then cover that over with touches of odd intimacy—Billy reaching out to adjust the collar of Morris's jacket in the middle of calling him a dumb, syphilitic jerk-blind ox; the two of them sitting side by side and pelting empty shell casings at the indig dish wogs who roamed the field tent and mess mopping spills, gathering cups, and stealing everything that wasn't nailed down. Every time one of them would look their way, Morris and Billy would make to be looking somewhere else and whistle through their teeth. The indig would do this grin thing that meant not happy, exactly, but embarrassed, uncomfortable, confused. Then he'd clap or bow or clap-and-bow and move on, another bit of .303 brass bouncing off the back of his head as soon as he'd turned away.

Carter sat through it, laughed through it, had a couple drinks and waited for his extremities to thaw, deaf with the echoes of shearing winds and roaring engines still living in his head. The whole time, he half wanted someone to haul back and punch him in the spine to pop the bubble of tension that'd collected there. He didn't ask though because, had he, someone surely would've obliged and slugged him.

It was dawn when everyone found out that Durba hadn't been killed outright as had originally been suspected. Apparently, the shelling that Carter'd originally witnessed hadn't been the first to hit his position, but the beginning of the second round, followed by a third and a fourth and a fifth. Barrage upon barrage. It was hard to believe he hadn't seen the first, what with it being blushes of rosy light in a dark place and all that, but he hadn't. It wasn't like he'd been looking.

"Might as well have been looking for Santa Claus or the Easter Bunny, right?" Carter had asked, hardly noticing the odd looks this inspired. "But I'll tell you: From now on, I'm keeping a sharp goddamn eye out for flying fucking reindeer as well. I mean, artillery on Iaxo? Fuck that."

Around the tent line, his small soliloquy had been listened to with something like reverence. As though it were poetry, or something finer. Almost a philosophy, though the only part of it that had any resonance was the last line. *Fuck that*. Like "Think warm thoughts," for an hour or two, it'd become a saying: "Artillery on Iaxo? Fuck that . . ." Then there had been laughter that almost always trailed away into uncomfortable silences. Then it'd gone away. Still too soon.

The initial strike had caught Durba's First IRC completely unaware, either above ground or lounging in their open, shallow fighting positions. Their first thought had been that they were being bombed by the pilots accidentally and Tony Fong had put in a frantic wave-off request to Flyboy control, which had been taken by Tanner, passed along to Diane, and had been what had inspired her to send for Ted and bring him in. It'd taken less than a minute to get things straightened out, but a minute was all it'd taken for the lot of them to get blown to bloody chunks. A good number of Durba's men had run, no doubt thinking that the sky was falling—though, in the confusion, they'd advanced rather than falling back and had charged headlong into a unit of bad indigs waiting just out in the darkness. They'd been cut to pieces. Then the artillery had hit the survivors again and again. It was a mess. One of Durba's indigs had made one final distress call on an open channel, then gone silent.

It took all night, but eventually what was left of Durba's Rifles— thirty indigs plus two of his command element—found their way back to the headquarters area five miles from the ford on the friendly side of the river. They'd carried about ten of their wounded along with them on their backs. For Durba, they'd made a travois out of rifles and shattered timber, tied with nylon belts. Antoinne had apparently spouted scripture the whole way—raving, promising hell and damnation for those who'd laid him low—and called out for his daughter, Marie. He had a piece of shrapnel lodged in his head just above his right eye and a foot-long hardwood splinter run through his guts, but he was alive when they brought him in.

Died not long after, but he was alive when they brought him in.

| | | | | | | | | | | | |

When Carter'd landed Roadrunner, Vic had been there to do the post-flight check. He'd smiled at her (which he knew, in retrospect, had probably been unwise), lifted his goggles, and winked as if to say, *Survived another one.* Like that was something special. It was just part of the habit of being a pilot—the swagger, the arrogance, the laughing at death once death is safely in one's slipstream. Reflex. Like running across empty airstrips or rolling through turns as if always under fire.

He'd taxied into his spot outside the longhouse, climbed jauntily down out of the cockpit, and flipped his scarf back over his shoulder. They'd said a few words to each other, Vic and Carter, before he'd gone to the field tent and she'd gone back to the flight line. That, he knew, had probably been a mistake, too.

Later, once he'd switched from pop-skull to coffee, from the field house to the mess, and after most of the other revelers had finally retired or simply dropped in their tracks, Vic had come in grinning. She'd stood across the table from him and laid down three stubby arrows. Having been half-asleep sitting up, still hearing the sound of engines in his head and feeling the phantom vibrations of nine cylinders cranking in his bones, he'd just blinked dumbly at her, thinking how nice it was that she'd come to visit him in bed.

"Crossbow bolts," she said. "Steel tip. Aluminum shaft. Imported, apparently."

Carter picked one up and rolled it between his palms, trying to make some kind of connection, to appear thoughtful even though he had no idea what she was on about. "Imported, apparently," he parroted. "Apparently, apparently, apparently . . ." He wasn't trying to be difficult, wasn't mocking. He just liked the way the words sounded popping off his lips. It was a nice arrow, he supposed, but could come up with nothing particularly insightful to say about it, so he looked at her instead. He thought about how pretty she was when he was mostly asleep. He smiled at her again, thinking how he'd just done that not too long ago and that twice in one night was a lot. He looked away. One fresh glance had been enough. Like looking directly at the sun.

"Pulled them out of your wing, champ. Your elevator. Congratulations."

The bolt was light, tip-heavy, and viciously sharp, nocked at the tail in a cross. The flights were hard plastic. White.

"Congratulations for what?" he asked her, rubbing at his eyes.

"You're the first Flyboy to take a hit since we got here."

He touched a finger to the tip of the little arrow and made a face. Sharp. "Hmm," he said. "Lucky me."

Vic took a step back from the table. "Jesus Christ, Kevin. We're friends. They're souvenirs. I saved them for you."

He couldn't think of anything to say. Something other than the memory of the engine was roaring in his ears now. He looked down at the table, arranged all three bolts into a nice, even line, patting each into precise alignment with the palms of his hands.

"Say thank you," she said.

"Thank you," said Carter. He didn't look up.

It was quiet for a minute. They were the only two in the mess just then. He could feel her staring at the top of his head.

"Prick," she muttered, then walked out.

| | | | | | | | | | | |

What Vic had said wasn't exactly true. Not about Carter being a prick. That was spot-on. But about the two of them being friends. They weren't. They were something else entirely. Also, she'd been wrong about Carter being the first pilot to take fire while flying.

When the company had first arrived on Iaxo, the indigs had shot all sorts of things at them. Sticks, rocks, spears, arrows—they'd tried it all. And the pilots had gotten quite a laugh out of it, actually, thinking the entire situation rather pathetic and silly. For a time, they'd made it into a game, scoring the abos on their bravado, their ingenuity, their aim, the amount of frustrated rage they expressed—shaking their fists, jumping around, howling at the sky. Winners lived. Sometimes they'd go out between missions with pistols, fly real low, use the natives for target practice. "Just keeping my piece lubricated," they'd say by way of explanation or excuse. "Just to keep it working, tip-top."

This went on for a while. Until Danny.

Danny Diaz. He'd been a good man, a good pilot. He had Earth-born parents but had been a natural citizen of Free Luna where he was conceived and born, and where he grew up. This made him overly tall, a bit more delicate in appearance than the full-gravity lugs, and generally ill-suited to long hours in the cramped cockpit of a Vickers or Camel.

And maybe that'd been enough to single him out, to make him a target for part-time bullies looking to go rough on someone. Though he drank with the other pilots, flew with them, fought with them, never shirked, didn't complain any more often or any more loudly than the rest, he was just a little quieter, a little more reserved, stuck with the effeminate cast of low-g elegance that Luna had worked into him, and that made him an easy target. Skinniest kid on the playground. Something like that. And there wasn't a man on Iaxo who, at his best, was much better than an overgrown fourteen-year-old anyhow.

Ted especially hadn't liked Danny. Again, there was no particular reason that anyone knew, but Ted, of all of them, was hardest on Danny.

And if Ted was the worst, then Vic was the easiest, even shacking up with him for a time, taking special care of his favorite plane—a D.VII called Angelina—and by and large going through all the motions of actually liking him.

All of this made it worse that Danny had to be the one of them to go—to buy it in action. Made it almost a cliché, which is a bad thing to be in any war, no matter how ridiculous. Were they ever to talk about it, most of the pilots would also say that that this all made it obvious that he was going to be the first to go. Highly superstitious, sensitive to the ironies and truisms of war, they would say *of course* it would've been Danny. Anything else would've just felt wrong. But then talking about it was the one thing that they'd never do. Superstition: To talk about death was to invite it close. To talk about *dying* was fine. That they did all the time. But death—real death—was different. The finality of it was like a curse that had to be spoken to come true.

Old-time fliers used to call what got Danny the Golden BB, that one shot in a million, the one you never expect and never, ever see coming. It used to refer to small-arms fire—to some grunt on the ground spraying bullets up into the air at a plane flying a mile overhead at six hundred miles per and getting truly, phenomenally lucky. Hitting the jackpot. Ringing the bell. A ten-cent piece of lead alloy bringing down a multimillion-dollar aircraft.

On Iaxo, it meant some indig with a bow and arrow who managed, somehow, to put one right through the gap in a vent panel and clip one of the radiator hoses on the D.VII's liquid-cooled engine. Danny hadn't even noticed it at first. Not until the engine temp gauge began to spike and he saw the long stain of scorched coolant blown back all along the flank of his plane. He'd radioed it in. He'd been laughing about it. But then his engine had seized and he'd gone down.

He'd been flying low: twenty, maybe thirty feet off the deck up on the high moors, and Carter knew this because they'd all been doing the same thing, playing Great White Hunter, just sporting around. This was about a month after the big battles on Sispetain, but they'd caught a cavalry troop out in the open on the flatlands and were running the horsemen down. Sidearms only. Those were the rules. They'd been keeping score. And Danny'd been playing, too, though rather half-heartedly. Killing—especially the pointless, up close and personal kind like they were doing that day—had made him uncomfortable sometimes. Not something he talked about, just something everyone knew. And even still, there was nothing too strange in that. In their better moments, nearly all of the pilots would claim that the killing was appalling, exasperating, a drag and a taint on their otherwise pristine moral characters. And then, mostly, they would laugh. Carter the hardest, the longest.

Danny, though, mostly meant it. Some of the others did, too. Occasionally. And while one might wonder why, then, had Danny or any of them become fighter pilots—*mercenary* fighter pilots at that, where it often seemed as though the slaughter was more or less all they were about—this was an easy question to answer.

It was because Danny loved to fly, same as the rest. Simple as that. And he knew that there was no better test of himself than to do the thing he loved, the thing he was best at, under stress and all the most difficult conditions. No pilot flew as well or as often as a combat pilot. And no combat pilot had ever flown in such strange, challenging, or varied conditions as a Flyboy pilot did most days before breakfast. Danny had understood that. Danny loved to fly. And if, in the course of getting to do what he loved best of all, he had to put himself in situations where his better nature was dipped repeatedly in shit, then Danny had understood that, too. It was a popular fiction that, like their pomp and swagger, fighter pilots also possessed some strong core of combat élan—a streak of gentlemanly decency, a book of rules not held to by the dogfaces, doughboys, and mudfoot grunts of the other military professions. Danny knew better. He was not deluded. He'd been with the company long enough to have learned that if there was any such thing as gentlemanly soldiers, Flyboy had a policy against hiring them, and that all men who voluntarily made their living by the gun were, by trade, dirty fuckers and destroyers of lovely things.

But at any rate, Danny had gone down, victim of that million-to-one shot by the luckiest indig on Iaxo. The other pilots had immediately broken off their game to go and get him, figuring he had to have been just fine because even a brain-damaged chimp could've brought a ship in for a glide landing from thirty feet up. No one had even been worried about him, and Carter recalled being on the radio making jokes about how, if anyone was going to be brought down that way, well then *of course* it would be Danny fucking Diaz.

And the truth was, Danny had landed it and he had survived, though later, the pilots would all kind of wish he hadn't.

They found the plane but no Danny. All of them had put down in the field where he'd been stunting to check things out (which had ultimately been the mistake that most of them felt made Danny's dying their fault) and then had stood around like idiots with their fingers in their noses for a good five minutes. There'd been no blood, no body, no sign of Danny at all. Lots of hoofprints, though, which, for a couple of minutes, had seemed like nothing until, all of a sudden, it became very important indeed.

The indigs on their ridiculous horses had gotten to Danny quicker than the pilots could in their planes, and by the time the pilots had all gotten their engines cranked up again, their planes straightened out, a taxiway chosen, and themselves back into the air, those horses, those indigs, and Danny were all long gone.

They'd searched all the rest of the day and on into the night, but found nothing. Connelly had been up on the ragged skirts of the moors then (digging in the remains of his troops for what was to be the ultimately pointless defense of the cities on the river), and Durba had been camped with his riflemen not too far away. Since there were favors owed and kept, they and their men went out looking, too—on foot, raiding and killing and questioning prisoners. There'd been another fellow, a man named Workman, stretched far out on the northern flank and commanding a five-hundred-strong company of native cavalry. They were light horsemen, mostly indig but with a dozen-odd Earth-side officers, and they linked up with Durba to help. Some bored engineers from Cavalier did also, along with another gang of redneck sharpshooters who'd hired on as reavers and kept their own indig scouts chained up in pens like dogs. Together, they'd scoured the high ground for any sign of Danny. The entire war was put on hold while the humans looked for one of their own.

And this had gone on for a week, progressing with a grim sort of calculating passion. Word traveled. No cruelty or expense was spared in the searching. Men who'd never met Danny, who'd never heard his name or seen his face, poked into every hole they could think of, rode hard, marched nights, put their own lives at risk for him just because that was what men (if not always corporations) did: They took care of their own. This, they thought, was what made them better than the abos. Danny was human, and no one wanted to think what might've been happening to him in indig hands. No one wanted to think that his fellows would do any less if it were him in duress and them left to look.

The pilots, of course, searched twice as hard. They were in the air around the clock, spotting and marking terrain, attacking everything that moved. They appreciated the help to the tune of owing all involved more favors than could possibly be repaid. But for all the cost, vigorous brutality, and appalling acts committed in Danny Diaz's name, it came to nothing. After a week, the search was called off at Ted Prinzi's insistence.

It was a decision that made him no friends, but deep down, all the pilots knew it was the right choice. It was a big country they were covering, and one that the natives knew better than anyone. If they didn't want something found, it generally didn't get found.

So Ted had grounded everyone, threatened a general confinement to quarters after some of the men got it in their heads that there must've been a spy among the camp wogs, and began trying their unskilled hands at interrogating the dishwashers and postriders and laundresses. Some indig huts were burnt, a couple of the locals were killed. And when those men were pulled off the indigs, they spoke about what they were doing as though it'd all been very sane, rational, even *important,* in words that weren't even words, and sentences stripped of all meaning by their grief.

Carter hadn't been involved in that, but only because he'd already voluntarily confined himself to quarters, along with Fenn, Porter Vaughn, and Billy from first squadron, in order to wake Danny—a period of mourning that had taken the form of a drinking contest and ended badly all around. Things at that point had started getting very weird. The jargon of retribution blew around the camp like bullets. And then, two days after they'd given up all hope, Danny came home. Or what was left of him did, anyway.

It was a ratty mob of Workman's light horsemen who brought him in. They'd found his corpse being carried in a caravan they'd raided two nights prior, far to the north, and had ridden day and night to deliver him. They'd come with prisoners as well—three of them—and through translators, the pilots learned that Danny had been picked up away from his plane as he'd been making for cover, then tortured for most of the week by indig elders and wise men.

That much they could tell by the condition Danny's body had been in. He'd been very systematically beaten, flayed, and brutalized. Most of his bones had been broken. He'd been primitively blinded, likely by having his eyes burnt out. His fingers and toes were missing, as well as some other bits and pieces. There was indig chicken scratch burned and cut into his graying skin, sigils that the horsemen wouldn't even look at, let alone read aloud. And at some point, he'd been split open like a fish, throat to belly, then crudely stitched back together. That was the part that Carter'd remembered most clearly: the incision mark, in a Y, just like a body carved up for autopsy. Everyone was wondering how much of it he'd lived through and praying to their human gods that it wasn't very much.

In a fury, the company men had turned on the three prisoners from the caravan and demanded to know why. And how. They wanted details to justify the terrible things they all wanted to do to the prisoners, were *going* to do to them regardless, and were shouting—at the prisoners, at Workman's light horsemen, at their own translators and at one another. It was madness. They learned that it wasn't out of blind cruelty that this had been done to Danny. Neither was it in revenge or out of plain malice. The indigs who'd taken him had been curious, more than anything, and however vicious their methods, they'd had a reason for what they'd done.

They'd wanted to know where Danny's wings were. How he became like a bird. They'd been trying to make Danny teach them how to fly.

| | | | | | | | | | | |

Carter could still remember that morning. The strangest details had stuck with him. He remembered the day and the hour and the light. He remembered the sound of the abos all talking at once. Like stones in a can. He remembered the sweet smell of their horses, ridden half to death and washed in sweat that stank vaguely of what he imagined damp hay would smell like (as if he'd ever smelled such a thing), and a little like high-grade machine oil—plasticky and warm.

Carter remembered the pounded mud spatters on the horses' feet, black and thick like old blood, and thinking how he didn't know what that part of a horse was called. Not in the language of Iaxo, but any language. The part above the hoof but not quite the leg. Its ankles, he guessed. On a plane, it would be the shortening linkage or the torque link assembly, but horses were not planes and, really, these were not horses. He didn't have any other name for them, though, so found himself lost in the language and, soon enough, the problems dissolved into violence anyway until, at a certain point, after the tenth or twentieth or fiftieth punch or kick he'd delivered to the prisoners, he'd had to stop. He was tired, yes. His hands ached and one of his toes felt wrong inside his boot. But more than that, he'd stopped to consider what kind of line they were crossing. It wasn't an ethical line or a moral one he was considering. In this cold and damp and occasionally blazing but mostly just scourging alien environment, any sense of morality had already been corroded out of them. Carter understood that. He wasn't a child.

It was something else. Another kind of line. Tactical, maybe. Certainly physical. Panting, standing bent with his hands on his knees, ceding his turn at the prisoners to someone else with fresher hands, it'd occurred to him that this was the first time he'd touched one of the indigs on purpose. The first time that he was hurting them up close. Personally. With his hands and his feet. It was the first time he'd been able to look into their heavy, wet eyes and say, "See this? This is *me* that's doing this. And motherfucker, you are going to *die* today."

He didn't much like it, truth be told. It'd taken him a while to realize it, but when he did, the intimacy of it disturbed him on a level he'd been previously unaware he possessed. After a time, he'd walked away to stand in the circle of men and watch rather than participate.

That had felt better. Not clean, exactly. But better.

|||||||||||||

After that, the war had picked up again and continued on like normal. In the aftermath of Sispetain, the neighborhood was lighter on humans than it had been before. Many of the gangs and companies that'd fought there had been beaten right off-planet, had given up and gone home to cut their losses. Workman had stuck it out for a little while but vanished not long after. Connelly was reinforcing from among the native fighters. And among the pilots, each man now carried a single TCM-40 fragmentation grenade in his flight bag, just in case. For a while, they'd flown with them taped to their chests, called it "putting the Danny on." But in time, that'd come to seem rather ridiculous. Uncomfortable, too. So now, they just carried them. Either way, no one ever wanted to end up like Danny had. He was shipped out in a steel coffin, sealed, the outside of it marked REMAINS UNVIEWABLE. Among all the many ways to get off-planet, it was roundly agreed that this was the worst. A terrible way to go home.

| | | | | | | | | | | |

So Carter hadn't been the first to take fire in combat like Vic had said. Danny Diaz was really the first, even though his memory had been banished, his name scrubbed from the history. No one liked thinking about Danny and no one talked about it, ever. There was nothing to be learned from death by dumb, bad luck.

On the day that Danny had come back to the Flyboy camp, Ted had shot the three prisoners in the head with his pistol, appearing out of nowhere with his sidearm drawn and walking up behind them—*pop pop pop*. He'd done it before any of the pilots could do worse, seen the light horse troop paid off for its efforts, and ordered his men up. All of them. On scouting patrol for twelve hours. Radio silence. Alone with their thoughts and hatred, they had nothing to do but let it all bleed away into the cold gray sky.

After, Vic had come up behind Carter while he was walking to the field house and taken his hand in hers like a girl. That was all it took. And, later still, lying with her, feeling confused but also rather proud of himself and wrapped up in grief as much as in her, Carter would ask, "Why me?"

He remembered Vic saying, in a completely matter-of-fact way, like it was the most obvious thing in the world, "Because you're next."

Vic had a thing for tragedy and death. Everyone knew that. Danny hadn't been her first love to die, or even her second or her fifth. She had a strange sense for seeing the reaper coming at great distances, people said, and was more in love with that than she'd ever been with any pilot. So Vic had been wrong about her and Carter being friends, too, because Carter, at times, wanted Vic not to exist at all or, at the very least, to be as gone from his thoughts as Danny was.

Because you're next. There were times when Carter felt like just another number. There were times when he felt as though he was being stalked by her—hunted, her steps just a little bit quicker than death's. And he'd tried to forget her a hundred times, but it never took. All too often, when she wasn't even around, he would find himself conjuring her in his head: the curve of her neck, the arch of her eyebrows, the sound of her heart pumping, her gasping breath, the tight skin on the small of her back and the close smell of her when they pulled a sheet up over their heads like two children hiding from monsters.

He'd buried his traitorous thoughts and emotions (and other, arguably more salubrious organs) in some of the other company girls whenever opportunity and communal desire presented itself, but he always came away feeling even worse. He felt that Vic was bad for him, physically and spiritually. That she would get him killed. And he kept telling himself that, even if he would then be assailed with thoughts of the sweetness of her sweat, the tightness of her cunt, the heat of her breath in his ear when she whispered his name, and have to get up in the air and make something die just to be rid of her for a moment.

Absently, he fooled with the three crossbow bolts she'd brought him, fingertips running down their smooth shafts, teasing the stiff plastic fletching of their flights. Finally, he tucked them carefully into his flight bag, stood, and made for the tent line. He was exhausted.

WHEN CARTER WOKE UP, IT WAS STILL MORNING—icy, damp, and bitter. The cold season on Iaxo wasn't bad because it was dry. Same with the hot season. It was the time between those two brief respites that got to him; when the chill and the wet seemed to sink right through the skin and gnaw at the bone. On Iaxo (which had a parabolic, 440-day rotation), it was like having an entire year of November broken only by a couple weeks of August on one end and a couple weeks of February at the other. In time, it came to bother everyone.

Like Lefty Berthold's list of Ted-isms, Carter, too, had tried to make a list once. About a year back, he'd tried to make a list of everything he hated about Iaxo. Really dig in and lay it out there. Permanently. On paper. Everything he hated, all in one place.

He hated the land, and that, he'd felt, was a good place to start. He hated the trees that were so like other trees he had known, only different, and he hated the other ones—the blue ones—that were totally and completely alien. He hated the mud when there was mud and the ice when there was ice, and he hated the way the air tasted almost all the time. He hated the animals. Most of them. Although there weren't that many of them around to hate. The disgusting, scabby flying rats that skulked around the edges of the tent line at night eating garbage. The heffalumps they hunted from their planes when there was nothing better to kill. The horse-things with their shovel-blade heads and too many feet. He hated the indigs, though he couldn't say precisely why. There were a million small reasons, though all variations on a theme. The vastness had stymied him.

He'd given up right about there. A list like that would've been just too massive—long like the Bible was long.

Sometime later he'd adjusted his tactics, deciding on making a list only of the things he liked—all the good things that Iaxo had produced. This was easier, but he'd given up on it as well because it was too short. He'd been able to come up with only two things.

One, this war, which had given him gainful employment and an excuse to fly. It was a good war, with all the necessaries of one. It was far away and exotic. There were all manner of interesting people around, either doing bad things for good money or trying to do good things for none at all. The planet itself, through a history that he didn't comprehend, had thoughtfully provided two groups of natives angry enough to kill for reasons he'd never understood and hardly cared to investigate, and came endowed with resources enough (mostly in the form of land and prom- ised rights thereto) to pay the company that'd sent him for his services as a combat pilot. There was little chance of him, personally, being killed, which he appreciated. And the natives treated everyone from the com- pany like something close to gods, with a god's perfidy and murderous flair, which was also nice. Finally, no one besides the principals involved seemed to care a rat's dong for what happened here. It was a playground game of war, serious only to those who died of it. And in Carter's expe- rience, though situations like this were not all that hard to come by, it was still nice to have a good war around when you needed one.

The second thing on his list had been Cat. Not exactly a pet. More like a mascot. Carter had fed the thing once, not long after their arrival in this place, and forever after, it'd just been around more often than it was not. When Carter'd left his tent to head for the flight line last night, Cat had been peacefully laid out asleep and wheezing in a pile of ratty blankets by the tent door. Now he could hear it rooting around some- where beneath his bunk. And he'd often said that when the time finally came to leave this place completely, Cat would be the only thing he took with him for the big ride other than the lice.

Cat looked something like a bug-eyed Burmese kitten swallowed to the neck by a snake. It (since the issue of he or she had never been determined as neither Carter or Fenn had ever known where to look) had a mashed-in face, pointed ears, a head the size of a fist followed southerly by a long, snaking body covered in furred scales that felt like the green on a pool table, eight stubby legs, and a docked stub of a tail like a Doberman's. Cat was brown some of the time, or mottled white, or a deep and golden tan depending on the season, but furious always. It spit when angry. Like a cobra, it had a hood on its neck that would stand up when Cat was annoyed and turn a bright, angry scarlet when it was about to kill something. The flying rats that Carter hated, for example. Or Fenn.

The three of them, Carter, Fenn, and Cat, shared their unlovely tent accommodations the way the British and the Germans had once shared the Somme, gaining and losing ground by inches, creeping around in the night to seize, here and there, tiny bits of valuable personal real estate.

Captains Fenn and Carter got along well—a relationship substantially lubricated by drink and common misery. Carter and Cat had an understanding based on conjoined need. Cat needed Carter because Carter provided it with a warm, safe place to sleep, some measure of entertainment, company when it was desired, and the odd scrap of food when the hunting was poor. And Carter needed Cat because Cat gave him something to like about Iaxo that wasn't all tied up with dying.

But Fenn and Cat did not get along at all. Though Fenn's dislike of the creature was rather diffuse and generalized, Cat's dislike of Fenn appeared heated, passionate, and dire. For reasons beyond the ken of the tent's two human occupants, the animal loathed Fennimore Teague more than any other thing on a planet that, in Carter's opinion, was just full of detestable things.

But Carter liked the bug-eyed little monster, and Cat, for its part, tolerated Carter to the extent that it did not sneak into Carter's bed at night and try to kill him as it did at least once a month with Fenn. Carter always found this hilarious—seeing his friend leap up half-naked in the middle of the night, screaming bloody murder with Cat attached at the teeth to one of his legs or the back of his neck. Fenn, needless to say, did not see the humor in it, though it was perhaps a measure of his friendship with Carter that he hadn't yet simply put the barrel of his sidearm to the thing's head one night while it was sleeping and blown its brains into the dirt.

So that had been it. Carter's entire list—the total extent of what there was in Carter's mind to recommend Iaxo—came down to Cat and the war. Everything else could burn for all he cared. The summers were hot, dry, and short. The winters brutally cold. The drugs were revolting, the food primarily inedible, the landscapes just familiar enough that every little difference between Iaxo and Earth stuck out like a cockroach on a birthday cake. And the way Carter saw it, the battles between the two antagonistic gangs of abos that called Iaxo home had been entirely savage and Neanderthal undertakings until the company had come along to civilize them.

And even still, they were *mostly* nasty affairs. Bunch of fucking monkeys poking each other with sticks and bashing each other with rocks, he would say. The indigs themselves—both sides—were dirty, simple, smelled bad, and seemed themselves possessed of only two emotions: murderous rage and adoration. As Carter would readily admit, this might have been because he'd only ever seen them in two positions—either bowing to him in passing or in the bead of a gun sight—but this didn't make his essential belief any less true. And even if he'd never cared to know them in any other context and detested the miserable little world that'd created them in full, it had always been his proudly stated position that he was here only for their money and their blood, in that order. Nothing more.

That was another list, of a sort. Not a nice one but, really, none of them were.

Lying in bed, Carter coughed. He had a taste in his mouth like he'd been chewing nickels wrapped in lemon all night. He rolled over and spit into the dirt next to his rack, wishing to God he had just one cigarette. Just *one*. He felt the aching tightness of need in his chest, the itch in the back of his throat, the dampness of his palms from wanting. He thought to himself about the one that Ted had given him last night or yesterday or two days ago or whatever it was now. How that'd been cruel, really—just one being enough to retrigger the frantic yearning, certainly not enough to put it back to bed.

Rolling onto his back again, he stared up at the tent canvas. He crossed his arms behind his head, then threw one over his eyes. He was cold, so he dragged his blanket higher. Looking down the length of himself, he saw the toes of his boots poking up, uncovered. He'd slept in his boots. In most of his gear. Again. *Pig,* he thought.

But then, past the tips of his boots, he saw something else. On the trunk at the foot of his bed were two cartons, each about the size of two bricks, shrink-wrapped in black plastic and labeled as TINNED MEAT in large, white letters. For an instant, he thought they were a mirage, that maybe he was still dreaming.

Quick, he told himself, *just close your eyes and wish for fresh eggs, orange juice, a nice, fat beef steak, and a teenage prostitute to bring them to you,* but it was no good. *Tinned Meat* was like abracadabra to him—powerful magic words. *Tinned Meat* was how cigarettes were labeled when they had to be shipped through the colonial customs blockades. And just then, he wanted tinned meat more than anything. More than love or money or a steak or real orange juice or pussy or even another breath. It was like there was a hand grown from the middle of his chest, already reaching, and dragging him along after.

He heard Fenn laughing quietly in the bunk next to his. "So, what did you wish for for Christmas, little boy?"

Carter said nothing but descended on the first carton with all the cool and poise of a drowning man reaching for a life preserver, scrambling the wrong way down the bed, over sheets and blankets and his own feet, one hand groping for his ankle where, in his boot, he wore a trench knife; fumbling around it, getting tangled in bed linens, fighting free, then drawing it and, slitting the plastic like a throat, tearing at the blank white cardboard to fumble out a pack, strip it open, and pry out one clean, white, and perfect filtertip cigarette with a dirty fingernail. He stuck it in his mouth, snatched away the lighter Fenn held out to him, lit it and sucked it down in an ungoverned panic as if, at any moment, he might realize that this really was a dream and wake, wanting even worse than before.

When the first was half-done and slobbered into limp wetness, he chain-lit a second off the stump, threw the first aside into the dirt, and fell back down amid his thin blankets, musty sheets, worn canvas, and two lumpy pillows, feeling as plump and luxurious as a pasha, done in by the effort and a little high. He smiled stupidly. "My God . . . ," he said softly. "Oh my God."

"You know, I'd had this thought." Fenn was sitting up in bed cross-legged, a cloth spread in his lap laid with the disassembled pieces of his sidearm. "I'd had this thought that it would be funny to get two actual cases of tinned meat and set them there for you to see. Would that have been too cruel?"

"I would've killed you," Carter said.

"Yeah, that would've been too far. Pushing it too far. But still, I thought about it. I think it would've been hilarious."

"Maybe. To someone else. Not to me."

"I've never seen your eyes as big as when you first saw those cartons, Kev. And watching you drool all over that first one? It was really rather disgusting."

Carter shrugged dreamily, feeling etherized by the sumptuousness of lying there watching coils of pure white smoke twisting up toward the roof of the tent. "So don't watch. I haven't many vices left, Captain. Let me enjoy those I have."

Fenn scratched in mocking thoughtfulness at the grown-out shag of a blond crewcut. "Not many vices, dear? Now let us see . . . There're cigarettes, apparently. Whiskey, wine . . ." He counted on his fingers.

"Count those two together. For simplicity's sake. Drunkenness."

"Fair enough."

"Women, lechery, gluttony, sloth." Carter counted them on his fingers.

"Those are sins, not vices."

"Same thing, darling. They're sins if you feel bad about them. They're vices if you keep doing them anyway. Trust me, I know from sin."

"Do you?"

"I do. Add covetousness, too. I coveted that bottle you left by your bed last night. Then I drank it to remove me from temptation."

"Thievery then as well, you shit." Fenn eased the barrel assembly into the slide and pushed it back into its seating. "That's quite a list. Anything else we'd like to get off our narrow, bony little chest?"

"Killing," Carter said. He reached over the side of his rack and tapped ash into the dirt.

Fenn chuckled. "Ah, yes . . . Manly recreation." He set the recoil guide, fitted the pistol's slide onto the frame rails, and pushed until the barrel linkage clicked. "Speaking of which, young William is out flying reconnaissance and damage assessment with first squadron. They should be back in an hour or so." Carter could smell peppermint on Fenn's breath when he spoke. "Care to join me for breakfast, Captain? We can meet Billy on the field when they come back in."

"Ted out with them?"

Fenn pointed the pistol at his face, then set the barrel bushing, the recoil spring, and plug.

"No, actually," he said, and, for just an instant, the barest hint of concern darkened his face. It was quick, noticeable only at all because Fenn's was a face that Carter saw daily, altogether too much, and knew it to be rarely touched by gloom. It could've been something with the gun, sure. A piece mis-fit. It could've been some other fleeting thought entirely. But it wasn't, and Carter knew it wasn't, because he knew and understood Fenn's imperturbable serenity at close range as the maddening and damn annoying thing that it was. Thus he saw even the briefest flicker of dark against the face of that tranquil spirit like a cloud blotting the sun. He took it as assurance that no one was truly as calm and placid as Fenn pretended to be, just that some could fake it better than others. It was validation of his belief that everyone was just as jangled, miserable, and spoilt as he felt most of the time.

"No," Fenn continued. "Our dashing commander has been shacked up with Fast Eddie in the comms tent since late last night and hasn't poked his head out once. Either they're in love or there's trouble, and neither sounds very appetizing, so let's not think about it until after breakfast and possibly lunch, too, okay?"

"Deal," Carter said. He sat up, scrubbed at his face with the palms of his hands. He was badly in need of both a bath and a shave. It had been too long. "And you were kidding, right? What you said before? It's not really Christmas."

"No lie, G.I." Fenn jacked the slide, dry-fired his piece, smiled beatifically at the sharp snap of the hammer falling. He pushed a loaded clip into the magazine, set the safety, and put it aside. He looked across at Carter. "It's December twenty-fifth back home. Merry merry."

"No shit."

"No shit."

"Wow."

"Yes. Wow, indeed."

"Then I need coffee to go with my Christmas cigarettes. Or something. Is there any coffee left anywhere?"

Fenn's smile brightened even further. "Oh, we can do better than coffee, my boy." He stood and offered Carter a hand, dragging him roughly to his feet and then putting a hand on his shoulder to steady him. "Unscheduled resupply came in last night while you were off saving the world. I saved out your share while you were up, hid it down in the mess away from the grabby hands of our mates."

And to Carter, this came off as a stunning kindness in this place that generally felt short of everything nice and long on anything mean. Standing, he wondered for one dumb second whether or not he would've thought to do the same for Fenn, but needed only that second to know that he probably wouldn't have even thought of it. Stammering, he blurted out an awkward thank-you to cover his embarrassment and flushing shame.

Fenn just grinned, virtuous and cool. "Merry Christmas, Kevin."

Toothpaste, toothbrushes, and soap that smelled like lilacs and dust. Dried fruit and hard candy, squares of weatherized chocolate, manufactured cigarettes beneath their tinned meat labels, scotch and Kentucky sipping whiskey shipped in black plastic bottles with VITAMIN SUPPLE-MENT stenciled on their sides, and vodka by the five-gallon jerry. There were telestatic copies of pages from pornographic magazines wadded up and used as packing material in crates of medical supplies, cans of condensed milk, batteries, cereal, freeze-dried beef from real cows. Little indulgences like bottles of olives and cherries, jars of peanut butter, rock sugar, breakfast cereal, high-density data chips packed with music and magazines, news reports, movies, and ball games; letters from family for those who had them and personalized cards from the company for those, like Carter, who didn't anymore. Pens, lighters, and vacuum-packed bricks of coffee were tucked in among smuggled cases of ammunition, spare parts, and tools.

There were big things, too. A digital projector (which arrived broken beyond repair), a new generator, tires (the planes ran through tires like crazy, banging them out of shape from always landing on stubble fields, dirt, or grass), twenty thousand gallons of high-grade aviation fuel, six fresh engines for the planes (four 250-horse Royce Eagles and two hybridized Hispano-Suiza/Daimler air-cooled thirteen-cylinder behemoths that one of the company's engineers had designed specifically for the improved Sopwith Camels). There were structural parts, bolts of fire-retardant cloth, lots of bomb parts that came packed (alongside cases and cases of beer) inside sealed caskets stamped with biohazard trifoils and those words, REMAINS UNVIEWABLE, just like on the one they'd sent Danny Diaz home in. The irony of bombs in a casket, they'd all appreciated. The fact of receiving a shipment of caskets at all, none of them did.

For the medical area there was an ice machine that Carter thought was almost a joke because of the cold, but then not, because it meant that the pilots could now drink their whiskey on the rocks like gentlemen ought to, and that was like luxury beyond imagining. When he mentioned it to Fenn, his friend just smiled. "I knew you'd get the joke of it."

All told, it'd been a sixty-ton orbital drop, wholly unexpected by any of those who claimed secret knowledge of company resupply schedules. A Christmas miracle, then, whose origin or cause no one among the pilots wanted to examine too closely lest the mistrust in their black and suspicious little hearts would somehow make it all disappear. While Carter had been asleep and dreaming, or walking maybe, or up and in flight, it'd been delivered by a speedy blockade runner who'd done his job so well that he'd nearly flattened the machine shop with one of the armored containers. No one had even needed to leave camp to retrieve the riches. Santa Claus, it appeared, had gone high-tech now that all the good little children had become so greedy and scattered among the stars.

Portions of each man's pay were delivered. A small percentage, and only in company scrip, but that was fine. It wasn't like there was anything to buy with it, but it was enough to make the card games more interesting for a time.

Promotion reports, wage adjustments, a company stock report, and mission summary were delivered as well, in a sealed bag keyed to Ted Prinzi's greasy fingerprints. Copies were already tacked to the walls in the field house. Not everything, but the important stuff. Carter had received a 1.72 percent pay raise. Billy Stitches was given the rank of flight lieutenant. Some of the reports were old but, to them on Iaxo, everything coming from the real world arrived old. Time and travel. Distance. Carelessness. It didn't matter. News that was new to them was new news, and they devoured it like it wasn't due to happen till tomorrow. Flyboy Inc. stock was doing well and, through their negotiators, the company had haggled up its stake on Iaxo to something in the neighborhood of eight hundred million acres in exchange for services. They owned (or *would* own, eventually) a sizable fraction of the total continental land mass, one entire ocean, and someday—once the place was civilized—the company could then sell that off to developers, mining conglomerates, real estate speculators, and land rapists of every stripe. Put in a casino, some strip mines, chain restaurants, a whorehouse, level the mountains, take out all the trees, drain the rivers. Show the indigs what modernity really meant. At that point, each of the mercenaries (mercenary pilots, mercenary mechanics, mercenary cooks and computer operators and lawyers) would get a piece of the profits, and the indigs on both sides, if there were any left at that point, would get screwed all over again. It was the company man's retirement plan, so to speak. And it wasn't a bad deal at all, provided you weren't an indig.

|||||||||||||

Carter and Fenn had themselves a huge and leisurely breakfast of local bread with grape jelly manufactured a hundred light-years away, powdered eggs (because every army everywhere has had to eat powdered eggs for breakfast since the day some jerk had first come up with the notion that such a thing as powdering an egg was a good idea), condensed-milk sandwiches with ground sugar, and slabs of the native equivalent of ham steak, which was, in actuality, nothing like a ham steak at all except that it came salty from the cure and cooked up the proper color. It came from an animal that looked something like a fat, legless rabbit, like a fluffy slug with big, floppy ears, and not the kind of thing anyone wanted to picture while eating. Tasty, though. And they were so dumb, they could be hunted with a hammer.

Most important, they had coffee. Gallons of coffee. They drank coffee until the entire tent smelled like the inside of a grinder and Carter felt like he would burst. Coffee sweetened with condensed milk and bourbon whiskey, and made sweeter still by the fact that they hadn't had anything but instant in nearly two months and had even begun running short on that in the last week.

So they drank coffee. They sat with their boys from second and third squadrons who straggled in, bleary with sleep, dragged forward like zombies by the smell of fresh joe and frying slug-bunnies. Everyone helped themselves to the supplies. There were no arguments, only munificence and sweetness and men who, some days, acted as though they couldn't stand the sight or sound or stink of one another, heaping one another's plates with food and lighting one another's cigarettes. They smoked, laughed, joked, swore, and kept wishing one another a merry motherfucking Christmas until the air inside the mess tent was warm, close, blue and foggy with smoke. It was, in Carter's memory, the greatest Christmas party he'd ever been to until Fenn, reaching over behind the back of Jack Hawker, punched him in the shoulder and pointed out one of the plastic windows at the blurry form of Ted Prinzi stalking purposefully across the compound, headed in their direction.

Fenn grabbed him by the sleeve, dragged him back and out of the general melee of conversation. "Here we go, Kev," he said. "I've seen this coming for a year." This struck Carter as strange because he had no idea what his friend could've seen coming or why he wouldn't have told him about it if there'd been anything about anything he'd suspected for a whole year. They'd had entire conversations about their feet, the two of them; they'd spent hours talking about tent canvas or toast because they'd run out of meaningful things to say to each other so long ago. Suddenly Carter felt as though Fenn had been holding out on him and would've said something cross about it except that inside the overcrowded tent, a couple of people had seen Captain Fenn point. A few more saw them looking out the window and, before long—in the space of a breath or two or three—their fine and blasphemous Christmas party had gone from cheerfully effusive, piggish, and juvenile to sepulchral. Half the pilots were on their feet and seemingly ready to make a dash before Ted even stepped through the door—the idea being to put a bit of running distance between themselves and whatever ill tidings Ted eternally bore. Raoul, one of Vic's mechanics, had Lori Bishop, a flight controller, on his lap, and they'd frozen together like that, a tableau of holiday merriment with her arms thrown around his neck and his hands creeping high along her hips. Ernie O'Day from Fenn's 3rd had his eyes squeezed shut and was muttering curses under his breath. Beside Carter, Jack Hawker, his squadron leader from the second and not at all a religious man, appeared to be praying.

|||||||||||

Ted had followed his feet across the field, thinking *Christmas* with each step. *Christmas*, step-step. *Christ-mas, Christ-mas*. He didn't know what he was going to say. He felt as though he should look like he knew what he was going to say. But he had no earthly idea.

He pushed through the flap door and into the mess, his face bruised by exhaustion. And for a broken second, he stood there, just inside the door, swaying slightly, drinking in the warmth of bodies, of breath. He felt like a drowning man suddenly given one more gasp of air. His back was straight. His eyes were bright. The rest of him felt like it could turn to liquid at any second.

"First squadron took fire over Mutter's Ridge five minutes ago and are coming home hot. Two planes damaged. One pilot wounded." He swallowed. His throat felt hot and distended, like he'd swallowed a billiard ball halfway. "I don't know who, I don't know how, I don't know sweet fuck-all, so don't ask me any questions. I want crews on the field with emergency gear and all pilots to their planes double-quick."

Ted looked around. He tried to catch each man's eye. There was a lot of blinking but for one terrible, long moment no one spoke, no one moved, no one even breathed.

And Ted could've yelled. He knew he could've screamed his head off to snap everyone out of their collective trance. And maybe he should have done that, but he was so tired, so spent. Scared. Sick with it.

So instead, Ted just spoke. One word, dropped with all the intensity of an atom bomb as, in the background, everyone heard the grinding moan of the scramble siren beginning to wail.

"Now," he said.

And the tent was empty before the word hit the floor.

CARTER WAS ON THE FIELD WITH ENGINES HOT, the squadron arranged behind him in scramble formation, and the ground vibration was enough to shake his vertebrae like dice. They were ready to go, ready to fly, but instead they sat, boxed together for fast takeoff, idling impotently on the west end of A strip with orders to go exactly nowhere.

Carter was still thinking about breakfast because breakfast was preferable to death. Breakfast was preferable to most anything, and death, obviously, was among the worst things in the world.

Carter was thinking about toast. About real toast. Not too long ago—less than a year, maybe—he and Fenn had had a long conversation about toast. Real white toast made from real white bread by a machine, perfected across centuries and made to do nothing else.

Toast. Seriously, they'd talked for hours. How toast, made well, was one of those things a person didn't ever think about missing until it was gone and then missed with an ache that was incalculable. How toast might be the one thing he'd wish for if he were suddenly granted one wish and, of course, couldn't wish to leave, to go home, to be just gone and, of course, wealthy and, of course, dog-piled by naked girls.

Ridiculous, sure. Ask them on any other night and it would've been something else, some other stupid little thing that no one ever thought about until it was unavailable.

Toast. Golden brown, still hot from the toaster, dripping with butter until the middle of a piece of it got a little wet and squishy but the edges stayed crisp. How even *bad* toast was great toast when compared with having no toast, and was fucking phenomenal toast when measured against the coarse, gritty, heavy local bread toasted over a fire or in a pan on the gas stove in the galley. The bread on Iaxo was terrible. What bread must've been like when bread was first invented, before anyone knew better. It tasted green and almost moldy even when fresh. And the toast made from it suffered accordingly.

Toast. Hours of talk about toast until they were mad for it. And now, all Carter could think was that this was one of the things they'd talked about, wasted their time on, when Fenn wasn't saying whatever it was he'd claimed to have known about for a year. If it'd been important, he thought—important enough to mention now, important enough and right enough that he'd copped to it just a minute before Ted had opened his big mouth—motherfucker should've *said* something.

Carter hadn't been able to ask Fenn about it in the mess. No time. Certainly, he hadn't been able to ask when they'd broken in a frantic sprint for the tent line—for their gear, their gloves, their warm coats and collars; scrambling for them and then running out again, whooping and cursing, for the flight line where the planes were being shoved out of the longhouse like boarders late with the rent. And now it was bothering him. And now he really wanted some toast, too.

First squadron had come down on the southern tip of C strip, which was the emergency strip, while Carter and two squadron were taxiing into position and before Fenn and his squadron had even gotten their planes out of the longhouse. Consequently, no one had seen what sort of shape they'd been in. No one had been able to count planes and guess at who was hurt, who was down, or anything. No one in the control tent was taking questions. Ted couldn't be raised on the radio.

Sitting, waiting, Carter could see the tail and body markings of Fenn's plane, Jackrabbit. It was the best of the company's D.VIII models, square-bodied, boxy, with the odd little fin on the tail and Fenn's painting of a rabbit, running, just below the cockpit. A huge penis had been added, drunkenly, by someone who may or may not have been Fenn, at some later date. So, too, had a top hat. A cigarette holder poking crookedly from the rabbit's mouth.

Lined up with him were Charlie Voss and George Stork in the company's two Airco DH.2 pushers, each loaded down to the axle stops with 250 pounds of bombs. It'd been a DH.2 that'd killed Boelcke, the aerial tactician, October 28, 1916. Boelcke had written the book on air-to-air combat, was a genius, died at twenty-five. Carter'd read the book. So had everyone else.

Carter knew that it wasn't really a DH.2 that'd killed Boelcke, but rather a collision with his wingman during a dogfight with a squadron of DH.2s, but that was close enough. The DH.2 was what pilots had flown before there was anything else to fly—one of the first planes that didn't kill them instantly.

Behind Voss and Stork were Emile Hardman and Ernie O'Day at the sticks of two Vickers Gunbus F.B.5s, two-seaters, with Max, the armorer, and Willy McElroy, the machinist, on the guns in the forward observer seats. There was no legend to the Vickers. They were ugly, cranky, and slow. No one liked them at all.

Two squadron was in formation. Carter and Jack Hawker, the squadron leader, were sitting side by side with fourteen feet of space between their wingtips. Tommy Hill was behind Carter. David Rice was behind Jack. Lefty Berthold was in drag position.

They were trained to lift this way, five seconds between pairs, which was dangerous but quick. When Carter looked again, he saw Fenn's third squadron laid out on the south end of B strip with their bombers and ground support planes, arranged the same way. With two squadrons using both strips, the controllers could lift ten planes in less than a minute. It'd never been necessary before, but they'd practiced it. A few times. A long time ago. They'd drilled things like fast lifts and combat descents, squadron flying, rush envelopments, and all the nasty tricks of the dogfighter. After a while, it'd seemed ridiculous, so they'd stopped, comforted a little by thinking that they could probably still do it if they had to. Now it was what was on everyone's mind: whether they could and whether or not they'd have to. Whether this, finally, was the moment when it might matter.

Except that they weren't doing anything but sitting. On the ground, they were useless, harmless, vulnerable. Ask Danny Diaz. Though they might play at it with their feet rooted to the earth, it was only in the air that they became elder gods, avenging angels of decrepit technology, all roaring engines and blazing guns, raining fire from the heavens, death from the clear blue sky. In the air, they were wrath. They were furious might. They were power without bounds.

On the ground, though, it was all backaches and leg cramps, boredom, the wasting nervousness of sitting, clenched and waiting.

Carter recalled a month or a year ago sitting in the tent with Fenn, talking bullshit. Not even about anything because neither had anything to say, but just talking. About socks, say. Or weather. Didn't matter.

But he recalled the moment it'd turned. When, in the middle of the bullshit, Fenn had stopped and said, "Now Vic . . . Vic is . . ."

Carter'd said, "What? Vic is what?" because it'd occurred to him then that of everything they'd talked about—and they'd talked about *everything*—Vic was something they hadn't. As though sacrosanct. Or maybe precisely the opposite.

Still, hearing her name on Fenn's lips had gotten Carter's hackles up for some reason. A gut reflex, her name like a slow lightning bolt touching him, climbing the ladder of his spine.

"Vic is . . ."

And Carter'd waited for it. *Vic is unlucky. Vic is a death sentence. Vic is bad for business.* He'd heard it all before—the kinds of conversations that dried up the minute someone realized he was close enough to maybe hear. Him and Vic—that was no secret. Especially not from Fenn. Him and Vic had been him-and-Vic ten feet from him, just one bed away. Fenn knew everything.

And at the time, it'd been almost nothing. A conversation instantly forgotten, except that it hadn't been, because now, a month or a year later, it was all coming back to Carter. Another thing they'd talked about that wasn't what Carter now wished they *had* talked about: Fenn's secret wisdom.

Instead, he remembered Fenn saying, "Jesus Christ, Kevin." Using his full name, which Fenn only did when he was very drunk or very serious or both.

Fenn saying, "That is the saddest goddamn woman I have ever known."

Fenn saying, "For real," and "Kevin?" and "You okay, Kev?"

Two squadron was all arrayed in Camels like Carter's Roadrunner. Fighter cover for the bombers. And the noise of those five sputtering engines grinding all around him was like an earthquake that wouldn't stop, hitting him right in the guts, throbbing through him in waves, almost hypnotic but for being so loud that he couldn't hear, couldn't speak, couldn't even think clearly.

Carter closed his eyes, trying to love the droning noise, trying to climb inside it like a blanket of sound. It was the reverberation of death, fast approaching; the language of the machine that he cherished. He spoke to himself, to his plane, in words that were drowned by the throbbing, crashing walls of noise. He slapped the breech on the cannon open and closed, open and closed. He adjusted his safety belts. He lowered his head and pressed it against her instrument panel, thinking how, after all that coffee, he wished he'd taken the time to put on the catheter.

|||||||||||||

Twenty minutes passed, became thirty. Only after all that did Carter finally hear the squawk in his ear of the radio calling him. He'd been sleeping, he thought. Just a little.

"Two squadron clearing for takeoff."

"Jack?"

"Yeah, Carter."

"I was sleeping, I think."

"That's weird."

Looking up, Carter saw Lambert and Rockwell, two of Vic's ground crew, come jogging out of the comms tent to flag him for takeoff. He shook his head, pawed at his eyes with fingers gone numb from the vibration.

Rockwell pulled his chocks, then Jack's. Lambert, walking backward, held two yellow flags crossed in one hand, giving them the slow caution.

Carter and Jack began to roll—a lazy, creeping taxi, hard wheels bumping over the close-cut grass and a million small stones.

Finally, Carter thought. *Finally.*

He'd done this hundreds of times before, but his stomach still boiled with butterflies. Modern jets, transatmospheric fighters, shuttles, dropships, spacecraft especially—they were all designed to remove the pilot from the experience of flying; to insulate him from the elements, from wind, weather, engine noise, exhaust fumes, and that sickening, giddy, here-we-go sensation of actually leaving the ground and taking to the air.

But in an open cockpit, there were no illusions. Every bump, roar, clatter, and stink came directly at the pilot. Burning oil, wet leather, the screaming of an over-revved engine in a dive, the throaty chugging of machine guns firing and *tac tac tac tac* of spent brass caught in the slipstream bouncing off wings and cowling. In his plane, Carter was loudly, plainly, often painfully aware that he was trusting his life to little more than an uncomfortable chair bolted onto a lawn-mower engine, surrounded by nothing but a rickety, sparse conglomeration of sticks and fabric, bombs, bullets, and modern aircraft fuel. Everything around him was flammable, explosive, or both. And once he was up, he knew that there was nowhere to go but down.

Lambert gave them the green and, in unison, Jack and Carter throttled up. As he watched the speed indicator starting to climb, Carter was still thinking how crazy it was to do what he did and how very much fun. He gnawed at his lip with his teeth and felt the churning of nervous adrenaline in his stomach. He passed critical speed (that point at which there was too much forward velocity and not enough runway left to slow down should something go terribly, catastrophically wrong) and spared a quick look at the rearview mirror mounted to one of his wing struts just to make sure that David and Tommy were under way and in sequence.

But they weren't. Lambert had red-flagged them both, and Carter could see the cottonball puffs of blue-gray smoke drifting away above them, a sure sign that they'd killed their engines.

Carter and Jack reached speed. Carter felt the shudder of breath on control surfaces, and he and Jack lifted together, both at full throttle, easing away from each other and nosing up into thirty-degree climbing turns for a circle around the field as planned.

Tipped over on their wings, they both had a good view of the east end of C strip and the field house where first squadron had come to rest. There were three D.VIIs, all jumbled up on the runway skirt, and people rushing to and fro. Vic was down there somewhere in that mess. Carter couldn't pick her out individually, but he could feel her moving through the personal space of his own swelling panic. He knew that three D.VIIs were one plane too few for the number that ought to have come home. Heavy smoke clung tightly to the ground like fog, getting whipped into rococo curls behind Jack and Carter as they turned close overhead.

Passing the longhouse that ran parallel alongside B strip, Carter saw Fenn's Fokker already up, the two DH.2s lifting, and a fourth plane—Billy's two-seater Bristol—trundling along close on their tails. Ground control capture was just starting to show planes in flight on his map display, and none of them belonged to Fenn's second squadron. He was busily shouting nonsense into the radio, demanding that ground crews launch his wingmen, cursing, spitting. There was no effect. By the time Carter and Jack had made their first turn, two squadron was already on its way back to the longhouse.

Roadrunner and Jack Hawker's plane, Fast Nancy, moved into position above and behind Fenn's Jackrabbit, snap-rolling to dump speed as the chugging, heavily loaded Aircos struggled to catch up and keep ahead of the much-faster Bristol riding drag position. Forming up, the radio was filled with control chatter, but no one was answering Carter, or Jack, who'd gotten into the shouting, too, threatening the lives of all and sundry and demanding to know why the rest of his squadron members were now enjoying coffee and donuts in the field house rather than being up in the air and on his tail where they belonged. And no one was answering Fenn, who'd started cursing his own pilots for cowardice or dereliction in cruel, soft tones almost drowned out by the more strident voices of protest.

It was Ted who finally answered, calling in on the all-hands channel from the gunner's seat of the Bristol with Billy Stitches on the stick.

"Come about to course fifteen degrees north-northeast, level at one thousand feet. Two squadron plus five hundred and kindly quit your goddamn whining. Fighters to high cover. Charlie, Stork, make your target a downed Fokker approximately eighteen miles out. Look for the smoke. Bombs away on my mark only."

Ted paused and, for a second, there was nothing on the radio but the sound of static. He allowed the shock to root in deep before continuing. "Captain Teague, you're wing leader. I'll be going in with Billy to inspect the wreck. You and first squadron will cover. Two squadron covers you. Understood?"

The pilots consented with their silence, as if speaking would've broken the cheap, stunned solemnity of the moment. It was Fenn who finally ruptured the hush. "Copy, command. Jackrabbit is flight leader. Coming around to fifteen degrees at one thousand short. Flight, follow my lead."

They turned in formation, stacking up behind and above Jackrabbit, wobbling on the unsteady air, drifting like bad dreams looking for a place to settle.

"So who was it, Ted? Who went in?"

And Ted didn't answer immediately, as if debating whether to tell the pilots at all. Like it was a state secret or something and not just a matter of them all counting heads in the mess that night and seeing who'd turned up missing-presumed-dead.

There was a moment of quiet, the radios popping and sizzling like bacon frying, the pilots all imagining a different friend or partner mashed up inside the crumpled wreck of a D.VII. Death by fall. Death by flame. Slow death, choked by smoke, seared by an engine fire, bleeding out in the cold, terrible quiet. A quick death, maybe—on impact or by bullet through the heart or head. Infinitely preferable, though the endings all came out the same. Danny Diaz . . . Who could help but think of that story just then?

"It was Morris," Ted said. "Morris, goddammit."

Carter thought how Morris was no friend to Ted—no more than any of the rest of them were—but that they'd bunked together briefly about half a year back after a storm that had blown away some tents and temporarily jumbled up the living arrangements. The two of them, Ted and Morris, had shared an affinity for pinochle that none of the other pilots understood, and they had spent a couple of long weeks waking together, smelling each other's dirty socks and bad breath and listening to each other snore. That sometimes passed for closeness between men and was damn close to carnal intimacy for a man like Ted.

"Everyone shut up and do their jobs," Ted said, the spotter's radio handset held too close to his mouth, fogging the channel with the rattle of his sucking breath. "No more talking. Jackrabbit, you have the lead."

| | | | | | | | | | | |

The crash site was easy to spot by the finger of greasy, black smoke reaching up into the sky. Carter and Jack, Fenn and the two DH.2s went into split circles at one thousand and fifteen hundred while Ted, Billy, and the Bristol went in for a rough field landing close to Morris's plane, the Delta Doll, drag-assing along a flattish, grassy swath that had probably looked a lot more favorable from the air than from the ground.

From their height, Jack and Carter could see the smudge of troops moving a few miles off. They weren't yet close, but had most definitely made their way across the river and into Flyboy's side of the lines.

Jack called Billy. Billy told him to sit on his hands. Ted called in the bombers from the ground. "Morris cashed his check," he said. "Plane is a total wreck. Grease it." Two passes and the area was a smoking crater. Close by, the Bristol was still on the ground.

Everyone would find out later that Morris had gone radio silent about two minutes after the pilots on the ground had gotten the call to scramble. The Delta Doll had been limping at the tail of the flight back from Mutter's Ridge, and Porter Vaughn—flight leader of first squadron—had dropped out of formation to check on him. He'd called flight control to report that the Doll was trailing smoke and losing altitude, pilot unresponsive. Thirty seconds later, he'd called in again to say that Morris had rolled over and was down, no radio contact. Ted had given the order to pull the extra planes out of the lineup. He'd grabbed Billy straight off the strip, muscled a ground crew into hauling the Bristol out of the longhouse and into drag position. They'd primed her, thrown off all weight they could manage, dumped in a hatful of gas, and put her in the air. The thought was that if Morris was still alive, he could be loaded into the gunner's seat and Ted could hobble home in the damaged Fokker. If the Doll was inoperable, he could ride on someone's lap. And if both plane and pilot were unrecoverable, the order would be to bomb both to keep them out of the hands of the unfriendly indigs who'd crossed the river before dawn at the now-unguarded ford and were currently headed their way.

Jack and Carter circled and circled, doing a crossing-eight pattern above Fenn, who was in a holding pattern above the bombers who'd gone in low and slow so as not to accidentally splash Billy, Ted, or the Bristol with their drop: HE and incendiary five-pounders, laid out by hand. The bombers were lugging their way back up to altitude, still fat with bombs, and with each passing minute, everyone was expecting to see the Bristol climbing back into formation. But it didn't. And then it didn't again. On each turn they were disappointed, further confused. The unfriendlies were split now into two distinct groups, the forward of them quickly outpacing the rear. Carter called down for permission to break and hit the advancing troops, but he was denied.

"Remain in position, guys," Billy radioed back. "Chief's orders."

So they circled some more. Carter fished the spotting scope out of his jacket and took a look out toward the river at the enemy advance. The rear group was indig infantry, jogging along in rank, nests of spear-tips glittering in the sunlight. The forward was cavalry, riding under the whip.

He called Billy again. "Billy, those are horses coming your way, you know."

"Thanks for the update, Captain Obvious. But we can see them just fine from here. Simon says stay put." Over the radio, Carter could hear him racking the bolts on the Bristol's machine guns.

Two more times around, he told himself. *Then we go in anyway.* Carter switched channels to talk to Jack and told him the same. Jack agreed.

They made one circle. Roadrunner carried two .303s in the nose cowling, which he primed and racked, plus a block-mount cannon. He cleared the plug from the external breech, lifted a five-round clip of 37 mm RDX explosive shells from the magazine box, and dropped it in. Carter knew all too well that the failing of the cannon was that, when the shells ejected, they hit him right in the knees and then rattled around loose on the floorboards, always in danger of fouling the pedals. It was an imperfect weapon system, but pulling the trigger was like firing a beer bottle filled with dynamite, so there was that. Just one round would flatten a small house, so one picked targets with a certain amount of discretion. Carter knew that he had to hate something and want it blown to small pieces quite badly to justify the pain and bother of going to the cannon. He knew that the popcorn guns would settle up anything short of a serious loathing just fine.

He popped the safety catch off the cannon's trigger.

But then, as he and Jack came around through their second and final turn, Jack spotted the Bristol airborne, punching a hole through the cloud of dust and smoke raised by the bombing. It was struggling to gain altitude, clawing at the air. Jack cut his turn outside and dropped back into position. Carter followed through onto his wing. Across a gap of sky, he looked over at Jack and Jack shrugged.

Ted's voice broke in over the radio. "Home, gentlemen," he said. "Jackrabbit, I have the lead. All wings fall in. We're going into refit and lockdown till I say otherwise. Until we find out what the fuck is going on around here, no one flies."

|||||||||||

Not another word was said by anyone until every plane was safely back on the ground. They made best speed for the airfield behind the Bristol, but that wasn't very fast. Billy's plane was sluggish and off-balance. It waggled discomfortingly in the crosswinds. Once they were down, the pilots found out that this was because Billy and Ted were carrying Morris's body with them. He'd been thrown from his plane in the crash and vaulted partway up a tree, still attached to part of his seat. Ted had kept Billy on the ground while he'd gone up to cut Morris down, then rode the whole way home with the corpse in his lap, Morris's head pillowed against his shoulder.

So even once they were back on the ground—after hearing that and seeing Ted standing there beside the Bristol with Morris's body in his arms, his shirt covered in gore, waiting while Doc Edison chattered in his ear and someone went to grab a tarp for wrapping the body in—no one said much of anything either.

Ted had already given the lockdown order so, obviously, the planes weren't going to fly.

And this was how the war on Iaxo began for them in earnest.

PART 2
A PRIVATE LITTLE WAR

TED HAD LOST TRACK OF THE DAYS SOMEHOW. He hadn't slept. Something in his head felt rattly and broken—some vital component fogged or ligature snapped. Carter had come home. The bombers had come home. A patrol had gone out, flying bomb-damage assessment, and Morris Ross had died in a way and for reasons that Ted couldn't quite fathom. There was a disconnect somewhere. It didn't make any sense.

Ted understood that there was a problem. The final orders had stated clearly that the operation on Carpenter was "outside compromised," meaning that someone knew they were here, meddling, trying to get rich. Someone wanted them to stop, or to get rich themselves, on their own terms, so was feeding supplies now to the other side. Though their technological advantage here was massive, it was also tenuous.

Fact: A bomb, a machine gun, a man in a biplane—all of that was glorious witchcraft to someone who didn't even know where the wind came from. But it didn't take much to trump that. As easy as it had been for Flyboy to get here—to ship in the men and the materials to make two years' worth of one-sided war—it would be just as easy for someone else to do the same. Up to this point, though, their indigs had been the only ones paying. Cavalier, Eastbourne, Palas, Flyboy, and

141

the rest—none of them were working here just for the fun of it. No one was here because they believed in anything. They had their orders. Distant companies had picked the side that was going to win this game of war, pushed their bets with guns and bombs and men and airplanes, and had known that, once all was said and done, everyone would profit handsomely for their work save the dead. Had things been different, they might've been fighting for the other side. It wouldn't have mattered. The other side just had nothing to negotiate with.

But now Morris Ross had died. Ted had carried him on his lap. Ted had held his head against his shoulder, felt the weight of him, smelled the terrible smells that death hangs on a man. He'd been chewed to pieces by someone else's machine gun, and when Ted had returned with the body, he'd lost control of things. He'd felt it leaving him, that control—a sensation like reins slipping through his fingers, the threads of command dissolving or hanging slack.

He should've said something, but he couldn't. His brain wasn't functioning; it was filled only with a blankness that he couldn't think around. He'd clung to Morris's body as though the weight of it were the only thing holding him rooted in place. Without it, he thought he might just float up and away forever. Or worse, sink. When hands had finally taken Morris from him (to lay him down gently onto plastic, to arrange his arms and his legs in some semblance of order—Billy crouching over him and staring into Morris's slack face like he was just waiting for him to wake up and say "boo"), Ted had staggered at the sudden lightness. He'd walked off quickly so no one would see him fly away.

There'd been a wake. It'd gotten out of hand. While the men were grieving, he'd washed up, shaved, changed clothes. The indig who did his laundry wasn't around, so he'd piled his gear in a corner and kicked it. Then kicked it again. That had felt good. He'd stalked the length of his tent and back again a hundred times, then cleared the comms tent and sat in it with Eddie, with maps, with plans. They'd behaved as men do, with coffee and pens and lists, grinding their way through the past two years of violent history and trying to make something good of it. Something that would appease and mollify their corporate masters— some proof that all hadn't been wasted and that, somehow, their inexplicable failures and thousand wrong moves had all been part of a path to ultimate victory, riches, success. They made lies of everything, but pretty ones.

"Who reads these reports?" Ted had asked of the air, then answered himself. "No one, that's who. There are only two communications that matter to the company: the one that says we've arrived and the one that says we've won."

In the tent, they waited on the final call from corporate—the confirmation of their final orders. That it had only been twenty-four hours surprised Ted. How could it only have been that long? How could this disaster be only a day old? He was losing track of time somehow, the entire business growing distended and strange. Like a bubble in a vein, choking off the orderly flow.

It was cold. Ted blew into his hands and rasped his knuckles against the edge of the table. Together, he and Eddie wrote a new history and predicted a new future in anticipation of that call: victory in a month. Or a week, why not? A minute. All they were begging for was time. A new clock to be started. Mercy. It would be the only chance they'd get. A moment where, perhaps—with the right words, the right numbers— their future could be changed. So they'd hunched together, head to head, light spilling across the table from a lamp, and they'd waited. They drank all the coffee and when it was gone, there was nothing but the lingering warmth of the cups.

When the final call from corporate came in, Ted crouched silently beside Eddie with earphones pressed to the side of his head, listening to every word. Eddie was polite, businesslike. He said all the right things. He laid out their position in the brightest possible light. He bargained. He made impossible promises. None of it mattered. Eddie grew strident, then angry, then desperate. The voice on the other side (Loewenhardt, Ted thought, though he wasn't entirely sure) was cold and distant the whole time, speaking with implacable tones like a cash register ringing. The voice said no and no and no some more, and Ted felt himself falling into the void of it, a gentle rush like the nearness of death. At a certain point, he closed his eyes. The voice gave spreadsheet reasons that were difficult to argue against. "We cannot, at this time, see a way to profit from any further expansion of the Carpenter mission and have shifted resources away to more likely theaters."

"I'm not asking for any expansion, sir, just—"

"At this time, the company can't commit any additional resources, owing to a rapidly shifting political situation."

"Sir, we don't need resources. If you could—"

"Currently, your operation is in danger of jeopardizing other ongoing company projects, and any further direct action from the company would only expose us to more risk. I'm sure you can understand this from the shareholders' perspective."

"Sir, I think that the shareholders would be anxious to—"

"As far as this company is concerned, this operation was never intended to be a sustained commitment. As observers, you were never expected to single-handedly fight this war."

"Observers? But we never—"

"And we thank you for all your efforts in the past two years."

"I understand that the company might need to—"

"Good. We're glad you understand. This hasn't been an easy decision for any of us. And as soon as the situation, both on the ground and in council, becomes more tenable, we look forward to renewing a relationship with you on Iaxo."

"Wait, what?"

No answer.

"Wait. You can't just leave us here."

No answer. Dead air. The whistle of empty, impossible distances.

"We just need a fucking ride!"

Ted laid a hand over the controls and killed the connection. He shook his head, suddenly deprived of the power to speak. This was his fault. This was all his fault. He stood up, dragging his fingertips across the FTL relay until his hand fell leadenly off the console.

"Wait. Commander, this is ridiculous . . ."

Ted just smiled at Eddie—a thin and brittle thing. He had an overpowering urge to pat him on the head like a child. *Loewenhardt,* he thought. It must've been Loewenhardt. He'd met the man before. A couple of times, in passing. Better days. No one else in the world was able to talk that way. To speak completely in a language of abstractions. To wring assent out of words like squeezing oil from a stone with his bare hands.

"Commander," said Eddie.

Ted pushed things around on the table with numb fingers. He stacked cups and gathered the pens, tried to shuffle the papers together.

"Ted," said Eddie.

He turned down the light of the lamp until it was barely a firefly glow. Conservation of resources. Everything they had was suddenly finite.

"Tell me this isn't what they mean, Commander. We're being left here?"

"We're being lost," Ted said. His voice sounded very loud inside his own head and though he thought he'd spoken in barely a whisper (conserving even breath, never knowing which might be his last), he thought he might have been screaming.

"Why?"

"Am I shouting?"

"What? No. You're not shouting."

"You sure?"

Eddie nodded. "Why are we being lost?"

"That conversation? It was all being recorded. It'll play if legal sanctions are ever brought." Ted smiled at Eddie again—a doddering old man's grin, lips peeling back from his fake teeth. "Am I shouting?"

"You're not shouting."

Ted turned off the lamp. He folded the thick stacks of paper and shoved them into his pockets.

"We were observers," he said. "Subcontractors, unrelated to the company, who came here and decided to fight a war without the company's knowledge. That's how it'll sound. In court, I mean. Later."

"Not if we say different."

Ted tilted his head. He took the two coffee cups by their handles, looping a finger through each of them, and looked at Eddie quizzically. "How would we do that?" he asked. "We're all going to be dead."

After that, Ted had gone out and gotten drunk. He'd burned the papers full of plans he'd taken from comms and then tried to burn the coffee cups, too. After that, Ted had found Eddie in his tent, sitting with his head down, forehead touching stacks of other papers piled into high palisades around him. Ted had walked right in. Things had been thrown. Things had been broken. Ted told Eddie to not say anything to the pilots. Not now. Maybe not ever.

"This isn't over yet," he'd said, and slapped Eddie hard on the shoulder. "Not yet."

Then he'd staggered out into the dawn and, in doing so, couldn't recall whether Eddie had been awake. He turned around. He pushed through the door again. Eddie was lying on the floor, curled up and weeping. Ted nodded once, sharply. That, he thought, was a man finally coming to terms with his situation.

The sun was coming up. Or would at some point. He'd gathered pilots. He'd broken planes out of the longhouse. With a powerful urge to do some damage, he'd organized a dawn patrol with the idea of, beginning now—beginning *right fucking now*—taking over the whole of the planet for himself. Becoming King for Life of this wet and backward shit hole and ruling Iaxo like a despot. Teach these monkeys a little something about civilization right quick, he thought. With his planes, his pilots, he could do it. Maybe talk to Connelly, too. See what he thought about being queen.

They flew the Vickers and Billy's Bristol. Albert Wolfe from first squadron went up in Carter's Roadrunner. Max, the armorer, had wisely stripped the planes and locked the armory as soon as he'd seen the bottles come out, and then had locked himself inside with the key for safekeeping. Having no guns or bombs, they'd headed out looking for trouble with their sidearms, the pockets of their flight rigs stuffed with beers just like in the good old days before Danny Diaz. They went up with empty glass and clay bottles and rocks, with bows and arrows stolen from their own indig guards at gunpoint, and a few Molotov cocktails made out of aviation fuel siphoned off the fresh tanks at the field.

They spotted an indig supply caravan well north of the river, moving contentedly through badland and in the lee of a low rise of hills. This, they went after with some vigor, banging away with pistols, throwing the rocks and bottles and then the bows and arrows, too, when it became clear that one couldn't properly operate them while in flight and sitting. They started a good-sized grass fire with the Molotovs, but it sizzled out too quickly, and Ted even managed to piss over the side of the Bristol and onto the heads of the column from a hundred feet up. He'd stood with one foot wedged behind the gunner's seat, the other braced in the empty Foster mount, and let go over the side while holding one-handed to the top wing. Lots of style, little effect. But when Carter heard about this stunt later, it would make him like Ted a little bit more.

The planes went up. The planes came down. It was an inauspicious start to the reign of King Ted. When he landed, he went to see Eddie. Eddie was in the comms tent again. Eddie was waging his own private war. A lawyer war. He had more papers—new papers, stacks of them. He had memos and orders and a pen in his teeth. When Eddie heard Ted come in, he'd looked up and the two men had stared into each other's eyes and maybe saw a little too much madness there, a little too much sudden kinship. The reflections were jarring.

"Call them in," Eddie had said. "We need to have a meeting."

"Who?"

"The pilots. Officers and squadron leaders. We need to talk."

"We don't have anything to tell them," Ted said.

"I do. You're not the only one who has old friends back home."

"Eddie, we *can't* tell them . . ."

"Call the meeting, Ted. Gather them up. Dig them out. I don't care. I have information now. We need to talk."

IT WAS THE SOUND OF THE DAWN PATROL LANDING that woke Carter and triggered the instant onset of a brutal hangover that made him wish he'd never been born. A just punishment, perhaps, for the previous evening's indiscretions. But still, it was mean.

Most everyone had gotten drunk as hell the night after Morris Ross was killed. Spooky drunk, mostly. Quiet and focused, at least at first, but by midnight the quietness had worn off and the party spilled out of the mess and the field house, across the airstrips and up and down through the longhouse. To those involved, it must've felt like an affirmation of life in the face of the death of one of their own and, in that spirit, they broke things, hit one another, and accidentally burned one of the tents to the ground. To the camp indigs, it seemed like something else entirely and, in quiet places, away from the quaking epicenters of grief, they gathered to softly discuss it among themselves, hunkering in the shadows cast by guttering flames, away from the shouting, casting their eyes occasionally skyward as if expecting heavenly reinforcement or, perhaps, retribution.

As should have been expected, Carter woke up beneath Vic at some point during the night with her knees straddling his hips, her fine, pale skin glowing ghostly in the moonlight. He didn't remember going there, getting there, nor being there, but he did remember Vic, that was sure. He remembered warmth, softness, aliveness, and her dark hair running like oil through his fingers when he reached for the back of her neck to pull her down closer on top of him.

Now it was only cold. And in the thin, watery blue light of morning, waking wrapped in a blanket out in the tall grass next to B strip, they were both probably half-dead from hypothermia. Leaning over her, Carter saw Vic's hair crunchy with frost, her lips pale in the bitter, hard chill.

A truly awful landing by Wolfe in Roadrunner nearly ended the war for both of them, but the near-death passing of his wingtip over Carter's head when he sat up only made him laugh, goggle-eyed with wonder. He recognized the insignia of his plane and said aloud to himself that he really shouldn't be flying in his condition.

He spent the next twenty minutes throwing up beside the longhouse, and when he came back, weak-kneed and stark naked, to the spot where he'd been lying, Vic had gone and taken the blanket with her. There were no clothes to be found. He knew for stone certain that he'd been fully dressed at the start of the night, was less sure at what point he'd become undressed, and hadn't a clue as to where those clothes might be now. It was precisely these sorts of things that Carter felt ought to concern him more, but they didn't. Maturity, one might say, is always knowing where one's pants are, but weak-kneed and naked was how Carter'd stumbled back to his tent that morning.

Morning at the Flyboy camp looked like the aftermath of a bad night fight with no survivors. There were bodies everywhere. Max had fallen asleep locked inside the armory. Tommy was found by Doc Edison, the Carpenter mission's medic and least busy man on all of Iaxo. He was facedown in the middle of C strip, arms and legs spread like he was trying to make a puke angel. Davey Rice was sprawled close to the remains of the burned tent, smears of blood dried across his nose and cheek. Charlie wasn't far away, half-frozen in all his gear. They discovered Emile inside an empty shipping container beside the machine shop, buried like a tick in cast-off packing materials, his head pillowed on a mound of slick pornography.

Raoul and Lori Bishop, having obviously picked up where they'd left off the last morning, were all tangled together on a table in the mess like a horrible accident at a contortionists' school and were left alone to wake to their own misery, the growing search party of mechanics, ground crews, and communications personnel led by Doc Edison backing out quietly, smothering grins behind their hands.

Carter found Fenn in the tent where he belonged, but stretched out in the dirt beneath his rack with his boots off and his helmet on, a halo of empty beer cans ringing his head. Cat had taken a predatory interest in one of his bare feet and was stalking it with a cold and lethal intensity.

Slowly, they put themselves back together and got on with the painful business of being the living.

|||||||||||

Carter and Fenn could feel Ted coming before they saw him. It was like a game. Once a man got the feel for it, he could sense Ted coming a hundred yards off, and the first one to say his name won. Or lost, depending.

It was a few hours past dawn and the two men were recovering, not really doing much of anything and most surely not in the mood for company. They could barely tolerate each other's; they weren't speaking, breathing too loudly, or even looking in each other's direction. Cat lay curled in a tight ball on Carter's stomach, snoring while Carter scratched between where he thought some of the little monster's shoulders ought to be. It would wake periodically, just long enough to open one eye and spit at Fenn before dropping back into a heavy, blissful slumber. For a while, Fenn had been spitting back, but he'd quickly lost interest.

Carter said, "Ted."

Fenn said, "Fucker."

Ted walked straight in. He didn't knock.

"Captains," he said.

"Commander," said Fenn.

"Ted," said Carter.

"Good to see you both conscious."

They both nodded. Neither saluted or came to attention or even sat up, for that matter. Ted stood straight as a rail, was showered, clean, and shaven so close and so recently his chin and cheekbones looked blue. It was, in Carter's opinion, obscene.

Ted stood a moment, surveying. The two pilots and one cat-snake, the empty bottles, cigarette butts crushed into the dirt, the wreckage and general slobbishness of their bachelor officer quarters. There was no doubt that everything in his sight offended Ted—from Fenn's socks drying on the potbellied pig-iron stove they heated the place with to the tattered, vicious girlie spreads and war porn hung everywhere by way of decoration. But when he spoke, he did so slowly, as if trying to initiate a friendly conversation but not exactly sure how to go about it.

"So . . . Morris, yeah?"

"Yeah," said Carter.

"Morris," said Fenn.

"It's a shame about him. He was a . . ." Ted sniffed, but apparently thought better of breathing too deeply, so grunted instead. His hands were clasped behind his back, but Carter could see the twitch of the muscles in his shoulders and arms, as though he were wringing his hands behind him or digging his nails into his palms hard. "He was a good man. No sense of direction and not the best flier, but a good . . . a good guy."

"Not very lucky at cards," added Fenn.

"Social skills of a walnut," said Carter. "But a good guy."

"Yup," said Fenn.

"Yeah," said Ted, then, "Right," and, "A good man." He looked from Fenn to Carter to Fenn again, squinted his eyes, then, to the pilots, seemed to shake off whatever momentary bit of human compassion had seized him. "Right. So anyway. Enough fucking eulogizing. We've got a fight coming, so I want you two, all the squadron leaders, and Billy in the comms tent with me in fifteen minutes, got it? Senior staff. Go dig 'em up from whatever holes they crawled into last night and carry them if you have to. Fast Eddie wants a word or two about . . . something . . ."

Ted's voice trailed off. His eyes drifted around the tent again, head revolving on his neck like a turret traversing and his tongue clicking against his fake teeth. Fenn and Carter shot quick glances at each other but kept quiet. Ted wobbled a little on his feet but, again, seemed to recover himself—to jink free of whatever kept grabbing at him.

"Well, anyway, the man wants a word," Ted finished. "Get it done."

"Right," said Fenn.

"Aye aye," said Carter.

"Good," said Ted, then turned and was out the door without hesitation.

"Such a pleasant man," Carter said to Fenn after he was sure Ted was out of earshot. Cat got up, stretched, then slunk off to its bed by the door.

"Yes. We should really have him over more often. Lends a bit of class to the place, don't you think?"

They both reclined quietly on their cots, Carter smoking, Fenn gnawing the ragged end of one thumbnail, neither in any rush to jump to Ted's orders, and still not so sure about speaking. Carter couldn't recall what they were mad at each other about. Could've been any one of a million things, he thought. Didn't much matter.

"I think he was sizing us up," Fenn finally said, spitting a sliver of thumbnail off the tip of his tongue and into the dirt. "Don't you think so? Coming in here, talking about Morris and all that?"

Carter considered that a moment, having to cast Commander Prinzi into a whole new man just to get his head around the thought of him doing anything calculating or emotional. "What did he think we were going to do? Weep?"

"Quit, maybe? Give up our commissions?"

"And forgo all this splendor?" Carter put out his cigarette, popping the ember off with a finger and stashing the dog-end in his pocket.

"It is a war, after all, isn't it? People get hurt."

"People get killed. It's to be expected."

"But not the good people."

"—Good people."

"The good guys."

"What do you mean by that?"

"Not us."

"We're the *good* people?" Carter hucked out a short laugh. "Christ help the wicked."

"I just mean that none of us expected *this*," Fenn said, swinging his feet over the side of his cot and planting them firmly in the dirt in probable expectation of eventually getting up and doing as Ted had asked. "At least not like the way it went. And not Morris, certainly."

Carter opened his mouth to speak, closed it, looked up curiously. "What do you mean, 'not Morris'? Why not Morris?"

"I just mean no one expected Morris to be the first to go." Fenn paused. His brows came together to make a single straight wrinkle in the middle of his forehead. A fresh topography, as though no wrinkle had ever perturbed that place before. "Or next to go, rather."

"But why'd you say it like that? Like 'of course, not *Morris*'?" Carter stretched, popping joints from toes to fingertips, and it felt good. He wanted to sleep just two or three more years, he thought. Two or three more years and then maybe he'd be able to find the energy to get up and fight this war in proper good humor. "You're talking like there was a pool going or something."

"There was," Fenn said.

"What?" Carter pushed himself up on one elbow, actually facing Fenn. "Why didn't you tell me about it? You know I would've kicked in."

Fenn stood. "Because you were on the top of the list, Kev."

Carter thought about that for a moment, then bounced to his feet all in one quick motion—a trick he had for fooling his brain into accepting a new orientation before the lingering hangover could make him all dizzy and nauseated. And it worked, more or less. At least he didn't fall over.

"You should've told me about it anyway," he said. "I would've put fifty bucks on me, too."

It hadn't been what he'd wanted to say, but it was what he said. Then he clapped Fenn on the shoulder and led the way through the door and out into the world.

| | | | | | | | | | | |

Carter'd taught Cat a trick a while ago. It hadn't been much of a trick, but it was something. If Carter could get the thing's attention—and if Cat was feeling frisky—he could throw a ball, a sock, a wadded-up bit of paper across the tent and, no matter where it landed, Cat would pounce on it and destroy it, shredding it to pieces. It didn't matter what Carter said once the object had left his hand, but he usually said something like "Kill it, Cat! Kill!" just to feel like he was involved somehow, like this was something he'd accomplished by long training, not just the exploitation of instinct and Cat's own murderous temperament.

If it rolled into the mess under Fenn's rack, Cat would pursue it. If it bounced out the door, Cat would rocket off after it. And when the little monster was done demolishing its target, it would return like a dog to exactly the place it'd been when Carter started the game and wait, expectantly now, to see if he'd do it again.

One night, not paying attention, Carter'd absently thrown a crumpled ball of slick photo paper that had ended up between the legs of the potbellied stove, resting in the scorched dirt beneath the blazing hot body of the thing. And Cat had gone after it, of course. Only it was too large to fit, even slithering on its belly.

The creature had screamed as it dragged its back along the underside of the stove, snapping at the paper with its jaws and howling like nothing Carter or Fenn had ever heard before. And even as they'd both leaped up, they could smell Cat burning—a stink like flaming hair and charred meat and some greasy filth.

Fenn, in a strange instant, had panicked. Carter remembered him standing, bouncing on his toes, and waving his hands up and down in front of his chest, squealing, "Help it! Help it!" It was so unlike him that it'd stuck in Carter's mind. For his part, Carter'd grabbed Cat by the back legs and dragged it out, yelling the whole time. Not words, just unintelligible noises of fear and anger.

There was a bloody chunk missing from Carter's hand now that'd scarred terribly. Cat'd bitten him, had torn the flesh from his arm in ribbons that required dozens of stitches from Doc Edison who'd been so happy to have something to do that he'd made most of a day out of it. Eyes rolled back, terrified, Cat had thrashed and fought and finally squirmed free of Carter's blood-slick hands, hit the floor, and then went right back under the stove again, right back after the paper. In the end, Carter and Fenn had had to hold Cat down, wrap it tightly in a blanket to quiet it, get the paper, and throw it out the door. Carter's first instinct had been to feed the paper into the stove, but Fenn had stopped him.

"Cat'll go after it," he said. "It will. Just throw the paper away."

So Carter had, tossing it out the door. And as soon as they'd unwrapped the blanket, Cat had gone after it, just like Fenn had said. And when it was done, Cat came back—burned and meaty, scales blackened, panting from pain—to sit right in the spot where it'd been when Carter had first thrown the paper. It'd stared up at him with wide, rolling eyes, waiting to go again. There were wet, red stripes on its back where the stove had burned it raw.

"Well done, Kev," Fenn had said. "Nice trick you taught it."

"Fuck you," Carter had said, feeling bad enough already and turning his back on Cat, staring at the wall.

"No, really. You taught it to be just like you."

This moment came back to Carter when Fenn told him that it was the sound consensus of all the other pilots on Iaxo that if anyone was likely to die here, maybe *deserved* to die here, it was him. That was some heavy dope. It would hang on him for a good, long time. He recalled the smell of Cat burning. The crazed fixity of the little monster when, hideously wounded, it'd gone back under the stove a second time for no better reason than it hadn't yet gotten what it'd gone in after. The ridiculous pride he himself had felt when Cat'd come back inside to sit, waiting for another turn.

You taught it to be just like you, Fenn had said. But Carter knew that was wrong. He was nothing like that. He told himself that he'd quit in a minute if there was a way he could finesse it. That he'd gladly walk away. The day that their ride off-planet finally showed up, Carter told himself he'd be the first one aboard. Bulkhead seat, no baggage. And he'd never look back. Not ever.

That was what he told himself. When asked, that was what he would say: *First one aboard, motherfucker. Race me.* He pretended like he dreamed of that moment every single night.

15

CARTER, FENN, AND THEIR CHARGES MADE IT to the comms tent in under a half hour, and they were only that quick because they'd found Charlie Voss and Billy together by the machine shop trying to coax Jack Hawker down off the roof by poking at him with long sticks. Porter was in the longhouse with the mechanics seeing to his planes, and they collected him along their way. Vic wasn't there, and Carter was thankful for that at least.

The comms tent was part of what was generally referred to as the field house—a large, square, pavilion-like affair with canvas walls, a metal roof, and grate flooring to keep everyone out of the mud. It might have been festive if it'd been colorful and garlanded for Christmas, but it wasn't. It was military-regulation gray-green, the color of mildew, of Chongju or the Marne, and festooned with ratty camouflage netting. Since no one was flying, the ground control electronics were going unmanned, though Jimmy McCudden, one of the day controllers, sat off in a corner with his head down and fat, coconut-shell phones over his ears, ostensibly monitoring the radio and microwave traffic, but probably just sleeping. Every device in the place had some manner of alarm attached to it so that whenever anything at all happened, one gadget or another would immediately start screaming. A human head between the earphones was more a backup system than anything else. A brain to parse the static and background radiation for whispers in the dark. And Jimmy's head was as good as any. The company didn't miss much.

At the back of the tent there was a ready area—the kind of arrangement one almost always saw in movies about fliers, where the pilots all sit in chairs with desk-arms and listen in rapt attention while some crisply uniformed senior officer tells them how the day's bombing and mayhem is supposed to go and then warns them all not to be heroes.

Here, the area was supposed to be used for preflight briefings, tactical and strategic planning, pep talks by management. It was intended to buzz with talk and busy action, to be full of young men pushing chits around a map and talking in hushed tones about axes of advance and diversionary maneuvers. And in anticipation of such productive use, it'd been outfitted with whiteboards, tables, maps, computers, fancy and expensive projection equipment. There was even a podium, as a setup like this would've seemed naked or incomplete without one.

Mostly, the space was used for card games, office space, storage of extra equipment, or as a bivouac for off-duty controllers sleeping between shifts. No one gave the Flyboy pilots pep talks. Their strategy and tactics consisted entirely of shooting anything that moved and bombing anything that didn't. Preflight briefings—if they occurred at all—were normally held over drinks or consisted of orders screamed at a pilot as he jogged out onto the strip toward his plane and, in either case, were invariably misheard, misunderstood, or just plain ignored. The pilots knew what they were doing most of the time anyhow. Things had not been complicated here. And as recently as this morning, all of the expensive war gear had been covered with tarps and dust covers, pushed off into corners, ignored. To make plans for fighting the indigs, it was thought, would've been giving them altogether too much credit. Simpler just to kill them and be done with it.

But now, just a very few hours gone from the freewheeling innocence and egotism that'd died with Morris Ross, there was Ted, standing surrounded by all this gleaming, uncovered technology, glaring at it like he was afraid that if he took his eyes off it even for a second, it would all slink off into the woods somewhere and defect to the enemy. Fast Eddie stood with him, but Eddie was behind the podium because Eddie was the sort of man who, if there was a podium around anywhere, seemed most natural behind it. He was leaning easily on its top when the men all stumbled in, looking as comfortable and at ease there as some men do behind the wheel of a car or with their elbows down on top of a bar. Had he been feeling better, Carter would've laughed. It wouldn't have surprised him at all if he were to find that Eddie'd brought the thing with him as personal baggage.

| | | | | | | | | | | |

Eddie had been the one who'd uncovered all the equipment and pushed it into useful alignment. He'd wiped the dust off things with a cloth he'd found and made sure everything was plugged into the generators. On the podium, he had a stack of handwritten notes. He'd slept a little, cleaned himself up, and turned out for the meeting all polished, prim, and proper. He'd fussed because fussing was what he was good at. Meetings were what he was good at. This was his element, where he felt most comfortable, and after years spent fighting very different kinds of battles inside the dark and clubby confines of the company headquarters, he could slip on the aura of calm and competence like putting on a jacket.

Ted had followed him in a few minutes later and had stood off to the side, watching Eddie shove and polish and straighten.

Like a goddamn maid, Ted had thought. *Straightening up. Fretting.*

"Saw you in your tent last night, Eddie," he'd called out while Eddie crouched to drag the podium into place at the head of the room. "Crying like a girl."

Shame had flared in Eddie's cheeks. He'd felt the heat of it prickling his skin, but hadn't responded. Instead, he'd shuffled the map projector around until it was sitting just so and made sure the proper information was loaded into it and would be waiting. He liked his meetings to run smoothly, with a minimum of glitches or distractions. There was an art to it. He knew that half of appearing in command was simply controlling the environment. More than half.

Ted leaned against a stack of discarded shipping crates and looked at his hands—making fists, then releasing them, watching the play of the muscles beneath his skin. "Finally hit you, didn't it? What's happening here?"

"I am well aware of what's happening here, Commander," said Eddie. "More aware than you are right now."

Ted didn't rise to the bait. "Nothing to be ashamed of, you know. I've seen men break down worse. Not many of them, but still. It's good you're so in touch with your"—he spit onto the grating, making a little popping sound with his tongue and his lips—"your feelings."

"We should discuss our order of speaking," Eddie suggested. "We have a lot to get through."

"How do you figure? We've got a real fight now. A stand-up fight. Everyone needs to toughen up a little bit, that's all. Get some things done around here."

"Like you did this morning? I heard about your little stunt. I'm sure that just impressed the heck out of the natives."

"Better than lying around in the dirt crying for my mommy."

Eddie looked up. "Do you see me crying right now, Commander?"

Ted said nothing. He stared at Eddie, eyes hard. Eddie stared back, face a mask of calm, a twitch of a smile jerking at the corner of his mouth. He felt strong here. A decade of boardroom ambushes, career assassinations, back-office street fights, and paperwork sieges had hardened him in ways that a creature like Ted Prinzi would never understand. He'd been unprepared last night, on the relay. Two years on the front lines had left him soft and vulnerable—afraid only of bullets and bombs, the cold, the natives, and dying, which, Eddie knew, was far from the worst thing that could happen to a man. But he was over that now. He had his armor on tight.

"I have notes," Eddie continued. "We can work from them together if you like. You can talk about the operation and about Mr. Ross. I'll take care of the rest." Standing behind the podium, Eddie held out the stack of papers he'd arranged earlier. He rattled them a little. "I have a couple surprises you might be interested in."

Eventually, more out of curiosity than anything else, Ted came over to take a look. At which point, Eddie squared the papers up and placed them back on the podium. "It'll have to wait," he said, jerking the point of his chin in the direction of the door where the first of the officers were starting to filter in. "But try not to fall asleep before the end. I have some news that I know you'll want to hear."

He waved Ted off and turned to concentrate on his notes.

Controlling the environment, Eddie knew, was half the battle.

| | | | | | | | | | | |

All around Carter, the men settled into seats as though even this simple action was something entirely new to them. They fiddled with the folding arms, scrabbled their chair legs around on the flooring, and shifted their weight uncomfortably. Everything about them was red-meat raw. Everything hurt. Carter was still thinking about Cat and the way it'd sat there, staring, waiting to play again.

Eddie talked. He smiled more than was comfortable, or probably necessary. Ted spoke barely at all. For the most part, no one else had anything to say. Once things got going, it was just a meeting, same as any other, save that those who weren't still drunk from last night remained terribly hungover and all of them felt more than a little guilty just to be breathing. It was just like a meeting except that their action items, talking points, and memoranda all had to do with bloody death and destruction.

Point one: Morris was dead. They mourned him now in the most banal of all possible ways: by committee. From behind his podium, Eddie informed the assembled men that the company would be sending official condolences to his family. Carter hadn't even known Morris had one.

Point two: funeral. Ted, with his arms folded across his chest and his eyes constantly shifting to watch his flanks, said that everyone was ordered to attend a brief service for the dearly departed scheduled for later that same night. Full dress. Show off their fancies and hard hearts for the wogs. The pilots all cursed him under their stinking breath.

Point three: arrangement and disposition of forces. To be determined at some later date, unspecified. First squadron was now two men down, Danny first, now Morris. They were a weak link, to be officially assumed strong until further word and a rejiggering of the roster. Billy Stitches was to be commended on his unexpected promotion as flight lieutenant within first squadron now, please, with polite applause. That done, it was suggested that his brand-new lieutenant's wings would count as an extra man, or something like that. Carter was paying very little attention.

At the front of the room, Ted shifted uncomfortably while Eddie spoke. When it was his turn to talk, he said as few words as possible. When Eddie stood behind the podium, Ted kept looking at him like he was waiting for a snake to jump out. He wore a look the whole time as though half his mind was going. Like it was actually trying to squirm its way free from inside his skull.

"Commander Prinzi is going to run through the details of yesterday's action," Eddie said. "I think there are things here that we can all learn from."

| | | | | | | | | | | |

Point four: the action. Ted took the floor. He switched on the map projector, the other electronics around him, punching their buttons with a little more force than absolutely necessary. Eddie leaned, beaming, against the podium. Ted discussed the last flight of Morris Ross, working a laser pointer like it was a club, smashing it across the three-dimensional map projection that grew out of the wall. Everywhere he pointed, map marks would light up. They would dim again as he moved on. It was a nice effect.

"Bomb-damage assessment," Ted said, then something else, then, "First squadron here. Formation breaks east, hooks around the edge of the ridgeline here," then something else again. Carter watched as four little blue triangles lit up on the map, altitude, heading, and airspeed indicators spelled out in even tinier blue letters beneath. The little triangles did just as Ted said, pausing when he did and moving when he spoke. "Now, two planes break to dive," he said, and the triangles moved.

Carter was tuning in and out, watching the little blue triangles follow Ted's merciless direction. It was all very slick, but there was a feeling like he was making Morris die all over again with his words, making the triangles break, move into position for the coming kill. Part of Carter wanted him to stop—as though interrupting the presentation could suspend the terrible thing that was coming. Carter wondered if Ted had rehearsed this, too, while he'd waited for him and Fenn to go and gather the officers. Sitting there in the audience, Carter wanted Ted to say, *Happily ever after,* clap his hands, and make everything right again, but he didn't. He just droned on, moving Morris's triangle closer and closer to death. Jack Hawker was staring straight ahead with his mouth open like he'd been hit in the back of the head with a sack of nickels and was waiting to fall. Beside Carter, Fenn was asleep. He had a knack for doing it with his eyes open, like being dead himself. Porter, the first squadron flight leader, was staring at the floor.

Ted again: "Billy and Albert here, flying high cover at six thousand. Porter, this is you and Morris, down at one thousand, dropping speed for observation of the target area, yeah?"

Porter nodded. And as if his neck were on a spring, once he started nodding, he didn't seem able to stop.

Eddie was watching the action on the map with the vapid, distracted grin of a game-show hostess. To Carter's eye, there was something so terribly deliberate and false about his every motion and every twitch of his pretty, pretty face. Even his teeth were perfect, and he seemed somehow to have far too many of them crammed into his sucking little mouth. He thought about Vic and had to shake his head to make her face go away. It was reflex—his body jumping at the barest scent of her presence, real or imagined. Vic leaning over him in the dark, her hair falling like curtains around them, blocking out the greasy light of the fires in the distance. Vic leading him by the hand away from last night's festivities, turning back to look at him over one shoulder, smiling with a sadness so deep it was as if she'd swallowed an ocean.

"They make their pass here, directly over the strike zone, and come up clean. Right, Porter?"

Porter's head kept nodding.

"Porter?"

"Right." He didn't look up.

Carter was thinking about Fenn.

You were on the top of the list, Kev.

He wondered how much of that was because of the interest Vic had taken in him, how much of it he'd brought on himself, how much was the prescience of pilots for just knowing somehow who among them was going to go. It wasn't a measure of skill. Not about like or dislike. Rather, it was a determination of hardness, of armor. Some pilots shone with it—an aura that clung to them like skin and spoke of invulnerability. Others didn't. Others had chinks, bits of softness that were like psychic weakness.

Carter thought about Danny Diaz.

"Breaking here. Still in formation."

It was still a crapshoot, though. Luck, good and bad. People's internal numbers got skewed, odds tumbled. Luck was the only real divinity of the battlefield, and it broke to no amount of praying or sacrifice. This time, the pilots' pool had been wrong. Carter wondered where Morris had been on the list and who was profiting from his demise.

"We've got planes high and low. Porter and Morris descending, making a second pass."

Of the many, *many* things Carter hated about this place, its people, the situation as a whole, he thought sometimes that the thing that drove him most secretly crazy was how the stupid indigs wouldn't fight back. *Couldn't* fight back, really. Not against the company and its flying machines. Because while he supposed that they tried, it was rarely to any effect. Things might be different on the ground, but from the sky, fighting the indigs was like punching a baby. It was like shooting some dumb animal chained to a post. It was safe, sure, but there was little dignity in it.

And it wasn't like Carter cared about honor or fairness—at least not that he would ever admit to out loud—but he'd hated the indigs for the fact that they just died without having the self-respect to make him feel good about it by putting up a fight.

He squirmed in his seat while Ted talked Morris Ross closer and closer to his little death. Contrary to his standing in the pilot's pool and his comradely offer of betting heavy on his own dying, Carter didn't want to die. He wasn't a suicide case. He didn't want the filthy little indigs to kill him or Danny or Morris or anyone else, either, but sometimes—*occasionally,* he would say—he did want them just to hit him back.

That was all. Even in the cloister of his own mind, Carter was careful to halt his imaginings right there. No one needed to die, but there was a dark and wet and awful part of him that *wanted* to be hurt—that hated the indigs for being stupid and backward and powerless, for just rolling over and dying in his gun sights for the past two years; that wanted them to fill the sky with tracers and blacken it with flak and shoot him all to hell and back.

He'd dreamed of it. Not often, but some. On those nights when, if asked, he would say he'd been dreaming of nothing more than the lead-weight pressure of six gravities of acceleration and the long burn for home, he actually dreamed of the indigs punching holes in the skin of his plane and the flesh of his body. On those nights he dreamed of them burning his eyes out the way they'd done to Danny or carving into him with bullets and shrapnel as he'd done to them so many times before and making him hurt the way he'd been hurting them for so long. He dreamed of waking, bloody and screaming, in a medical tent with pieces of himself left scattered on these alien fields and to thus be granted—finally—a pure fury. A clean and justified rage. A clarity of purpose and a singularity of intent that would give him a reason to kill and maim and hate without guilt, without doing it just because he'd been told to. He wanted to love himself and his machine and the job and his weapons. He wanted the unquestioning faith in rightness that Durba'd had before he died, raving, with a hole in his head and a spike of wood through the belly. He wanted Ted's upright coldness, Billy's joy, Fenn's calm. He wanted an enemy, not a victim.

Only then, on that awful morning with Morris dead and Ted droning on and all his wishes coming true, Carter *still* wasn't happy. He wasn't sad either. He wasn't grateful and didn't hate any more or less than his usual amount. He wasn't even angry. If he felt anything at all, sitting there in his uncomfortable chair, watching the Ted-and-Eddie show, it was only the slow relief of an unbelievable pressure of waiting. He caught himself whispering without moving his lips. "Now," he said. "Maybe now," over and over again while Ted's triangles danced around, drawing closer and closer to the kill. Carter spoke as though blowing breath onto sparks, hoping for a flame, hoping to kindle that love he'd been looking for—its heat pale and tentative and delicate.

"Now as reported," Ted was saying, "the artillery site was hammered real good. Carter had 'em lit up, so it was tough to miss. Fokkers one and four pull up into a turn here, moving to rejoin formation, and here"—the map paused itself—"just as you're starting your turn, Porter, you call in movement in the tree line."

Porter nodded. "Just on the edge of the strike zone."

"Just on the edge of the strike zone," Ted repeated. "Right, Porter?"

"Movement in the trees," Porter said. "Didn't know what it was. Figured it was nothing."

"Yeah, well, you were wrong. Nothing's nothing. Everything is something. And that's why you're a shitty card player, too." The little blue triangles were frozen against the map, an instant away from the sharp end. Ted coughed and cleared his throat. "Anyway, as per standing orders, Porter, as spotter, takes point. Fokker four—that's Morris—is on your wing. Fokkers two and three dive to come in on your tail. The whole squadron turns out wide and comes in to, what, Porter?"

"To investigate."

"To investigate. Fucking right."

"They were waiting for us," Porter said quietly. Carter looked over at him. His hands were folded in front of him, his eyes on the floor. Pose of the penitent, of regret.

"Of course they were waiting for you," Ted said. "We've been blowing the shit out of these dopey, primitive shits for months. You think they haven't been watching what we do? I guaran-fucking-tee you, gentlemen, our planes have been the single most carefully observed thing on this whole stupid planet since the day we showed up, so every one of those shit-eating monkeys out there knows exactly what we're going to do before we do it. And we did just like they expected, didn't we?" He slashed at the map with his laser pointer. "The flight drops speed, comes in low and slow from the north to investigate Porter's nothing in the trees, puts them in the kill box here, in the ideal position to be shot at. Porter? You want to take us through what happens next?"

"No," said Porter.

And Ted whirled, his body a taut wire of rage, like something inside him was afire. "Yessir, you mean. Yes fucking sir. Porter, take us through what happens next."

For a minute, Porter worked his jaw without any sound coming out. When the words finally came to him, they dropped leadenly from his mouth, in short, clipped sentences with a breath between each. "They opened up on us as soon as we crossed the strike zone." Breath. "Three guns in the near tree line." Breath. "Fourth at the northeast end. To our flank. We were down close to the treetops—"

"Three-seven-five feet," Ted clarified, turning back to the display.

"At choke speed."

"Ninety miles per," Ted said. He was close enough to the projection to read the indicators.

"The forward guns got Morris and me on approach. They had tracers. We flew right straight up on them. Impossible to miss. I think the flanking gun tried for Billy and Albert. It missed. They just got lucky with Morris and me."

"That's not luck, Porter. That's planning. That's wanting really, really badly to kill you right goddamn dead." Ted turned to face the room once more. He tucked away his pointer. "What's luck is that you aren't." He stuck his hands in his pockets, drew himself up with a breath, and finished out the narrative. "First squadron breaks for evasive with two planes damaged, overshoots the site, climbs to safety, and changes course for home."

On the map behind him, both Porter's and Morris's triangles had turned to red.

"Fokker four had serious engine trouble, splintered prop, oil leaks. He was shot to shit and probably would've never made it back even if Morris hadn't also been hit. He took seven rounds we could count. His suit stopped five, but he took one penetrating wound in the belly and one in the hand that mostly took it off at the wrist. Morris passed out from blood loss before going in and wrecking eight miles short of the field. Upon investigation, he was found KIA on-site."

Morris's triangle turned black, fell out of formation, then winked out.

"Everyone here knows the rest."

Eddie jumped in. "I don't want to be a prick about this, guys, but odds are airman Ross would've survived until a pickup could be scrambled if he'd been wearing his emergency gear. I can't understand why he wasn't, actually. But I've been informed that this has become common practice over the past year, and it ends right now. This stuff is here for your protection, so from now on, no one goes up without a complete kit. That means helmet, protenolol and hemosclerex injectors, web gear—everything. That's a direct order, understood?"

"They get it, Eddie," Ted said, then to the pilots, "And we're back to putting our Danny on as well, gentlemen. Just in case."

Off to the side, Eddie nodded as if he had any idea what Ted was talking about. Ted shrank the map image to half size. He fiddled with this and that. Carter was feeling sick to his stomach. Probably, it was just the hangover.

Point five.

"Speculation," Ted announced, and then began talking about weapons—those that Durba had lost in the rout, those that had gotten Morris, and how, odds were, these were not the same weapons. He talked of guns and bombs and said many tough things that were lost on Carter just then because all Carter could think about was the image of Morris's hand blasted away by a bullet, by a kicked-back shard of prop or engine shrapnel punching through the firewall. He couldn't get his head around the pain it must've caused, but he could see the wound in his head, Morris's face at the moment of realization, the sickly feeling of suddenly seeing a piece of one's self shattered, blown into hamburger, missing. The faces around him, with the exception of Fenn's, were all gray. Porter was almost white and was shaking gently in his chair, still nodding, his mouth working even though he'd gone silent again.

At the front of the room, Ted was backing away, turning to Eddie, who had laid a hand on his shoulder and was taking the floor with a grin. Eddie had a laser pointer of his own—small and metal and about the size of a bullet. He toyed with it, walking it back and forth across his knuckles while he talked. It was a trick he probably did in bars to impress girls in places where there were bars and girls to impress.

"All right, guys. Here's the situation . . ."

Fuck you and your situation, Carter thought.

"Had the fire come from the guns captured from the rifle position, it would've been bad news, but not awful. We would know they had only the three light machine guns and a finite amount of ammunition for them. Only now, we know that the fire came from four guns, not three, and that the rounds recovered from flight leader Vaughn's plane were of a larger caliber than those used by Antoinne. They were . . ."

He paused, looked back at the podium where Carter thought he probably had a stack of notes stashed: *Be casual. Smile. Curse more.* And a list of nomenclatures under the double-underlined heading, NOMENCLATURES. He aimed his pointer at the projection screen. A picture of a Federated Arms light support gun came up, a belt-fed 8 mm.

"Nope," Eddie said. "Not that one. Dammit." He waved the pointer around until another image swelled: a water-cooled .30 caliber antiaircraft machine gun. Simple but tough, efficient, easy to maintain, and the least necessary application of force to counter the advantage given by the company's heretofore uncontested command of the skies over Iaxo.

"Okay," Eddie said. "There we go. It was probably something closer to this."

Ted grumbled something under his breath that none of the pilots could hear. Carter silently measured in his head. A .30-caliber round was about as long as his middle finger, as big around as his pinky. Almost identical to the ammunition in his own plane's guns, the difference essentially cosmetic. Eye for an eye.

"We also know from Captain Carter's flight that the Lassateirra faction had field artillery pieces at their disposal. Reports from survivors of Antoinne's unit estimate something in the . . ." Eddie checked his notes again.

"One-oh-fives," Ted said. "Modern shells, trained gunners or computer rangefinders, imported tubes and hardware mounted with native carriage. Least force, most bang."

Eddie nodded. "Exactly. There were four that we hit, but there's no reason to think there's not more out there. Also, on the night you guys hit the artillery position, Captain Carter took ground fire from crossbows using imported arrows."

"Bolts," Ted corrected.

"Bolts," said Eddie, tapping his notes with the tip of his pointer. "Right. Says that right here. Aluminum shaft, steel tip."

There was sniggering in the ranks—first sign of life in some time. Fenn, suddenly awake, leaned over to Carter and whispered, "Geez, Kev. Why didn't you tell me? Being shot at by crossbows? Sounds so *dangerous.* Why, all you had to defend yourself with was an airplane, a couple of machine guns, and a whole wing of bombers overhead. You're so brave."

"Must've slipped my mind," Carter grunted. He crossed his arms over his chest.

Eddie plowed on. "Right. So anyway, this is serious. Corporate has been suspicious for some time that someone had finally gotten through to the Lassateirra with off-world supplies, but until this morning we didn't know who or what or how much."

"Gotten through to the who?" asked Jack.

"The Lassateirra faction," Eddie repeated.

"That the bad guys?"

The pilots laughed. Carter laughed. Porter didn't laugh. Eddie's mouth turned into a hard straight line, and he tried to stare down Jack Hawker but failed.

At the front of the room, Ted was balling his hands into fists, then releasing them, balling them up again. "Get to the point, Eddie," he said.

"In good time, Commander," Eddie replied. "There are important details here. Recently, the company has been in communication with sources on the ground here on Iaxo—"

"I thought we were under blackout," Billy said.

"We are," said Ted. "Eddie?"

"We are," said Eddie. "Corporate is not. These were back-channel conversations, mostly, so don't go getting any ideas."

"Well, what sources then?"

"Other mercenary organizations," Eddie continued. "Some well-placed friends of ours in various foreign aid groups and noncolonial charities. That's in addition to their contacts in several of the large shipping conglomerates and guild spacers. And for some time, the company has been very concerned about other groups moving supplies through the blockades. With this recent turn of events—"

"Eddie . . . ," said Ted, warningly.

"Not to mention their substantial investment in material resources here and the usual risk of legal sanction involved in such an operation, there has been some discussion—"

"Eddie!" snapped Ted.

Behind his podium, Eddie Lucas turned on his thousand-watt smile, passed it over the assembled pilots like a searchlight. He could tell them everything. That was in his power. He could crash this entire mission with a word or two. But that wasn't the surprise he had. He looked at Ted and saw him leaning forward, waiting, maybe, to tackle him. To hit him. Eddie loved this. He really, really did.

"It's bad news," Eddie said.

"Fucking out with it already!" someone shouted, and Carter was surprised to discover that it'd been him.

"Stow that shit, Captain," Ted barked.

"I spoke with a couple friends of mine in the legal department back home just a couple of hours ago, and they informed me that . . ." He paused briefly and then Eddie came back, quoting from his notes. "A motion to provide humanitarian aid for Carpenter 7 Epsilon, also known as Iaxo, was presented four days ago before the Colonial Council, currently in session at Tranquility. The request was vague. No specific cause was presented before the officials, and there was no specific or implied mention of ours or anyone else's presence here. But it's there now. It's in the hands of the council, which means that Iaxo is now a real place. It's on the map, so to speak. And while the company feels it likely that the motion will be dismissed without a formal hearing, the operations department feels that it is only a matter of time now before someone comes and pokes their noses into our business here."

Carter was drifting. Repeated shocks, his hangover, the nausea of relived death—it was all numbing him. He'd had some very specific reasons for taking this job when he did. One of them had been that he would never again have to sit in a little room, in an uncomfortable chair, and listen to someone lie to him about how concerned his bosses were for his health and well-being. Another was that he would never have to talk (or hear, or even think) about politics, corporate or otherwise. He'd had enough of that in his other life—the one that'd come before this. Before Flyboy. So sitting there, he decided that Ted and Eddie could talk at him all they liked. It didn't mean he had to listen. He closed his eyes and put his chin on his chest. He was going to sleep. No one could make him care against his will.

"But after the events of the past two days," Eddie continued, "it has become obvious that this filing was only part of a larger strategy. Off-world supply has been coming in to the Lassateirra for some time now." He paused again to look at his notes and shuffle through the pages. "No one seems sure exactly how long. But there is equipment in theater, and potentially quite a bit of it. Most deliveries have been coming in far up-country . . ." He looked at his papers, running a finger down a page. "Arkhis Mountains," he muttered. "And the coast."

Carter told himself to sleep. He *ordered* himself to sleep. He thought he knew what was coming—could imagine the worst thing, suddenly, as a real thing. And just like Ted talking Morris's plane onward toward death and Carter's wish that he could've just stopped, just changed the path of the past with a word, so, too, did he want to not be here when Eddie said what he thought he was going to say. He wanted to not hear it, to go forth in ignorance, unworried. Part of him cheered Eddie on, begging for the worst. Another part dove for the deep, dumb blackness of sleep. If he didn't hear it, things wouldn't have to change, get worse. To hear the words, that would make it real.

"That's not the worst of it," Eddie plowed on.

At the front of the room, Ted took a step toward Eddie. Next to Carter, Fenn leaned forward in his chair, thinking that this was like the greatest show ever. And if not, then at least it was something new. Carter squeezed his eyes more tightly shut and shouted *Sleep!* inside his own head. *Sleep, goddammit. Sleep!*

"The motion for aid was filed through the Office of Cultural Affairs by Native Rights Intersystem."

The room and everyone in it exploded.

They yelled. They cursed. Ted did both at the same time because, apparently, this was the first he'd heard of it, too, and Eddie had been keeping it from him. Billy shouted pointless questions toward the front of the room, and Porter turned his face skyward and howled. Eddie stood behind the podium, looking terribly proud of himself. This was what he did. This was what he was good at. No one could take command of a meeting the way Eddie Lucas could. No one could control the environment like him.

Fenn was smiling a lost, beatific smile. Jack was laughing so hard that tears ran down his cheeks. Charlie Voss was on his feet, stabbing a finger toward Eddie and his podium. And Carter, as though feeling some supporting structure inside himself let go the instant Eddie said the words, had sagged into his seat, thrown his head back, and now was just shouting nonsense up into the air, his mouth wide, eyes still pinched shut, just because it felt good to make noise.

At the front of the room, Eddie turned to Ted. His smile shone like a burning strip of magnesium. "Commander? Anything to add?"

Ted stepped forward. "Dismissed!" he shouted.

|||||||||||

The officers stepped out into the sunlight and cold as if walking away from a mine cave-in—blinking, gape-mouthed, unsteady on their feet. It was quiet in the camp. The air was still. A perfect day.

Jack Hawker took Carter by the arm. "We're all going to die here," he said, speaking with exaggerated slowness, his eyes wide with shock.

"No," Carter told him. "We're not."

"Can I have your bunk when you go then? It's more comfortable than mine." He doggedly held to Carter's arm, his eye.

"Sure thing, Lieutenant," he said gently, trying to brush Jack's hand off his arm. "Anything for a friend."

Jack smiled, stuck a cigarette in his face with his free hand. Fenn appeared beside them, grinning, his cheeks ruddy with excitement. He put a hand on each of their shoulders. "Gentlemen," he said, "are we dancing?"

"We're all going to die here," Jack repeated.

"We're not," Carter said. "They'll pull us out before NRI comes. Before the marines. They have to. No one is going to die here, Jack."

"Promise?"

"Cross my heart."

Jack looked Carter in the eyes searchingly for a few more long seconds. His hand was like a vise. Desperate strength. Fenn tried to guide Jack away, to move him, but Jack wasn't budging. He took the cigarette out of his mouth, put it in Carter's, pressed his face close.

"I don't believe you," he whispered.

"Ah, Jack . . . ," said Fenn. "No kissing among the commissioned ranks. You know the rules." He moved to pull Jack away now, and clamped a hand over his wrist. But Jack chose that moment to release Carter, turn, and walk away—toward the mess where, no doubt, things were about to become very ugly all over again.

"That wasn't very nice," Fenn said.

"He's just scared," Carter said, watching Jack stalk purposefully across the field, rushing to catch up with the rest of the officers. "He'll get over it."

"No, I mean you." Fenn reached up, straightened the mussed collar and pleats of Carter's uniform, brushed at its shoulders. "We had a deal. I get your bunk when you die. It really is more comfortable, you know." Fenn touched a hand to the side of Carter's face and patted it gently, then turned smartly on his heel and followed along after Jack.

Carter went in the opposite direction, toward the tents. All along the way he saw faces peeking out at him—from windows, behind tent flaps, everywhere. They were pilots' faces, mechanics' faces, technicians' faces, even indigs' faces, though those were rare. Everyone knew something bad had happened, was about to happen, was coming their way very fast. Carter had to fight to keep from laughing. He had to cover his mouth with his hand as sick giggles bubbled up from his chest.

He went to bed. He couldn't sleep. He felt light as a feather. Unburdened. He felt like he was flying.

"Now," he whispered over and over again. "Now, now, now . . ."

Back in the field house, Ted waited until the last of his officers' backs had gone out the door, then whirled, meaning to punch Eddie Lucas right in the face. Meaning to really hang one on him and beat him bloody for springing this ambush, this bushwhack on him and the men with no warning.

But when he turned, Eddie wasn't there. He was on the other side of the room because Eddie, though not a fighter, was not an idiot. He knew a dangerous, cornered animal when he saw one.

"Over here, Commander," he said.

"You knew?"

"Of course I knew. I told you: You're not the only one with friends at the company."

"You knew about this when we walked in here." Ted moved toward Eddie, hands hanging loose at his sides.

Eddie started circling away, backing off at equal speed, moving around the outside edge of the tent until he came to the door. "I found out this morning."

"And you didn't tell me."

"I told you I had a surprise."

"That's not funny."

Eddie favored Ted with one of his blinding smiles. He said, "Ta-da," then slipped out the door and into the sun.

Ted stood alone in the middle of the room, surrounded by chairs, humming equipment, and Jimmy McCudden, who sat at his post with his eyes closed, his head down, and his hands folded over the back of his neck. Last man standing, but once again Ted Prinzi had a feeling that he'd lost a fight without really understanding how.

NATIVE RIGHTS INTERSYSTEM, more commonly called just NRI or Natives R Us, was a political association, foreign aid organization, and lobbying group dedicated to the protection and preservation of indigenous cultures and native peoples the galaxy over. It said so right on the covers of all their brochures.

NRI had a snappy logo that looked nice on posters. It translated well to television and the Net. They had a very slick and practiced public relations department that made commercials and organized rallies and crafted public service announcements full of pathos and inspiring music. Their proficiency at fund-raising was almost unparalleled, gathering their treasure ten dollars at a time from softhearted university students and grade-schoolers and a million at a go from corporations aching for a whiff of social activism on their prospectus. The group also had a certain air of fanatical missionary zeal, which was attractive to those who really felt the need to care deeply about something but had neither the motivation to actually *do* anything nor the desire to examine their convictions too closely. NRI was full-service. Opinions, heroes, villains, smart catchphrases, and T-shirts were provided to the faithful, all in gross amounts.

As a political action group, NRI lobbied, lied, and campaigned for the interests of all the fine, indigenous populations who occupied all those planets that the evil human race wanted to exploit. They labored mightily to keep away the strip miners, the real estate speculators, carpetbaggers, and squatters, the adventure capitalists and the developers, the smugglers, thieves, and snake-oil salesmen. With the outward appearance of unimpeachable virtue, they struggled to keep both the legitimate military and not-so-legitimate mercenary companies out of all the endless squabbles going on in every miserable backwater of the galaxy. It was their deeply and passionately held belief that every culture and nascent civilization should be granted the opportunity to grow and develop freely, without meddling humans constantly trying to trade them Zippo lighters and whiskey for whole continents or getting them hooked on Coca-Cola, cheeseburgers, and color TV before they'd even discovered, say, the wheel. This, too, was in their brochures—though worded somewhat more eloquently.

And in his bed, in his tent, on an airfield very far from home, Carter knew that, under other circumstances, NRI would've been heroes. Champions for the downtrodden, voices for the voiceless—this would have all been a good and decent thing for them to do had the local galactic neighborhood been densely packed with planets and short on life. But the fact of the matter was, the opposite was true. Because while yes, the galaxy was fairly fucking teeming with planets, nearly every goddamn one of them capable of supporting life, did.

A century ago, when mankind first began exploring the stupid galaxy in earnest, this was taken to be a good thing. Such bounty! Such wild diversity and wondrous multiplicity of nature in all her guises! Life, it seemed, was tenacious and far more varied than anyone had ever guessed—capable of flourishing in the strangest places and under the most extreme conditions. For a while, everyone thought it cute how critters of all description thrived in lava chutes, beneath nitrogen permafrost, under waxy oceans made of liquid hydrocarbons, and in atmospheres made up entirely of sulfur and noble gasses. Cities were found beneath roofed seas where giant walrus monsters cavorted in blood-warm seas with salinity so high the things could almost walk on the water. Humanoid paleolinds on the icy second planet of 18 Scorpii got

their own dedicated broadcast channel with high-def cameras recording every step, grunt, and shit they took. The planets surrounding Alpha
Lyrae were the focus of much scientific inquiry because they contained
no life at all, only its ruins.

Still, after the hundredth or so populated planet was found, it just
became annoying. Wonder quickly transmuted to irritation. Discovery
fatigue set in. In rather short order, mankind gave up all pretense of
being careful curators of life in all its wondrous diversity and just started
whacking the little alien fuckers with bats whenever they got in the
way. And five minutes after *that,* Native Rights Intersystem was founded
and immediately called for a galaxy-wide ban on the production of
Louisville Sluggers.

Put simply, the local cosmic neighborhood was just flat-out packed
with leaping, bouncing, slithering, gibbering monsters. And if it wasn't
a peaceful, advanced society of intelligent and socially progressive giant
walruses on one planet, it was a bunch of slack-jawed, nose-picking
bipeds on another who'd yet even to come down out of the trees.
Nearly everywhere man went, it seemed there was already something
there waiting, watching, standing on some distant, foreign shore waving
arms, tentacles, proboscis, or genitalia at them and saying, "Sorry. All full
up here. Maybe try the next planet over, thanks."

And NRI was committed to defending the rights of every one of
them to grub around in the dirt, live in miserable poverty, die of curable
diseases, bash one another with rocks, and generally just lie around fling-
ing their own crap at each other until such a day came that they got
around to evolving, undisturbed by man, invented lawyers, and sued the
shit out of humanity for willful neglect. Carter knew that tomorrow, a
survey ship could discover a planet pimpled with solid gold mountains
and inhabited entirely by semi-intelligent gophers. When it did, NRI
would be right there, saying that everyone should keep their grubby
hands off until such a time (undoubtedly a few billion years down the
road) that the alien space gophers developed a sociocultural gestalt
advanced enough to deal with mankind on an equal footing.

Human instinct, of course, said poison the stupid gophers and take
their solid gold mountains back home to Earth where their value could
be properly appreciated. NRI said no. The gophers had an inalienable

right to life and the fulfillment of their unique cultural destiny so, there-fore, deserved protection from all such bastards who felt otherwise.

If this protection could be provided by the courts, then good. NRI had a lot of powerful friends in the Colonial Council. And while a good portion of their membership was made up of young and impressionable kids with too much disposable income, they kept on retainer even more high-powered attorneys.

When politics and the law failed them, NRI would use the media. In terms of public opinion, they swung a big weight because the defense of native species—like the defense of rain forests, the defense of displaced tribal peoples, or the defense of puppies, babies, and pie—gave them a moral high ground that was difficult to assail. It was hard to argue mani-fest destiny or resource scarcity in the face of sensitive, heartfelt docu-mentaries about the tragic plight of the noble space gophers or pictures of them being starved out of their gopher-homes and clubbed to death by a bunch of swaggering, grimy deep-rock miners. Many tried. Few succeeded. In most cases, careers were ruined the minute they ran up against the NRI media machine.

But if none of this worked, NRI had another side—a militant one that, while less easy to defend in public, was even more effective on the ground. With no sense of hypocrisy, NRI would lay aside the protest signs and injunction paperwork and use guns. Or bombs, flamethrowers, atomics, starships, and anything else at their disposal to go in and kick a little ass in the name of alien gopher solidarity. Nothing made them happier than when one of their own people—wild-eyed with fanati-cism, wearing a black NRI armband, holding a terrified space gopher in one hand and a rifle in the other—made it onto the news back home. It was even better if that person was being arrested and dragged away by the Colonial Marines while the cameras rolled. Made them appear fearless and unswervingly committed to their cause. And whenever one of their own got killed under the media glare? Jackpot. After something like that, the donations always came flooding in.

One of the most famous promotional campaigns NRI ever had—the one that brought in more money than any other, that showed up, in poster form, on the walls of more university dorm rooms—centered around a single picture. It was very dramatic, full of fire and action, and showed, center frame, the blasted, bloodied face of one of their young recruits. He sat with his knees up against his chest, his back pressed against a scorch-marked and twisted steel antitank barricade, his arms folded protectively around some froglike, babyish alien critter with huge, expressive eyes and a look of abject, shrieking terror on its reptilian face.

The kid, on the other hand, was almost smiling. There was a look of sublime peace on his face, a holstered pistol under his arm and, in the background, the twisted metal of a crashed aircraft, towering flames licking at a smoke-black sky, and the silhouettes of Colonial Marines in their distinctive, bulky power armor charging toward him.

At the bottom of the picture, NRI ran the simple caption: IF NOT US, THEN WHO?

And if you looked closely, you could see the kid's name stitched over the pocket of his black, NRI-issue jumpsuit: *Carter, Kevin H.*

It was Native Rights Intersystem that'd taught Carter how to fly.

| | | | | | | | | | | | |

In his bed, in his tent on Iaxo, Carter thought back to that day, that moment, that picture. He knew that he hadn't had that look on his face because he was happy. He'd been shot in the neck while piloting the rescue helicopter crashed and burning in the background. He was dying. And those marines certainly weren't headed his way to help. They were coming to arrest him. To drag him to his feet, stomp the little frog-thing he'd been holding beneath their heavy boots, popping its head like a grape; to dig their fingers cruelly into the wound in his neck until he screamed and cried for them to stop; then to beat him into unconsciousness—which, if he recalled correctly, hadn't taken much.

Carter spent eleven years in a military prison after that, and all of NRI's politicians and lawyers and rich members and documentary filmmakers and idealistic young followers and sympathetic supporters and soldiers and believers and faithful didn't do a goddamn thing to get him out. He was beaten regularly in prison. Left to rot in solitary confinement, on a diet of water and thin protein gruel all full of spit and piss and worse. He was raped. Humiliated. Passed around. Starved.

He was left for dead by guards more times than he could count, by men who *wanted* him to die because he didn't belong. Because he was a race traitor, a tree hugger, an alien lover. Because he was an aberration, an enemy combatant imprisoned among those against whom he'd fought. For eleven years he was kept mostly in solitary because, if left to the appetites of the general population for more than five minutes, no one would've ever found enough pieces of him to identify his body.

To NRI, he'd served his purpose, and was forgotten but for a once-a-year care package with some cigarettes, candy, toiletries, and a form letter from the board of directors thanking him for his brave sacrifice and saying how concerned they were for his health and well-being. It was the same goddamn letter every year. That Carter remembered very clearly. None of them could even be bothered to sign it themselves. He checked every year before using the letter as toilet paper, or to smear the blood of another beating from his face.

One year they'd even sent him a T-shirt with that picture screened onto the front and the NRI logo on the back, telling him he should wear it often, "to show his continuing dedication to the cause of native rights."

His name had been blacked out of the picture. He'd assumed it was so that no one who saw it ever asked, *Hey, whatever happened to Kevin Carter?*

No one ever did.

ALL OF THE INDIGS WERE EXPELLED FROM CAMP AT GUNPOINT the afternoon after the meeting with Fast Eddie. They were walked out en masse, a dozen Flyboys motivating them with hard looks, harsh language, and fingers on triggers; moving them past some invisible boundary of influence and ownership where their land ended and indig land began again, then leaving them there.

For a time, the indigs all just milled around, looking bewildered while a few of the pilots and mechanics lingered to call them wogs and monkeys and, occasionally, throw clods of dirt at them. There were more than a hundred indigs: sentries and postriders and laborers and cleaners and camp followers of all descriptions. And they were no doubt confused by this sudden and drastic turn in their fortunes. One minute, they'd been mixing with the Big Gods—doing their laundry, carrying their messages, burning their shit, and watching them while they slept. And the next, they were turned out. Cast down. Eighty-sixed from whatever weak Eden their belief system had led them to believe the pilots, the company, and their squalid little camp represented.

And they were all still standing there an hour later when Fast Eddie, looking neither left or right, stalked out to talk things over with them. Eddie didn't speak a lot of indig, but he could say a little. More than anyone else in camp. For their part, the indigs mostly stared—standing or squatting right where they'd been left, looking at Eddie or back mutely toward the airstrips and tents and just waiting for something else to happen. Eddie brought Ted with him and Ted was in full Godly kit—black leather and shiny buckles, the whole nine yards. His job was to just stand there and look indestructible, which, conveniently, was one of the things Ted was good at.

Carter didn't know what Eddie said to them, but after a few minutes, the indigs all came filing back in and went right back to their business with no trouble and without a word.

Having been unable to find sleep no matter how hard he looked, Carter'd been watching most of the excitement from the tent line—sitting wrapped in his warm coat, campaign blanket across his lap, in a chair he'd dragged over for a better view of the proceedings. He had a jug of coffee with him, spiked with vitamin supplement, and a tin cup, some cigarettes. It was better than television, except that he couldn't really hear anything. But he sat and made hard jokes along with Tommy Hill ("You look like a grandma," Tommy had said. "All you need are glasses and forty cats.") and Jack, who was looking significantly less spooked now, and had been one of the gang who'd marched the indigs out in the first place. Oddly, he couldn't seem to remember quite why it'd been a good idea. When Carter asked him about it, he claimed it was something about spies, about traitors. "Didn't much matter once the guns came out," he said. "It was something to do."

Seeing the indigs come back, Carter wondered how much doubt had been sown in the hearts of their ostensible comrades by that little misunderstanding. He wondered what happened to a people when their strong, alien gods and saviors were suddenly proven fallible, mortal—proven merely human, for lack of a better word. What happened when that façade of all-powerful omnipotence abruptly began to show cracks?

Nothing, to look at them. And Carter thought how maybe that wasn't so surprising. His mother was a born-again Christian, having drifted late in life into a sect of severe Pentecostal believers. She had, for a time, tried to instill a similar whiplash faith in the magic of Jesus and the Resurrection in Carter and his brothers. It never really took, but he remembered the way she'd believed so unquestioningly in everything.

God didn't make mistakes. And even when it was apparent that God had made a mistake, God *still* didn't make mistakes. It was all part of a divine plan, the details of which mere mortals were not privy to. It was all *intended*.

Convictions like that could make things very easy for the faithful, and Carter thought that maybe it was the same thing here. So long as they killed for the indigs, beat down their age-old enemies from on high, and spilled blood for their cause, maybe they didn't care much what else happened.

So when it was done—once all the indigs had stepped back across that invisible boundary and back into camp—Carter had continued watching, curious about what would come next until nothing did and, eventually, he grew bored.

Carter thought that maybe the indigs felt they'd done something to anger the flying gods and that it was only a god's infinite mercy for the chosen that allowed them back into their good graces. Believers, he knew, were big on that self-flagellation thing. The children of the Big Gods always seemed to believe that wrongness dwelt exclusively in them. That the objects of their devotion were made of stainless steel. At the time, he figured that must've just been the nature of the thing. He figured it was over.

| | | | | | | | | | | |

When they had their service for Morris Ross that night after dinner, many of the indigs crowded around to watch. They stood silently, just outside the ring of light cast by the hooded lamps the humans used to illuminate their mourning, and stared with big, damp eyes as the pilots, in turn, stood with their heads down, in full battle dress, and listened to Ted eulogize Morris. His coffin was already closed and sealed. When Ted was finished, each of the pilots approached and signed his name to the outside of the box with a laser etcher, and that was that. They'd done the same for Danny once. With Morris, it became a tradition.

It took all of a half hour, the ceremony. But as it ended and they all turned to walk away, Carter noticed that the indigs had vanished. Not just from the area, but from the whole camp. It was very quiet and very dark and suddenly spooky in the way that a house, abandoned in haste, can sometimes be—the setting grown suddenly cold in the absence of living things.

That night, they all heard explosions in the distance—artillery, almost definitely.

Carter and Fenn lay awake in their racks, smoking and listening to the faraway cacophony. For a long time, neither of them said a word.

It was only a few shells, and they never figured out who was shooting at whom. But that didn't matter. The fact that someone had been shooting at all was enough. And when it was done, someone had come and stood a moment just outside the flap of their tent. Didn't knock. Didn't come in. Just stood there for a few long seconds, then was gone. It was too dark to see who it was, but Carter knew.

A while after, he asked Fenn who it was that had Morris in their betting pool.

Fenn just lay there breathing for a minute. Carter could see him only by the glow of his cigarette. "Ted," he finally said. "Ted had Morris."

But Carter was pretty sure he was lying.

The next morning, Ted made another appearance in the mess. Most of the outfit was there, everyone on edge, delicate, moving as if afraid absolutely anything had the potential to upset a fragile peace that wasn't peace at all, but was just nothing having gone wrong for a minute, then two, then three.

"New orders," Ted had said. "Effective now." He dropped a few sheets of paper on the table closest the door through which he'd entered. Then he exited through the same without saying anything more.

No one looked. Not immediately. No one got up, no one went to examine Ted's leavings. By unspoken consent, they all pretended he'd been a bad dream best banished by ignoring it'd ever come.

But eventually, people had to leave. Had to go out into the cold and the world. And when they did, everyone went out through the door Ted had used and, on their way, looked at the papers he'd dropped.

Carter was no different. He walked a deliberately long path around the mess, but the table, the papers, they had gravity. They drew him. And when he looked, he saw a new roster, handwritten in a small, fiercely controlled hand; three pages so crowded with times and patrol orders and map coordinates that they all ran together into a bramble. There were day flights and night flights. Overlapping coverages. Crossing radials. So fat now with fuel and bombs and bullets, why not? Ted's plan was plain. He'd written it at the top of the first page, in letters scribbled in so heavy and dark that they'd torn the paper.

NO ONE DIES.

| | | | | | | | | | | | |

Later, Carter found Tommy Hill from his squadron and Charlie from Fenn's third in his and Fenn's tent, viciously stoking the fire in the little potbelly. They were jamming stick upon stick into the thing, working in tandem, each urging the other on. Tommy and Charlie both had night flights on the new roster—two of the first, and due to lift in a few hours. Fenn was on his bed, aimlessly thumbing a smartpaper copy of *Wind, Sand and Stars,* regularly touching the flip button without looking at the pages. Cat was backed into a distant corner, looking suspicious and pissed.

Charlie and Tommy took no notice of Carter as he came in, sidled around the perimeter of the tent, and hauled up close to Fenn's side.

"What are they doing?" he asked, squatting beside Fenn's rack, whispering because there was something so focused and unreal about the sight of the two of them blindly jamming lumber into the stove, stoking a fire that was already throwing off waves of blistering heat.

"Haven't the slightest idea," Fenn said, brushing the paper with his thumb and making it turn another page. "They showed up about a half hour ago. Said it was too cold in Tommy's tent and wanted to make a fire. Been at it ever since."

"And you don't think that's a little weird?"

Fenn looked at Carter, looked down at his lap, looked back at Carter. Carter looked down. Hidden by the paper was Fenn's sidearm—cocked and loaded—lying on his belly.

"I think it's a lot weird," he said, and went back to turning pages.

Carter stood, then stepped forward. "Tommy," he snapped. "The fuck are you two doing over there? Drop the lumber and step away from the stove."

Neither of them slowed. Neither acknowledged Carter had spoken. He looked back at Fenn and rolled his eyes. Fenn shrugged. *"'La vérité pour l'homme, c'est ce qui fait de lui un homme,'"* he said, and tapped the page without looking at it.

Carter shook his head, walked over to them, laid a hand on Tommy's shoulder. Tommy, who was closest to him, feeding sticks to Charlie. Tommy, who'd been his friend and his squadron mate for two years, been solid and dependable, been always on Carter's wing.

Tommy, who felt the touch of Carter's hand on his shoulder, spun and laid the snapped end of an inch-thick branch across the side of Carter's head with a snarl and shouted, "Get off me, you fucker!"

The stick did no damage, but it hurt like a lash, and Carter staggered back, mostly out of surprise. For an instant, his brain seemed torn between laughter and rage. His breath snagged in his throat in half a giggle. Then the red veil dropped over his eyes and he charged in, swinging. He hooked Tommy (who'd gone back to hunching over the rapidly diminishing woodpile) under one arm, spun him around, and gave him a jackhammer punch in the eye, his whole body weight behind it, dropping it on him from a height. Tommy went down to his knees and Carter hit him again. He tried for a third, but Tommy'd gotten his arms up, so he kicked him instead—heel of his boot into Tommy's side, pushing him over and stepping across him. When he looked up, he saw Charlie, his two fists, squeezed together, coming around like a bat.

Charlie was wearing his gloves. Lucky for Carter. But when the impact came, he saw stars anyway and fell hard, back and across Tommy, which, in any event, kept Tommy from getting up and laying in as well. Charlie was still coming for Carter as he went down.

Next thing, nothing. Charlie stopped in his tracks. Squirming beneath Carter, Tommy shoved him off and struggled to his feet. Carter rolled to his stomach, then scrambled up, bringing his hands in front of his face like a boxer, trying to look better than he felt. Then he saw Fenn standing with his legs spread, shooting hand braced, his gun leveled at his own squadron leader.

"Stand down, Charlie," he said, voice calm, unhurried. "You know I won't kill you, but I'll put one in your leg that'll have you in the sick line for a week."

Charlie actually whipped his head back and forth a couple of times as if he'd been possessed by something and needed to shake it off. He looked at Tommy, at Carter, at Fenn and Fenn's pistol. He smiled sheepishly, which was not a look that came easily to him because he was older and had a veteran's hardness about him. Tommy, on the other hand, had none of this. He was twenty-two. Iaxo was his second tour with Flyboy, his first with Carter, and he looked about to cry or laugh or throw up or all three at once. He'd had a cut opened below his eye—a ragged tear that was just starting to leak a film of blood into the sheen of sweat on his face. He reached a hand out to Carter, and he felt it scrabbling at the sleeve of his coat.

"We were cold, Captain. That's all. I don't . . ." His voice trailed off. From the look of them, Carter didn't even think they'd been drinking. "We were just trying to get the fire banked, and . . ."

Charlie stepped up. "Put it away, Fenn. It's done and we're sorry. I don't know what got into us."

"Nerves," said Fenn, carefully laying down the hammer on his pistol and lowering it. "Happens." He paused. "Not to me, of course." And then he grinned. Charlie laughed. Tommy did the same. Carter's head hurt, but he felt the anger whirlpooling out of him like water down a drain. Everyone was sweating. It was hot as an oven.

"Okay," Fenn said, then repeated himself. "Okay. Now that we've all got that out of our systems . . . ," and let it hang, incomplete. Without taking his eyes off Tommy or Charlie, he laid the pistol down on his bed, on top of his book.

"It's going to be cold up there tonight," said Tommy. "We were just trying to get a big fire going and—"

"It's all right, Tommy," Carter said, reaching over and cupping the back of his head in his hand. He did it with the one he hadn't hit the boy with. The other one hurt almost as much as his head. "Just drop it. You and Charlie feel a bit more civilized, you're welcome to sit awhile. You've got some time yet." He checked his watch. "Night flights don't lift for another few hours."

Charlie asked Fenn if he minded and Fenn said no, provided everyone made a solemn promise not to hit anyone else. And so they sat, the four of them, while their bruises swelled and blackened and their aches receded and the heat bloomed from the overstoked potbelly.

No one liked flying at night. It made a man strange, knowing it was coming. But in the end, Fenn and Charlie and Tommy and Jack all made their patrols and came back shaken but not dead. Carter, having finally found the knack for it, slept while they were gone, waking from a dream of flying just enough to count their engines as they passed over the tent line—one and two, three and four—then dropping back again into an exhausted slumber that seemed to last for days.

AT FIVE HUNDRED FEET, when flying at nearly two hundred miles an hour, the landscape became a very personal thing. One got to know it intimately, though not as this tree or that bush, but rather as a minute of green blur here, a few seconds of brown over there. It was like a fondness for maps—for looks, not land. It was like the distracted passion of a man who loves pornography but loathes an actual warm and real woman. The land, the pilots must've come to hate because they'd done so much violence to it. The topography, though, was spectacular.

Roadrunner was in the shop. Over the following three days, Carter got friendly with Li'l Red Rooster—a hinky Fokker reproduction that was both slower and less graceful, but easier to fly. Together, the two of them got to know a whole lot of terrain. Hundreds of square miles of it, crossed and recrossed and re-recrossed by defensive patrols taking off and landing nonstop, all around the clock. Artillery was their big concern. The airfield could be crippled by one solid barrage, decimated by concentrated fire. After artillery, they were concerned with troop movements, supply caravans, lone riders who might be scouts or forward observers. And after artillery, troops, caravans, and scouts, they were worried about everything else.

The new orders were followed. No one died. Gone were the days of just flying around like idiots and banging away at random. Everything was methodical now. Businesslike. No hunting parties, no harassment, no provocation of any sort. On Ted's orders, no fighters were to engage any targets under any circumstances. If they were shot at, if they saw anything, if they were even looked at funny by anything on the ground, they were to call in the location to the bombers (who circled constantly at ten thousand feet, specks of dust on the lens of the sky), then get the hell out of Dodge most fucking ricky-tick.

They worked the sky in three-man teams, split squadrons, with two fighters low and a bomber high, each sortie moving them fractionally deeper into Indian country; observing, reporting, everyone checking roads and forest paths, hilltops, and their favorite hidden landmarks for signs of movement, for gun emplacements, for fortification—looking everywhere for anything. Nothing was nothing anymore, just like Ted had said.

Until better intelligence was received as to the kind of materiel support being provided by NRI, these were the new rules. It was, in most everyone's opinion (excluding Ted's), a chickenshit way to fight a war, but necessary. At least for the moment, there were too many unknowns on the ground. Too many questions. And if there was any consolation at all beyond the fact that, for a few days, no one died, then it was only that the other side had found an even *more* chickenshit way to fight: by not showing up at all. The fighters were bait, flying low to the deck, trying to draw ground fire and give the bombers a target. Only most days, the bombers came home fully loaded. Most nights, the pilots ended up the same way.

It was a new kind of boredom. One with a knife-edge of real, bright danger wavering somewhere just out of sight. Not shattering like actual combat could be, but grinding, fraying—the kind of fear-spiked and blistered boredom that ate at you hour after hour, that obsessed you even when you weren't in it. The danger was the danger of the unknown, and the boredom was the boredom of not knowing when the boredom might, quite abruptly, end. Every moment that Carter wasn't in it, he felt like he was preparing for it or decompressing from it. He felt, oddly, as though he didn't have the time for anything else *but* it. And he was not the only one. Suddenly everybody had lucky socks and wore them all the time. Every loud noise, every minute change in the weather became a harbinger of something. Every cold, sick feeling of directionless dread in the night was a premonition. Everyone became a prophet. It wasn't unusual at all to see a man, in the dawn or at the dusk of the day, standing at the head of one of the airstrips and trying to smell out the positions of the enemy on the wind, his eyes closed and his hands hanging slack at his sides. And after two years in the field, everyone's internal resources were already so depleted by distance and lack and hate and nearness to death that they cracked like eggshells under the least application of pressure.

| | | | | | | | | | | |

Ted spent most of his days on the radio or furtively fighting with the FTL relay like he was touching something he wasn't supposed to. This was when he wasn't on the field or getting in everyone's way down in the longhouse or chasing after Eddie.

Diane watched him when she wasn't at her post. Or when she was at her post, but with nothing going on. She watched him hunch his whole body around the machinery—arms laid flat on the table, shoulders folded in, head down. From certain angles he appeared to be hugging it, and she could never figure out who he was talking to, only that some of the news was good and some of it was bad. She'd learned to tell the difference only by the angle of the back of his neck and the weary curve of his spine.

| | | | | | | | | | | |

The pop and hiss of the radio on traditional frequencies became a kind of music to Ted; the low triple-tone hum of the microwave transmitter/receiver finding nothing but dead channels a droning intonation, the Om that began and ended his every conversation with the infinite. He could close his eyes and feel the waves stretching out over alien fields emptied of friends, of support. Early, there'd been a few contacts. He'd spent part of a morning talking with a group from Healthwatch

I.S.—a group of doctors who'd come to the boonies to try and help the blighted monkeys and now found themselves stranded in the mountains with a hundred displaced native women and children watching as cities burned in the distance. He'd listened in on the orderly retreat of a band of off-world engineers and their native bodyguards—the calm and collected withdrawal of forces from a half-dozen positions being casually overrun by indig infantry with flamers and explosive breaching charges. The engineers were firing all their equipment as they pulled back, destroying their Rome plows and Caterpillar tractors and workshops with white phosphorous grenades or blocks of C4 strapped to acetylene tanks; denying the enemy valuable spoils. The last thing they did before loading up into the transports was open up on their own indigs with machine guns because they were trying to force their way aboard.

He'd caught a detachment of distant air cavalry from Applied Outcomes who'd been operating far to the south just as they were preparing to pull out. He'd raised their radio op late in the night and asked him what their situation was.

"Situation? We have no situation, man! We are *gone*. We're fragging the lifters and pushing them into the sea. Dust-off is en route. What are you guys *doing* up there?"

"Holding fast," Ted had said, mostly because he couldn't bring himself to speak the truth and couldn't yet make himself ask for the help he needed—for a ride out, offering anything and everything they had for lift weight and space for fifty-odd troopers stranded far from home.

"Holding fast? Holding fast to what, Chief? Charlie Mike is on the way, and he don't much care for our sort."

Charlie Mike: the Colonial Marines.

"Roger that," Ted had said. "How are you flying out?"

"Ranger hot tails, straight from the home office. We are out, friend. Eighty-fucking-six and good-bye. Do you have exfil waiting?"

"Yeah," Ted lied. "In orbit, but we're sticking it out."

"Crazy, man. I'd hate to think of you stuck here, though. We've got orbital flares reading north of us, maybe near you. Supply runners. You heard that Natives R Us is dropping in on this party, right?"

"I'd heard that. We've been getting a little action from them."

"Yeah, that was our sign to bug out. If I'd wanted a fair fight, I would've joined the army."

"Tell me about it."

"Hey, you know Connelly? That ape from Eastbourne Services? He's staying, too. You should call him and try to talk him into hitching a ride with you when you go."

Ted had cut the connection after that. He couldn't take it anymore. Hour by hour, day by day, the radios were growing more quiet, the planet of Iaxo slowly being returned to those who'd had the misfortune of being born here. He kept the planes flying, kept the patrols going, but he would not commit to any engagement—afraid of what might be waiting for his men, his planes. If he was going to be abandoned here, left all alone, then he needed to conserve them. Husband his resources. Wait for his company to come to their senses, call him, say that all was forgiven and a ride was on the way.

He was afraid. With the Om in his ears and his eyes squeezed shut, he could see everyone leaving him behind—the bright sparks of transport freighters maneuvering in distant, high orbit, and the shuttles, the hot tails, climbing for them atop pillars of fire.

Too late, he had fluttered his fingers at the radio, trying to call back the radio op from Applied Outcomes. He would ask him for a ride, offer him anything, admit that he'd lied—that his company was abandoning him here to death or prison or worse, and that there was no exfil waiting for them in the sky. No ride. Nothing.

He'd beg if he had to. Promise anything. He'd punched in the frequency and waited.

"Hello? Alpha Oscar radio op, this is Ted, do you read? This is Commander Prinzi. Do you copy?"

But there was nothing. The frequency was cold and dead. And slowly, the silence grew.

In the longhouse, planes were rotated in and out for refitting and maintenance. Engines were tuned up for combat, guns were changed out, broken down, cleaned, and tested. Any machine showing stress from two years of inconstant use was put through a thorough overhaul, and that work alone was enough to keep the lights on day and night. Blackout curtains had been hung to keep that light where it belonged—inside, and not spilling out into the darkness where it might give away the airfield's position to any sneaky indig with a howitzer in his horse cart.

The Akaveen indigs—the ones on whose side the company was currently not fighting—took the opportunity to pour troops across the ford and into what was previously enemy territory. From the sky, the pilots watched long, snaking files of them tramping across the lowland plains and dreamed of strafing them just because there was nothing else to do; they dreamed of attack angles, the hard hammering of machine guns, and the sweet release of weight as undercarriage bombs were let go.

Infantry, archers, gangs of cavalry, and long, shuddering supply trains moved into positions that stretched for miles up and down both banks of the river and ten miles deep into the other side. To the south, the bridge was taken with surprisingly little effort by a mixed force of local indig light infantry—raggedy-ass militia armed with spears, pikes, clubs and farm implements. They'd been the vanguard of a larger sweep downriver and held the position until help arrived in the form of heavy, organized infantry and native engineers who cleared the area and set about lazily building muddy fortifications.

The remnants of Durba's Rifles—those who'd survived the artillery barrage that first night—had re-formed under one of the surviving first IRC platoon leaders, a man named Garcia. They'd reinforced their numbers by absorbing a troop of native postriders and light cavalry, becoming mounted infantry. Garcia's Horse Rifles, they called themselves, and they had abandoned their encampment to the south of the Flyboy airfield and moved in to hold the ford for Connelly. Rather than trenches, they built a stockade this time—a half-moon wall of stout timber with firing positions for their guns and a paddock for their horses. To replace their lost equipment, Fast Eddie okayed a loan of two FI-60 field radios and, on the sly, Ted gave Tony Fong a rebuilt microwave transmitter so Garcia could keep in touch with him at the airfield and be Ted's eyes on the front. The transmitter was the backup to the company's primary microwave transmitter, which Ted clung to like a life preserver.

Tony had survived Durba's worst night only because his radio post had been a ways back from the front line, but he had still managed to catch a piece of hot shrapnel in the ass running away. Tony told them that Garcia himself was simply the luckiest son of a bitch on Iaxo. He'd been right in the middle of the shelling and had somehow walked away without a scratch.

When Ted had tried to ask Tony if there were any plans for Connelly and his surviving humans to leave Iaxo, Tony had laughed.

"Where would we go?" he asked.

"All the other companies, they're pulling out. I've talked to some—"

Tony's eyes grew hard. "Quitters and cowards," he said. "We have a job to do."

"Has Eastbourne called in a dust-off for you?"

Tony spit in the dirt. "Quitters and cowards," he repeated, thanked Ted for the loaner, and promised that he'd be in touch.

|||||||||||||

To the north, the Akaveen indigs pushed their lines until they were in sight of Lassateirra-held Riverbend, then called a halt—massing troops in a huge encampment on the friendly side of the river and spotting smaller, provisional units under off-world command out ten miles on the other side to cut off roads and any quick reinforcement from the south. Trouble was, there just weren't that many human officers left. Fewer every day. So the blockade of Riverbend became the worst siege in the history of sieges, the lines full of holes and gaps that a tank division could've rolled through.

But organization was not the natives' strong suit. The Akaveen militia spent their days shouting up at the walls of Riverbend while the regular army marched back and forth on their side of the river, shaking their shields and spears and making occasional one-man charges on horseback—riding their mounts into the water, splashing through the low current, and rearing the beasts up to wave their too-many feet at the city walls. Every time one of the company's planes flew overhead, the Akaveen went nuts, whooping and cheering and waving their weapons in the air.

The prevailing wisdom in the field house was that the Akaveen must've thought Flyboy had done this—driving back their age-old enemies or whatever, and sending them running for the hills and the safety of their walled cities. Whether or not this was true was debatable, though not, actually, debated, save in private. The indig commanders and elders and officers dealt only with Fast Eddie because, besides Billy Stitches (who spoke a little), Eddie was the only one who spoke any indig at all. And since the pilots still believed that Fast Eddie answered to the company, which in turn depended on him (and Ted) to make sure the fight was going well and all their investments would someday pay off, no one thought Eddie was going to try very hard to convince the wogs that the pilots weren't, in fact, the heroes they thought they were.

Thus, any display by the Akaveen indigs became cheering and adulation. Any sounds at all became utterances of love and faith and thanks and, as with the supplies, the pilots grew fat with that as well—bloated and waddling with adoration.

And they sucked it up as though starving, hoping silently that this blind presumption was right and that it would sustain them even as the Lassateirra haunted their dreams, vanished in daylight, and their own camp indigs were stealing away in the middle of the night and lighting out for badland.

Still, they told themselves that they were winners. Terrifying and impervious as stone. They told themselves that they were loved as only liberators could be loved, a boon to friends and death to their enemies. They roared low over the lines and made the indigs jump. In the mess, they circled around Morris Ross's coffin and used it as a table for cards and drinks and breakfast. It was just a box. What was inside no longer mattered.

| | | | | | | | | | | | |

On the fourth day of the new patrol schedule, Connelly's 1st (now Garcia's Horse Rifles) and 2nd companies were pulled forward to the bridge, his 3rd moved across the ford and up to the base of Mutter's Ridge where the artillery position had been, while his 4th—which had seen the most action recently—fell back all the way to just east of the airfield, now a good thirty or forty miles to the rear of the new front lines.

And the pilots flew. They flew constantly. Once Connelly's 4th moved in, they burned lights on the field without fear of being spotted because there was nothing that could approach their position under cover of darkness without being spotted itself, nothing that could come in range of them without being utterly destroyed.

Carter looked at the maps. He knew that the Akaveen Something-or-Others were solidly in control of nearly eighty miles of river now, including the bridge and the ford. They had troops covering the forests on the far side all the way up to Mutter's Ridge, cavalry patrolling the two cut roads that ran through the area, and their forces were in sight of Riverbend to the north and just a day's hard march from Southbend to the south. Those two fortified towns were the anchors of the other side's presence in the area, and if they fell, or were taken, the river would open back up again for three hundred miles. The fight would then move back up to the high ground east of the river again, back onto Sispetain. From the moors, it would be on to the plains beyond, then the mountains beyond that, the cities that crouched at their feet, the far coast, which none of them had seen except briefly when they'd arrived from orbit.

Conversations of tactics obsessed the pilots now. Miniature Trenchards and Hoeppners, they crouched in the dirt and drew pictures with sticks, pounded their fists on tables, jiggling the saltshakers and glasses of whiskey they used to denote fallback positions and axes of advance. They would move *here,* of course, then set up a secondary field *there.* They imagined turning Immelmans over the fortified walls of Riverbend, the shriek of twenty-five-pound bombs being dropped from a height. Everything looked simple to them from here on out: They had only to take the towns, take the moors, take the high plains, jump over the mountains, and then fall on the coastal cities. Two years, they'd been wasting their time out here in the back of beyond. The coast was where the action was, where this thing would be decided. It was like they'd spent all their days bombing and machine-gunning a bunch of farmers, furry hillbillies with pointed sticks and poor personal hygiene, while the lights of an alien Manhattan burned, just out of sight, over the distant horizon.

So fuck the NRI. Fuck the off-worlders sticking their noses in at this late date. Fuck everyone but, most important, fuck the Lassateirra and the Akaveen and all the indigs, whatever they called themselves. The pilots were going to take this goddamn planet if they had to bomb every inch of it into submission. And it was all starting now. It was all going well *now*.

Except for one thing, which was the nagging refusal of the other side to show up to the fight. The pilots—some of them—were beginning to take this whole God thing to heart, Carter thought. Because, to look at the situation another way, Riverbend and Southbend were the two opposing jaws of the vise that the entire friendly indig army had just charged headlong into, and the next time any of them saw the glittering cities of the east and that coastline would be from orbit again, in chains, in the brig of the Colonial Marine transport shipping them all off to prison.

That was what Carter thought. It was a glass-half-full, glass-half-empty kind of thing and, for the most part, he kept his speculation to himself. The important thing was, for several days, nobody died and all of their planes came home whole.

| | | | | | | | | | | | |

Five days passed. Six. Things were growing frantic. The no-contact missions, the no-fire policy—it was eating at everyone. On top of this, there was Ted's sudden, desperate need to keep every square inch of ground under constant surveillance. In daylight, it was all big talk and victory and men shooting each other vicious smiles as they made Vs with their fingers. But in the dark, the pilots granted mystical powers to the enemy indigs. They could vanish and appear at will. They could move faster than Superman. They had networks of tunnels under the ground through which they traveled like moles. In the morning, the men mocked them the same as they always had, but when the sun went down and the moons rose, it was different, malicious, spooky.

Sometimes they spoke of the enemy in tones of reverence or respect for the amount of punishment they'd endured from their heretofore untouchable tormentors. Sometimes it was plain fear. Sometimes it was more. "The wogs," Carter'd heard David Rice say one night, his voice full of awe after returning from another night flight where nothing had been seen and nothing had been killed. "They've gone imaginary. The wogs understand it all."

Nights were when the pilots feared the most about the least. Nights were really starting to fuck them up.

| | | | | | | | | | | | |

On the seventh day, it rained. A mist at first that was close to freezing so that walking in it felt like brushing up against snow and even a fast jog between, say, one's tent and the mess for hot coffee and the thin pleasure of dull company—of, at least, hearing one's own language spoken in this alien place—left a man feeling as though he'd just fallen into a bathtub full of icy water.

Ted ordered up regular patrols but kept them near to home in case the weather worsened. And when it did—the rain, at first, falling like little silver needles from a sky that was dark, close, and bruised with sickly light—no one went anywhere. All flights were grounded and the men mostly sat in gray silences, watching the drops of rain grow fat and begin to pour down with a kind of vengeance, to shatter themselves against the cold, hard ground until it seemed to be raining upward as well as down.

"If it keeps up," Carter heard Ernie O'Day say, "he'll have to cancel the night flights. No one would fly in the dark *and* freezing rain."

"Ted might," said George Stork.

"And the indigs might march in it," added Wolfe, from first squadron, holding a white mug of hot coffee between his palms and rolling it slowly back and forth. "How much ground do you figure they could cover in twelve or fourteen hours, unmolested by airplanes?"

"A lot," said Ernie.

"A lot," said Stork.

"Damn right, a lot. This rain would be good for them. Good for their business."

"Monkey business," said Stork.

"Motherfucking monkey business."

And all three of them laughed, the conversation trailing off into the awkward realization that there really wasn't much else to say. Ted would or he wouldn't. The pilots would or they wouldn't. And the indigs, the same. There was no figuring it.

"Motherfucking monkey business."

Later, the mess grew crowded and all the talk was pretty much the same. They discussed the rain and the cold, compared it to other rains and other colds. Johnny All-Around cooked freeze-dried steaks that he rubbed with some purple leaf that tasted a little bit like garlic, but not completely. Everyone sat down to dinner, but Emile Hardman refused to eat his steak, saying he wasn't going to eat anything that'd been touched by some monkey plant.

"A patriot!" Fenn shouted from some corner of the mess. Carter hadn't even known he was there. "I'll eat his."

The pilots laughed. Emile ate six cans of pears in syrup stamped with Earthside expiration dates that'd passed a year ago, and everyone drank cold beers pulled from the well of the ice machine and scotch by the bucket. They talked about fucking an indig lady and how much they'd have to be paid to do it. A hundred thousand dollars was the going rate. Fifty if they could do it from behind.

And yet still, there was no letup, no stopping. In the night, the rain turned to sleet and everyone cowered from it, hunkering down wherever they were, and the mess became like some big slumber party with everyone huddled up close and intimate and the ovens all turned on to heat the place. Around dawn the next day, the rain finally pissed itself out and the ground all froze. At the first glimmer of light in the sky, Ted came through the doors looking frozen into his uniform and ordered the planes up. They flew missions. They landed. They hopped out of their cockpits into ankle-deep, waxy mud as everything started to thaw, helped the ground crews slog their machines into the longhouse, helped them roll a new plane out onto the apron, ran to the mess for a cup of coffee, to the field house for a couple benzos from Doc Edison's medical locker, a cigarette, then were back out on the strip again, agitating for clearance to go up, unscheduled, for kicks or for cover.

The day went on, and then the night, and then another day. And Ted, haunting the comms tent now like some kind of unquiet spirit, pacing the length of the longhouse or the aprons of the airstrips all day and all night, acting as unofficial flight coordinator whenever he wasn't on the board as official flight controller, always said yes.

"Up!" he'd yell, jerking two thumbs to the sky. "Gas it and go!" And then a string of map coordinates, a sector to advance, some mystical schedule of ground coverage that existed, organized, in the scrambled-egg mush of his sleep-deprived mind alone. On one day, Lefty Berthold from Carter's second squadron saw what he swore was an entire copse of trees moving across the horizon. Ted scrambled a bomb run (he'd had to fly one of the DH9s himself, being short on pilots) and blew it to matchsticks. It was nothing. Just trees. They'd only been moving in Lefty's overheated imagination.

"Nothing is nothing," Ted said—his new motto. And anyway, defoliation was denying the enemy valuable cover.

Eight hours later, Albert Wolfe, against orders, machine-gunned a rock that'd looked a little like a tank from a thousand feet up and in just the right light. To be safe, Ted ordered Wolfe home and had the rock bombed, inflicting casualties only on the surrounding flora and whatever fauna might've been unfortunate enough to have chosen that particular outcropping on which to warm itself in the thin, inconstant sunlight.

"Nothing is nothing."

The men began to wonder whether Ted was losing it. Knowing that they were afraid of *something* (even if that something had no specific name), they began to wonder what had him so scared. What he knew that he wasn't telling them.

Fenn got lucky. He was the first to receive the clearance, to be loosed against a positive target in badland, and to vent some of his fear and fury through the chattering breech of his guns.

He was flying close to the river, had spotted six wagons and thirty horses running across open ground for the cover of trees just on the other side. They'd no doubt heard his engine too late and gotten caught out.

He was flying Jackrabbit. Was loaded with incendiary rounds. Had plenty of fuel and a solid identification, support from the rest of his wing, and about fifteen minutes of daylight left. The situation was perfect for an engagement. It wouldn't get any better. The closest bomber was ten minutes away, minimum—having been called out to bomb Wolfe's tank rock—and in less than five, the caravan would've reached the cover of a heavy wood less than a mile from them. There was an almost subconscious sense among the pilots listening in on their radios that if Ted didn't release Fenn on this target, then there was something more to his reticence than plain caution, something more than a sudden unwillingness to allow his fighters to engage ground targets or spend them against anything more dangerous than the landscape.

There was a pause—a gap of silence between Fenn's lackadaisical request for free-fire clearance and the response. A gap of doubt, perhaps, into which everyone poured their worry that Ted had gone soft, gone insane. Everyone silently hoped it was a gap of somber, calculated, and bloodthirsty thought.

Then the call came back from Diane, fresh on her shift, sitting in the radio chair and with the scent of Ted Prinzi all over her voice. "Jackrabbit, control. Order is engage. Repeat: Engage, engage, engage."

It was over in less than a minute. Three close passes. Three hundred rounds of ammunition from Fenn's twin Spandaus. He hit everything that moved and then, to be sure, hit everything that didn't move. The phosphorous rounds burned blue in the air, sparked as they hit the ground, bounced, and danced. The wagons caught fire. All observers reported secondary explosions. And then it was done.

|||||||||||||

In the tent, Diane had gotten the call from Captain Teague. Ted was already there. It'd been him who'd sent Ernie O'Day in to bomb that rock. Coughing, red-eyed, drinking coffee from a filthy tin cup, Ted had checked the maps, the computer projections. He'd leaned close, putting a hand on Diane's shoulder that'd made her want to recoil, partly. Partly wanting to lean into it. He squeezed, probably without thinking about it. His breath was awful.

Then he'd stood back, as if to get a long view, as if this were momentous. Jimmy McCudden was there. He'd been afraid to leave the comms tent for days and had set up a disgusting little nest in the ready room. Tanner, the backup radioman, was there. Shun Le, the second controller, watching the split flight of three squadron over the near-south sector. They all watched him. Diane looked up at him, something pleading in her eyes, her own sweet breath coming low and rough.

All Ted had done was nod once sharply. Then he immediately turned and left the tent.

"Jackrabbit, control," Diane had said, something like a butterfly beating its wings against the cage of her ribs. "Order is engage. Repeat: Engage, engage, engage."

But what she'd really been saying was kill. *Kill, kill, kill.*

Ted had gone directly to the strip and stood there, unmoving, watching the sky until every plane touched down safe and sound.

After that, the action came easier for a time.

AT TELLER S-2, during the guild troubles, Carter'd flown missions off a naval carrier. It was a huge thing, like a city in orbit. He'd fly—mostly defensive patrols, guarding the carrier and other blockade ships against a terrestrial splinter government that had no space fleet—and then he'd come home, back to his steel and plastic apartment near the center of the massive ship. He had better accommodations than any navvie below command grade could've dreamed of. He lived alone. Two rooms. Private bath. Murphy bed and an entertainment center. It was just him and fifty Flyboy mercenaries, only nominally under the authority of the Colonial Council, the Terran navy, and spacers guild, and they were generally left to their own devices. It would take him most of an hour to get from hangar seven where his squadron was berthed to the tier where he was quartered. It was like commuting. There was a train—two trains, actually—and a lot of walking involved.

He would get home, strip out of his ready blues, shower. He would pick a restaurant at which to eat, because there were forty or fifty different messes on the carrier and each was different, nicknamed something like Lucky Louie's or the Eggery, good at some stuff, bad at the rest. Just like real restaurants. He'd hop a train. He'd eat. Maybe he'd see some Flyboys out, maybe not. He'd decide: Did he want drinks? A movie?

Company? A quiet cycle at home? He could go to the gym, the simula-
tors. If he wanted some action, he knew where to find it. Sometimes
he'd find a girl. Sometimes not. There were 12,344 people living and
working aboard the *TEF Alabama*. Navals, contractors, families, officers
and enlisted men and women. A man could get swallowed up in that,
easy. When he was tired, he'd go to sleep, wake up, make his call time,
fly, do it all again. One sortie per thirty hours, no more than five sorties
in any seven-day stretch. It was a job. Like working in an office, except
that Carter's office could fly and kill you from a thousand miles away.

Strapped into the acceleration couch of his ship (a pure space fighter,
no gear for making atmospheric translation), he'd had more electronics
in his helmet than the company had shipped, in total, down to Iaxo. If
he thought hard and closed his eyes, he could still remember what that
kind of boredom had been like. Totally different. He could remember
his call sign, his radio protocols. *Alabama-indy seven-oh-one calling home:
Boxing one thousand and coming back to formation. Nothing to report.* He
could remember the thrill of exo-atmospheric maneuvering, the different skill set, the isolation of being one ship in a thousand square miles
of space, and the blood scent of catching the reentry burn of a blockade
runner from one hundred degrees of arc away. *Alabama-indy seven-oh-one
to Alabama actual: Target acquired making entry. Permission to engage.*

Permission granted, Alabama-indy. Weapons clear for free fire.

And then the rush of falling, throttles open, nosing down toward
the death that the atmosphere represented (the same as falling toward
the earth); skipping like a stone across the hard halo of firming gasses
and reaching fingers of gravitation; following a ballistic arc described
for him by the targeting computers, rushing to make a firing solution
against a closing angle of arc.

Finally, the sweet tone of a positive lock, in range. One button: weapons away. Maneuver engines blowing clouds of vaporizing LOx as he
pulled up and out in a backspin spiral, eighty self-tracking darts of
molybdenum-alloy flaring outward toward a distant point of conver-
gence, to slam into the body of a blockade runner at a velocity of ten
thousand feet per second. One touch was lethal; could punch an inch-
wide hole in a ship's heat shielding, knock a tile loose. When they died,
the ships flared like shooting stars. It was instantaneous.

Then home. He carried only one weapon, one offensive package, one shot. After a kill, five days off. A reward. He'd watch movies, sleep late, eat well. After five days, it was back to the grind.

It was strange, the entire experience. There was always this moment of odd domesticity, like wanting to brag about a good, successful day at the office. Signed the contract. Sealed the deal. Made a kill. There'd been a deep sense of accomplishment in it. All the waiting, the flying, the training, the endless patrols—all of it, paying off in that gratifying chug the ship would take as the kinetic weapon detached and went screwing off through space toward the inevitable. Once the siege had done its job, the carrier had dropped its complement of Colonial Marines onto the surface: one brigade, plus support elements. It took them one day to organize on the surface, one day to crush the opposition government's forces. When they came back, the marines had seemed hardly out of breath. There was a small ceremony, a banner in the carrier's assembly area that said MISSION ACCOMPLISHED. Carter and the rest of the Flyboys were paid off and stayed aboard to catch a ride back to the nearest station.

It was a job, Carter knew. Like this one. But it was different. And if he knew how, he'd explain it to himself—sit himself down and clarify— but he didn't. He couldn't understand it at all.

| | | | | | | | | | | |

Ted was no longer flying with his squadron at all, leaving them two men short after losing Morris and, technically, three short since Danny Diaz had flown with the 1st until he died and didn't anymore. Bad luck to be in Ted's flight, it seemed. He refused to make any transfers on the roster because the 1st had been overweighted by one pilot to begin with (originally having six men rather than five, with Ted holding the commander's slot) and because they'd been operating as support for most of the tour anyhow. He wanted two full combat squadrons on hand no matter what, and was running split flights on the roster—short three/one and two/one combinations—so that there would always be five pilots at the field and ready to fly should anything requiring their immediate attentions pop up. Carter thought he had a screw loose— perhaps more than one.

Instead of flying, instead of taking the fight to the enemy, Ted had devised a new tactic and hunted Fast Eddie instead. Apparently convinced, in opposition to all available intelligence, that the airfield was going to be overrun at any moment, he wanted defensive weapons: razor wire and land mines, field lasers, motion trackers, and caterpillar mortars. He wanted more planes to take the place of the three lost in the past two years. He wanted *better* planes. Jets, fighter/bombers, transatmospherics, and the technicians, crews, and equipment necessary to keep them flying. He would spy Eddie in the mess or moving between the tent line and the field house and fall onto his tail like it was a dogfight, shouting at the little lawyer to make it work. To find a way. He wanted Flyboy to hire another mercenary company to provide airfield security because he thought that the camp indigs (of which there no longer were any) were all spies planted by the other side, and possibly secret assassins. Come to find, it'd been his bright idea to have the lot of them escorted off the premises in the first place; had drafted the first dozen willing (all too willing) humans he'd come across to be his muscle, then had sat (much like Carter had sat) and watched the whole thing get done. It'd been stupid. Now who was going to wash everyone's shirts?

He told Eddie he wanted sheaf rockets and cruise missiles. He told Eddie to buy them, beg them, or steal them somehow. To conjure them from thin air. Carter hadn't heard that conversation, but Emile Hardman had. He'd told everyone about it in the mess one morning, doing a fair impression of Ted and a very good one of Eddie, with his shoulders hunched and his ass in the air, running the hell away. Ted wanted the raw materials to build and outfit a patrol boat for the river (he had even drawn up the plans for one in a careful and surprisingly competent draftsman's style that he'd shown to Fenn while Fenn was trying to eat his breakfast), and one night he got on the tight-beam FTL relay himself, called corporate, and tried to ask for sixty canisters of Virox nerve gas.

Carter was alone in the mess tent drinking cold coffee and playing solitaire with a deck of Charlie Voss's girlie cards (which made it more like fortune-telling than card playing) on the night after Fenn had made his kill, the night Ted had tried to call home. He came storming in with Eddie, now hot on his six, in kill position. Eddie was yelling—something Carter had never seen him do before—and Ted was in retreat—something else he'd never seen. They both hung up at the doorway when they saw Carter, likely not expecting to find anyone in the tent at such a late hour while, across the camp, everyone else seemed to be celebrating a productive night's work. For his part, Carter froze, too—redheaded Irene, the queen of hearts, in his hand. Suddenly, he wished he weren't there either.

Ted broke first. "Carter," he barked. "Nerve gas."

"None for me, thanks. I'm fine with coffee."

Ted made for his table, slapping his hands down hard on its surface, leaning down, eyeballing Carter with crazy, sparking intensity like his eyes were two lightbulbs shorting in the socket. Eddie stood where he was in the doorway, shaking his head and mouthing, "No."

"Don't get smart, Captain. Virox. Fifty or sixty cans. We can just kill them all. Gas the fuckers. Let 'em choke. Then we can all just go home before anyone else shows up to ruin our little picnic here, right?"

Carter looked at Ted. He was a man badly in need of reinforcement. He looked past Ted at Eddie, who was silently waving his hands like an umpire signaling safe, shaking his head, mouthing, "No, no, no."

Ted jinked his head on his neck, bringing it back in front of Carter's with a snap. "Don't look at that little snake, Carter. Don't you look anywhere but right here. I am your goddamn commander. You look at *me*."

He did. Irene was still in his hand, biting her lip, sitting on her heels amid a rumple of pure white sheets. He laid her down in her place and stood up. Ted followed him, tight on his every move. There was a serious fear in Ted. Carter could smell it on him like rotten lemons. See it in his fixated, unblinking, red-eyed stare. He folded his arms and turned to face Eddie across the empty room.

"I'm with Ted," he said. "Nerve gas. Nukes. Burn all the little savages right the fuck up."

He did it because Ted was his chief, no matter what. He did it because Ted flew (and well) and Eddie didn't at all. He did it because if he hadn't, he honestly believed Ted would have lost his shit right then and there, and because, frankly, going all crazy and just carpet bombing this whole boondock nowhere, raining nuclear fire down on it from on high, really ripping and torturing the land, sounded like big fun. Mostly he did it because he didn't like lawyers.

Ted turned back to Eddie with a smug look on his face, a told-you-so glare of total and complete victory, as though Carter's opinion was all he'd needed to make his case for depopulating an entire planet and going straight home before supper. To prove, maybe, that he wasn't absolutely out of his mind.

Eddie shook his head, turned, and kicked his way out the door. Before it slammed closed, he caught it, stuck his head and shoulders back inside, pointed a finger at Ted, and said, in level tones, "You know better than this, Commander. Don't go near the relay again. That's an order."

Ted laid an arm across Carter's shoulders and gave Eddie the finger.

Eddie left. Ted, removing his arm from Carter, straightened up, smoothed the front of his wrinkled and stained shirt, and did the same—going out the opposite door without another word. He was muttering to himself plenty. He just didn't appear to have anything further to say to Carter.

And Carter, for his part, just stood there—bewildered last-man-standing, survivor of some sharp and speedy melee that he couldn't begin to comprehend. For an instant, it felt like Ted had taken all the oxygen out of the room with him when he left. Then it didn't feel that way anymore, and it just felt strange to be standing.

So Carter sat. He squared up the cards. In his head, he tried to figure what had Ted so scared. Having someone funnel supplies to the other side was bad, no doubt. It would ruin all their fun here. But really, it was almost to be expected. And now that it'd happened, it was surprising only in that it hadn't happened sooner. NRI was bad news for sure. The possibility of the Colonial Council sending in the marines was worse. And the thought that either organization might actually come to Iaxo—and that he and his friends might find themselves flying souped-up biplanes against jump ships, assault helicopters, orbital corvettes . . . That would get weird and out of hand very quickly.

But no one was saying that this was going to happen. For sure, they'd be long gone before the marines arrived. No private military contractor could afford the kind of trouble that would come from that. They might lose this fight, and probably already had, but no one would ever know about it. The company would lose a two-year investment in the Carpenter mission and the chance at owning a gigantic stake in a viable planet. That would hurt, sure, but it was only money. When things got wrong-sided enough, the orders from corporate would come. They'd strike their camp, bury what they could, burn the rest, and then vanish like they'd never been here. That was the way it was done. There were plans, procedures—corporate directive memos that detailed specific steps that needed to be taken. Or at least Carter hoped there were. Personally, he'd been trying not to think about it. Ted, obviously, had been thinking about it far too much.

Carter slowly began to deal out another hand. Halfway through, it occurred to him that he hadn't shuffled. Didn't much matter, though. He could never win. The ace of spades was missing from the deck. In any military outfit, there were never enough aces of spades to go around.

CARTER WAS BETWEEN FLIGHTS—stoop-shouldered, exhausted, his hips and tailbone, one elbow, both shoulders, a patch between them and the balls of both his feet all numb from the constant vibration of flying, the repetitive motion, the rub of straps, components, whatever. Fenn had been feted last night for his clean kill on the caravan. The party had occurred mostly in the tent, so Carter was hungover, too. Toast upon toast to the killer instinct of his friend, to his glamorous victory over, what? A bunch of filthy monkeys and some horses. Brilliant.

Carter had ducked out. He'd gone to the mess tent, and that'd been where the Ted-and-Eddie show had erupted all around him.

Gas the fuckers. Let 'em choke.

Fuckin'-A right, Ted-O. Fuck 'em all and let's go home.

An hour later, a three/one flight had come back from badland. Stork, Hardman, and Porter Vaughn. There'd been cheering. Carter'd heard it even from inside his own weird bubble of distraction—still in the mess, dealing hands of solitaire but getting nowhere. After a time, he'd just taken to spreading the cards and trying to pick redheaded Irene out of the deck with his eyes closed. When he heard the noise, he'd gone to investigate.

|||||||||||

They'd been standing right on the apron when the flight had come down, waving bottles and goggles and white scarves. Everyone who wasn't due up with the dawn patrol was hammered. Lori Bishop had her tits out. Vic was there in her leathers. She'd spotted Carter and smiled at him while brushing prop-whipped hair out of her face—an image he'd take to bed with him later that night and up into the air again the next day.

It'd been another solid kill, he learned—a maneuver element moving under cover of darkness on the extreme edge of the engagement zone, deep in Indian country, target approved by Ted. Vaughn had estimated a file of a hundred indigs, passing through a three-mile-wide gap in the siege lines, humping big packs, and making for Riverbend, double time. Machine guns, cannon, and ten-pound white phosphorous bombs had settled them. They'd left nothing standing. Carter watched McCudden pour whiskey straight into Hardman's open mouth. He heard someone say, "All that hair, they burn like goddamn *candles*." Cheers all around.

|||||||||||

Carter'd walked off, avoiding the hot glare of celebration like tiptoeing around the glow of a lamp in the dark. He'd wandered the tent line and found himself at Ted's, with light burning inside and spilling out through the windows in a way that seemed, after the worries of the past few days, almost obscene.

He heard Eddie talking in low, angry tones while still in the lee of the walls, standing with his hands in his pockets, in the shadows.

"You can't do this, Commander. The blackout was put in place for a reason, and you breaking it is not helping our cause with the home office."

"We have no cause. No one is coming, Eddie."

"They will. We just have to hold out. You just have to let me do my work and not be sabotaging it every time I look away."

Ted coughed violently. When he spoke, his voice was hoarse and strained. "Your work? What work have you done? Have you called in one of the other companies before they're all gone? Found us some smuggler that'll take us out of here?"

"No. Absolutely not. There are channels, Ted. There are ways that these things are done."

Carter crept closer. Hunched down below the bottom edge of one of the flap windows, he peeked inside the tent and saw the wreck of Ted's quarters—maps and papers covering every surface, his bed a mess of tangled blankets and odd bits of gear. It was the room of someone who was still at war, and Ted sat in the middle of it with Eddie hovering over him, both of their backs to the window. Eddie had his hands balled into pale fists, the muscles of his jaw standing out like iron cables. And Ted did nothing but stare at a clock on his bedside table, seeming to mouth out the seconds as they ticked past.

| | | | | | | | | | | |

Carter'd tried to sleep. Failed. Done dawn patrol. Landed. He was angry at everything, bored, so tired, coiled up inside from impotently waiting (there'd been no action that morning, none that he could even invent), and knotted with stress. He had a sick, empty cramp low in his belly that felt like sexual frustration and was, though for a different kind of intercourse entirely—wanting so badly just to fuck something up. The thing with Ted and Eddie last night had put him on edge. It'd put in his head the thought that there really was something more wrong than he understood. Since he did not know, his imagination had filled in the blanks with a hundred worst scenarios, all of them corrosive, eating away at him slowly until all he wanted was to go up in the air and destroy everything he was afraid of—to kill this place before it killed him.

But there'd been nothing. Just sky and earth and nothing between. And when he'd come down, he'd almost been doubled over with the pain of it—violent blue balls cramping him into a ferocious thing, crippled with aching, directionless, frightened fury.

On the ground, Vic saw all of that in him. She watched him surreptitiously, from distances—pacing a perimeter the way he'd walked the edge of the light last night. Carter could see her. And when he couldn't see her, he could feel her. The weight of her attention like a hand on the back of his neck. She circled him like a carrion bird, waiting.

For lack of anything better to do, Carter went up again. Extracurricular. He cobbled together a three/two/one reconaissance party with Charlie, Wolfe, and Tommy Hill and made straight for the river. Three D.VIIs and him in the Vickers with no one in the second seat, freezing half to death in the draw from the pusher-mount prop, the carriage garlanded with fragmentation bombs and jellied kerosene napalm with magnesium contact igniters. They found nothing. Six hours in the air. Absolutely fuck-all.

The ground crews were wasted. There were fewer of them than there were pilots, so with all the pilots going up and coming down all the time, it meant that they didn't get any rest, any sleep, any time away. Machinists were conscripted onto the flight line, controllers on their downtime. Even still, when Carter brought his flight home, circling low and lazily in cover position while Charlie, Wolfe, and Tommy brought their machines thumpingly back to Earth—there was no one there to meet them.

They'd rolled, on ground once again frozen stiff with the chill of winter rolling down out of the mountains, edging their planes onto the sidelines of the strip, goosing their engines, and trying to give Carter room enough to land the clumsy, overloaded, skid-foot Vickers.

But something had seized hold of him—all his rage and frustration compounded by the lack of a ground crew, by his wasted day, wasted hours aloft. Compounded by nothing worth killing. Compounded by the image of Vic tossing her hair, of Vic smiling, Vic stalking him through the tumult of the field, that'd kept fogging his vision all day, insinuating itself into his view across the Vickers' sloped nose until he was periodically blind from it; jerking his head back and forth like he was trying to get his bearing around the hazy edges of his own traitorous memory or just shake it free from his brain like a burr.

So he'd slammed the Vickers down into the close grass, dead center of the strip, doing a forced combat descent the overloaded antique had never been built for. He hadn't been thinking about the bombs he carried. Hundreds of pounds of fused explosive wrapped in brittle aluminum ribbon and fragile shells of home-brew napalm. He hadn't been thinking about the death that, in the instant he touched down, brushed perilously close.

He felt something in the skid assembly snap when he hit, pulling up out of the sharp dive, belly flopping the plane. She'd tried to catapult on him, end over end, but carried most of her weight in her middle and had enough forward velocity left that Carter was able to bog her front skids and slap her tail back down, burying the rear-end gear, slewing off to the right, clipping the ground with her lower wing, and crumpling the straight braces. The wheels at the back end of the skids were twisted on their short axles; Carter and the Vickers limped to a halt ten feet short of where Wolfe and Tommy and Charlie sat frantically scrabbling at their safety belts, trying to get themselves untangled from their own planes lest Carter be unable to prevent himself from smashing straight into them.

He didn't, though. And once the machine was down and stopped, he pulled the emergency release, hopped out of the cockpit, and walked away, turning his back on the plane as though he'd never seen it before.

Vic had been in the longhouse. She'd seen the flight come down, seen Carter's landing. She'd rounded up Rockwell and Meleuire, woken two of her other mechanics (asleep in the grease pits, heads pillowed on bolts of patch cloth) to act as crew, and helped Wolfe and Tommy and Charlie push their planes through the doors and into the house.

Carter'd stomped off, twenty feet maybe—clear of the smell of aviation fuel, the stink of hot oil. He stared silently past the southern end of B strip, attempting to compose himself, clear his head, control his breathing. When he thought about how close he'd come to killing himself, he had to fight not to laugh. He lit a cigarette, coughed until his eyes teared. He tried to think of nothing.

After a while, he could hear Vic behind him, looking the Vickers over, banging on this, shoving at that. He wouldn't turn around. He heard her curse at it once. The sun was almost down. It was dark and getting cold. B strip was quiet. Wolfe and Tommy and Charlie had retired, backing away from Carter without a word, like he was a wounded animal, although one of them had thrown a helmet at him and missed by a mile. Vic's mechanics had gone back to the house. It was just her and Carter, but he still wouldn't turn around.

"Something wrong with your plane, Captain," she finally said, her voice conversational.

"Yeah. It's broke," Carter said.

"Was it broke before you landed it?"

"Probably not."

She was quiet for a minute. So was Carter.

"We're gonna have to leg this. Brace up the wing. Need light and some tools."

Carter said nothing.

"Come with me, Kev. I need an extra set of hands."

And he did. They didn't talk any more. She had to bring out the tractor to tow the generator lights. Carter walked. For an hour, they worked in silence with jacks and splints, raising the tail, getting a temporary wooden strut under the crushed straight braces of aircraft-grade aluminum, cutting away the broken skid plate and axle and putting a gimp on it. When she hooked the tractor's tow chain to the Vickers, Carter killed the genny, waited for her to drag the half wreck into the house and then come back for him. He attached the lights and generator to the tractor and hopped up onto the foot plate for the ride back. When, in a crosswind, a bit of her hair brushed across his neck, he felt as though he'd been whipped by fire.

Inside, Vic pulled the big sliding door shut. Together, the two of them muscled the Vickers over into one of the repair bays and got to work rebuilding everything Carter had broken. They talked a little, just hand-me-that and where'd-you-put-my-whatever. It took another hour to get a new front skid mounted, twenty minutes to leg the tail. The wing was more serious. They stood side by side staring at it and then, without any discussion, got to work with cutting torches and strutters. It was the middle of the night before they'd finished, and Carter felt empty. He felt good.

| | | | | | | | | | | |

The scramble sirens went off at thirteen o'clock, and if anyone noticed Carter arriving from the direction of Vic's tent, no one made any mention of it. He was still warm from her skin, wet from her, drunk on her—except that he was technically sober. That'd been a first for him, coming to her without the soft armor of drunkenness and its excuse. It was different.

The alarm had been nothing. Chasing ghosts. Vic had lain for a time, not knowing, watching the path Carter's plane had followed at takeoff as if its motion had torn a hole of emptiness in the night that she could still see—the fading track of his passage from her and into the sky. She'd been naked, of course, and chilled by the suddenness of his absence as if something almost precious had been taken from her.

The planes all came home and Vic, dressed now and aching, had put her boys under the whip—lighting the strip, flagging down pilots, wheeling machines into bed. She motivated them like they were under fire. Drove them, stopping only every now and then to look up into the cold, hard sky, barely lit by the shards of the double moons, to try and spot Carter's plane. It was no good, though. Painted up for night fighting, she was as good as invisible.

In the air, Carter was doing the same thing, trying to pick Vic out of the play of harsh shadows, the severe glare of runway lamps, and shifting beams of nightsticks. He knew she was down there somewhere in the baffling dark. He could feel her and imagined that, circling, stacked up six deep, now five, that he was circling only her. Like there was a string tethering him, its knot tied high in his throat like something he couldn't quite swallow.

| | | | | | | | | | | |

On the ground, Vic counted three planes, then four. The accounting was in her head—the order of things, tomorrow's busywork—but she didn't allow much room to this collection of simple numbers, mental spreadsheets, constantly pressing against the soft walls of the movie playing behind her eyes.

The sex hadn't been nice. There'd been nothing friendly about it. It was rough and it was hard and that'd been fine. It'd been good because that was what he'd needed and she'd wanted and, so, what she'd taken from him. After the longhouse, he'd followed her back to her tent like a puppy—slinking, shy—and that'd been a disappointment. But once inside, behind a closed door, there'd been a moment. A spark like a starbursting short. The closing of a switch. She'd been doing something. He'd been doing something else—moving across the tent, talking some kind of nonsense. And then suddenly he'd stopped and she'd stopped, and their eyes had brushed each other and his hips had twitched around as though she'd caught him with a fishhook in the belly and pulled.

It was all in the tilt of her head, the turning angle of his body, and the coils of barbed wire that looped along the trajectory of their gazes—into each other's eyes, electric with the sure knowledge of what was coming next.

Vic was there in that moment. She knew that. And then she wasn't there because she became like a doll to him, an object to be used and bent and turned this way and that; a target on which he could spend some terrible rage.

He fucked her without sweetness and that, too, had been fine because he had no sweetness to offer and none that she wanted. And when it left her hot and sore and breathless and (at least temporarily) mindless of anything but his skin and his mouth and his cock and the sound of his breath in her ear, she was happy because that was what she'd wanted from him and because she knew that, as she'd been there, fully present, in that first charged instant of connection, so, too, would she be there on the other end, as what would be waiting for him on the other side.

And she was. He hadn't been sleeping when the scramble siren had gone off, but he was peaceful, something she knew he hadn't been in a long time. That was her gift. What she knew she was capable of giving.

"I know what they say about me, you know," she'd said to him in the moments before the quiet was split by the siren's grinding wail. "It's not true."

Carter'd known exactly what she was talking about. He hadn't lied and pretended he didn't. She'd appreciated that.

Eventually, Carter brought his plane down. Second to last. And when his postflight was done, he followed Vic again, back to her tent, without hesitating. He'd followed her down to the ground already. Had felt her reel him in safely, dragging him from the sky to the earth. This, then, was just more following. He hadn't yet been cut free and didn't fight the hook at all.

She was taking her clothes off before even getting inside. Undoing buttons, rasping zippers. It was need, same as his. Not even desire. The bite of cold against her bare skin only served to remind her of the heat she now craved like water, like oxygen.

And three hours later, the siren went off again. Carter brought his head up from between her legs and growled, still starving, like her. He dressed, then ran for his plane. This time, it wasn't nothing. It was a true target. And now that it was his turn, in the wan, sad hour before dawn, he'd done like Stork, Hardman, and Vaughn had done, like Fenn before them. He killed without any dignity at all.

They cheered him and his flight on the ground, and Carter felt disgusted by it. When he saw Vic, he went to her, but she'd stopped him—laying a hand gently on the frozen leather of his chest.

"No. Celebrate. You need it and so do they."

"I don't . . ."

"Go. I'll be here when it's over."

And she was. There was nowhere else to go.

CARTER'D HAD THIS GIRLFRIEND ONCE, BACK ON EARTH. She was pretty and young and, at the time, so was he.

They'd met in school. He was finishing his third levels in math and physical sciences, prerequisites for the engineering school at Swan that'd already accepted him. She was on an earthbound track, something artistic and soft. Fiber crafts, maybe. Papermaking. It was hard for him to remember now. She'd been a commune kid, born and raised, so the artistic tastes had been no surprise. Her father was a laborer who painted a little—mostly other people's houses. Her mother did something strange with pottery and was, in that world, quite well-known for it.

Carter was the exact opposite—an engineer born of engineers and raised among engineers just outside Midland Spaceport, he'd never once had cause to question the path that'd been laid out for him since birth. His father designed solar-electric panels, his mother varial-g structural components. Their parents, Carter's grandparents, had all been engineers. Grandpa Carter had designed light pumps for orbital stations and darkside colonials. Grandma had been heavy into food science. On the other side of the family—his mother's—the grandparents had both been architectural engineers, one on the public works side, the other in the private sector, though Carter could never recall which had been which and who'd done what.

In any event, they were engineers who made more little engineers (Carter and his two brothers), socialized them only with other little engineers, entertained them with engineers' toys, and saw them schooled inside primary and secondary academies where engineering was treated almost like a religion, with all the same fervor and promise of great reward. Mark, the oldest, quickly showed a flair for genes, Jacob (ironically) for aeronautics. Kevin Carter, the youngest of the three, was a bit slower, but by sixteen he had found his niche among the mechanical engineers and had flourished. He was happy. He lived a life without doubt, without the stress of wondering what he'd be doing for the rest of his life, because there was never any question of what he'd been born to do. Mark, Jacob, and he had each come out in the top five in their respective first levels, in the top three in their second levels. In turn, they'd each earned off-planet berths—valuable seats on big birds that would take them off to university programs, which would lead to further off-planet postings where they could carry on their life's work, find girl engineers (or, in Jacob's case, another boy), make more little engineers and so keep the cycle going. Carter was the last, but he was doing nothing more than following a course already well charted by Mark and Jacob before him.

Then Carter'd met Sara—the girl, the fabric artist or painter or whatever she was. She'd been at the school doing a contract art installation: some mural of glorious engineers doing glorious things like building bridges, DNA helixes, the skeleton frames of spacecraft with classical geometric and physical formulae wreathing their bulk like halos of pure math. It was hideous, but fairly standard—social realism being the only artistic tenet that engineers embraced that couldn't be expressed as a neat equation or theorem—and Carter had known enough not to blame the artists for the brutish heavy-handedness of the thing. They were artists. They did what they were told or they didn't eat.

Sara had been there, along with her father and six or seven other apprentices from the commune. And Carter remembered exactly how they'd gotten to talking: She'd spilled a bucket of paint on him. Not exactly subtle. And though she always swore that it'd been accidental, she always swore it with a mocking grin.

It took less than three months for Sara to undo Carter completely, to lift him free from the path of his onrushing future and show him, for lack of a better word, options. One of the reasons he'd been so content in his course was that he'd never known anyone who'd done anything different. He'd never known anyone who wasn't an engineer or an engineer in training. For the life of him, he couldn't have understood then why anyone would've wanted to be anything *but* an engineer. He felt proud, fortunate, blessed, even, that he'd been lucky enough to have been born into exactly the right family that could allow him to become exactly what he'd always wanted to be.

He learned different on the commune. When he would sneak out of the academy dorms to go see Sara, he would see people who couldn't describe the physical action of a lever or read the point stress of a T-beam if their lives depended on it. Yet they seemed happy. Or at least they pretended very well. They cared about things that he had never considered. Valued things that he thought of as superfluous, if at all. Something in that freedom had appealed greatly to Carter and, completely against his wishes, he'd fallen in love with the girl.

When he missed his flight out to Swan Station where he was to meet with the dean of the mechanical engineering school there, his parents became concerned, but by then it was far too late. He and Sara were already on a rather different flight: terrestrial, just a little ways south to Matagorda Island and the Villachez Spaceport, where seats were waiting for them on a commuter jump out to Unity Station (anti-motion-sickness Therazine caps and anti-emetics pressed into their hands as they rushed to the gate at the last moment, the standard effects-of-high-and-low-g safety lecture abbreviated by their late arrival) and then a ride on a small guild cruiser to Mars. Sara was outbound, headed for the university at Chryse, and Carter was more than happy just to tag along. Their liberal arts program was second to none.

For a few months, everything was wonderful. They lived together in a tiny capsule apartment under the dome—on the cheap side, but not far from the university. Sara attended classes in art and design. Carter even audited a couple, though he quickly lost interest and took a job on campus instead, using all of his years of careful education and cloistered study to patch seals and polish pipeworks at the Chryse water-generation plant. At Sara's insistence, he avoided all attempts at contact from his brothers and his parents. They wouldn't understand, she told him. All they wanted was for him to come back and build their stupid spaceships again. Curled together like quotation marks on their apartment's narrow bed, they convinced each other that this was the start of their great adventure together, that everything was going to work out fine.

And when Sara eventually broke Carter's heart for the most banal of reasons and saw him thrown out of their combined quarters and his job at the campus plant to boot, he found himself suddenly at loose ends. Gone was the security of the groove cut by his time as an engineer's brat. Gone was the heady rush and careless bravery of rebelling against all that for what he'd thought was true love. With two brothers, a strong family unit, and years of boarding school, he'd never experienced aloneness before. He'd never faced down a day without knowing the purpose meant to be fulfilled at the end of it. It'd scared the crap out of him.

Joining NRI was what Carter'd done to replace all that he'd lost. In them, he saw a sort of salvation. They had goals, discipline, plans for the future—all that he felt he lacked in his moment of weakness. They were doing good on a galactic scale, fighting for a cause they believed in. There was other stuff, too. He couldn't remember what, exactly, but he could remember Sara having several NRI posters on rotation on the media wall of their small container apartment, each blazing with vaguely inspirational slogans. And those slogans must've burned in deep enough that Carter was able to recognize the NRI logo when he saw it a couple of days later, hung over the door of a recruiting office just off campus. Looking back now, Carter knew he might just as well have walked in with *Fresh Meat* tattooed across his forehead. They took him in like they'd been looking for him for ages.

The NRI training camps were unpleasant places. He liked that about them. At first, being there felt like vague punishment for sins he barely understood having committed. Earthside, they had one in the Han Republic, what used to be far northern China, which was austere to the point of invisibility; another in South Africa, which existed by dint of a look-away agreement with the local government and had, as its main feature, an urban bombing range laid over what used to be Bloemfontein; a third in Washington Free State, not far from Seattle, which was where Carter first visited.

There, under the mystifying greenness of an old-growth canopy forest, he learned small-unit ground tactics, the strategies of protest, both nonviolent and active, how to deal with tear gas, riot police, stun batons, and fast-insertion. The basics of escape and evasion he picked up fast, trying to avoid the come-ons of the aggressive, militant omnisexuals who felt that the standard boy/girl-girl/girl-boy/boy modes of intimate expression were just another form of gender oppression that could be lifted only by the consumption of potent, homegrown hallucinogens and frequent participation in their creepy forced gang bangs. He also sat for interminable hours on a tree stump being harangued by various extremist commissars of the movement, told how the human race was made up of ruthless conquistadors, cultural rapists, and murderers on a genocidal scale. He was told how his presence here among the wise trees, giant slugs, and moldy assault courses wasn't nearly enough and that he should also be willing to give up all known banking codes his family used so that their wealth might be "equitably redistributed for the defense of all native species."

He didn't, but refusal wasn't easy. He'd also kept from them that he'd come from privilege and private school, from engineers who'd probably designed some of the things that these people so obliquely hated. His brief commune past with Sara served him better, made his arrival more obvious and easier to explain. He was nineteen years old.

On a salvage ship called *Band of Brothers,* a blind former Colonial Marine commando called Applebaum taught twelve of them the delicate art of bomb making and schooled them in the less delicate theories of engineered demolition. Theirs were not the simple butane-and-nails terror bombs or the wasteful compound-4 jacket of the suicide martyr, but rather structural explosives, sabotage bombs, and complicated implosion chains that could take down entire buildings. It was fun. And while no one there pretended not to know why they were being taught all of these fascinating things, neither did anyone talk about it. Maybe someday they'd be called on to blow something up. Save a space gopher. Whatever. In the meantime, they were kept busy.

They practiced first with dummies in the few pressurized compartments that remained on the *Band of Brothers,* then moved into soft vacuum for the real thing; gleefully blasting huge chunks of the derelict superstructure and learning the chemical intricacies of zero-atmosphere demolition.

Carter had the knack for destruction. It was nothing more than the opposite of engineering. And he was enjoying himself right up until one of his fellow scholars—a short, fat, normally gifted chemist named Barley—made a tragic miscalculation with a concussion tamper and blew himself and his kit straight into space.

The *Band of Brothers* was in a constantly decaying orbit around Calisto, its tumble corrected somewhat by the explosions that would bump its trajectory, more by the transit bubbles that would always land and lift from its down-facing Calisto side. Equal and opposite force and all that. At any time, there were a dozen or so of these little single-use engines with life-support bubbles attached and glommed onto the wreck, each with a little fuel left over from its single trip out from whichever NRI transport had delivered students into the vicinity and Colonel Applebaum's tender care. And it was to one of these that Carter charged the minute he saw Barley blown off in the general direction of Venus, several million miles away.

Long story short, he caught him. In his vac suit, Barley was able to cling to one of the bubbles' debarking clamps while Carter got it turned around and headed back toward the *Band of Brothers.* Unfortunately, he knew nothing about orbital mechanics, relative velocities of bodies in space, or piloting in general at the time. After catching up to Barley, matching his velocity, maneuvering in close enough for him to grab on, getting the bubble turned and faced in the direction he'd come from, the *Band of Brothers* was long gone. Carter found her in the glass, rapidly receding, then made the one mistake that probably saved his life—aiming low, past her horizon, and giving one long, hard acceleration burn.

Then his bubble ran out of gas.

It took most of a Calistan day, but his ballistic trajectory eventually merged with that of the *Band of Brothers,* his faster relative speed and lower orbital arc allowing him to draw close enough that he could start screaming for help over the suit radio. Colonel Applebaum, having assumed them both dead of misadventure and adding them to his long mental list of the same, dispatched students with tethers to rope Carter, Barley, and their bubble in like a wayward, floating calf, and Carter, having now gotten a taste for it, was in love with flying. It was childish and instantaneous, but real. Something he knew in his blood.

When NRI got wind of Carter's dumbass heroics, they called him back from the *Band of Brothers* and had him thrown into a torture cell for six days where interrogators (mostly students, one of whom fainted after putting the battery cables to him) did their best to prove that he was actually a spy sent to infiltrate their ranks by any one of a dozen colonial or federal agencies that they believed (wrongly) gave a damn about anything they did. Carter was used as a demonstration case, a live subject, and he broke under questioning a hundred times but never gave them anything that made them worry. NRI was concerned with grand conspiracies. About the motivations of the faithful and their small betrayals? They couldn't have cared less.

On the seventh day he was cleared, his physical wounds dressed, the rest apologized for in the most bureaucratic of terms, and he was farmed out in secret to a small conglomerate of belt miners who made some side money letting rookie NRI pilots in training crash their machinery for a while. He was shifted again to an agrarian/utopian colony on Ceti Z, which alleged to grow food for starving aliens under the boot of colonial authority but actually grew gengineered drugs for sale on the black market and operated as a cover for an NRI training and development unit that flew low-g crop dusters and reconfigured rescue helicopters into and out of simulated crisis situations. Ceti Z was far out and well off the galactic plane, a distant colonial experiment that attracted only those who wanted extraordinary isolation. As such, this was where Carter got his first taste of live fire and serious indoctrination. This was where he was taught not just to fly, but to kill. There were targets first—twisted metal or rag bags. Then there were the 'phants—club-footed pachyderms that traveled in herds around the ragged edges of the terraced fields. The meat that the 'phants were turned into at the business end of the trainees' guns was used to feed the settlers, the NRI staff, and the pilots. "No waste," it'd been explained to him. "It wouldn't do to waste the gift of life being offered us."

So much for the defense of species. Carter didn't know any vegetarians on Ceti Z. The meat tasted a little like he imagined frog might taste. Or lizard. Dark and oily and rank. It tasted considerably better after smoking a little of the settlers' product—a strain of cannabis kafiristancia that grew ferociously fast and was shipped in toward the hub in containers packed with thousand-pound bales—but it never tasted good.

He made it back to Sol before his twenty-first birthday and took drop training on Luna, of all places. It was a commercial course for pilots looking to become orbital certified, paid for by NRI through a shell company. Carter adopted the name Tino Vasquez for the duration and spoke as little as possible. It took a week and was the most civil time he'd experienced since leaving Midland. He thought about going AWOL (if that was even the word); of vanishing, finding passage back to Earth, trying to pick up the tatters of his old life. There was a party on the first night for the eleven pilots taking the course—cold beers and real steaks, fiddle music, potato salad, and backslapping. They were staying in a surveyor's dome—little more than an emergency shelter but compared to what Carter had become accustomed to a palace: fresh, clean oxygen, seals that didn't leak, beds that were actually beds (not repurposed pallet decking or hammocks woven from fronds), and people who didn't talk incessantly of the need for armed, violent insurrection against the tyranny of the colonial-industrial complex. Instead, they talked of paychecks and benefits packages, of their children and wives and husbands and families back on Earth or Mars or among the belters; of birthday parties and bad bosses and the weather. Carter missed his family terribly. When someone noticed him crying, he said it was a bad reaction to some antihistamines and went inside to lie down for a while.

They made drops on both the light side and the dark side of Luna, practiced emergency procedures, and sat through classroom lectures in ballistics, physics, and orbital mechanics. They learned how to plot courses and calculate falling trajectories, how to make everything go right, and how to recover when everything went wrong. Then they practiced all of it and then they ate and then they slept and then they started all over again the next day.

At the end of the week, there was another party. Everyone exchanged contact information. Carter's was all fake, but the sentiments were real. He liked these people. He would miss them. He thought again of escape but knew there was no way. NRI had retained all his real identification. He had no money, no credit. All through the final party, he'd hung close to the center of the celebration, drinking fast and hoping that someone, anyone, would ask him what was wrong. Why he had this look in his eyes like he was drowning a little bit at a time. But no one did. He hadn't become close enough to any of his classmates to just come out and ask for their help. NRI was his only ride out, his only refuge. And there was still a part of him that was a little curious about what they had in mind for him next.

Re-education. Cold tofu and protein porridge. An iron bunk welded to the bulkhead of a poorly pressurized cargo hold where he and two thousand other quote/unquote volunteers sweated out the wait before their ship could make the translation to Alpha Lyrae. Everyone was sick. Everyone had raging ear infections, bleeding from the sinuses, lung problems, DCS skin rashes, and seizures.

Carter cut his teeth in the Alamora campaign, Lyrae, on a planet called Oizys in eccentric orbit around Vega. A bare twenty-five light-years from Sol, it was a rather close thing—a jungle hell of greens and poison being logged naked by competing resource interests, none of which had any patience for one another or for NRI.

Carter flew—fast-insertion boats full of bewildered volunteers and cadre leaders and commandos and commissars, launched from orbit and falling like shooting stars through the heavy, dense atmosphere. The dropship was one of the favored transports of NRI because it allowed them to unload hundreds of protestors or soldiers or lawyers into anywhere with all the speedy shock and surprise of an orbital bombardment. And this was exactly what Carter did, delivering his human cargoes to programmed coordinates where they were hustled out, down the combat ramps in some semblance of military order, to confront the loggers and their machines with cameras rolling. Under cover of the frenzied, panicked, choking volunteers being herded by the commissars, the commandos would slip away to sabotage machinery and burn fuel dumps. The cadre leaders would take groups of volunteers in riotous charges toward armed loggers or instruct them to chain themselves to trees standing before the onrushing clear-cutting apparatus. Meanwhile, Carter would lift, return to orbit, take on another cargo and some fuel, then do it all again.

This went on for days. On his return trips, he would ferry the wounded and corpses back into orbit. He would clean the decking of his ship's bay with a high-pressure hose and, under orders, spray air freshener so those in his next load wouldn't smell the stink of blood and puke and shit and death on their way down into the grinder. The native species the NRI volunteers were allegedly protecting killed said volunteers in droves. The plants killed them. The environment killed them. It was a wonder there were any left for the human loggers and their mercenary security teams to put bullets into.

This was how NRI truly operated—a scene that would be repeated over and over again for Carter throughout the next two years. Sometimes there was more death, sometimes less. He ferried soldiers and he ferried paralegals. He delivered supplies. He made night drops on alien shores, guided in by infiltrators with IR strobe lights who, when he set down to unload whatever he was carrying, would always say something like "You didn't see nothing here, Chief. Nothing at all. You were never here."

Occasionally he fought, flying air cover or bombing missions in air-craft that could barely take to the air and were only craft at all by the loosest of definitions. Again, he didn't understand how killing anything could possibly be in sync with the goals of NRI, but he never raised a fuss about it because it never particularly bothered him. He did what he did in defense of alien species and alien planets simply because no alien had ever abandoned him or beat him or tortured him or brainwashed him. No alien had ever called him pussy or faggot or traitor or terrorist. He would defend them not because he loved them more than his fellow man, but because, at that point, he hated them slightly less.

That changed, of course, but not until Gliese 581c, called Frogtown, where he was shot down, apprehended, and incarcerated. Not until the marines came for him. Not until NRI discarded him, forgot about him, and left him to suffer and rot.

It was funny, but when he was in the mood for telling himself the truth, Carter blamed it all on the girl. A bucket of paint, a chance word, a warm smile as alien to him then as the worlds he would someday see—these were the things on which his entire life had pivoted.

And he had never forgiven her. Not even a little.

CARTER WOKE LATE AND VIC WAS ALREADY GONE. He liked her tent. It was cleaner than his, smelled nice. She had no roommate, no Fenn, no real neighbors even, save the planes and the longhouse.

He rolled over onto his back and stared up at the canvas. He thought about the girl—the artist—in a variety of savage ways and then stopped when it began to make his chest hurt. He tried to think about his brothers, his mother, but had difficulty conjuring their faces. His memories of them all felt so distant, like he was trying to imagine a family he'd never quite had but had heard described once, a long time ago.

He closed his eyes and tried to think of something specific. A concrete moment. He remembered a night that his mother, who was not a drinker at all, had come home from a party a little bit drunk and the way she had kicked her shoes off, each attended by a little whoop of joy that was so unlike her that it'd made him burn with a childish kind of happiness for her. She'd been wearing a dress made of something sparkly that looked like lightning made flat.

He thought of Jacob hunched over his drafting table, drawing pictures of airplanes and rockets, pink tongue poking out of one corner of his mouth. He tried to think of himself and Mark crouched in the short hallway just outside their shared room, peeking around the corner of the door, watching Jacob, and biting their lips to keep from laughing.

Kevin was twelve, maybe thirteen; Mark and Jacob both older. He and Mark had taken pages from Jacob's drawing tablet and replaced them with pictures of penises, testicles; of naked men sprawled clumsily on beds and smiling into invisible cameras. It'd been a joke—boys being boys, pranks passing endlessly between the brothers almost like a form of currency. And Kevin and Mark waited, breathing shallowly, watching Jacob and knowing that, sooner or later, he would have to turn the page, and then . . .

It ended up being the day he and Mark had realized Jacob was same-sex. For the longest time, Kevin had felt guilty—as though he'd somehow *turned* his brother this way, having flipped a switch in him somehow with a few scraps of paper torn from bound medical journals and porn downloaded from their home terminal. But he hadn't understood that it just didn't work that way. Watching Jacob from the doorway, seeing him reach out so gently to touch the pictures, as if they were electrified and he expected a shock; watching him look around furtively, slowly slip them free from his tablet, and carefully fold them into one of his pockets—Mark and Kevin had stared at each other open-mouthed, wide-eyed with revelation.

The next day they'd caught Jacob in the room alone and beaten him for not telling them earlier—smiling and laughing and offering their congratulations, only slightly tinged with jealousy. His life was going to be so much easier than theirs, they knew. So much less complicated, even if he became a carrier for the next generation.

And then, just like that, Carter had them again—his mother in her party dress, his brothers' faces. It was that moment that'd triggered the recall: the memory of him and Mark grabbing Jacob by the arms and shaking him, pounding him on the back, and Jacob's bewildered expression at the sudden, violent attention. He smiled in the perfumed quiet of Vic's tent, Vic's bed. He started to laugh, remembering Jacob's sputtering denials being subsumed by giggles, his fluttering hands, his finally bouncing up and down in place like he was dancing. He'd been happy, too. He'd refused to give back the pictures.

Carter's eyes teared. He squeezed his lips together. He finally had to pull one of the crumpled pillows from behind his head and press it over his face, at which point he was washed in the scent of Vic's hair, Vic's skin, and, like changing gears, his brain suddenly went in a completely different direction.

Raised voices outside, on the flight line, interrupted him. He got dressed quickly and went to see what the clamor was all about.

|||||||||||||

It was nothing. Or anyway, not much. Lefty Berthold and Lambert rolling around on the ground in front of an audience, planes scattered on the apron. Everyone was getting a little hinky from the stress, the drink, the lack of sleep. It manifested itself in strange ways. Carter watched while Emile Hardman flicked a cigarette at the two men knotted on the ground. Someone else slapped Lambert on the ass. No one moved to break the two men up until Ted was sighted striding in the direction of the flight line and then, all of a sudden, everyone did.

No one was hurt. No one could even remember what it'd been about. Carter had seen Vic from across the field and she had seen him, too. Their eyes had met and there was a jolt as from a low-grade electric shock—not as powerful as last night, but still there. They'd spent some of their charge on each other, and what they'd gotten back was less than what they'd put out.

That'd been the point, Carter thought. But he wasn't sure.

|||||||||||||

Carter flew. Carter landed. Carter flew again. Roadrunner was released from the shop after a complete overhaul and refit. Roadrunner was put back into the shop under specific orders from Ted that one of the new engines be put in her. A massive fifteen-cylinder monstrosity with turbochargers like corded muscle. Without even laying a hand on the stick, without even *seeing* her, Carter knew what the results would be. Slow to climb, hard to lift, wicked through the turns and screaming hell in a dive. Also, he thought, it would probably kill him. It was an experimental engine, and though the Flyboy engineers were good, "experimental" often meant recalcitrant, temperamental, explosive, or worse. The airframe had originally been designed for a few hundred horsepower, stabilized somewhat against the pull of the rotary. This new monstrosity would put out almost a thousand and torque enough to twist the entire plane into a giant's corkscrew.

In his off hours, Carter would try to sleep. He would read. He and Fenn would talk about nothing or just lie, in silence, and stare at the fluttering canvas, though the two of them seeing each other was rare now, one or the other of them always being up with their squadron. He'd tried once to tell Fenn about what he'd heard outside Ted's tent that night—about Ted and Eddie, the nerve gas, the conversation he'd overheard in the tent and how Ted was still fighting, still in it, counting the seconds on that clock of his like he was just waiting for Eddie to be out of his hair. It'd sounded to him like Eddie was ready to chuck it all and pull out. To run like a coward now, just when things were getting interesting. Carter'd tried to bring it up, but the moment was just never right.

He would see Vic or he wouldn't, depending on variables too complex to calculate. One day they had coffee together like two normal people, sitting across from each other at a steel mess table, holding tin cups in their hands, and smiling like they were somewhere else. Carter told her the story about him and Mark and Jacob and the penises, and she'd laughed—the sound of it seeming to push outward and form a bubble around them where nothing could go wrong. Later, they'd carried that bubble with them to bed and rolled around in it, on musty sheets in need of laundering. Vic lay with her head buried in a pillow to muffle the rough noises she made, her dark hair spread like a fan across the pale skin of her back. Carter had shoved a crate against the door so they wouldn't be interrupted. They weren't fooling anyone, but it didn't matter. They kept it up until the warmth of the two of them together beat back the cold and the damp and the war, and then they lay side by side, faceup and facedown, one of his legs thrown across one of hers, and listened to the sounds of things falling apart.

In the strange moment between dark and dawn, they were awakened by a dull, hollow booming that seemed to rattle the sky.

"Artillery?" Vic asked, rising up against the heaviness of Carter's arms and struggling free of his attempt to hold her.

"No," he said.

"You're sure?"

Carter nodded sleepily. "Orbital insertion. Supply drop, or a decelerating dropship. They're sonic booms."

"How do you know?"

"Just do."

"But you're sure?"

"I'm sure. It's not something you forget."

She settled down against him again, but stiffly. When Carter moved to spread her legs, she wouldn't be budged.

"No," she said. "Not now. Just . . ."

"Don't say it."

"Okay."

They lay with their eyes open, staring at nothing, while around them the stars fell.

| | | | | | | | | | | | |

Eight days had passed since Ted's new orders had gone into effect. Or nine. Or ten. Carter could no longer keep track and no longer cared to. He came home guns-hot or guns-cold, heavy or light. Rumors careened down the tent line like ball lightning. All talk became hard talk, and every shooting star in the night sky became an orbital drop coming in, rock-solid proof of a landing-in-force by whatever organization encompassed one's worst nightmare scenario.

One evening just on the sweet side of dusk, passing between his tent and Vic's, or maybe the flight line and the field house, Carter had stopped to watch the scything course of a ship making orbital translation. It was low to the horizon, fifteen degrees above the plane maybe, and traveling in a retrograde arc that made it appear to be fishhooking in the sky.

He caught himself counting off the cadence of insertion in his head, the sequence he'd learned from NRI and practiced a thousand-thousand times. Angle lock, deorbit burn, reaction engines prime, lock surfaces, go-for-react, primary roll . . . His hands twitched as though wanting to find again the controls to which he'd first trusted his life.

The ship on the horizon was a fast-insertion boat going through its first or second roll, one of the long S curves that would bleed off the fantastic speed it'd built up during translation. Standing there in the frozen mud, Carter tilted his head, catching a sudden phantom whiff of superheated plastics and vomit—the hundred kids in the back of his dropship all losing their lunches simultaneously as he rolled her over to eighty degrees, dropped flaps, and executed a deceleration turn at six g's, burning like an impossible comet across the sky of Oizys, Sparta, Ananke, Gliese.

Carter did a little fast math in his head to estimate a landing point and guessed at something like eighty statute miles from its current point of incidence. Close. He spit into the dirt and, silently, almost guiltily, wished the kid behind the stick a little luck.

"Don't die, you fucker," he whispered. "There's so much worse to come."

And while he spoke to the night and the sky, he saw a second bright slash mimicking the course of the first. Then a third.

Once he'd counted ten, he closed his eyes, turned, and walked away. Behind him, unseen, he could feel the lights popping like tiny fireworks all along the horizon.

| | | | | | | | | | | |

Ted had begun to flake like flint—every glancing contact on the ground splintering off sharp and razor-edged pieces. Fenn grew quiet. When Roadrunner made her second trip to the shop, Carter'd joined her briefly, thinking to help, but Vic eventually chased him out. That was her world again, alone, so he'd waited. After a certain point, Carter could barely speak without growling, something feral and wanting in his chest rising into his throat and finding no words with which to express itself. Eventually, his plane was done, and Carter found Vic again that night and wrapped himself in her, falling into a place where no words were necessary.

Stork got shot. He was wearing his gear, so it turned out okay. Later, on the ground, he picked the crumpled slugs out of his silk and arranged them on a shelf beside his bed with what Ernie O'Day, his roommate, described as way too much care. He stared at them for hours. The gun that'd tagged him got away—first failure of many to come.

Ted and Eddie fought like they were married. They fought like they wanted to kill each other and, Carter thought, they probably did.

It was all over supplies, contingencies, plans for the future. They tried to fight in private (like parents hiding dire news from the children who couldn't ever understand), but the Flyboy camp was a small place and word got around. It actually got so rough that some of the pilots started feeling bad for Eddie. Not Carter, necessarily. He'd chosen his side and on some level appreciated the viciousness with which Ted pursued his chosen enemy. But there were some who felt otherwise.

| | | | | | | | | | | | |

One night Fenn invited Eddie over to the tent for drinks just to get him out of Ted's gun sights for a couple of hours. Carter was out on a flight—he and Jack sortieing; just play-fighting, turning barrels, and climbing rolls to stay awake and keep the blood flowing in unusual directions while Tommy Hill clattered and clunked along above them in one of the horrible DH.9s. They found nothing in six hours, having done a grid-pattern search of twenty square miles above the river, then turning (against orders) toward the walls of Riverbend just before the sun went down. They'd wanted a peek was all, so took one—almost daring each other to drift closer and closer at the apex of lazy, slipping turns.

Even then, there was nothing much other than stone. In the failing light the shadows played tricks. Riverbend could've been sheltering an entire armored division and they wouldn't have been able to see it. And even if it wasn't, the quietness of it and its forbidden essence frayed their nerve until, boasting and saying how they hadn't really wanted to get any closer anyway, the three of them started for home. Below them, there was nothing but dirt, bare deciduous trees looking like skeletons reaching up for them with clacking, bony fingers, and slick patches of ice where the murky groundwater was beginning to freeze. The pilots had all started greasing up their faces against the chill slipstreams, caking on petroleum jelly along their cheekbones, their foreheads, and under their eyes. ChapStick was becoming as valuable as gold. Doc Edison had given an impromptu lecture on the dangers of frostbite one morning in the mess—a word-perfect recitation of one he'd given last year at the same time. And when it'd become plain to him that no one was listening, he'd broken off midsentence, retired to the medical tent, and etherized himself into a long slumber just for fun. He'd used starting fluid to do it—priming spray borrowed from the mechanics. He certainly had personal access to more advanced narcotics, but Edison had always had a streak of the romantic in him.

On the ground, it was brisk. Chilly. Freezing only occasionally. Up in the air, it was bone-breaking cold all the time, miserable and painful and dull, which Carter knew was the way most wars were most of the time, everywhere but in war stories.

When he came down again, Ted debriefed him.

"Anything?"

"No."

"Map grid?"

Carter rattled it off. Ted nodded.

"Sleep. You're up again in six hours."

And that was that. Carter wanted nothing more than a hot bath, a couple of large drinks, and a quick lie-down before his next turn in the rotation. He had a couple screamers in his jacket pocket—little orange pills cadged from the medical box in the field house—and he knew those would get him up and keep him that way for the duration of the six-hour dawn patrol, but he was tired now and could feel the need for sleep prickling his skin and tying weights to the nerves behind his eyes. Even the walk from the flight line to the tent line seemed impossibly long, his legs heavy and numb, his head aching. And when he finally made it, he found a lawyer in his bed, sharing a bottle with his best friend.

"Negotiating our divorce, Fenn?" he asked, pushing through the door and then shutting it tight against drafts behind him. "After all our years together?"

"Yes, Kev. I'm sorry. Your feet stink, the house is a mess, and you haven't cooked me a warm meal in months. Eddie and I were just discussing who gets custody of this bottle." He raised a half-empty jug of the local delight and shook it at Carter.

"Wait a minute," Carter said. "How'd I end up the woman here? You're lying around, sitting on your pilot's license, and drinking with Eddie while I'm out there, slaving over a hot machine gun, trying to make the galaxy safe for human exploitation. Fuck you. You're the woman. Give me that bottle."

He tossed his helmet on the bed next to Eddie. Everyone had started wearing them again. Most of the time, anyway. And he wasn't trying to hit Eddie with it, but he wasn't exactly *not* trying to either. In any event, it bounced off his back and Carter didn't feel bad about it. The lawyer wriggled over a few inches and Carter sat down hard beside him. He pushed his shoulder and Eddie moved a few more inches, until he was pressing his hip against the bed's foot rail. Carter felt like pushing him again but didn't—only because what he really wanted was something else to hit him with but could find neither the appropriate object nor the energy.

Eddie just grinned—charmed, Carter thought, by all this authentic, careless, vaguely homoerotic pilots' banter. Or maybe he was just drunk. Carter also didn't have the energy to care. The talk was all crap anyhow—variations on a theme, a riff he and Fenn had kept going for as long as Carter could remember, the thing they did with their mouths when there was nothing else worth saying. It was easier to talk than not, better than lapsing into resentful silences or just complaining all the time. It was a show. A put-on for an audience of none. Reality was nothing more than a sore back, dead legs, numb hands, aching eyes and a wicked headache that no amount of bitching would ever cure.

"Machine guns?" Fenn asked. "You and Jacky find something?"

Carter waved a hand dismissively. "Figure of speech." He hung his head and pinched the greasy bridge of his nose between his fingers. "Six hours over target and we didn't see shit. Tommy was falling asleep at the stick when we landed." He cracked his neck and saw spots exploding in the darkness. Then he started patting down his pockets for cigarettes. "Why aren't you up right now? Didn't you have a two/one this afternoon?"

"Scrubbed." Fenn shrugged. "Ted's orders."

Carter snorted. "How long you have to spend on your knees each day to get favors like that?"

"Less than you'd think, darling." He passed the bottle across the gap between their beds. "Drink. You'll feel better."

Carter took it, drank, didn't. Twisting against the bed rail, Eddie held out a pack of cigarettes, and Carter extracted one dubiously. "You don't smoke," he said to the lawyer.

Eddie smiled wanly, something lost and sick about it. "I started. I don't think I have to worry about them killing me at least."

Carter turned, raised an eyebrow at Fenn, then turned back around and snatched the rest of the pack out of Eddie's soft hand. "You don't get to talk that way," he snapped. Then he threw the pack back at him hard, bouncing it off his chin, scattering perfect, white, manufactured cigarettes in the dirt.

Eddie flinched back, wide-eyed. Carter looked back at Fenn. "He doesn't get to talk that way. Tell him. Not in this house."

"Throttle back, Captain," Fenn said calmly. He lifted his chin in the direction of the bottle. "Take your medicine."

Eddie started collecting cigarettes off the ground.

Carter had another drink, set the bottle in the dirt. "Fucking desk pilot," he said to the top of Eddie's head. "I heard you, you know. The other night. In Ted's tent."

"What other night?" Eddie asked.

For a hanging second, Carter had to think how to answer that question, then shook his head and snapped, "Don't try to fucking confuse me! The other night. You were in there crying about finding a way off this rock. Trying to run. Trying to talk Ted into letting us catch a ride with some smuggler." He lit his cigarette with Fenn's lighter. "Whining little pussy."

"That isn't the way it happened at all," Fenn said.

"It was. I was listening. I was going to tell you about it, Fenn, but . . ."

"That's not the way it's happening," Eddie seconded.

Carter whirled on the lawyer. "Fuck you, Eddie. I heard you. I saw you. I saw Ted. We have a job to do here and he's trying to do it, and you're trying to run? You're a fucking chickenshit coward." Carter

slapped at the pack of cigarettes in Eddie's hand again but failed to con-
nect, so shoved him instead. "A fucking lawyer!"

"Shut up, Kev." Fenn was fiddling with the bottle's cork, absently
picking it apart with his fingers. Eddie had his head down.

"You defending him now?" Carter asked, turning back to Fenn.

"No. I'm just telling you to shut up or leave."

"So you're throwing me out now?" It was no longer a joke. "Because
of him?"

"I invited him, Kevin. Be nice."

Carter took a deep breath. He and Fenn had fought only once the
whole time they'd lived together, which was really saying something,
considering the closeness of the quarters and the amount of time they'd
both spent in them. Regardless, Fenn had beaten Carter pretty completely. They didn't talk about it, but it was there—a solid truth of their
relationship. It'd taken Carter a week to recover. And right before, Fenn
had had a look on his face like he had now, watching Carter from his
rack. Not anger, but just the absence of his usual levity. A look with
some real cold, dead weight behind it.

That first fight had been about good manners among houseguests,
too, if Carter remembered correctly—a particular pet peeve of Fenn's.
And for a moment, Carter thought about making a go at his friend
again, on principle, because he didn't like that look much at all and
didn't like how Fenn leveled it at him like a gun across Fast Eddie's
back.

He decided against it, though. He was too tired, and fighting over
Eddie seemed like a ridiculous thing to do anyhow. But he let Fenn
know that he *had* been considering it before he looked away. Maybe he
would've had a go had the hour been earlier, had he not already been
hurting enough.

"Sorry," he said. "Long day is all."

Fenn nodded. Eddie popped back up between them and clapped a
hand on Carter's shoulder. "It's been a long day for everyone, Carter.
That's okay."

And friends or no friends, manners or no manners, Carter could've
choked him just then. So priggish. So terribly, terribly stupid. He was
already bringing his hands up to do it.

But Fenn was on the verge of laughing as he reached over and removed Eddie's hand from Carter as quickly and delicately as if he were picking up someone else's underwear, and Carter had never been able to not laugh when Fenn did.

"Oh, I don't think you want to do that, Eddie," Fenn said, fighting down a smile he couldn't quite bury.

And Carter's anger fizzled like a fuse pinched off. "Yeah, you really don't," he said, smothering a grin of his own behind his hand as he took a long drag off Eddie's cigarette.

"Sorry," said Eddie. "I just—"

"Yeah, don't." Carter edged back a little on the bed and took another drag. He looked away from Eddie. He bit his lip.

"So," asked Fenn. "Nothing from nothing then, Kev? No action?"

"None," he said. "Quiet as anything. We were thinking about bombing Connelly just to get some fun started."

"Oh, Connelly's not out there right now," Eddie said brightly. All of a sudden, Carter wondered how old he was. So expertly preserved, he could've been anything from twenty to sixty, easy. His skin was smooth as a girl's, mouth a perfect little bow. Eddie motioned to the bottle at Carter's feet and Carter handed it to him warily. Eddie took it with both hands like a baby, had a good swallow, passed it along to Fenn, who gave Carter a little nod in Eddie's direction as if to say, *Listen close.*

"He's in here," Eddie continued, dabbing at the corners of his mouth with his fingertips. "At the field house with Ted, I think. That's what we were talking about before you came in."

"Not possible," Carter said. "Saw Ted when I landed. Did a debrief."

"Full debrief?" Eddie asked.

"Full as they ever get now. Twenty words maybe."

"In the field house?"

"On the apron."

Eddie nodded. "Connelly's there. Ted was stopping you before you came in. Diverting you."

Carter looked at Fenn, who just shrugged and lifted the bottle to his lips. It was red wine they were drinking, though only by the loosest of definitions. Locally made, it was closer to fruity, red liqueur with a sweetness like rotting mangoes and a kick like a mule. It'd been a favorite of the indig officers before they all left, an acquired taste for sure. Carter knew that you had to be careful with it and either drink it slow so you didn't go out of your head or fast so you didn't care.

He took the bottle from Fenn again. "He serious?" he asked, meaning Eddie.

"No. Eddie's too short to be taken seriously. But he is correct. Connelly is here. I saw him walking across the field myself, six of his natives with him, all decked out like he was late for a costume ball." Fenn gestured grandly at all the wrack and clutter of the tent and present company. "Hence this little garden party. I figured Eddie could use a break from getting screamed at."

"Oh, I'm accustomed," Eddie interrupted. He turned and looked straight at Carter. "No one likes lawyers, right, Captain?"

Carter opened his mouth, but before he could say anything, Fenn continued. "Also, I was thinking that if we got him drunk enough, he might be able to let slip some of the family secrets. So tell us, Edward." Fenn leaned forward with a leering smile. "What do you know?"

"Eden," said Eddie.

"Excuse me?" Fenn's smile went crooked, then vanished. For an instant there was a look on his face like Eddie'd said some kind of secret word.

"Eden. That's my first name. Not Edward. My parents were . . ."

"High?" Carter offered, smiling to himself at his wit.

"Different," Eddie said. "They were settlers. Pioneer family. They settled three different colony worlds before I was born, helped found one of them. I was first-born at Serenity, on Challos, and the tradition was to name every first child Eden."

"Missionaries," Carter said, thinking of his mother.

"No. Mormons. A Dominionist sect. Pretty common outside Sol."

"Mormons don't smoke," Carter said.

"Or drink," added Fenn.

"I took my manumission at eighteen and went to law school on Earth. London, actually. Never looked back."

The three of them were silent for a minute. Carter found it somewhat more difficult to dislike Eddie now that he knew something about him. Now that he knew they had something vaguely in common. He still hated him but had to work a little harder at it, which was forever the problem in getting to know the enemy.

"Well," Fenn finally said. "Not the kind of family secrets I was talking about, but if a man is willing to admit to a name like Eden, I think the drink has done its job."

"Not yet," Eddie said. He took the bottle and tipped it in Fenn's direction. "Here's to damnation." He drank deeply. Carter thought to tell him to take it easy, to be careful, but he bit his tongue. When Eddie was done, he gasped, cleared his throat loudly, and passed the bottle along to Fenn, who rolled its squat neck thoughtfully between his palms.

Once he'd recovered the power of speech, Eddie asked, "Have you seen Connelly lately, Captain?"

Carter thought for a second. "Not since . . . No. Not for a while. Months, at least."

"He's gone a bit around the bend, I think. Captain Teague saw him. He can tell you."

"Gone bwana," Fenn said, his eyes focused on something else. "Long gone. He was always a little bit, uh . . . *close*, you know? To his indigs. But now it's something different."

"He orders the Akaveen around like dogs. 'Sit here,' 'Stand there,' and every time he gives an order, they do the clap-and-bow thing for him like he was one of their own. Like they've adopted him."

"Looks it, too," Fenn added distantly. "Filthy. Hairy. Always lumped up in a pile of his officers. Paints up his face. Carries a big stick with all this junk hanging off—beads and batteries and shell casings and chicken bones. I don't know."

Eddie nodded. "He's big magic these days. Talks just like a native—far better than I do. He forgets himself midsentence and just starts going on. That really pissed Ted off."

"You were in there with them?" Carter balled up his two thin pillows behind his back and reclined as best he could. He could already feel the liquor working its evil voodoo, a warm, liquid numbness licking at the edges of all his aches, leaching the spite out of him like drawing deep splinters out of his skin.

"For over an hour," Eddie said. "They were——"

Fenn held up a hand to shush him. For a second, Carter couldn't hear anything. Then he could. It was the buzzing of another flight coming home.

"Is that first squadron?" Carter asked.

"Too early," Fenn whispered. "It's the two/three, I think. Lefty, Charlie, and Stork."

"They're late."

Fenn nodded and all three of them waited, heads cocked as they listened for the engines to roar over the tent line so they could count them. The fire was crackling in the potbelly, the lantern light guttering. It was a slow approach and there was the sensation of the entire camp waiting, breath held, silent, until the communal exhalation—one, two, three, everyone home safe. They could breathe again, and did.

Eddie'd waited politely, his eyes pinballing back and forth between Fenn and Carter as the drink settled into him. Fenn had gotten up and gone to the door, standing poised, waiting still—looking out into the dark and listening for the scramble siren, for raised voices, signs, omens, perturbations in the false calm of the night like vibrations in a high-tension wire. He was tall, Fenn was. With one hand resting on the scrap-wood lintel of the door, he was able to lay his forehead against his knuckles—a pose as old as worry.

Carter silently motioned for Eddie to continue. He was waiting, too; had edged forward on the bed until his feet were on the ground again, one hand stuck inside his jacket, caught searching for another cigarette and frozen that way. Iaxo had no crickets, but Carter imagined their chirping anyway, overlaying memories of a familiar night's silence over this wholly unnatural one.

"They're cutting a deal," Eddie said, voice low, almost conspiratorial. "Ted and Connelly. You didn't hear right in the tent that night, Captain. Not completely. It's not just me trying to get us out of here. The *commander*," he said, singing the word mockingly, "is convinced that we're going to be overrun any minute and wants to be able to defend the airfield." He started picking at the filters of the cigarettes he'd stuck back into his pack, inexpertly trying to extract one. Carter, his hand breaking free of its entropic ice, took the pack from him, slapped it against his knee, and took out two cigarettes. He handed one to Eddie, who placed it delicately between his lips with all the grace of someone for whom the action still felt somewhat awkward. He nodded his thanks and began fussing with a Zippo lighter. "Not that I blame him, actually," he added awkwardly, around the filtertip in his mouth. "He's probably right, too."

"We're going to be overrun?" Fenn asked from the door. The wind blowing in around him was positively frigid, seeming to suck the blasting heat right out of the stove glowing in the center of the tent.

Eddie leaned forward, blinking away the smoke that curled directly into his eyes. "Actually, if the Lassateirra really want this place, they can pretty much take it whenever they want. What've we got to stop them, really?"

"Ten thousand friendlies and forty miles between them and us," Carter said. He thought about Ted in the mess tent. *Gas the fuckers and go home.*

"And nine thousand nine hundred of them armed with sticks and stones, concentrated mostly on the flanks of the line, who'll run away the minute someone comes at them shooting. And with Garcia moved out, once the Lassateirra cross the river, there's nothing at all between them and us but *us*. Fourteen planes if we put every pilot in the air at once. The fight would be over in a day. Maybe less. And we'd lose. Bet on it." Eddie grinned with a sudden, dark humor that didn't suit him and looked, in fact, almost like a soldier's—albeit a different sort of soldier. "Matters of consequence, right? I know because I did the calculations for Loewenhardt at corporate. I gave us a thirty percent chance of holding out at this location for another month if the Lassateirra are being supplied now through foreign contractors. And I was being optimistic. Assuming every best possible break in our favor. Past thirty days, our odds drop off rather precipitously."

"They have, what? Actuarial tables for this kind of thing?"

Eddie nodded. "I wrote them."

Carter and Fenn lapsed into another silence then. Eddie smoked inexpertly and, for the moment, Carter decided to forgive him for what he'd first seen as a pretender's affectation toward toughness. Those were rough numbers. Heavy dope that Eddie'd been carrying around alone, in his head, and, in them, there was death the same as in any bomb or machine gun. Worse, they described his own life and possible fate as accurately as they did the pilots'. They did not discriminate between the pilot in his plane, the controller in the tent, the lawyer behind his desk. It occurred to Carter that the actual difference here was that Eddie had already fought their battles for them, seen them (and himself) lose seven times out of ten. He'd seen himself die in a pie chart, on a table, as a statistical abstract.

Carter hoped Eddie was bad at his job, but probably he wasn't. If there was one thing Flyboy was good at, it was hiring damnably competent men. But because he didn't know, he asked.

"Eddie, are you bad at your job?"

"You know, it's funny. I've been asking myself that same thing all day."

Quiet returned to the night. Down on the field, engines died with a sputter. The dark swallowed voices. Carter thought again about home and remembered, all in an instant, the lay of his childhood and his house and his brothers' rooms and how it felt to walk in the night through a place he'd known since birth, to be warm and safe and protected on all sides, and to feel the comforting wisdom of knowing every step before he took it. He thought about what he'd traded for that. What he'd lost in the exchange.

"Well," said Fenn from the doorway. "Well."

"Sorry," Eddie said. "You wanted the family secrets."

"Sobering thought." Carter stood and started working his way out of his gear, fumbling with the buckles, his fingers gone stupid with shock.

"Poor choice of words." Fenn stepped away from the door, and it blew shut with a bang, loud in the hushed gloom. "Should we be expecting any help from on high?"

Eddie opened his little mouth, then shut it again with a snap. For a moment, he seemed to be considering his answer, which, to Carter, meant debating whether or not to lie. Carter unstrapped the pump from his arm and bent his elbow back and forth, running his fingers over the sore places. He unbuckled his belt and dropped it, clattering, onto the bed.

"Do you really want to know this?" Eddie finally asked, his voice having taken on something of a plaintive tone. And he held up a hand to stall off the obvious response. "I mean, I know. I *have* to know. It's my job. Ted knows and, Captain Carter, you've seen what it's done to him. But you don't have to know."

Fenn looked at Carter. He dropped his jacket on the bed behind him and rolled his shoulders. "We had a moment," Carter said to him, shaking his head and remembering Ted's eyes in the mess, the way he'd jinked his face in front of Carter's every time Carter'd tried to look away. *Gas the fuckers. Let 'em choke.* "There was never a good time to tell you about it. Anyway, it was nothing."

"Nothing's nothing, pilot."

Carter shook his head again. Redheaded Irene and solitaire with a deck missing an ace. An unwinnable game. "Let it go."

"You don't have to know," Eddie continued. "It's like flipping ahead in a book and reading the last page. Knowing doesn't change anything. The story still goes the same way." Sitting on the edge of the bed, he looked almost pleadingly now at Fenn, stepping carefully across the floor toward the stove, now at Carter, standing in front of him. "You can do your jobs perfectly well without knowing, is all I'm saying."

He squirmed a little. Fenn stared at him unblinkingly. Carter did the same, pinning him there on the bed like a bug.

"We can talk about something else." His cigarette was burned out, forgotten, between his fingers. "Anything else."

Because in war stories, that's what men do. Pictures of sweethearts, stories of home. Carter unclipped his dog collar, pulled his shirt off over his head. He had no sweetheart. This was his home. The whole time he'd been in prison, no one had visited. His parents had never written once. Neither had his brothers. He imagined their thoughts, how, as far as they were concerned, he'd died on a poster somewhere. In a photograph. On the news. An embarrassment and a failure and now, hardly even a memory. It'd been twenty years.

Eddie looked from Fenn to the door to Carter to the door to Fenn again. "Eden, right? What a ridiculous name." He laughed weakly.

"So, Eden," Fenn said slowly, "should we be expecting any help from on high?"

Eddie's face hardened. "I know what you all think of me," he said. "I mean, I'm not stupid."

Carter sighed and sat down beside him. He started working on his boots. "Eddie, none of us have really thought about you much at all."

And Eddie laughed—one short, sharp bark. "None," he said. "No help. And no ride home." He slapped his hands down onto the mattress, palms flat, dust and hair and dead skin puffing up around them. "Is that what you want to know? Two years we've been here, you fucking idiots. More. And what have you done? Drank, smoked, walked around like arrogant pricks in your uniforms. We had native support, and you chased them off. We had will on our side, and you squandered it. You had planes, bombs, machine guns, computers, everything. Everything the company could give you. And what did you do with it all? You *lost*! To a bunch of cavemen! This mission should've been over in three months, but what? You were all having too much fun, weren't you? Playing soldier. Acting like all of this was so awful, so *hard* on you because you didn't have the right movies or climate control or whores and ice cubes for your drinks? You are all fucking *embarrassments*! I've spent every day—every goddamn day for two years—talking to corporate, telling them how well we've been doing, how we're worshipped by the natives, how we're winning every day. But you have accomplished *nothing*."

"Hey, Eddie . . ." Fenn started forward, a calming hand extended. Carter sat frozen, hunched over, his boot half-off. Fast Eddie was coming unstuck right in front of him. He found it fascinating.

"No," he said, pointing a finger at Fenn, which was not a smart thing to do under the best of circumstances. "You wanted to hear this, Captain. Now you're going to hear it. Every other military contractor has been pulled out on this continent. All of them. If the Akaveen lines collapse, which they will, or if the Lassateirra break through at some point and come our way, the company is looking at a one hundred percent material loss. It's already been written off in the next quarter's projections—materials, death benefits, legal, everything. And it's not like we're talking about a lot of materials or anything. A bunch of antique planes, a few engines, a few guns—that's nothing. The comms equipment and flight control are worth a few dollars. So is the equipment in the longhouse and the machine shop. But even with everything put together, the company has spent ten times more shipping everything here than all the stuff is actually worth. Subtract two years of depreciation, factor in a nice, fat insurance bond payout, outstanding costs amortized, and the seven years it will take before any personal compensations are paid to your next-of-kin because none of us will actually *die* on paper, just be listed as missing, pending investigation. In the next shareholder report, Flyboy will take a small financial hit, which it will spread over several quarters, passing along any losses to its investors and future clients, while we are all forgotten as quickly and completely as possible. Buried. Carter thinks I'm such a coward, but he hasn't had to watch the commander listening in on the radios as everyone else has left. We're under communications blackout, but Carter hasn't had to try and stop Ted from calling up the company every night and screaming at them for nerve gas or new planes or a recovery mission. Ted has lost his mind, Captain. It's mush. Gone. He finds me in my tent and demands cruise missiles, for God's sake! A boat! He asked me for a *boat*! He's the one that's been trying to find us a ride off-planet with one of the other companies, but he couldn't manage it. He is *useless*! And we are now officially a lost cause because you pilots couldn't turn a thousand-year technological advantage into a victory. And do you know what I spent last night doing?"

Eddie looked around. No one said a word.

"Writing letters to your families, describing the unfortunate circumstances of your deaths in our employment. Apologizing on behalf of the company for your tragic losses. Saying how brave and hardworking you all were and explaining how all benefits would be withheld until the conclusion of a standard investigation. But you know what the real kick was? I got to write my own, too. Addressed to my wife and daughter. You smart bastards killed me the same as you did yourselves." He dropped his cigarette, crushed it under his heel. "Nice work. Any more questions? No? Good." He shot to his feet, none too steadily. Neither Fenn nor Carter moved to help him. "I think I'm leaving now. Thanks for the hospitality, Captains. This was just what I needed, you know? Drinks with some friends. First time in two years you could be bothered to ask. Instead of me . . . you know . . . in my tent with everything."

Eddie made no move to leave. Carter and Fenn made no moves at all.

"Okay," Eddie said. "I'm going to sit back down for a minute."

He did, and heavily.

"Jesus, that wine packs a punch."

"Yeah," said Fenn, approaching gingerly, like Eddie was a wounded animal, a ticking bomb. "It'll get right up on you if you're not careful."

Carter quickly kicked off his boots and moved clear of the area of effect in case Mormon Eddie decided to blow. He stripped off his jumpsuit to the waist, pulled off the catheter and (empty) bag, reached beneath his bed for a filthy rollneck sweater and put it on.

"Sorry, guys," Eddie said. "I'd leave if I could, but I can't feel my legs. I just need a minute."

Fenn looked at Carter behind Eddie's head and Carter shrugged, wide-eyed. He didn't know what to do with him. He certainly didn't want Eddie puking in his bed. This night was turning into something quite different than what he'd expected.

"Uh, that's fine, Eddie. Just . . ." *Don't puke; don't puke; don't puke.* "Just take it easy, all right?" Carter looked up again and growled at Fenn, jerked his head in Eddie's direction as if to say, *Do something!* What, he had no clue.

Fenn shook his head. He stepped close, laid a hand on Eddie's shoulder, crouched down, asked if he could get him anything.

"You're not going to hit me, are you?" Eddie asked.

"Why would I hit you?"

"Because of what I said?"

Fenn laughed. Carter laughed because Fenn laughed. Eddie looked up with unfocused eyes and an expression strung out somewhere between misery and mystification. "What's funny?" he asked.

"Family secrets," Fenn said, picking his words like he was choosing his steps through a minefield. "The thing with them is, they're never really secret." He looked across at Carter and motioned for him to speak, opening and closing his thumb and fingers like a duck quacking.

"Yeah," Carter said, still looking at Fenn. "Right. I mean, I don't know if I've ever had my worth spelled out for me quite that way, but I've heard that speech . . ."

"Or something like it," Fenn added.

"Right. Something close. I don't know, two or three times at least."

"A half dozen easy."

It came easier now, a flood of words—anything to delay the inevitable, to talk down and beg a moment of grace from Eddie vomiting, sure, but also from death, because Eddie had just killed them. Eddie had just drawn a hidden, secret gun and painted the stinking canvas walls with their brains.

"Worthless pilots. A bunch of drunks and fuckups. Doom and gloom from the company."

"Heard it from Ted just yesterday."

"Got the same thing on Proxima Three when things started going bad there."

"Palas," Fenn said. "Barson's World. It's always the same."

But still, there was a moment. Between the snap of the hammer and the terrible impact. There was a moment when the bullet was in flight, and that moment could be forever. It could be extended, warped. Death came, but it was flexible. They were dead and they knew they were dead, but it hadn't happened *yet*. The bullet was in flight. It was coming. Seven chances out of ten. They talked to expand the distance. To buy time because there were still things to say, stories to tell.

"Oh, but you were eloquent, Eddie. Don't get me wrong. I mean, that was a good speech."

"Top-notch."

"But if you've been holding this in all this time?"

"Yeah, if you've been trying to, like, protect us or whatever?"

"That's sweet of you, really, but—"

"But we've been written off more times than we can count."

Eddie blinked a couple of times, his eyes clearing. "Really?" he asked.

The two pilots bobbed their heads like they were on springs. They smiled like they were being forced at gunpoint. *Totally, Eddie. Absolutely, Eddie. Nothing at all to worry about, Eddie.*

And Eddie folded like an envelope, collapsing forward into his own arms, his head resting on his knees as he hugged himself. And he stayed that way for a good five minutes—maybe weeping, maybe not—while Fenn and Carter had a silent, mimed argument over the back of his neck about what they were supposed to do now.

"Uh, Eddie?" Carter asked. "Now that we've got this little problem cleared up . . ."

He didn't move.

"Eddie?" Fenn tried.

"Is he asleep?"

"No," Eddie said. "I'm not."

"You okay down there then?"

"Yeah." He straightened up slowly. His eyes were red-rimmed, his nose running. Eddie was most certainly a weeper. "I'm okay. Thanks." He smiled, and the snot trickled down like the handlebars of a mustache.

And then Carter and Fenn both said, "Good man," and "All right," and slapped Eddie on the shoulder like men do, but they weren't quite finished with Fast Eddie just yet.

Seven chances out of ten.

"So, okay," Fenn said once Eddie had repaired himself somewhat with his sleeve and a handkerchief he'd produced from somewhere and the two pilots had spent a minute silently slapping at each other, shoving each other into the honor of being the first to reopen the breach. "Now, I know what you've heard from the company, and Ted and I know you've had to do some pretty awful things recently."

"Terrible things."

"Just hard, terrible things and all."

"Which is, like, rough. We know."

"Right. And had we known what you were having to do in there, in your tent, we would've totally bought you a cocktail or two at the O Club."

"Absolutely would've."

"But now seriously, Eddie. What do you think the home office is *really* thinking. You, Eddie Lucas. What do *you* think?"

Carter butted in, glaring across the top of Eddie's head at Fenn, who, in his opinion, was tromping all over the delicate approach. "Fenn means what they're not telling you, Eddie. Knowing what you know now—like that we've heard all this before and how they're really not just going to completely abandon us here. What do you think their first move will be?"

"Well," Eddie said, straightening up and slipping a little blearily back into good-time-lawyer mode. "I mean, with that in mind. With that good news—and it really is good news. *Good,* good news. And I can't tell you just how good and great and . . ."

Eddie's wheels were spinning. Fresh tears hung from his pretty eyelashes like ripe fruit. "My daughter, you know? It's going to be . . ." He coughed, reached up, and screwed his small fists into his eyes, cursed at himself, and rallied. "Okay . . . Okay, look. I know they're not sending any more supplies. These new complications . . ." He coughed again, and Carter lit him a fresh cigarette out of Eddie's own pack, which he'd already pocketed while Eddie was resting and crying. "This new information we have—the foreign supplies and lack of success we've had thus far—means two things for sure. First, the company is not going to spend *more* money shipping more worthless equipment to what is beginning to look, to them, like a lost-cause mission. And two, they're certainly not going to pay to have all this antique junk pulled out of here. Easier to just lose us, you know? Like, on paper. To let NRI and the marines wipe away any trace that we were ever here. Deny that we were operating on behalf of the company." He shrugged. "Ted's been screaming at me for everything from a wing of A-40 Scorpions to nerve gas, as you well know, Captain." He winked at Carter, which was just weird. "And I've done all the rationalizing and begging I can do. It's just not going to happen. This last supply drop, on Christmas? That was scheduled and paid for six months ago. It arrived early, but it will be the last. That much I know for sure. The numbers just don't add up any other way. Ted and I received final orders from corporate ops that same night—the communications blackout, the news that there was no recovery mission planned. And then there was a confirmation a day later where we were told, like . . . I don't know. Sit here and play with ourselves."

"Okay," Carter said. "So tell me why we don't just throw in the towel and pull out now?"

Fenn answered for Eddie. "Because there's still a thirty percent chance things might go our way, isn't there? According to Mr. Fast Eddie's calculations. And a thirty percent chance is better than a guaranteed loss any day."

"Captain Teague is correct," Eddie said, making a gun out of his fingers and firing a round at Fenn, making a popping sound with his lips. He was slurring now, just enough to be noticeable. And his eyes seemed to have come unstuck in their sockets, rolling slowly skyward whenever Eddie wasn't paying close attention. "That's what I've been able to determine since then, talking with some people. The company cannot afford to get itself involved in a fight with NRI or the Colonial Council, so they've made it look like we're operating here without corporate control. If we all die here, there's nothing that'll make them legally liable. But there is still a chance that things could swing our way. And then we'd be heroes. 'Heroes, Eddie.' That's what one of them said to me. Someone from somewhere . . . Because with no other military contractors operating here, most of the continent would be Flyboy's for the taking. It puts our negotiators in a very strong position. It really is as simple as that."

"Right," said Carter. "Simple."

"The only thing we've got going for us," Eddie continued, "is that the Lassateirra would have to fight their way across the river, then march forty miles from there to here while being shot up and bombed by everything we've got the whole way. I figure that gives us maybe two days, two and a half, from the moment we know the Lassateirra have begun to move against us until the end actually comes. If it all goes bad. So that's two days for a smuggler or a blockade runner, a transport to get here, transition, land and pull us out. That is *if* there's one in range, *if* he or she can be talked into doing it. If, if, if . . . I make our odds on that long but not impossible."

"How long?" Carter asked.

Eddie lost control of his eyes again, pupils running for his perfect hairline. For a minute, he said nothing. His tongue, stained purple from the wine, poked from the corner of his mouth. Fenn and Carter had another frantic, silent conference—all pointing and eyebrows and mouthed obscenities.

"Ten-to-one," Eddie finally said. "But that's just a round . . . uh . . ."

"Guess?"

"A round guess. Exactly. I have certain, uh . . . Under extraordinary circumstances, I have certain powers and freedoms to make executive decisions. Ted and me together. There are orders and *abilities,* yes, to call in a recovery mission and to pay for it out of a fund. Gold or something. I have orders. But anyway, like you guys said, it doesn't matter, right? The company will come for us. You guys have never been abandoned before, right? Because you said. You said they're not going to just bury us here."

Sure, they said. *Absolutely, Eddie. Nothing at all to worry yourself over, Eddie. Happens all the time.*

And then, as quickly as the words had come to them, they dried up. Silence rushed back in to fill the vacuum. Carter touched his throat. Fenn brought a hand up to touch his forehead, to scratch an itch just below his hairline. He seemed surprised when his fingers didn't come back bloody. They were dead. Everything else was just waiting.

"This is probably why no one invites insurance adjusters to nice parties," Fenn said under his breath. Eddie laughed wetly. Carter didn't at all. He asked about Ted and Connelly—what they'd been talking about, why they were meeting. This had been the original topic of conversation before they'd become sidetracked by the scrying of actuaries, the pie-chart war in poor Eddie's head.

"A trade," Eddie said, chin bobbing and lips bubbling wetly as he spoke. His eyes were like fat glass beads now, pushed into a doughy face. When he closed them, he looked like a waxwork, something from the lawyer museum. "His help at what he's good at for ours at what we do . . ." He faded for a moment, lips pursed, pecking kisses at the air, but he pulled up again. "Connelly is smart, you know? Dumb but smart. He sees this whole whatever same as Ted and me. The lines—unbalanced in the middle, going to fold at the first sign of trouble. Connelly wants to go in and take Southbend now. Immediately. Before things get worse. Says that drops are coming in on the moors. Delivery. Off-world. We don't know because we can't see, but Connelly has scouts. Spies. The Akaveen . . . They want Riverbend worse. They're massing there, leaving Connelly with just his natives and a small holding force to the south, but he wants to make a move anyway, under air cover. Bombers to breach the walls. Ted, though. Ted is just, *whoo* . . ." Eddie laughed and buzzed the palm of his hand over his head, eyes blowing out wide like valves opening straight into his skull. "Ted wants some defense on the ground. He wants something standing in front of him when the bad guys arrive. They're making a deal. Us in the air for Connelly's second company here as a security force. Also, Connelly wants a safe place to receive an orbital drop. Ted's offering the airfield in exchange for a cut. Just arguing over how big a share. That's what they were doing when the captain here . . ." Eddie pointed to the stove. "Here." He corrected, pointing to the door. "Came to my rescue with your tricky custody battle to resolve." He smiled softly then, and Carter felt as though he could almost see the weeks of worry vaporizing through the pickets of his teeth. Rage spent, fears allayed. Now Eddie was just shitfaced. "Hope my services were beneficial to you guys. Okay if I take a nap here?"

"Not in my bed, counselor," Carter said.

"Good enough." In a gentlemanly fashion, Fast Eddie Lucas stood, dipped from the waist in a sketched bow, then fell over—asleep before he hit the dirt.

"Christ," Fenn said. "Now everyone's going to think we killed him."

Their laughter was loud enough to wake the dead. The drunk, however, slept on undisturbed.

| | | | | | | | | | | | |

This was later. A few minutes. An hour.

"So," Fenn said, leaning back against the door frame. He'd put his jacket on, collar turned up, his cheeks buried in its fur. The cold was bitter. "What do you think?"

"It's not good," Carter said. He hugged himself, hands buried in his armpits, rollneck sweater pulled to his nose, muffling his words.

"Not good at all."

"No."

Inside, they'd banked the fire. Carter had taken a musty blanket from his foot locker and thrown it over poor, inebriated Eddie, then grabbed Cat from its pile of rags by the door—catching the little monster by the back of the neck while it was still half-asleep—and had tried to hold it, balled up in his sweater for warmth and to keep Cat from murdering Eddie.

Cat was having none of it, though, and had clawed free, hit the ground spitting, and bolted for the door. It huddled ten feet off and stared at Carter and Fenn in the cold, just waiting to be allowed back inside. He and Fenn had followed Cat outside for a breath of air and to clear their own heads. Carter'd kept the lawyer's cigarettes and was smoking them now through a hole in the neck of his sweater, one after another.

"I think we shouldn't tell anyone just yet."

"Agreed."

"I would desert if I thought there was anywhere to go."

"I think that's all part of the plan." Fenn plucked the cigarette from Carter's mouth-hole, took a drag, planted it back amid the cabled wool. When he spoke, he exhaled thunderheads. "Leaving us with no options but to soldier."

"Damn sneaky if you ask me."

Fenn nodded.

"So, was any of what you told Eddie true?"

"You mean . . ."

Carter nodded.

"God, no. We won at Palas and on Barson's World. I shipped home with everyone else, sitting on my bonus payout. You?"

Carter shook his head. "Proxima was a wash after we switched sides. Spent six months plastering the place from a transorbital bomber, flew home on an Argo-Stanislav freighter after the truce. This is bad, though."

"True enough."

"Could still go our way. If Connelly attacks, diverts the Lassateirra. If NRI supplies don't make it into the field fast enough. If the marines stay away or the council ignores the NRI request. It could go our way."

Heroes, Eddie . . .

"Could," Fenn agreed.

"But it won't."

Fenn shook his head. "No."

Carter thought about the ships he'd seen the other night. The hooks of light on the horizon. He'd meant to tell Fenn about them, but hadn't. Everyone had seen something similar anyway. He'd meant to tell Fenn about NRI. About what they would do when they got here in force. The shock. The death. Cameras rolling while poor scared kids came tumbling out the back of dropships and veterans pressed grenades and pulse rifles into the hands of every native who reached. But he hadn't. No time. Or something.

"Look, I've been told by plenty of bosses what a fuckup I am," Carter said. "None have ever conspired to leave me for dead before. Eddie's got to be wrong."

Except that wasn't true either.

"Don't start believing your own propaganda, Kev. That's dangerous business. It's a lot of money on the line. A lot of legal troubles and bad press. I can see Eddie's point. It would be a lot simpler for all concerned if the whole bunch of us just disappeared one day."

"Well, not *all* concerned. I'd be pretty pissed about it."

"It's about the money, Captain. I think maybe it's cheaper for the company just to let us die."

"Bright and shiny, Fenn. Love the way you think. Really."

Fenn shrugged. Coming out of the dark, they heard the crunching of a native post horse approaching, its big, clubby feet crackling on the scrim of ice that'd formed, like walking over broken glass. They watched as it came on down the line of tents and crossed right before them, its rider upright in the saddle, reins held loosely, eyes like black pools—wet and reflective.

It watched them as its horse picked its way along, head down, swaying slightly. Fenn noted the loop of charms around its wrist—shell casings, buttons, a braided wire, a battery—and the way it seemed made of a single creature, the horse and its rider, each perfectly suited to the other. Carter saw the rifle in its scabbard of stitched plastic sheeting, the scraps of ballistic cloth sewn into a pathetic barding for the horse's barrel chest, and himself reflected in the absolute dispassion of the indig's gaze as it went by. The creature did not bow or scrape. It did not smile or move to clap its hands or look away. It simply watched, as though the captains were stones or clouds or something less, and only once it was past them did it make a sound—a breathy hiss in the back of its throat that might've been a command to the horse or might've not.

"That one of ours?" asked Carter, once horse and rider had vanished again into the swallowing dark.

"Oh, good," said Fenn. "You saw it, too."

Carter thought of a question he'd never asked Fenn before. Same as a question Fenn had never asked him.

"Fenn, what did you do before you joined the company?"

Fenn smiled and stared off in the general direction of the horizon. "Nothing at all. You?"

"Yeah."

"Yeah. Funny how that works, huh? None of us did anything before, I guess."

"I guess."

For a minute, neither man spoke. Neither man looked at the other.

Carter remembered reading somewhere once how the captains of Spanish galleons, after sailing their load of conquistadors halfway around the earth to the New World, would burn their ships in the bay, giving their men a very showy lesson in commitment and dedication to a cause. With their ships in flames, a point was succinctly made: No one was ever going home again. There was no retreat. No surrender. Win or die.

And Carter seemed to recall that it'd worked. The conquistadors—with their guns and steel and armor and horses and big, ridiculous hats—had decimated entire populations, had killed millions of indigenous peoples, murdering them with gunpowder, with swords, with plagues and starvation and, eventually, had installed themselves as rulers of a hot, sticky, smelly, and dangerous place, as alien to them as this place was to him even now.

Of course, it'd taken a century. And even at the end of it, there'd been plenty of indigenous peoples left to hate the Spaniards for what they'd done. It was a messy process, and there was a lot of dying to be done before the inevitable victory. Carter imagined that a lot of those dead conquistadors went to their graves thinking that the New World wasn't all that nice a place anyway, that maybe everyone would've been a whole lot happier had they all just stayed home, eaten some olives, screwed their wives, and left the New World to the people who were already there.

And he was willing to bet that all of them, to a man, thought that burning the ships had been a really shitty idea.

"What's on your mind, Kev?" Fenn asked.

Carter shook his head. "Ancient history," he said. "So what do we do next? I feel like we should do something."

"Cards? There's been a rotating game going on in Stork and Hard-man's tent for the last day or so."

Carter shrugged. It sounded as good to him as anything else. He figured he'd have plenty of time to sleep when he was dead, and told Fenn as much.

"Very cheerful, Captain. Be sure to tell the boys that one. I'm sure they'll appreciate it."

Together, they stumbled off into the quiet dark. Cat waited until they were gone and carefully slunk back inside to walk in slow circles around the stove and sniff at the drunk lawyer on the floor.

23

CARTER WON THIRTY DOLLARS PLAYING POKER. Vic was there. They were coldly cordial to each other, but neither of them could bluff, each knowing the other a bit too well. He took the two screamers about an hour before his next flight was due to lift, giving them time to work themselves in, swallowing them with a mouthful of cold coffee. In his condition, they hit almost immediately, and he was seized with a sudden urge to clean the tent. His, Stork's, didn't matter. His hands couldn't seem to stay still.

Dawn patrol was uneventful. He flew a two/three with Tommy Hill and Ernie O'Day. Exhausted, hungover, hyped up, and feeling poorly, he went up in the bomber, taking a little DH.2 called Scrambler out of the house and up near maximum altitude. He just hung there, glad, for a change, for the cold and the quiet and the thoughtless boredom while the boys talked about girls on the flight channel and tried to get themselves shot at. Scrambler had been refitted with a 250-horse replica Rolls-Royce Eagle and bomb grapples under its lower wing, triggered hydraulically from a finger switch on the stick. He kept all ten of his far away, not trusting his own hands not to just drop the weight wherever to make some pretty flowers.

The cold made him ache. He'd forgotten his helmet in the tent, and the grease on his face made his skin smell like a hospital. He ducked low, curling within the body of the plane, and looked up past the top wing and into the gray-blue sky. It almost never snowed on Iaxo—it was one of the small mercies of the place. Clouds grew, darkened, fattened, but what fell, if anything, was freezing rain or a mist that seemed almost to sizzle and made the eyes sting like tear gas if one stayed out too long in it. Real snow was a rarity. On some nights, though, he longed for it simply because it felt as though it ought to snow.

The plane flew like a brick. They were down around Southbend, still under strict orders to stay clear of the walls and outlying mud huts and tents that huddled close around the periphery. At fourteen thousand feet it looked like a scene out of antiquity—the fortified town almost like a castle, white-walled and standing at the river's edge. Peeking over the cockpit's side rail, Carter imagined peasants going about their daily business in the shadow of its squat, roofed towers and massive gate, and he wondered what this place must've been like before they'd all arrived—a Heisenberg riddle, just enough to keep his mind churning through the dull, looping repetitions of air patrol.

Southbend was the smaller of the two towns. Dirty flags snapped from the walls. The land around it was flat, gray-black, and ugly, denuded of trees by whatever mysterious industry went on within. Gouts of smoke rose from inside the walls. Through the spotting scope, it masked all but the most massive details, but when the wind blew just right, Carter swore he could see tarps, camouflage netting. He wondered if it was his imagination. Could be thatch. Could be someone's washing. Could be nothing at all. Every pilot reported the same thing when flying just a little closer than they were supposed to. Everyone thought the same thing.

He thought about how much difference 250 pounds of modern high explosives would make if dropped in just the right place. Trouble was, he didn't know which place was the right one.

He circled lower. Tommy Hill and Ernie were back along the river, trolling for action. He thought again about just buzzing the city, dropping indiscriminately, praying for fool's luck—black smoke, secondaries, tongues of fueled flame. Lower. Closing his eyes, he imagined the perfect strike: the bloom of black and orange, action-movie style. Bodies and debris blown into the air. The whuff of tortured air.

His hands shook. In the hours since he'd talked with Eddie, the whole thing had begun to feel unreal. How could he die? He was the hero of this story—its main and most lovable character. He had guns. He had bombs. He had a fucking airplane. And some smelly, simple, backward abo monkey with a rock or a stick was going to kill him? No. That wasn't going to happen. Eddie had been wrong. Carter stroked the red button of the bomb release taped onto the control stick with his thumb, running it over the smooth plastic, the simple plunger mechanism.

He rolled out then, climbed for the thin, high scratchings of the clouds, and flew awhile, sitting on his hands with the stick between his knees. Soon enough, he figured. And if not, he and Fenn would mutiny, lash Ted to a pole, raise their own air force, and blow the shit out of everything.

| | | | | | | | | | | |

By the time Carter's two/three turned for home, around midday, Connelly's first and second companies were on the march back from the bridge. The planes passed over them on approach and waggled their wings in greeting. Connelly's 3rd remained in place, securing Mutter's Ridge from any reinforcement, and the fourth had been detailed as manual labor, off-loading the supply drop that'd come in on huge parachute skids while the flight was out. Carter saw them as he came drifting down to land, packing a supply train of ponies and wagons that were chewing up the dirt of C strip.

Postflight check was smooth. Vic was flagging planes straight into the longhouse, and she looked beautiful, standing there in pilot's leathers over her coveralls, dark hair blowing out behind her in the mean, frigid crosswind that'd kicked up. She gave Carter a thumbs-up as he rolled past her. He smiled and saluted, something swelling in his chest, making him feel large in her regard. Like she'd been waiting just for him.

Ted's debriefing was the quickest yet, done in passing as Carter jogged off the flight line, looking for Fenn and some coffee.

"Spot anything?" he asked, holding Carter by the shoulder and shouting into his ear over the roar of warming engines as the next flight due out taxied into position.

"Nothing," Carter shouted back.

"Nothing?"

"Smoke at Southbend. Trees, water, rocks. Nothing. Connelly's first and second are on their way in."

"How long?"

"Before nightfall. Couple hours maybe."

"Good. On your way, pilot."

And that was that. Ted scampered off one way, into the traffic jam of planes coming and planes going, the choking breath of oil smoke and clatter of ammunition boxes. Carter went the other, jogging the length of the longhouse flight line, looking for Fenn, and heading in the direction of the armory.

| | | | | | | | | | | |

Ted, still carrying his own terrible freight of bad news, having carried it farther and for longer than anyone else on the field, stumbled as he moved from pilot to pilot and plane to plane. He was exhausted. The bags under his eyes were dark and pouchy. His skin felt alive with something other than him. He hadn't slept soundly in longer than he could remember because every time he lay down on his narrow cot and closed his eyes, he saw the columns of numbers that Eddie kept shoving at him every time he asked the little rat for help. With a pillow pressed over his face, throat open in a silent, never-voiced howl, he would hear the recordings of conversations with Eddie's friends in the Flyboy legal department that Eddie had so kindly offered him—the explanations as cold and sad and matter-of-fact as bullets. He would lie back and try to think of his perfect, clean, white place, imagining the sloping walls and gentle curves and the taste of the sterile, recycled air as his chest rattled with mud; but, in the dark, he would feel some nameless and dark thing reaching for him, slipping through the night, seeking him out. It had fingers, this thing. Arms. And it wanted him badly. In it—in his cold imagining of it—this black monster possessed some combination of comprehension and malice. It brought an understanding that had eluded him for two years, but also some dreadful knowledge.

When he slept, it wasn't sleep, only collapse. And when he collapsed, this thing came to him and tried to explain to him everything he had done wrong. It would whisper his name and tell him everything he'd done and not done, which, now, was going to get him and everyone he was responsible for killed. It sat beside him while he lay, paralyzed between sleep and not-sleep, struggling to breathe through the sludge in his chest, and it spoke to him. Told him stories about himself. Described the precise depth of the shit Ted Prinzi had gotten himself into.

He would wake with a start and have some idea—some new plan, new tactic. He would leap up from his cot, strip, press his uniform, wash himself, brush his teeth, and shave. He would stare into his own rolling, hot eyes in the small mirror hung from the nail on the tent post and work out the details of what wisdom had been granted him—knowing, on some level, that he was going mad, losing his shit, listening to ghosts, but also knowing that no other voices were currently available than the ones in his head and that no other advice was forthcoming.

On the field, he tripped over clods of dirt, over tufts of grass. He walked like a drunk on the downside, listing badly, and tripped over nothing at all. He thought of his wife. Ex-wife. Two ex-wives. He thought of the deal he'd tried to strike with Connelly. He thought of how much he despised the twin moons here, how one always seemed to be stalking the other across the sky. He thought about flying—as a wing captain on Forsmith, a mail pilot in the belt, as a rookie, two years washed out of civilian command school on Alpha Alexi, his first day in combat. His brain swirling, boiling with a froth of free association, all good governance blown, he thought of the children he'd never had, and missed them anyway. He thought of the places he'd never been, the places he had, the ones he'd dreamed. He thought of the board-room of the Flyboy office on Orion Station where he'd been hired—all earthy with its hardwood and distinguished leather. He'd never seen the London headquarters. Was never important enough to be called home to the nest. He thought of a bar at Serentatis that he'd liked a lot once. He thought of munitions stockpiles, of the liquid weight of aviation fuel, the cost (including manufacturing to spec, crating, transport, and storage) of a single round of .303 ammunition: two dollars and eight cents. He thought of his men, one after another, falling like a fanned deck of cards dropped, fluttering, to the ground. He thought about winning. How easy it should have been. He knew with the surety of a fanatic that he was going to die, and soon.

In the moments just before the worst of everything, Ted and Connelly had been standing together, side by side, at the door to the mess. After a night spent in the field house, they'd concluded their negotiations over the supply shipment now arriving courtesy of a fast, experienced smuggler who'd been supplying Connelly on the sly for years. They'd had breakfast, Ted and Connelly and a knot of Connelly's native officers, who'd kept, first, to their own table set with tin plates and silverware, ham and powdered eggs and bread and real coffee, but then had pushed the table out of the way in a fury of clicking, growls, and throat clearing and squatted on the dirt floor instead. This had done nothing to improve Ted's opinion of the natives, and he'd said so to Connelly, who'd laughed. He'd turned his head, clicking and croaking over his shoulder to his indigs, and they'd bared their teeth and made noises like ten men hawking before a spit.

"That's okay, Commander," Connelly had said, his voice syrupy and with a faint hint of some rolling Old World accent that Ted was never able to place. "They hate you, too."

Oh, they do not, Ted had thought, but didn't say it out loud.

In the comms tent, Diane was on the tight beam, talking to Connelly's swift blockade runner, just decelerating after translation and trying to find its parking orbit. Eddie was nowhere to be found. Unbeknownst to Ted, he was unconscious in the dirt beside Carter's bed, sleeping the first decent sleep he'd had in a week. Having unloaded his weight of worry and sorrow on Captains Carter and Teague and having been told that the tonnage he'd thought he'd been carrying all alone was not, in fact, his alone or really all that heavy, he'd slept with a lightness and ease he'd almost forgotten existed.

In any event, Eddie was absent—*had* been absent for hours—which Ted had taken as tacit permission to do precisely as he pleased for most of the night and on, now, into the morning: To sit with Connelly and make his deals absent any legal muffling, soldier to soldier. To use the proscribed transmitter to arrange for the drop, a nice piece of which he'd talked Connelly into handing over to him. Twenty percent was where they'd settled, plus providing a security force for the airfield in case of a determined advance on their position, in exchange for the use of Flyboy turf as a receiving area and the help of his pilots when the time came to take back the fortified towns along the river. Two patrols had been out right then, observing. Captain Teague was covering Riverbend, Captain Carter was watching Southbend. Ted had told Connelly that when they came back, plans could be made for taking the towns. An hour, two at the most. And in the meantime, the longhouse, aprons, and stubblefield were all active, and Ted found himself in the unenviable position of making small talk with a man who, now that their business was concluded, he could barely look at as a man.

Connelly smelled awful, like a rain-soaked carpet left in the muggy sun to dry. He wore some ragged fur draped over his shoulders, over the ruin of what had once been a fine suit of bespoke body armor aggrandized now with bits of steel, plates of scavenged plastic, and stitched hieroglyphs. He had some kind of paint or dirt caked into the creases of his skin, carried a tall, twisted staff that clattered with bits of junk and bones and garbage, and he spoke more indig than he did human of any variety. He was filthy and distracted by every little cough and whistle of his pets. Throughout their long night of negotiating, he'd regularly gotten up in the middle of some pointlessly protracted haggle over a pound of this or hundred-count of that and walked out of the field house into the dark to squat with them, bare his teeth at them, shake his magic stick, wrap a hand around the back of one of their necks and shake it like a puppy who'd just pissed on the rug, or just to stand there with them—close with them, shoulder touching shoulder, backs touching fronts—to stare up into the sky.

"What are you doing out there, man!" Ted had demanded once, after an absence of nearly an hour. "What, are your monkeys afraid of the dark, too?"

And Connelly had hissed at him, shook his stick, then grinned. "That what they say about me now, Theodore? That I'm afraid of the dark? That's funny."

"Funny?"

"Really more ridiculous. Telling."

"I'll fucking say."

Connelly had set in to scratching then, and for a minute he had said nothing at all. He'd looked around at the lights burning in the field house, the electric lights fed by the muted chug of a generator running on aviation fuel. He'd cocked an ear to listen for the scrape and sigh of the night controller shifting in his (or her) chair on the other side of the wall—listening for the pings and beeps of condensed radio communications being beamed across the heavens, for the scratch of voices in the sea of local static.

When he looked back to Ted, his expression had been soft, almost pitying. "You know why my . . . *indigs*"—he dropped the word like something exculpatory, evidence souring on his tongue—"won't fight in the dark?"

Ted shrugged dismissively. "Afraid of the boogeyman?"

Connelly smiled. "Because they can't *see* in the dark."

Can't see. That was his reason. Ted had laughed at him, and then they'd gotten back to discussing terms. Ted had thought he'd won something, because Connelly started conceding points left and right when he wasn't stepping outside to rub up against his monkeys.

Outside the mess, on the morning after, Connelly was standing too close. Their shoulders brushed and Ted shuffled a half step away.

"Stand still, Commander," Connelly said, and moved in again. His indigs squatted in a tight knot on the other side of the door, occasionally clapping their hands together, ticking and gurgling at each other. In the infield, Connelly's entire fourth company looked like an orgy of bearskin rugs.

"Stop climbing all over me then," Ted snapped back.

"It makes you look untrustworthy."

"What?"

"Pulling away. You're making my officers nervous. Stand still."

Connelly stepped closer.

"You gonna kiss me, too?"

"No. The Akaveen mating rituals are a bit more . . . aggressive than ours, if that's the word? Energetic? A kiss, they wouldn't understand. They'd think I was biting you."

"Then they'd think I was kicking your ass shortly after."

Connelly laughed. He bared his teeth. The two of them stood together quietly until Connelly spoke again.

"How long have you been here, Commander? On Iaxo?"

"Two years," Ted replied, making it sound like a thousand.

"I'm amazed at how little you've managed to pick up in all that time."

Ted huffed. He folded his arms. "Piece of fucking work, you are," he said, looking skyward through squinted eyes.

Connelly shrugged. "I work for them. They expect me to provide. To negotiate with the big fliers. Bring down the manna."

"Yeah. And understand their fuck rituals and wave your magic stick around. You'd kill at a costume party. How long have *you* been here?"

"Six years," he said.

"Your company is patient," Ted said.

"My company." Connelly smiled and looked out, as though over some far horizon. "My company. *This* is my company, now. These men."

"They're not men."

"Eastbourne is not patient, Theodore. Back then, we were among the first to come to Iaxo. Long before you. There were two hundred of us, dropped in with a one-year deadline. We were to infiltrate one side or the other, the Akaveen Ctirad or the Lassateirra, though neither of them had names then that we understood. Whichever side we chose, we would offer our services, off-world supply, ally with them, and negotiate a patch of four hundred thousand acres as payment. Land and mineral rights. Air and water. Everything. We had lawyers, xenobiologists, linguists, engineers. One hundred and fifty soldiers, armed to the teeth and with five hundred tons of arms and ammunition buried in the hills. We chose the Akaveen Ctirad because the Akaveen were warriors and because they were the first natives we stumbled across who didn't immediately try to kill us. That took almost the entire year. And by then, there were about sixty of us remaining. You know what I was?"

"No. What were you?"

"I was a geologist. I'd come along to take soil and mineral samples. But after almost a year, we knew that none of that mattered anymore. We'd talked to the company, to Eastbourne. We'd told them that we needed more men, more supplies, that there was something about this place that was . . . indefatigable. And do you know what they did?"

Ted looked away.

"Eastbourne abandoned us here. They forgot about us. Wrote us off. No, they are not a patient company. But the Akaveen are patient."

Somewhere amid the bangles, tatters, and fur of Connelly's outfit, there was a squealing chirp. Ted recoiled at the sound. "You pull a god-damn bird out of your ass or something, I'm going to be sick."

Not a bird. An old-fashioned microwave radio receiver/transmitter headset that Connelly scissored open and tucked around the shell of his ear. By the local standard, it was still miraculous, of course, but it was the sort of thing that made the cast-away gear Ted had at the airfield look brand-new.

The indigs by the door had fallen silent as soon as they'd heard the chirp. They all watched their magical human, looking up from their crouches with big staring eyes.

Ted knew three words of indig. There was *aka,* which meant yes; *nu,* which meant no; and a word that sounded something like *shipping* and meant something like shit-eater, or close to it—an all-purpose exclama-tion and terrible insult to the natives which, for a time, he and his men had used at every opportunity because it'd been funny to watch the camp indigs flinch at hearing it. Oddly, or perhaps only coincidentally, Connelly used all three in his call. And only those three.

Aka, he said.

Nu.

Nu, nu, nu.

Shipping.

It was the first native conversation Ted had understood in two years, and he'd felt wise for it. Finally wedded to this place and this planet.

Connelly had taken off the earpiece. He'd folded it carefully and tucked it among his vestments. Standing there before the mess tent, waiting for the shipment to come in, he'd looked Ted up and down, something in his eyes expressing a sudden sadness and understanding.

Then he'd looked at his officers and made a sudden, sharp cutting motion with his hand, a sound with his lips like *"Pssst."* Without a sound, they stood and lit out, loping, for the infield.

He turned back to Ted. "I'm sorry," he said.

"Sorry? For what?"

"Ten percent, Commander. Take it or leave it."

And Ted, wise for one instant, had suddenly felt once again as though great and terrible things were happening just out of his view. He was seized with the dream fear again of something sneaking up on his blind side, disaster personified and reaching for him. "Wait," he said. "Wait. Ten percent of what? What happened? Who were you talking to?"

Over Connelly's shoulder, Ted saw Diane step out of the comms tent and begin waving her arms. Ted pulled the radio handset off his belt and stared at it. It was turned off. He'd done that last night so he wouldn't be interrupted. He'd forgotten to turn it back on.

"Ten percent of our deal. As a courtesy, you understand. For letting us use the field."

Above them, a white and shining speck began to glow and grow larger. Orbital delivery, going through its first blazing molt.

"Our deal was twenty percent," Ted said.

"Yes. Ten percent of that. Yes or no."

Aka or *nu*.

"So, two percent, you're saying. Two?"

"As a courtesy."

"Wait. What happened? What's . . ." Ted was fumbling with his radio. His fingers were frozen from the cold, clumsy with a sudden, fierce frustration. "Wait. Just let me . . . " When he finally got it switched on, it erupted with voices—controllers and pilots and a hundred different words he did not want to hear.

"The Akaveen," Connelly said, his voice taking on a hectoring edge that Ted found unpleasant enough to want to hit him in the mouth, "the *free* Akaveen, mind you, not my troops—have just moved on Riverbend. Your planes have crossed into the highlands. Against orders, I suspect. Which is probably what all that yelling is about. As we discussed last night, NRI has been landing supplies behind the lines for the past five days. I tried to explain this to you, but—"

"You never said five days!"

"I didn't know until just now. I knew that they were there, but my information, my lines of communication, have been less than perfect lately. No one is sure any longer who is going to win this planet, and my informants—rightly, I should say—want to make sure they come out on the victorious side. There's no profit in doing otherwise. Something we taught them, I'm sure."

"So what are . . ." Ted stared at the radio barking and yelling in his hand. He felt a cloud muddling his vision, his plans.

"The Akaveen are going to be slaughtered at Riverbend," Connelly continued. "The lines are going to collapse. And now, the Colonial Marines cannot possibly be far behind."

"Okay, so then—"

"So two percent. I suggest you take it in food and water and decamp immediately," Connelly said. "You have to get out, Theodore. Now. Scrub the mission, call in your exfiltration, and get out as quickly as possible. My units can cover you for a day, but no more."

"What are you going to do?"

"Hide. Burn my communications equipment. Cache all my gear. Wait until this all blows over. Then take my troops back into the field when everything quiets down. Can't take more than a year."

"A *year*."

"I have a job to do, Commander. I have my men to think about. I don't intend to let them down." Connelly paused, looked skyward, straightened the mangy fur cape on his shoulders, and began to move away. "Two percent, then," he said. "Food and water. I'll have it saved out for you." He shuffled his feet in the cold dirt. "Commander?"

Ted had said nothing. Connelly took a few steps, turned back. Looking at Ted standing dumbfounded with his radio in his hand, he seemed to reconsider.

"There is no exfiltration waiting for you, is there, Theodore," he said.

"Of course there is," Ted had lied. "Just have to call them."

"Really?"

Ted had looked up. He'd looked Connelly in the eye. He would be damned before being shamed in front of this man, so he said, "Absolutely. Don't worry about us. But there's some time left. And I intend on using it to make those monkey motherfuckers regret ever leaving their little mud huts."

Connelly stared at Ted. Around them, everyone was clearing the infield, looking up with hands shading eyes.

"Ten rifles," Connelly said. "A thousand rounds of ammunition. All I can spare."

And Ted had nodded distractedly. "If it'll make you feel better," he said. He, too, looked up and watched the cargo drop approaching, burning off its first drag chutes—low enough that they appeared to jerk and flare like wings of flame. There, then gone.

"Ted," Connelly said.

Ted studiously did not look at him. Apparently, the man wasn't done talking yet. "Do you have any idea how long this war has been going on between them? The natives?"

"No." Ted watched the second parachutes deploy, billow for a second, then tear away. The container was dead on target. Someone up there really knew what they were doing. "Does it matter?"

"A thousand years, they've been fighting over this land. We are just an aberration. An eyeblink. One brief moment of magic and hope."

And then Connelly had smiled again—an expression that, at first, Ted had thought looked all wrong on his face, like maybe he'd just learned how to do it and was still practicing. But there was something almost beatific about it, with depths of sadness and personal vision, of joy at being just where he was, glowing under the pall of disaster upon disaster. Connelly was a happy man and Ted could not stomach that at all. "No one is going to write songs about us when we're gone."

| | | | | | | | | | | |

Ted shook himself. The conversation with Connelly he couldn't get out of his head, but the man himself had vanished. He couldn't think. He drew himself upright and debriefed Tommy Hill, grabbing him by the shoulder, listening without hearing his answers to any questions. Two squadron—Carter, Hill, and O'Day—had seen nothing. They'd been in the wrong position to see the action at Riverbend that'd just occurred, and had likely been too close to Southbend in the first place, flying against orders within sight of the walls. Ted no longer knew where he needed to send his planes to do good, only where he must ban to keep them from harm. He hadn't wanted anyone else dying here for no good cause. Danny Diaz had been bad luck. Morris Ross had been bad planning. He felt that, somehow, he should've known that was coming so it could've been avoided. Stork was luck again, only good. He had been terrified of doing anything, but now . . . Now he was only afraid of doing nothing. He was trying to encompass all the intelligence of an entire planet, all the possible plans of all his possible enemies, and to secure himself and his men against every one of them.

Once Connelly had walked off, Ted had run for the control tent. Captain Teague's flight had been up near Riverbend. They'd seen things happening there, had reported back with the worst of all possible bad news: That the end was coming. That everything was worse than anyone had wanted to believe. He'd demanded silence from the controllers in the tent. He might've threatened them with his pistol, but wasn't sure. That seemed extreme. He'd gotten back on the radio with Teague. "Just come home . . ."

He'd called all of the planes back in from their patrols. He'd felt that, if he just held out long enough, an idea would come to him. Some plan. Some scheme for turning it all around. His only responsibility, he'd thought, was to keep everyone alive until something told him what to do next. But things were happening now. The action was coming and time was running very short, so all he could hope was that the wisdom would come quickly.

Ted staggered again, turned out and away from the ruckus of planes and bodies moving to and fro and the pressure of motion all around him. After Captain Teague's flight had landed, Ted had given orders that all planes be turned around for immediate flight upon landing, hoping that he wouldn't need to send them out again but knowing that he probably would. This was it, he thought. Might be it. The beginning of the end. He'd spoken briefly with a god in whom he did not believe and asked for more time. Just a little. But he didn't think his call had been received.

Ted stopped, briefly, on the close-cropped apron of the strip and took a breath. There were things that needed to be done now. There were orders he needed to give. He looked up into the sky, one hand shoved deep into the pocket of his uniform trousers and fingers wrapped around his radio handset as he shaded his eyes with the blade of the other. And while anyone who saw him at that moment would've thought only that he was searching the skies for danger, for threats coming from unusual directions or, perhaps, the approach of planes that only he knew about, the truth was that Ted was only pinching himself through the pocket of his uniform and biting the inside of his cheek until it bled to keep from bursting into tears.

| | | | | | | | | | | | |

Charlie Voss and Emile were walking across the work yard wearing their gear and trying to enjoy the thin comfort of the sun that'd suddenly emerged from a break in the solid ceiling of cloud. They looked, oddly, like young men again in the light—walking in a bubble of strange calm through the riot of planes and men and weapons and mechanics. Like children almost, on a day out at the museum, stopping here and there to touch a wing, a strut, a bomb. They were talking about the marines coming because, today, that was the rumor: that the Colonial Marines were on their way. And that was the only thing that anyone was talking about, discussing what they thought would become of them when it happened, if it happened, if the company didn't come and get them first.

"We'll do jail, I think," Emile said.

"Jail for sure," agreed Charlie.

"But not for long."

"No."

"A warm bed. Hot meals. Quiet."

"No missions."

"No fucking indigs. And the company, they'll get us out, I think."

"Yeah, they will. Have to, I'd think."

"Have to. Be an embarrassment otherwise. And we're still worth something to 'em."

"Sure. Absolutely."

"It'll be a nice break, I think."

"You think?"

"I really do."

| | | | | | | | | | | | |

Fenn was still shaking even though he'd been down on solid ground now for almost fifteen minutes. His legs were jerking so much that he'd had to cross them at the knee like a dandy to keep them from jumping, sitting in the mess, on a bench, leaning back against the edge of a table in an attempt at looking calm. His face was locked in what he hoped was a look of bemusement. When he'd landed, he could barely walk. His hand on his coffee cup shook enough to make rings in the greasy liquid surface. His jaw was clenched against the chattering his teeth wanted to make, and he breathed in a hiss—drawing in air across his teeth, blowing it out his nose—while his heart (disloyal organ that it was) tried to hammer its way out of his chest or climb out through his throat. Go for a jog. Run.

He focused on breathing. On stilling the tremors that coursed through him. He didn't know how long he was going to have to sit there. He thought, perhaps, a very long time.

Emile and Charlie came in, saw him, sat.

"That was something, eh?" Emile asked.

"Something," said Fenn, favoring his squadron mates with a smile. "It truly was." All three of them had been up near Riverbend. All three of them had broken the rules, violated the cordon that Ted had put up around the walled cities, had poked their noses too deeply into enemy territory. They had seen the high moors, the invisible land just over the artificial horizon created by months of stalemate, covered in men and indigs and equipment. Hundreds of containers. Thousands of bodies. An army just sitting, waiting for them. When the battle had erupted on the ground, they had come together into tight formation to watch the sudden collapse of time frames, of anachronisms fighting one another in the dirt and frozen mud. Fenn had begged release from Ted to turn his flight loose upon the enemy, but he had been refused, had been called home with guns cold. That wasn't what had scared him, though.

"We were talking . . ."

"No good will ever come of that," Fenn interrupted.

"Hilarious," said Charlie, and Fenn gave him a wink, squeezing his hand tighter on his coffee cup, and sighing with what he hoped sounded like collected peace.

"So we were talking about going to prison, right?"

Fenn nodded.

"Because we figure, Charlie and me, that that's where we're going to end up."

"In prison?"

"Right."

"Like, just eventually? Or were you planning on doing something specifically illegal?"

And the two of them sat a moment, confused by the complex twists and turns of Fenn's logic before grinning together and breaking out laughing.

"You're joking," said Emile.

"Joking, right?" asked Charlie.

"No, gentlemen. Really, I'm not. Why would you be talking about going to prison?"

"For what we're doing here," said Emile.

"When the marines come," said Charlie.

"Oh," said Fenn. "The marines. Prison." He had to remind himself that the boys knew nothing of what he now knew. That he carried with him the specific and terrible knowledge of their own ending here and was one of only four who did, the weight of it enough to warp his every thought down toward the hard, cold center of fact: that they were going to die here, and likely soon. NRI, the natives, they would settle this and do the company's dirty work of eliminating all witnesses long before the marines arrived. And even if they didn't—even if, by some miracle, the Flyboy Inc. Carpenter mission survived the coming battle and won through by some impossible turn of fate—then when the marines did arrive, none of them would be going to jail. Of that, Fenn was positive. And short of flying an open cockpit biplane across hundreds of light-years to land on Victoria Street in London, at the front doors of the home office, Fenn didn't know how any of them would ever get home.

Through one of the windows in the mess, he spotted Carter walking the flight line, looking dazed by all the action surrounding him, and a little lost. *A boy,* he thought. *Lost among a tribe of boys.*

"Colonial prison," added Emile again. "When the marines come."

He looks half-dead already. And Fenn wondered, not for the first time, if he, too, looked as bad on the outside as Carter did.

With effort, he focused his attention back on Emile. "No," he said. "I really hadn't considered that."

"Well, shouldn't you then?" Charlie asked. "I mean, the way things are going, don't you think they'll come sooner or later? They'll shut us down and, the way Emile and me were looking at it, probably shut us up in jail for a bit, at least."

"To be completely honest, gentlemen . . ." Fenn paused, careful with his words and fighting to maintain the tattered curtain of nonchalance he pulled ever tighter across his throbbing heart and jittering hands, the heel of his boot tapping painfully against his shin. "I'd never truly considered prison as an outcome. Or, for that matter, the arrival of the marines."

"So you think they're not going to come then? Even after—"

"Even after," said Fenn.

"So you think we're going to be okay then, Captain?" Emile leaned forward, as though being closer to a man who he thought believed things were going to turn out all right would help him catch some bug of optimism, some invulnerability. "Because prison, you know . . . Charlie and me were saying that maybe it wouldn't be so bad."

"Compared to what?" Fenn asked.

"To this," Charlie said. He gestured, in the smallest way possible, with a tiny bob of his head, to everything and everybody in the whole, wide world.

"To what?"

"To missions. The goddamn indigs."

"To the food. And Ted. And flying in the dark and stuff."

"It can't be so bad."

"Have you ever been to prison, Emile?" Fenn asked. Emile shook his head. He asked Charlie, and Charlie, too, said no—that he'd always been just a little too fast. "Then don't fool yourselves," he said. "It would, in fact, be so bad. It would be worse."

"But that don't matter, right?" Emile asked. He was looking at Fenn's hand on the coffee cup and Fenn made an effort to relax it. When that didn't work, he carefully took it away and hid it in his lap. "It don't matter because you said the marines won't come, right? You said."

"The Colonial Marines don't take orders from me, Emile. They'll come or they won't. I just said that I hadn't been thinking about prison."

"Then what were you thinking about?"

Carter had disappeared again into the mess and riot of the airstrip, but Fenn stared out at the place he had been, wondering where he'd vanished to, how difficult disappearing might really be.

"Something even worse than that," he said to Emile.

| | | | | | | | | | | |

Carter couldn't find Fenn and had stopped looking very hard. He was in the field house, maybe. Or the mess. The longhouse. Doing something other than wanting to be found, which was fine by Carter. He was tired and had lost his taste for company halfway through the looking. Now, hands in his pockets, he just walked, watching clouds scudding in and closing like a ceiling over the world.

At the far end of B strip, down by the armory and weapons lockers, Max waved him down. He was sitting, reclined against a massive pile of loose .303 belts, with a stripped Spandau-style drum-fed machine-gun body across his knees and an unlit cigarette dangling from his lip.

Carter changed course and made for the sunlit corner where Max sat, grinning a gap-toothed smile and cleaning the Spandau's fouled chamber with a black toothbrush. He was missing his four front teeth—had lost them in a fight in a transfer station spacer's guild bar the month before they'd all shipped for the final, plunging leg of their trip to Iaxo—and was forever poking his tongue through the hole. He smelled like rotten teeth and warm gun oil.

"Hear the news, Captain?" he lisped.

Carter's heart stalled. Three squadron's flight was home. He'd counted all their planes. The one/two flight with Jack flying drag had been coming right in behind his patrol with no trouble reported. It couldn't be bad news, but it'd been so long since he'd heard any good news that Carter immediately assumed the worst. It was a habit. "What news?" he asked, bracing for it.

"Monkeys moved on Riverbend this morning while you was out gallivanting. About four thousand of them. That entire northern flank." Max removed his cigarette, spit in the dirt, and beamed maliciously. "And they got the shit blown right out of them, too. Three squadron rolled up just in time to see the little chickenshit yellow fuckers running. They never even seen the inside of the walls."

"Did everyone come home safe?"

"Ours did. Fully loaded, too. Guns clean. No one cleared to fire a shot. Indigs probably haven't stopped running yet."

"We headed back up there?"

Max raised a mangled eyebrow. "I got stripes on me I haven't noticed? If you are, no one's thought to inform me. All's I know is all planes are in turnaround now, Ted's orders, and I do see our fearless leader over there"—he gestured off toward the strip's apron with his toothbrush, to where Ted stood apart from the messy throng staring up into the clouds—"watching the skies with what I would call a particular focus, if you know what I mean."

Carter looked at Ted. He looked up and down the flight line at the planes coming and going, being pushed in and out of their berths in the longhouse; the activity had been nearly constant since flights had resumed. Watching it, he tried to weigh today's hurry against last night's and yesterday's and the day before. He looked at pilots and mechanics, ground crews, planes, bomb trucks, fuel hoses, and saw them all as one body, its internal systems going through the motions of regular operation, not yet galvanized by the spark of any specific action.

He turned back to Max. "You're the man with the guns," Carter said. "When we're about to go kill something, you generally know first."

"That is true," he said, nodding. "When's your next flight?"

Carter checked his watch. The face of it was frosted with condensation. Its hands had stopped. "Two hours," he said. "Two hours or so. Up to the Ridge, out and back."

Max licked a greasy finger and held it up as if testing the quarter of the wind. He cupped a hand around his ear and pretended to listen with exaggerated concentration. "Hmm . . . ," he said. "If I was you?"

"Yeah, Max. If you were me."

"I was you, I'd go look up your boyfriend in the mess. He was there at Riverbend and might know a bit of something that I don't. And then I'd get you a hot cup of coffee and a quick piss. Have a laugh. Rest that weary trigger finger. But I wouldn't stray too far, you read me?"

"Five-by-five, Max."

"Things around this place have been a bit too quiet a bit too long, you know?"

"I do. Thanks."

"Don't thank me, Captain. Just taxi."

Carter nodded and was about to say something else when Max looked skyward, squinting. "Motherfucker . . . ," he said, sounding pleasantly bewildered, surprised, almost happy. "Is that snow?"

Out on the field, Ted still had the radio handset gripped in his fist. He'd waited until all his planes were on the ground. He'd gotten all the intelligence he could from the pilots. He'd waited as long as he could wait, had walked off, had given it as much thought as he could, and then had given the order. He'd called in to Diane at comms, told her to hit the button, and now was just waiting for the scramble siren to sound. He felt like he was being pulled in half and stood now, his face upturned, his eyes closed. He flinched as if burned by a hot ember when the first heavy, waxy flake touched his cheek.

"Is that snow?" he asked. There was no one around to answer him.

|||||||||||

Charlie interrupted Emile in the middle of saying something that didn't matter a bit to anyone.

"Check that out," he said, pointing out the mess tent's window. "Snow."

| | | | | | | | | | | | |

Carter told Max he'd see him around and headed for the mess tent at a quick jog. Inside, Fenn saw him break suddenly from the edge of the strip, move into the grass of the infield. The clouds were all massed behind him, rolling in. Windblown flakes of snow danced in the air between them.

He didn't make it even halfway to the mess tent door before the scramble siren went off.

PART 3
THE LAST DAY

24

TEN MINUTES LATER, CARTER IS BACK IN A PLANE. Strapped down hard.
Idling on the taxiway at ready-one while the rest of the flight takes up
post positions behind him. He has Jack Hawker, Tommy, Lefty, Stork,
and Porter Vaughn on him. Fenn wrangles the remainders, the stragglers; lining them up right-oblique at the action end of A strip. There
are choking clouds of smoke, much shouting, and the flat slaps of hands
beating the sides of planes like anxious jockeys whipping horses still in
the paddock as Vic and Raoul and Rockwell, Willy McElroy, little Paul
Meleuire and Max, and anyone else with a free hand, come charging
through the swirling, waxy snow at a dead run, dragging bomb sledges
and ammo boxes and helmets and gloves, bits of stray gear forgotten in
the haste of siren panic. The radio is a disaster of voices.

Carter is back in Roadrunner, so fresh out of the shop she still smells
of oil and love and the arc flame of the welding gun. So fresh that, when
the siren had gone off and he'd gone running to her, he'd found her just
coming off the crane in the longhouse and had had to help put wheels
on her—the pneumatic squeal of the driver almost deafening, the first
buck of it jerking the pistol-grip right out of his hand.

The new engine is like a boy's heart put into an old man's body.
Its rhythm—the sound of it—is different. To Carter, it sounds like his

plane's voice has changed, her expression, mood, temper, all wrong. He is wearing combat restraints, a six-point harness, all his gear, his helmet, collar, injectors. He has no map. There'd been no time. His flight electronics have been repaired, recalibrated. The airspeed indicator is new. The pedals are stiff.

All over the field, electric ignitions bring engines choking and banging to life. The pilots yell, "Contact!" anyhow, just because it feels good. There is no time to drag or wheel planes into position, so the pilots drive them onto the trim of the strip, wiggle and inch them into place. Wheels are chocked and unchocked as the snow falls and sticks to goggles and windscreens or is blasted by prop wash. Flags wave. They go staggered: Carter getting the first green, then Fenn crossing behind him, then Jack and Tommy together crossing behind him, then Charlie Voss and Billy, and on like that until everyone is airborne; Fokkers and Camels crisscrossing, straightening course; mean, wicked slashings of color across the tumbling clouds as paint jobs whip into the sky, roll, curl and climb, clawing for the close, claustrophobic ceiling of the clouds even before the throbbing headset chatter of a dozen simultaneous shouting, cheering, cursing voices expends itself into breathless silence.

Ted is on the command channel: "Flight leaders, make course for Riverbend. You are free-fire cleared."

Carter has to force Roadrunner to climb, feeling as though he ought to get out and push. He'd needed the full length of the runway before feeling the bite and lift of the air beneath him. The new engine is heavy. Powerful. Big like a god is big, but ponderously, murderously heavy. It needs a pull that it doesn't have while climbing until he cautiously opens the throttle a little further, then further, listening for the point where the roar will become a scream, a shriek, then silence, seize, stall, and death. There is a sweet spot. He just has to find it. The two of them, he and his plane, will learn together or they won't. There is no safety net. No one on Iaxo wears parachutes.

He'll get it, he thinks. The two of them, Carter and his plane, will learn each other's quirks and tolerances, or they will die. And as he gives the throttle another nudge, he suddenly feels a sense of almost bottomless power in her, a reserve of strength that is massive, dangerous, and comforting. He throttles up again, and the engine barely changes its tone as, suddenly, the balance shifts and he squirts skyward like a jet, cleaving a path, his flight following in the messy chaos of his prop wash.

"Correction." Ted again. "Course now below Riverbend, far side of the river. Intercepting a large and moving force, numbers unknown. Hold."

A pause. Chatter from ground control. Chatter from the pilots. The confusion of the rapid deployment resolves itself after a single turn over the airfield and the flights fall into staggered lines, drifting apart, making space.

Ted: "Our indigs are wearing their asses for hats."

Brief conversation between Carter and Fenn. Voices upon voices upon voices. They call out their wings, break right and left and, with a mile of space between them, form up into terrible flying wedges, which, to the Lassateirra indigs, must seem the sign of vilest evil; of angry gods, roused to wrath, and bringing nothing but pain.

In a moment, they are at maximum throttle, the fastest machines dragging the slowest, engines howling. The sweetest sound in the world is the metallic clack of a magazine going into the centerline cannon. Carter knows this. The sweetest sound is the *skatch-skatch* of belt-fed machine guns being primed. It is the whip of air across cowlings, the howling of it in the stays, moaning as though he travels with an honor guard of ghosts.

He bounces the palm of his gloved hand over the aluminum fins of the bombs he has hanging in the shotgun loops and calls for a gun check while his flight is still in the clear. Rounds sing by his flanks, gleaming phosphorescent tracers streaking the sky, and he lovingly strokes his own trigger. Death, death, death.

At nearly 200 mph, they are baying down on the river in minutes. Horrifying creatures, raining down fury from on high. Finally, they have been released to do what they do best. Finally. And Carter thinks that, someday, many centuries from now, the indigs on Iaxo will tell stories of dragons that belched fire and smoke, of monsters that flew and murdered and consumed whole towns with their rage.

He thinks that, when they do, they will be talking about him.

Ted once more: "Indig siege force was rolled up forty-five minutes ago by explosives and rifle fire, type unknown. The A.O. is considered hot. I've got a comms intercept saying hand grenades and land mines at least. Gunfire in the trees. Automatic rifles possible. The Riverbend Lassateirra have moved out of the city and are chasing the friendly retreat, moving toward the bridge and northeast on the high flank under tree cover. Enemy in the open near the river and on the ridgeline. Tallyho, gentlemen. Send them the fuck home."

They cross the river south of the advance in a blink, come north, power down, split-loop out to get their bearings. Carter calls Fenn.

"Fenn, Carter. Play you high-low?"

"Done, Captain," Fenn calls back. "B flight has the high side."

"A flight has low then."

"Happy hunting, Kev. I'll meet you in the middle."

Carter switches over to the flight channel and releases his fighters like dogs slipping a chain. "A flight, this is flight leader. Enemy in the open along the river, south of Riverbend. We are free-fire and hot. All fighters, break and attack. Let's tear 'em up."

| | | | | | | | | | | | |

The battle would go on for ten hours.

On their first pass, Carter's flight descended in formation, swooping down on the vanguard of the pursuing force in a wedge and chewing great, bloody channels into the ranks before rolling out, pulling tight turns, and coming back for another run. And another. And another. They killed, at first, with the wild abandon of animals turned loose from their bonds; out of rage and frustration and anger at having been pent up so long. They killed sloppily, occasionally joyously, sometimes stupidly as though they were very, very parched and only killing could slake their desperate thirst. Before a quarter of an hour had passed, two of Carter's flight—Lefty Berthold and Porter Vaughn—had to turn for the field because they'd burned the barrels out of their machine guns, dropped all of their bombs, jammed the mechanisms of their weapons beyond all simple repair. On the radio, one of them was sobbing as he turned for home. Crying or laughing so hard that it was almost the same thing. Carter never figured out which it was.

With two men gone, Carter re-formed his diminished flight—turning out high and rallying the remainder of his planes for a precision-bombing run with whatever they had left. The intention was to lay down a stick of hell just forward of the advancing Lassateirra vanguard (mostly light horse) in the hopes of hobbling them, tripping them up, blowing the legs out from underneath the animals, whatever. The planes dropped from the sky like bombs themselves, in hard dives, screaming across the front rank of horses at fifty feet off the deck and dropping their ordinance right where it belonged.

The result was horrific. Smoke and dust and clouds of debris fortunately hid the worst of the details of the carnage, but they still left visible just enough to catch Carter's eye like a burr and sink deep into his brain: horses cut off at the legs, squirming on the tortured, icy earth; indigs catapulted from their mounts and torn by shrapnel; indigs then trampled by following lines of horsemen trying to control mounts blowing bloody foam, bleeding from the eyes and ears. These images would give him nightmares, he knew. Provided he lived long enough.

The precision application of explosives slowed the pursuit briefly but did not stop it. The enemy was determined. Or perhaps crazed. With two years of practice, of knowing what waited for them whenever they crossed open ground, they absorbed the casualties like scratches to the body and just kept coming. At that point, the indigs were roughly thirty-five miles from the Flyboy encampment and closing fast.

Carter signaled for his flight to re-form on him, took them up to five thousand feet, and ordered his remaining planes back to the field for reloading. He would remain on station until Jack Hawker returned to take his place, allowing him, then, to go home, rearm, reload, come back. The flight could not maintain the consistent, withering, demoralizing fire that Carter would like because they simply could not carry enough bullets and bombs and cannon rounds to keep up the fight for more than thirty minutes at a stretch. Carter crossed the center of the moving battlefield, tangling briefly with B flight's pattern, then rolled out to get a look at the larger picture and prime his cannon. In the strange, hanging gravity of the combat dive, he tried to place his shots with care, aiming for standard bearers or large concentrations of horses;

but following the first pass by the fighters, the enemy had immediately spread itself out, lessening the ratio of shots to kills, to wounds, to cripplings and maimings and terrible slow, cold death.

His .303s are nearly dry. He has run completely out of bombs. He calls Fenn as he sees all but two of his fighters chuddering off in the direction of the airfield and asks, "You, too?"

"Dry as dirt. Shot their wads."

"Hadn't anticipated this particular problem."

"Me either. Those odds are beginning to look more and more right. Eddie's odds, I mean."

Carter thinks for a moment. His finger strokes delicately at his machine gun's trigger—not firing, just teasing. "This isn't that," he says, finally. "I don't think this is that."

"Maybe. But it makes one think."

Fenn says something to his fighters, and his two remaining wingmen roll over and fall into fierce dives, guns spitting sparks of light—tracers that, when they hit the hard-packed and frozen ground, bounce. Unless, of course, they find a body to embed themselves in. Something soft and warm and welcoming. They'd gone after a small knot of horses milling briefly around a flag. When they are through, there are no more horses. There is no more flag.

Ted's voice crackles on the radio. "Command to A flight leader. Carter?"

"Copy, Ted. What's up?"

"What's the distance between the two parties now?"

"Parties?" As if this were a lark, an outing. Looking down, Carter can see a trail of wrack and ruin and meat and blood and death running back from where the horses are now to where the planes had first engaged them; a track, sometimes thick, in some places thin. A brief flurry of snow swirls between him and the ground—greasy, fat flakes offering a mercy of blindness.

"Between the retreating monkeys and the pursuing force. How far?"

"Mile and a half and closing fast. Maybe two miles." Carter brings his machine around like reining up a skittish mount. She turns to the left as if bee-stung, the torque of the engine dragging her whole body in a skidding, ferocious inside turn. Carter groans as he is shoved roughly back into his seat, then continues. "Retreating forces are backing up at the river."

"What about between the pursuing horses and the main body?"

"That's a long way. Five miles. More."

"How bad have you fucked up those horses?"

"Bad," Carter says, recalling in a flash the bomb drop, the screaming he'd imagined, of the damaged and the dead. "But they're not stopping. They're taking it."

"Connelly is not in position to intercept ground forces. If we don't stop this advance right here, there will be nothing between the Lassateirra and us to slow them up." There is a pause, static, whistle of distortion. Over the radio, Carter can hear engine sounds, shouts, the husking of the wind. Ted is still on the flight line. Carter pushes a fresh magazine into the cannon—one of his last two—then primes it. He takes a breath and blows it out through pursed, frozen lips, a thin line of steam almost instantly sucked back into the slipstream.

"Carter. A flight is scrambling in bombers. Lay off the horses. All fire to be concentrated on turning back the main body. Hawker will lead the bombers in. Berthold and Vaughn are ahead of them by a few minutes, already in the air."

"Roger that."

"Captain Teague is remaining on station to spot for me. Bring everyone else in to reload now—understand?"

"Understood, Ted. Roger and out."

Carter switches channels, drops his nose, lets two rounds go, curses as the ejected shells spang off his knee and he hits the switch. "Fenn? Carter. You talked to Ted?"

"I did. Lovely man."

"So you're staying."

"Eyes in the sky."

Carter hears a long rip from Fenn's guns, muffled but still audible.

"Save those rounds, pal. You're gonna be all alone up here for a bit."

"One of them gave me the finger. Had to teach him some manners."

Carter laughs. "All right then. Porter and Lefty are inbound, but a few minutes off. Call in whoever's left of your flight and put 'em on my tail. I'm headed for home."

Fenn does that. They all shoot their guns dry on the way, waggle their wings at the outgoing fighters when they pass, then again at the bombers just making their way to the strip, confusing things, causing delays. Carter calls his mutt flight off approach and puts them into a long, lazy circle. He tries to catch his breath. He hunches down tight in the seat and hides from the wind slipping past the cockpit coamings. His lips are chapped and numb. His nose is running, and when he reaches up with his gloved hand to try and wipe it, he can't feel his own hand on his face.

The bombers lumber into the air. Carter brings the fighters down. On the field, every hand is turned to loading death into the idling machines. There is very little talking. This is something they are good at. Carter is scooping spent cannon shells off the floor of Roadrunner's cockpit with his hands like bailing water. He is bouncing in his seat and slapping at his frozen face—the lower half of it, the part not covered by the helmet. He is straining his muscles as Max hands him up belts of .303 ammo to be stowed and, all the while, he is listening to Fenn's flight channel.

This is how he hears Lefty Berthold die.

Key

TWR: Transmission from lead controller Diane Willis

RAM: Radio area microphone, voice or sound source

RDO: Transmission from ground control

-1: Identified as Cmndr. Theodore "Ted" Prinzi

-2: Identified as Controller James McCudden

-3: Identified as Controller Shun Le Harper

OPS: Transmission from Iaxo operations control, Theodore Prinzi

HOT: Cockpit or pilot microphone, voice or sound source

-1: Identified as Cpt. Fennimore "Fenn" Teague, call sign "Jackrabbit"

-2: Identified as Sqd. Ldr. Porter Vaughn

-3: Identified as Louis "Lefty" Berthold, call sign "Bad Dog"

-4: Identified as Sqd. Ldr. Jack Hawker, A flight

-?: Voice unidentified

( ): Questionable insertion

[ ]: Editorial insertion

13:22:04
START OF RECORDING

HOT-1: Return flight one-two, I have you inbound.

HOT-2: This is one-two return. Where are you?

HOT-1: Not something a fighter pilot ought to be asking, flight leader. I'm just saying.

HOT-2: Ah, go fuck yourself, Captain. [Laughter] You in the soup?

HOT-1: Roger that. Five degrees your left. Eleven o'clock high at . . . ten thousand.

HOT-2: 'Kay. We're incoming.

HOT-1: I'm winking at you. Can you tell?

HOT-1: Descending now.

HOT-1: Passing six thousand. Split out and form on me for formation.

For what time he had remaining, Carter would hear the voices in his head. Ghosts that, once embedded in the soft meat of his brain, could not be dislodged. In bed, in flight, at peace and at war, they would be there, taunting him, joking, dying. There would come nights when he would wake with his ears sore and his scalp bloody from trying to claw off imaginary headphones. To make the voices stop.

HOT-2: One-two inbound to control. We're on-target. Spotter on capture.

TWR: Copy one-two.

TWR: Ground capture, one-two inbound approach to target.

RDO-3: Thank you, control. I have both targets.

HOT-2: Fenn? One-two inbound. I have you on capture.

HOT-1: Roger. I've got visual. I'm maintaining at five thousand. Pass below and come around.

HOT-2: Yeah, I . . .

HOT-1: Porter?

HOT-2: Yeah.

HOT-1: Cut out there for a minute, flight leader.

HOT-3: Over there. Uh . . . Your two o'clock-ish. Low. Way low.

| | | | | | | | | | | | | |

On the field, Carter only dimly acknowledged the sound of Lefty Berthold's voice. He was busy. No idle hands. The ammunition belts passing through his fingers were heavy and cold as if knowing their own freight and destiny. He liked the sound of them sliding over the cockpit coaming, a clatter like an abacus rattling. He smelled the snow on the air and the heat radiating off his engine and the sweet, thick stink of aviation fuel from the pumps near him and the pour-cans being run across the field. When he caught himself speaking aloud, under his breath, saying, "Come on, come on, come on," he willed himself into calm, unclenched his fists, closed his eyes. He barely made note of Lefty's voice in his ear. Not yet, anyway.

| | | | | | | | | | | | |

HOT-3: Way low. Passing over now.

HOT-1: One-two inbound, this is Fenn. What's the problem, gentlemen?

HOT-2: You are seeing things, Lefty.

HOT-1: [Unintelligible] (Fucking cold legs?)

RAM: [Flight sounds, navigation capture chime]

HOT-2: Fenn? Porter. What's the time to target on the bombers?

HOT-1: Uh . . . Dunno. Hold one.

RAM: [Clack of frequency change]

HOT-1: Spotter to A flight inbound. Do you copy?

HOT-4: Copy you, Fenn.

HOT-1: Jack?

HOT-4: Yeah. We're on our way. Do you have a heading for us?

HOT-1: Yeah, no. What's your time to the river?

HOT-4: Uh . . . Let me . . .

HOT-1: Jack?

HOT-4: Wait a second.

HOT-4: Ten minutes. Less, maybe. We're heavy.

HOT-1: Okay.

RAM: [Sound of engine cycling up RPM]

HOT-1: Okay. Make for the river. Call in when you're in sight.

HOT-4: Roger that. A Flight out.

HOT-1: Spotter out.

RAM: [Frequency change, groaning]

HOT-1: Porter? Ten minutes or less.

HOT-2: Okay, well . . .

HOT-3: Let's go already!

HOT-2: Uh . . .

HOT-1: One-two, what's the fucking problem?

|||||||||||||

Earlier in the day, on dawn patrol in the sky above Riverbend, Fenn had seen all he needed to of his future on Iaxo. He'd flown up with Charlie Voss and Stork and Emile Hardman. At play, they'd been. Their guns (and their everything else) cold in the thin morning air and thin morning light.

Scouting. Ted's new way of winning the war. As ridiculous as every other. Bored, Fenn had been thinking of home. His last real home, green among the gray. Volcanoes sketched in the hand of a child—three of them like inverted Vs. His wife, Rose, under the dome of geodesic glass. Round face with a permanent smile.

Fenn had thought about Eddie while he flew a route so common that his plane seemed to know the way all on its own. He thought about what Eddie had said in the tent a million years ago. A few hours ago. All his numbers. His matters of consequence and paper and figures of murderous accuracy. The cigarette he couldn't keep lit. He thought about standing in the cold with Carter.

What did you do before you joined the company?

Two years they'd been together. Carter had never asked him this before. A strange thing only in the realization of its absence.

Nothing, he'd said, mostly because he was suddenly angry that it'd never come up before. That Carter hadn't asked. That they'd talked of socks and toast and where they'd fought and the money they'd made or hadn't made and which rock was better than this rock—Carter's notion of meaningful conversation. *You?*

And Carter hadn't answered either. Maybe for the same reason. Maybe for his own.

They'd flown, line abreast, he and Stork and Charlie and Emile. Patrolling the nothing. The patchwork. The stupid ground. Orders from King Ted had been to stay well clear of the indig cities, but orders were only orders.

So Fenn had approached, dragging the wing along with him, and ten thousand feet became nine, then eight. The river had split the living ground laid out below them and then the walls of the city had risen; beyond it, the stepping land, the tabling moors. The horizon was smudged with dust in the slanting, early rays of the young, glassine sun, and Fenn had touched a little rudder, meaning to skid by, over Riverbend and the Akaveen siege force laid out around it, just to the east. The wing had responded smoothly. And then they'd seen—Stork had seen—the last of the braking flares, carving a hairline gleam just off the temporary arc of the rising sun's ecliptic.

"Was that . . ."

"Jesus."

"Altitude," Fenn had ordered. "Get up there. Everyone."

Planes had scrambled, reaching for height and a recovery from glare-blindness. It was the panic of small animals suddenly scared out of their wits, fighting for angular geometries of safety and vision they understood only in their most secret, animal hearts. The planes had snapped past Riverbend without giving it a second look, moving more deeply into Indian country as they poured power into their machines and ran for altitude. The only safety they'd ever known.

The high moors had been covered with men and materiel and machines, all arriving by the first blinding light of dawn when the radiance of sunrise would wash out the fires of their arrival. It'd looked to Fenn as though they'd been coming for days, though that, he was willing to admit later, might just have been the shock. It might have only been hours. It might have been forever—all of them arranging themselves behind the lines, just out of view, waiting.

Fenn went to call it in. He'd been reaching out to fiddle with the radio. And that was when the disastrous assault on Riverbend had begun. He had wheeled the wing clear at altitude. He'd talked to ground control, and then to Ted. Everyone was chattering on the radio, talking over one another. He dialed in the wing frequency and overrode them all. "Home," he'd said.

There was no response, but everyone followed him as he leaped on the shortest radial for the return flight. On the ground, the natives were getting their asses handed to them. They were experiencing hand grenades, learning about the wrong ends of rifles, discovering land mines in the worst possible way, all courtesy of the Lassateirra indigs and their NRI friends inside Riverbend. Fenn was too high to see the worst of it, and he'd been glad for that.

| | | | | | | | | | | | |

HOT-1: Porter, talk to me.
HOT-2: One-two to spotter, requesting permission to break and investigate.
HOT-1: We are fighter cover, one-two. Bombers are on their way. Come up to five thousand and form up. Now.
RAM: [Static. Increased engine sound]
HOT-1: Investigate what?
HOT-2: Fucked if I know.
HOT-2: Lefty?
HOT-3: Can't see it.
HOT-1: Lefty, this is Fenn. Talk to me.
HOT-3: [Unintelligible]
HOT-1: Bad Dog, repeat. What did you see?
HOT-2: Coming back, one-eight-zero degrees. Idiot. Fuck, Lefty. Break and come back.

HOT-1: Somebody say something useful, please? One–two, I have visual of you. Break and come around and ascend to five thousand.
HOT-3: There!
HOT-1: Porter, get him back now or I'm going to shoot his dumb ass down myself.
HOT-2: Copy that, spotter.
HOT-2: Hear him, Lefty? Think he's fucking around? Not today, if we . . .
HOT-3: There! There! Guns in the field. Repeat, weapons on the field. I'm passing over right now. Directly below me.
HOT-2: No way. How could they . . . Spotter! You copy, Fenn?
RDO-2: One–two inbound, did you [unintelligible]
RDO-?: [Unintelligible] (Sound of struggle?)
HOT-1: I copy you, flight leader.
HOT-2: Did you . . .
HOT-1: I heard him. Can you confirm?
RDO-?: . . . Off the fucking thing . . . Hold him!
HOT-1: Porter! Can you confirm?

|||||||||||

Ted came through the door to the comms tent at a dead run, shouldering his way through and cracking the thin wood at the frame, never slowing down. He ran until he hit the radio boards and then clubbed Jimmy McCudden right out of his chair with his forearm. Tore the headphones off him by the wire.

Diane saw it all from the tower seat. She screamed when Ted hit the door, but she didn't have her microphone keyed. For just a second, she thought they were being invaded, and it'd been like all of her nightmares were coming true.

Jimmy fell out of his chair. He'd been talking. Diane tried to fix all of these details in her mind in case they became important later. Ted had hit Jimmy from behind, swinging his arm like a bat. Jimmy fell into Shun Le, who was coordinating ground traffic and taxi orders. She yelled, too. Diane was on her feet, her microphone off, and she tried to shush Shun Le because she was in charge—lead controller—and there wasn't supposed to be any talking on the radio line that wasn't integral to each controller's duties. People got distracted so easily. They lost track of what was important. So Diane tried to shush Shun Le. She stood up and she waved her hands.

But Shun Le wasn't listening.

Ted was yelling at Jimmy: "Get off the fucking thing!" And he was yanking at the headphone wire.

Shun Le was saying that she'd had just about enough of this shit and was going to file a complaint.

In the air, the pilots were all shouting at each other. A flight—the bombers—were on the wrong radial and having to duck down below the lowering cloud base to get themselves straightened out.

And Diane was laughing. She was laughing at Shun Le because she knew there was no one left to file a complaint to. She'd overheard enough from the pilots—in particular the ones who never even noticed she was there; the ones who, after two years, didn't even know her name. She'd listened to them talk. She'd watched the Ted-and-Eddie show often enough and had placed many of Eddie's early-morning calls on the secure uplink. Maybe she hadn't always switched her channel as quickly as she ought to. Maybe she knew more than anyone thought she did. Like she knew for sure that no one was going to listen to any harassment complaint from little Miss Shun Le Harper, who was always finding something to scowl about anyhow. To make faces at.

So Diane laughed. She also thought it was funny because she'd never heard Shun Le say "shit" before. So proper, that one. So quiet, most of the time.

Ted was saying her name. Diane shook her head.

"Hold him!" Ted snapped, meaning Jimmy, who'd never done anything mean to anybody. Who'd never said a cross word. And for an instant, Diane thought about kicking Ted instead.

"No way," she said back. "Everyone stop yelling right *now!*"

Ted's face was mottled. There was a crust of something at the corner of his mouth that looked like blood. His hair was mussed. Like a boy, like an idiot, he'd been out on the field, running around and playing with the airplanes when he should've been inside coordinating. Leading. That was his job. He smelled of cold and exhaust and fuel.

Diane had no doubt he'd been getting in everyone's way, trying to help but doing just the opposite. Like a boy.

She'd told him before that he shouldn't be flying anymore. That there was no need. And she could do that, being lead controller. She felt as though she was able to say things to Ted that no one else could—that it was her place to point out things that, maybe, he wasn't in a position to notice.

He'd listened to her for a while, but then had stopped. Said who was she to tell him what was needed?

Lead controller, she'd told him. *That's who.*

You don't know what's needed, he'd said. *You don't understand.*

Oh yes, I do.

He'd been carrying one of the radio handsets outside with him, Ted had. Diane knew that for a fact. She also happened to know that he slept with it in his hand, curled into his fist, his fist on his chest, with the rubber whip antennae sticking up like a lily in the hand of a corpse. Every sound it made, his eyes would snap open like window shades. She'd watched this. She was the one who'd change out the handset batteries in the middle of the night, when it was quiet, so that Ted would never notice. For two hours, sometimes three, she'd leave the fresh batteries out. She'd sit beside him, bouncing them in her palm. It was the only real sleep Ted ever got.

Lead controller, that's who.

Ted was pulling Jimmy's headphones on. Ted was crouching to Jimmy's microphone. His eyes were wild in his head. Bloodshot and watering from the cold and the sudden sour, stinging snow that'd blown up.

Shun Le was slapping her hand on the flat shelf of the radio console—something she did when she was looking for attention.

Jimmy was scrambling to his feet.

Jimmy was grabbing Shun Le for leverage and hauling himself up.

Shun Le was pushing him off.

Diane was standing, waiting to see what would happen next. The pilots babbled in her ear. Her breath was coming low and in grunts.

Jimmy—who'd never done a cruel thing, who'd never raised his voice, who'd never been anything but cordial and sometimes had coffee or tea with Diane when she was coming off the night shift and he was coming on—raised a hand. Jimmy made a fist and punched Ted in the back. He put all his weight behind it.

Jimmy might just as well have punched a rock.

Diane smiled, her lips parted slightly, tongue touching the tips of her front teeth.

Ted was suddenly calm. Ted was suddenly in control. His eyes were still bloodshot. He still looked like death walking. But there was some weight in him now. A presence that Diane recognized but couldn't put a name to. He turned in the chair.

You don't understand.

Oh yes, I do.

"Hit him . . . ," Diane hissed under her breath, too quietly for anyone else to hear. "Hit him . . ."

| | | | | | | | | | | |

HOT-2: Fenn, is your radio down? I'm getting nothing from the controllers . . .

| | | | | | | | | | | |

There was an order, a method for getting men and airplanes off the ground and into the air. There had been plans—written down somewhere, studied, lost, found, memorized, practiced, debated over. There were words to be intoned and replies to be made, pious gestures and motions to go through, movements to make. Like anything important, it all seemed rote and pointless in those hours and days and years when none of it had been necessary; when a man and his plane might leisurely go up and come down, defying and then succumbing to gravity without schedule. And then, like anything important, in the sudden moment when the plan's purpose became borne out by the situation for which it'd been designed, the whole thing just went completely to shit.

In his plane, Carter watched the chaos on the ground and it made him smile. All this action, this furious activity—it was exciting, was what it was. Finally, there was something to do. And it didn't matter to him if they did it well or did it poorly. He just didn't want to miss all the fun.

| | | | | | | | | | | | | | |

HOT-1: Control, this is Jackrabbit. Over.

HOT-1: Porter, come around sharp and put on some fucking altitude. Now. Lefty, you follow.

HOT-2: Roger that, spotter. Coming around to two-four-five. Breaking.

HOT-2: Lefty?

HOT-3: Heard him.

RAM: [Increasing engine noise]

RAM: [Navigation capture chime] (possibly from HOT-1?)

HOT-1: What the hell is that?

HOT-1: Control, Jackrabbit. Do you copy?

HOT-4: Fenn? A flight inbound. Is that me you're reading?

HOT-1: A flight, hold one.

HOT-1: Porter, Lefty, bug out now. Come to ten thousand on any heading.

HOT-2: Ten thousand, roger.

TWR: Jackrabbit, this is control. Are you—

HOT-1: 'Bout fucking time . . .

HOT-1: Control, I have an unidentified potential target. Off the river at—

RDO-1: Fenn, pull them up and out immediately. Come to two-seven-zero and get back across the river at altitude. Go to ceiling.

TWR: I have the target. Marking it as a navigation point. It's on the ground at—

RDO-1: I am going to OPS frequency now. Tower, scramble the fighters. Close C for takeoffs. Landings only. Emergency crews and equipment to the field.

RAM: [More chimes, increasing engine sounds]

HOT-4: I have three unidentified captures. Are these targets?

HOT-4: Four now.

OPS: A flight inbound, maintain course and heading. Rally at ten thousand, over the bridge at the third nav beacon. Box it.

HOT-4: Roger, Ops.

RDO-3: All fighters to ready position.

RAM: [Sound of siren from ground]

HOT-3: Cavalry is breaking up, Porter. See that there?

RDO-3: Fighters in taxi. Ground crews are still on the strip. Field crews shifting. Ops, do you want them to finish loading the fighters?

HOT-2: Yeah, come out and around, Lefty. We've got altitude. Just stay clear.

OPS: No. Put 'em in the air. We're re-forming by wing in the air at . . . Give them north by north, five miles clear. Form up and hold for attack orders.

RDO-3: Copy that.

TWR: A flight inbound hold and box at ten thousand at nav three. Jackrabbit and one-two inbound, crossing the river and going to ceiling.

RAM: [Sound of click from HOT-3—similar to rudder maximizing]

HOT-3: We're going to come back and—

RAM: [Sound of tearing]

RAM: [Sound of stick shaking begins. Sound of solid metallic impacts]

HOT-3: Oh God.

| | | | | | | | | | | |

Carter had seen Ted taking off like a dart for the comms tent. He'd been waiting on fuel, hunched down in Roadrunner's cockpit, sitting on his hands to keep them warm. He was listening to the radio.

Raoul came with the gas—hand pump on a dolly meant for moving file cabinets or furniture. He got a call to taxi to ready-one. He responded with a negative. "Waiting on the fuel truck, baby," was what he'd said.

He had machine-gun rounds. Belts of them, and then extras stashed in folds behind his seat. Max was walking the stubble field, passing out bombs like Halloween candy. Carter had eleven rounds for the cannon and could've stood ten or twenty more. He was heavy, but unconcerned. Breathing through his mouth, he felt dizzy with anticipation and frozen by the scattered action on the field, like he was looking in on it all from outside. Like they were in a snow globe he was shaking, far beyond the concerns of the tiny people inside. He heard Fenn yelling at Porter and Porter yelling at Lefty. They were having fun. He didn't want to miss it. He wanted to play, too.

Raoul finished with the gas, slapped Roadrunner on the flank, and moved on. Carter pulled a hand free and stuck his thumb up. He called ground control. "Ready for taxi," he said, and got no response. He closed his eyes and tried to imagine sunbeams on his face, the smell of anything green and living. The new engine growled like something caged and sent rumbles of power jittering up through Carter's tailbone. It made him have to pee.

Lefty saw something; he was yelled at some more. No one knew what he'd seen. Lefty was an idiot. Fine pilot, but an idiot. Jumpy. Bad eyes. He'd been Carter's drogue man since day one on Iaxo—fifth pilot in a squadron that generally sortied in pairs—and it never seemed to bother him. Carter snuggled down deeper into his seat, ducking his chin down to his chest and breathing into the fur of his collar. He pursed his cold lips. "Lefty," he whispered. "Lefty, Lefty, Lefty." His radio reception was spotty. It popped and crackled in his ear.

Orders began coming through. "Roadrunner, clear to taxi. Runway B left. Splendor, Havoc—three and nine at runway B left. Three squadron shift to runway A left. Ground crews away. All clear runway C."

Carter checked his mirror. He straightened his legs and squeezed up against his restraints, looking across the cowling and through the spinning prop before goosing the throttle and trying to rumble forward. The plane bumped and went nowhere. He was chocked. Keying his radio to the ground crew frequency, he felt a sudden sparkle in the air, an aliveness and tension that was like a fog lifting, a sudden adjustment in some global focus knob that brought everything into bright and sharp contrast.

"Roadrunner to ground. I'm chocked. Somebody pull these fuckers."

He thought he might be hyperventilating. Or having a heart attack. "This is just one of those things," he said to himself, aloud, and watched, wide-eyed, the swirls of waxy snow drifting and spinning across the field. The bare branches of trees like skeleton fingers on the verge. Rockwell kicking viciously with his steel-toed boots at the wheel mount of George Stork's Fokker, Iaxo Hustler, and the remains of first squadron, Albert Wolfe and Billy Stitches, wheeling their planes, Havoc and Splendor in the Grass, into their places in the taxi order, and Vic, somewhere out there, stopped like a wound-down toy, head cocked, one ear to the wind—paused in midstride because, as Carter knew, she'd felt it, too. A physical change in the atmosphere, like a pressure drop. Max was flagging planes, wearing a wide, gap-toothed smile. Meleuire came at a run, jinked around Roadrunner's spinning prop at the last second, yanked the chocks, and then popped up on the other side of the fuselage, spinning the chocks on their cord. He signaled Carter to roll.

"Roadrunner taxiing, B left."

In his ear, the radio bellowed with the clear voice of the ground controllers, ordering all fighters to lift immediately. They were to scramble and re-form, north by north, five miles clear.

The klaxon, the ground emergency horn, added its voice.

And Carter was already moving when he heard Lefty get shot.

HOT-3: Oh God. Oh . . .

HOT-2: Uh, control? We have . . . There's ground fire here.

HOT-3: [Unintelligible] (Laughing)

HOT-1: Iaxo Ops, ground fire. Ground fire.

OPS: All fighters, pull out to far beacon at ceiling.

HOT-3: Motherfucker . . . [Unintelligible] . . . coming (hard right?)

HOT-2: Lefty, repeat. Are you hit?

OPS: A flight, this is Ops. Time to target?

HOT-4: Ops, A flight. Target or . . .

OPS: The bridge, Jack. How far?

HOT-4: Climbing to it now. Three minutes.

||||||||||||

Carter didn't love Lefty Berthold. He didn't even like him in any particular, specific way. Funny that on a planet that hosted maybe a couple thousand humans all told—in a place that encompassed about fifty—there were still people he hardly knew and didn't much care to. He had flown with Lefty, yes. Fought beside him inasmuch as anyone did anyone when alone in a bathtub at ten thousand feet. And there was, as he understood it, supposed to be this profound and unspoken, unbreakable bond between men who were at war together, a sense that, in having had the shared experience of killing and facing death together, they were bound by some deep and communal connection that would link them for all their given days.

It was a job. Some people he liked. Some he didn't.

He gave Roadrunner some throttle. He wasn't waiting for any fucking flag. "Lifting now," he said, radio tuned to a wing frequency. He'd already squeezed through between Wolfe's Havoc and Billy's Splendor in the Grass. "Keep up. Stay tight. Let's go get some."

Across the field, B strip, planes were shuffling around one another like bad dancers, trying to find a clear taxi. The system had broken down completely. There was no order, just a deep need to be in the air and doing some damage. There was a bomb dolly lying half on the A strip apron, and he jigged around it until he felt his right wheel biting stubble. Once past it, he was in the clear. Wolfe and Billy would have to come single file. He saw another plane wobble into the air, another Camel that he thought was probably Tommy Hill. Just barely made it airborne, the fool. Carter punched his throttle forward and felt the new engine cycle up and begin to roar.

He hardly knew Lefty, save that he lived two tents down the line from him and Fenn, loved eggs, cut hair for some of the men (though not for Carter), had fought a day or two or ten ago with Lambert from the ground crew, had once bragged of laying Shun Le Harper, one of the controllers, which was a complete lie because Shun Le didn't even talk to pilots, let alone whatever else. Davey Rice had called Lefty on it, Carter remembered, during one of the slow seasons when there was nowhere to go and nothing to do but talk shit and scrounge for excitement.

"That one," Davey had said, meaning Shun Le, "doesn't even open her mouth to pilots, let alone her legs."

"Not to you, maybe," Lefty had said.

"Not to anyone," Davey shouted. "Motherfucker, I bet you got *Shun Le Pussy* written on your fucking hand." And everyone had laughed, even Lefty, because damn if that wasn't funny no matter what the truth was.

In the air, Carter checked his six, his twelve, and then his thirteen, fourteen, and fifteen, too, just for good measure. He would do a lazy circle, collect his wing, then go fuck some shit up. This was the new plan. His.

Lefty Berthold had once played out a lucky streak at the poker table for almost twelve hours until he fell asleep on his winnings and woke with shell casings and boot laces and coins from a dozen worlds stuck to his face. He had a family back home (though Carter didn't know where home was for him, exactly) who sometimes gave him problems and sometimes didn't. Lefty'd hurt himself once, drunkenly picking a fight with a horse. Lefty'd asked him once about Vic, and Carter'd told him to shut up. Lefty had an actual first name. Carter thought it might've been Hugo. He didn't know the man at all.

And now he loved him. Now he was going to risk his life saving him, helping him, avenging him, because Lefty was shot and being shot was special and different and, if he *did* die, Carter would mourn him like they'd been lovers or brothers—already, he felt rage and grief packing up like a hot ball in his chest.

That bond, that mystical whatever that soldiers and pilots were supposed to have? Carter knew it only meant that they would die for one another. But until the moment of dying came, it didn't really mean much of anything at all.

|||||||||||||

HOT-2: Lefty?
HOT-1: Tower, this is Jackrabbit. Bad Dog inbound is showing smoke.
TWR: Copy that, Jackrabbit.
TWR: Bad Dog, this is tower control. Are you damaged?
HOT-3: [Laughing]
HOT-2: I see that smoke. Coming back . . .
RAM: [Increasing engine noise. Stickshaker, indicating a hard climb]
HOT-2: Control, more ground fire.
OPS: Do you have a location on that ground fire?
TWR: Bad Dog, respond.
HOT-2: Right below and behind me. Um . . .
RAM: [Two clicks, rapid decrease in engine noise]

HOT-2: Jesus, fucking accurate, too. Multiple contacts. All over the bad side of the river here.

RAM: [Engine noise increasing. Two clicks—similar to flaps locking.]

HOT-2: Taking fire.

HOT-1: What the hell—

HOT-4: Ops, A flight. Two minutes. A.O. in sight.

HOT-1: Ops, I have . . . Is anyone else seeing this?

HOT-4: Jesus . . .

HOT-4: Ops, permission to engage immediately.

HOT-3: Tower, Bad Dog. I'm hit. I'm hit.

OPS: Negative, A flight. Climb and hold.

HOT-3: Oh mother . . .

TWR: Copy, Bad Dog. Come around to two-eight-three at any altitude. Bring it home.

HOT-3: Bleeding.

HOT-1: Ops, I'm seeing what looks like . . . I don't know. Orbital flares?

HOT-2: Lefty? Speak, pal. What's happening?

HOT-3: [Laughing]

HOT-3: [Unintelligible] . . . Fucking shot. I can't . . .

HOT-1: Insertion flares, maybe.

TWR: Bad Dog, control. Make any return heading, any altitude. Find a—

OPS: Bad Dog, repeat.

HOT-2: Repeat, Lefty. Come on, man.

HOT-3: Oh God. I'm gonna die.

| | | | | | | | | | | | |

Porter didn't see them—the flares. Later, he would say he had, but he hadn't. He would sit with Emile Hardman in the ugly, rancid remains of the mess and, over coffee that was cold before they poured it, describe the beautiful, arcing comets of light. How they'd lit like fireworks, dragging long tails of fire across the cloud-stricken bowl of the sky. How, in fact, they'd almost seemed to *boil* the clouds as they passed through them—punching holes like wounds into the clotted masses of wet, gray banks and then sizzled along their bellies like worms made of fire.

"It was like nothing I've ever seen," he would say, staring into the cold, oily surface of his coffee, shaking his head as though he almost believed what he was saying. Which, all things considered, wasn't difficult. It *was* like nothing he'd ever seen because he hadn't actually seen anything. He was just talking so that he didn't have to talk about Lefty.

That, he had seen. And Porter didn't want to think about that ever again.

| | | | | | | | | | | | |

OPS: Medical to the field. Clear C. Clear the infield aprons.
TWR: Bad Dog, pull up and out. Come left, east by east, and we'll walk you home.
HOT-2: Fenn?
HOT-1: Hold post, Porter. Stay with me.

| | | | | | | | | | | |

Carter had ammunition belts rubbing against his ankles. Clawing for altitude, running from the airfield as though from a fire, and with the rest of his hodgepodge wing trailing behind, he felt the weight of the bullets subtly altering the flight characteristics of his fighter. There was the weight of the fuel in the tank behind his head, sloshing backward toward earth as his pitch increased, and the weight of the bombs he carried. The cannon rounds in their flimsy metal clips (which broke constantly, keeping the machine shop forever busy at mending) weighed him down as he struggled for the shifting, clotted soup of the clouds. There was the weight of his guns, the weight of the machine dragging behind him—of flaps and rudder and wings and tail and his seat and the radio and instruments, all of it being yanked forward and upward by the chopping of the propeller, the firing of the pistons in their cylinders. There was the great, solid weight of the engine itself. And there was the weight of him. Of his damp, cold leathers, his helmet, his jumpsuit, his sidearm and pocket lint and gloves and boots; of his blood and bone and brains.

All of it wanted to fall. Everything wanted to go to ground—the most natural thing in the world. And Carter would let it. He would give to gravity what it wanted soon enough. When he came to the apex of the parabola he was describing, the highest point in the hump of air he climbed over the distant earth, he would hang an instant—weightless, like he'd been two years ago in the instant the dropship that'd brought him here had fallen clear of the clamps—then roll over and descend like wrath. He would go, dropping weight as he went, spitting out bullets and shedding bombs, burning fuel and loosing the weight of held breath and expectation as he howled down upon the enemy that had been chosen for him. To fight them, finally, with fairness and equanimity. Guns with guns and bombs with bombs. To give them their fair shot at him, meet them in the interstices between sky and ground, see them in the open where neither of them could hide.

Carter called in his flight to rally. He circled to let them gather and form up. Below him, terrible things were happening. And as he reached his chosen point in the sky, he rolled over, pointed his nose toward the ground, and became a terrible thing himself.

| | | | | | | | | | | |

HOT-3: Tower . . .
HOT-1: Ops? What are we doing here?
HOT-3: I gotta . . . Down, down, down.
TWR: Bad Dog, this is control. Do you copy?
HOT-1: Ops! I saw entry flares. Ten and two, high, coming in and headed for the moors near Southbend. Past, maybe.
OPS: Jackrabbit, hold one.
OPS: A flight, this is Ops. Form up.
HOT-3: [Coughing] I need a . . . [Unintelligible] (Doctor?)
OPS: Jackrabbit, Ops. Do you have a visual of the target?
HOT-3: I can't . . . Oh God. There's so much blood. I don't . . .
HOT-1: What target, Ops? The landing site?
TWR: Bad Dog, you are drifting. Come back on your heading.
HOT-3: I'm gonna try to . . .

OPS: The ground fire, Jackrabbit. The weapons. What landing site?

HOT-3: Down. Put down.

HOT-3: I don't want to die. I don't . . . I don't want to die now.

HOT-1: No. Not unless they're shooting at us, Ted.

OPS: Not now.

HOT-1: We're at almost twenty thousand feet here, Ops. No, I can't.

HOT-3: Not now. Not now.

OPS: A flight, any visual?

HOT-3: No. No. No. [Coughing]

Hot-4: No, Ops. No visual.

HOT-3: No!

HOT-3: Tower, Bad Dog. Coming around to two-eight-zero. I'm coming home.

TWR: Copy that, Bad Dog. Can you—

HOT-3: Blood all over the thing. I'm hurt pretty bad.

TWR: We're waiting on you, Bad Dog. You're going to be fine.

HOT-3: [Sound of grunting or heavy breathing] Gonna be fine. Coming home.

RAM: [Sound of banging—similar to engine oil pressure drop or failing cylinder]

HOT-3: I can see the—

TWR: Bad Dog, altitude is—

HOT-3: Flaps.

OPS: Come on home, Lefty.

TWR: Altitude is low. Come up. Come up.

RAM: [Sound of flash-over, engine sound decreases, spooling down]

HOT-3: [Screaming, unintelligible, continues to end]

HOT-4: Oh my God.

TWR: Bad Dog, do you copy?

HOT-4: Flame out! Lefty's on fire! On fire!

TWR: Bad Dog?

RAM: [Sound of roaring—similar to engine fire or flash-over]

HOT-1: Fuck you, Ted.

RAM: [Sound of impact]

END OF RECORDING

HOT-1: Fuck you, Ted.

Fenn had kicked Jackrabbit into a long, dancing turn, standing her high on her wing and watching the wet compass spin before nosing down into a shallow dive. He'd throttled back his engine, the glideslope seeming to pull him toward the ground with a slow-mounting tension of mass and alien gravities.

"Porter, follow me. Low six."

"Roger that, Jackrabbit. Falling in."

Lefty was like a dud firework. He was the last flare in the box, drifting to ground unnoticed. Fenn killed his channel. He didn't need anyone else's screams to haunt him, though he knew some of the others—Carter—would suckle at them, drain every last decibel like an alcoholic tonguing the neck of an emptied bottle. While he was at it, he killed the Ops channel as well.

"A flight, this is Jackrabbit. New target information."

Fenn explained. Looking up and back across the open spine of his plane, past the shark fin tail, he saw the wing of bombers moving like motes in the diffuse sun, the face shield of his helmet polarizing until he could just make them out waltzing the box.

They were going to hit the guns that'd got Lefty, easily identified by sporadic radio pickups on the navigation computers and, closer to the ground, by the fact that they'd be the only things shooting back. He felt ridiculous saying it, giving the orders. The tough-guy dialogue coming from inside him staled on his lips, the lusting after pointless vengeance an easily recognized cliché in a heart that spent so much time agonizing over past stupidities and judging the actions of every other organ surrounding it.

But Fenn did it. He spoke the words and he gave the orders because it was important—because, for a minute, it might make him feel better about having watched Lefty Berthold burn to death and go candling off into the long dark. Hitting these few guns wouldn't matter in the long run, but Fenn felt it needed to be done regardless. Also, he didn't believe any of them had much longer to run anyhow, so when they were done with the guns, they would hit something else. And they would keep hitting, Fenn figured, until he didn't have any punch left in him. Then he'd stop. Then he'd see what happened next.

"Copy, Jackrabbit," Jack said once the orders had been given. Then there was a squelch as he switched channels to relay orders to his wing of bombers. Then another as he came back. "Uh . . . Ted's giving us orders to stay put, Jackrabbit. To hold for fighter cover."

"My radio must be malfunctioning then, Jack, because I didn't hear that. You have your orders. Come down to visual range and fuck them up. Porter and I will draw fire. You follow."

"Roger that, Jackrabbit. A flight is rolling hot."

Above him, Fenn watched the bombers drop like stones, making fast for attack altitude. It was lovely sometimes, diving from such height. To come crashing down upon the earth with the promise of such fantastic violence. It wasn't Fenn's thing, as such, but he understood it. He hoped, looking up, that Jack had the joy of it. He thought it was about time someone had some fun in this droll little war.

Fenn turned around then to face the warped air beyond his spinning prop and eased his stick forward.

"Uh, Jackrabbit?" Porter's voice, half whispering like he was leaning over Fenn's shoulder. "We're gonna do what now?"

| | | | | | | | | | | |

There was an instant—the interval between the first bright flash of the guns opening up and the first hiss and spanging doppler of their bullets' arrival—when Fenn was able to think what a fantastically bad idea this was.

There was an instant to wonder whether he'd underestimated the skills of these novice gunners, rolling their pieces out for the first time, stunned (Fenn hoped) by the savagery the pilots had shown and stricken (Fenn prayed) by the slaughterhouse ambiance they'd made on the ground. An instant to wonder at their ability to hit a fast-moving target with a nearly flat approach angle, their excitement at finally being able to get their licks in—firing at the first thing that showed up in their offset gun sights even if that thing happened to be him. Smart gunners, adroit or artful gunners, would wait for the following targets lumbering down slowly upon them. They'd hold their fire for the good kill. The defensive burst. But Fenn had told himself a story about these enemies laid out before him, already sparking their cannon at him—that they would be scared and angry and anxious and bloodthirsty all at the same time and, because of this, would be less excellent than he was, and so would die. It'd been a reasonable gamble at five thousand feet. Seemed less so at five hundred.

There was an instant to think how this might be his last instant, and that one seemed to last forever, encompassing all the other instants, leaving him plenty of time to think of anything he wished. The faintly remembered touch of yellow sun on his face. A view of Iaxo from on high that might've been the view of any one of a dozen worlds. The dim, almost childish image of home—a geodesic over an abandoned pressure container, a boy, a mom, and a dad standing like stick figures before it, hands linked in scribbles, smiles on each round face. A conversation he and Carter had once had about toast and the simple, dumb, sweet and easy longing it'd invoked, like magic, into their hearts in place of the grief there on the day after Danny Diaz had died.

Toast, his last memory.

Danny.

Carter.

And then the instants all shattered around him, blowing back in a rooster tail of turbulence because he was through the gauntlet he'd made for himself and, behind him, all his doubts became nothing but the past as, behind him, the bombs were falling.

|||||||||||||

In the end, they'd driven the enemy back. They'd saved the day, at least for today, and then kept at it, beating the indigs not just to beat them, but to cripple them. To put the fear in them. And even after the worst of it—in those moments when the indigs had seemed to turn tail, melt into the ground, disappear into the terrain like ghosts—they'd chased them. Trying to make it so they'd be afraid to ever walk on the land again.

The pilots had attacked for a time, firing their guns dry, burning their barrels red. They'd been organized. They'd been disorganized. They'd flown in terrifying, meticulous formation and then, losing control of themselves, no human tenderness left in them, had broken, here and there, into cataclysms of rage—destructive, wasteful orgies of bombs and bullets—and flown around madly until the sky was tattered with smoke and the ground bruised by fury.

When the enemy advances had been turned back, the pilots had attempted to block avenues of retreat and counterattack. They would run back to the field for fuel, for ammunition, and then get right back in the air again—each time returning a bit more battered, holed, ripped and pocked with wounds that made their machines bleed and creep closer and closer to failure. They'd fought machine guns on the ground, hidden in stands of bush and copses of trees already shattered by bombs that would only need to be shattered again. They'd chased feints, advances that must've been meant as withdrawals, confused by the day when all directions went wrong—up being down and back being forward because, in the charnal house of that field, every direction was death. There was panic, some of it even from the enemy.

And they fought not only the Lassateirra. As the day wore on, cobbled-together squadrons would run after ground trucks that'd been seen whipping out in mad flanking maneuvers, around the backs of the horsemen and the infantry. For the first time, the Flyboy pilots mingled the blood of men with that of indigs—tearing up both together until they lay entangled in wet, vital solidarity. It was NRI. They knew it. And almost all of them felt that death was just exactly what they deserved. On the walls of Riverbend, they'd met rifle fire from disorganized packs of humans when they wheeled too close and, once or twice, saw the twisting columns of smoke upon which rode the hard, bright hammers of surface-to-air missiles that went corkscrewing off into uselessness or exploded low in white spiders of smoke. There was something in the fuel mix that was bad—burning sickly in the alien air and damp—but everyone knew it was a mistake the other side would not make again.

They'd flown to make recoveries of the lost. Lefty (who was easy) and then Stork (who was shot from the sky again, but lived) and Fenn, too, who'd been up longer than almost anyone and who was brought down by a failing engine, purely mechanical, but glided to a peaceful stop near a stand of squat, bluish trees and was found sitting cross-legged on the ground with his pistol in his hand. Waiting.

Fenn, they would say later. *You know Fenn. Sitting there waiting on us, happy as can be. Might as well have been getting a tan or admiring the scenery Stood up when we landed, said, "Gentlemen, fancy seeing you here," like some kind of lord or dandy.*

Later, Fenn would see Carter and say that the only thing he could remember was the smell. Even in the cold, the stink was terrible. The dying had been enormous, and he'd landed in a still-warm Golgotha.

"There were brains on my tires, Kev," he'd say. "There was no ground to land on that wasn't full of them."

They'd flown until they couldn't fly any more, exhausting themselves and their machines in a spasm of violence that just wouldn't quit until engines seized, eyes clouded over, mechanisms failed, and their guns gave forth only smoke. At the end of it, those still able had been reduced to flying low over the flood plain and assaulting the dead with harsh language. And when it was done, the pilots had blown icy breath through frozen lips and wondered where the energy had come from. They all felt so tired.

| | | | | | | | | | | |

Ten hours, then they'd come down. All of them. It was night. No one would fly at night. Everyone was crazed, exhausted, deaf, shot, sick, in pain, shattered, haggard, doom-struck, and lolling. Pilots would drop in their tracks, these youngish men—healthy and well fed—just going down like they were under sniper fire, to sleep for five minutes or ten in the mud and icy grass. It was scary the first time you saw it. The second time, you just stepped over the body and shuffled on.

George Stork was shot. So were Jack Hawker and Billy. George was missing a leg before morning and could no longer fly. Only the injectors had saved him—alien clotting factors and blood-thickeners keeping him from bleeding out completely before he could put his plane on the ground. Billy, too, though Billy hadn't even known he'd taken a bullet until somebody'd pointed it out to him—the back of his jumpsuit, tail of his jacket, even the tops of his boots all wet and sticky with blood that Billy hadn't even known was missing from him until he saw it, then stalked, cursing, to the shattered mess-turned-medical-tent, demanding explanations, ballistics, muzzle velocities, and shedding gear like he meant to go streaking.

Charlie Voss was dead. Porter was shot, too, but lived. Ernie O'Day had been shot in the face but was saved by his helmet. Doc Edison had taped a combat dressing that still smelled of the packing case it'd sat in for two years over the gouge in his cheek, then Ernie'd gone up again, where he'd been pinned in the sky by tracer fire, exploded, and fell like a comet crashing to Earth. Raoul was burned from a lashing of fire that'd flared out of an overheated manifold when he'd touched it with aviation fuel soaking his sleeve. He wasn't expected to survive.

Shun Le Harper was dead. She'd eaten the business end of a sidearm, but no one would say whose it'd been. She'd finished out the battle from her seat in the comms tent. She'd seen all the planes down and organized the first triage of men and equipment, coordinated all the messy taxiing of aircraft into the longhouse, and then she'd gotten up, found a gun somewhere (it wasn't like there was any shortage), walked out toward the verge, past the stopway of C strip, put the gun in her mouth and pulled the trigger.

Among the pilots, the question of whether or not she'd been loving Lefty on the sly seemed settled by this one determined act. By the fine spray of blood frozen into the grass like a pointillistic rendering of some hot, exotic flower and the shroud of snow she was wearing when found. There was a lovely storybook finality to it. An ordered progression of grief that, in its way, was comforting to those being fucked around by uncontrollable circumstance.

Diane was not so sure. True, Shun Le had been sleeping with Lefty Berthold. They lived together, the two women. It wasn't something Diane could not know. But sitting on her bed, in their tent, beginning the process of going through Shun Le's things and stealing anything she thought might be useful or valuable, Diane told herself that because she knew Shun Le, she knew Lefty wasn't the reason.

Diane had a theory that those who listen—controllers, radio ops, relay specialists—began like empty vessels of varying size, some large, some small. Over time, they began to fill up with the terrible things they had to hear. Last words. Final breaths. Bad orders. Fear. Worse, joyous slaughter. Eventually, everyone reached their maximum volume and the terrible things began to spill over. Some controllers went crazy. Some turned to drinking or drugs or began fucking everything that moved or started killing people. Diane had seen many variations. All of them were, to her eyes, attempts by those afflicted to either enlarge their internal vessel or to drain off some of the horror it contained. The trick of it was, it couldn't ever work. The vessel was the vessel and the voices were the voices. They never went away. Both the size of the vessel and the things it contained were immutable. Permanent.

So the way Diane saw it, Shun Le had simply reached her maximum volume. And because she was the way she was—so quiet and proper—she'd killed herself before she did anything embarassing or untoward. She'd done it because it was the quiet, polite thing, and she'd done it away from everything and everyone so as not to leave an uncomfortable mess. It was the overfull-vessel thing, for sure.

Johnny All-Around had tried to kill Ted. Ted, for most of the night, was suspiciously absent. Porter Vaughn was found, stunned, silently weeping in the cockpit of his Camel when the crews had come to wheel it into the longhouse; the floor awash with congealing blood and a hole in his foot big enough to stick a thumb into. Davey Rice had been missing most of the day and part of the night. When he'd come walking back into camp hours later minus one biplane, no one saw him but Emile Hardman, who, thinking he was a ghost or, worse, a hallucination, had almost shot him.

Emile went weird after that. And later, when asked what'd happened, Davey said he'd been forced down by ground fire that'd holed his tail, shattered the tip of one wing like bone, damaged his engine, and destroyed his radio. When no one came for him, he'd walked home—miles over the ground that'd so long been his enemy. He said there was nothing like it. Nothing ever. And then he'd popped the clip out of his pistol, ejected three rounds from it with his thumb, and dropped everything in the mud. He'd lifted that day with his sidearm and forty rounds. Those three bullets were all he had left. He didn't want to talk about where the other thirty-seven had gone.

| | | | | | | | | | | | |

Roadrunner had been one of the last planes down. Carter had fought as well and viciously as anyone, and when he'd come down out of his plane, he'd collapsed, his legs giving way as if they were made of paper the minute he'd stepped to the lower wing edge, the rest of him following after; falling into the cold, rutted muck outside the longhouse and barely feeling it because if there was a piece of him that wasn't dead from sitting or numb from the cold, then it already had hurts of its own that took precedence. Willy had seen Carter fall. He'd come and helped him to his feet.

"S'okay," Willy'd said. "We're taking bets, you know? Every one of you's fallen but one."

"Which one?" Carter'd asked.

It'd been Fenn, of course.

FENN HAD WATCHED LEFTY BERTHOLD DIE. He'd heard it, same as everyone, but he'd also seen it. Lefty'd barely managed to make it ten miles clear. Fenn had seen the fire. The distant spark of it against the dark, patterned ground. He'd known just where to look. Then he'd ordered the bombers in.

The bombers hit the guns that'd maneuvered, under cover of the slaughter, into advantageous positions in the tree line along the river. At the time, he'd wondered whether they were NRI gunners or native gunners, but it didn't really matter because, shortly, they were only dead gunners, which, all things considered, was better than any of the other options.

The fresh fighters arrived. They all flew around for a bit and did what they did. Fenn went home to rearm, went up again, went home to rearm, went up again. Each time, different men followed him. As they started to be shot down and die, there were fewer, but that was only math. Somehow, the equations and odds kept missing him, so, when he became tired and bored, he shot himself.

His plane, actually. Jackrabbit, who'd been so good to him for so long. He knew every inch of her skin, the simplicities of her insides, and exactly what went where, so he knew just where to put the bullets from his sidearm.

Fourteen rounds through the floor, between the rudder pedals, being careful not to shoot his own feet and not to aim too low where he would catch the edge of the protective bathtub that made up the cockpit. This, he thought, would probably sever the rudder linkage, but it didn't. It would probably cut the fuel lines, which it might have. It would almost certainly clip some of the bundles of oil and hydraulic hoses that ran in tangles around the base of Jackrabbit's big engine like the descending aortas of her many-chambered heart, which it did.

His gauges had skittered crazily for a moment, then went limp. He lost oil pressure like air going out of a balloon. The stick went heavy. He holstered his pistol and began looking around for a nice place to crash, but there were no good places. Some survival instinct made him fight the dying airplane. Adrenaline made him curse her for falling so quickly, for turning too slow, so that rather than whispering good night to her and sending her spinning into the ground (as had been his plan), he found himself screaming at her in frustration and calling her names as she died. He felt bad about this later, but not in the moment.

He landed the plane alongside a copse of trees, in a harrowed patch of blood and bodies and brains. His plane did not weigh a lot, but it weighed enough to pop the heads of the corpses he rolled over, to break the broken bodies further and desecrate them worse than had the bullets and the bombs that'd ended their pointless little lives. He hadn't meant to do that.

Later, he felt bad about this as well, and the bad feelings would nearly make him shoot Willy McElroy, which would've only made him feel worse.

When the plane had crunched to a stop, Fenn climbed out. He reloaded his pistol. There were wounded in the area, calling out in voices that sounded like echoes of Lefty Berthold's, even if the words were different. Or maybe they were the same. Pain and dying seem to give everyone a common language of anguish, he thought. For the first time, he felt as though he truly understood the indigs. Then he went around and put a bullet into the head of each of the wounded. This, he didn't feel badly about at all.

When that was done, he sat down and he waited. His friends would come or his friends wouldn't come. He had no stake in the matter except for a small amount of frustration at the tenacity of a living thing to remain so, a disappointment in his own lack of convictions, and a dull ache of tiredness that made him want even for the terrible bed he'd slept in, alone, for the past two years.

Fenn thought about his son, Andre, who'd lately been much on his mind. About his blond hair, dry and thin like straw, and the way his head had smelled right out of the bath. About him lying on the floor, surrounded by papers and crayons, drawing pictures of monsters and maps of lands that existed only in his head. Of squatting beside him inside the dome that was the newest and last home he knew and pointing out the stars at night, naming them because they were so new there that none of the constellations had been claimed yet, no pole stars chosen. They'd been like explorers that night. The whole of the universe, seen from original angles, became new all over again.

"That one," Fenn had said.

"The dog."

"And that one?"

"The duck."

"And those way out there?"

"Octopus."

"Good."

"Those are good names?"

"Yes."

"Are they right?"

"It doesn't matter. Right now, the stars are what we say they are."

And Andre had nodded as though that pleased him, furrowing his small forehead and the nearly invisible featherings of his brows. He'd scanned the sky with what, to Fenn, had seemed like a sudden panic, then settled.

"There," he'd said, and pointed in toward the old neighborhood, Sol and the Centauris, Ross, Groombridge, and Barnard's—all of them invisible at this distance but, somehow, sketched into the boy's DNA until he was like a good compass that always knew true north. "That's where home is, right?"

"Yeah, baby. You're right. That's the way home."

"I found it?"

"You found it," Fenn had said. "You can be my navigator any day."

And now, very far from that place, that moment, Fenn knew that if the indigs came, he would wedge the front sight blade of his pistol into the notch of his lower jaw, aim for the horizon behind himself, and pull the trigger. He also knew that if the indigs didn't come, he wouldn't. He didn't know why, and with no good explanations forthcoming, he simply sat and waited to see what came next.

| | | | | | | | | | | | |

Billy Stitches had come. Billy in his Bristol and Davey Rice flying cover low over their heads. Fenn had looked up at the sound of their engines. He'd even waved. He'd done it with his gun hand.

Billy had brought the two-seater in and landed it a couple hundred feet away, on a nice stretch of grass on the other side of the trees. Fenn had waited for him. The last moments had been the worst. The smell—a terrible, soupy, shitty, meaty stink of violent death—was all over him like he'd rolled in it. Like he'd swum in it with all his clothes on. The final poses of the dead, like terminal contortionists, like fatal lovers locked in shameless, public embraces, had overreached his capacity for metaphor and appeared to him now as only accusatory. When he heard Billy's footsteps, he'd raised the gun.

"Hey now, Captain. Why don't you holster that Python, all right? It's only me."

"Apologies, Billy. Never can be too careful."

"Uh-huh. You think I was sneaking up somewhere the other side of your neck?"

"Scratching my chin was all."

Fenn had smiled. He'd put the safety on. He'd holstered his sidearm and stood on legs that almost didn't hold him and walked on pins and needles away from his resting place while Billy stripped the guns and ammunition off Jackrabbit, put a bullet through her navigation computer, opened her engine panel, yanked her plug wires, and then delicately balanced a primed hand grenade between the base of the engine block and the firewall, its weight holding down the activator button so that the littlest disturbance would set it off.

"Sad, I know," Billy had said when Fenn ambled back. "She was a good girl, though. Did you proud." He laid a gentle hand on her nose. Fenn distractedly stroked a splintered blade of her prop. In the distance, they could hear the tectonic rumblings of impacts, the soft, almost delicate pop of machine guns firing. No way to tell anymore whose was whose. The moons were breaching the distant horizon, the day nearly done. How things had changed in so short a time.

Together, the two of them carried the salvaged guns and ammunition to the Bristol, loaded it all into the spotter's seat, and then Fenn squeezed in among them. The smell of them was crisp and bitter and mechanical after the savory stink of the dead. All the way home, he rode stroking the warm, oiled body of a .303, rubbing the gun oil between his fingers, touching it softly to his face.

They set down. Fenn sprang nimbly from the spotter's seat, scrambling down across the lower wing even as Billy was turning the Bristol for a taxi past the longhouse where he would take on a splash of fuel, then get up in the air again. Everywhere he looked, there was such delightful motion. Men running. Machinery moving. The cargo container that Connelly's drop had come in was sitting like something beached in the middle of the field, the ground around it churned and beaten into a sluggish mud that, overnight, would freeze harder than cement. He saw Emile Hardman walking like a zombie from the longhouse to the mess, which had become a medical tent. He saw David Rice—Davey who was always happy as a puppy to do anything, leaping into planes, panting with excitement; always joking and saying inappropriate things because he still had the Teflon soul of youth, the stored energy of a long life stretching out before him to infinity, untarnished by mortality. Davey stood off by himself, feet rooted, all motion drained from him but for his repeated, frustrated attempts to light a cigarette. He was drooling. The cigarettes kept slipping out of his mouth and falling into the dusting of waxy snow at his feet. Fenn didn't know it, but Charlie Voss had just died. Exploded out of the air as if by mean wishes. And Ernie, too— Fenn's faithful wingman. Davey had just heard about it. Every cigarette he stabbed between his numb lips, he would slobber out or drop. Fenn watched him go through five of them before he walked over and lit one for him, placing it carefully in his mouth.

Davey dropped it almost immediately. Fenn had given up then, smiled sweetly at the boy, and left him to gravity. He'd gone to the longhouse and Ted had caught him there to ask him what he'd been thinking, switching off his radio in combat, ordering the bombers in to hit the guns that'd killed Lefty. Ted's eyes were sick and glossy with the madness of failure.

"Wasn't your call to make, Captain," he said.

"Yes it was, Commander," Fenn replied, curling the fingers of one hand against his palm and examining the ragged crescent moons of his nails, his own madness kept well in check now, bitten back, bound, smothered under a muffling layer of practiced cool ten feet thick.

They were standing in a corner of the longhouse, near the machine shop, and the smell of wounded airplanes was so thick that the air seemed almost chewy. And Fenn would quote to Ted directly from the Flyboy Inc. employee handbook and pilot's manual: a document almost mythic in its very mention because everyone had one, had been issued one—an actual physical object, words on paper—on the day they signed their contracts with the company, but no one had ever actually read it. In its mystery, powers beyond imagining were sometimes ascribed to it. Promises of vacation time, legal explanations of the sexual harassment policy and payout schedules, details of deployment intervals and the dental plan. Every secretary, every cargo specialist, controller, supply clerk, pilot, mechanic, and junior counselor had been handed a copy on his or her first day. That much they could remember. Some could even describe the logo stamped on the front cover: a swoosh, rampant, over a field of stars, picked out in a very nice silver that would smudge the moment it was brushed against. But everyone, in the hot thrill of new and unusual employment, overawed perhaps by the slick glamour of a steel-and-mahogany boardroom or disappointed by some far-flung cubicle office out in the deep nowheres, had tucked it in among their things and then immediately forgot about it. The Flyboy Inc. employee handbook had never been read by anyone.

Except Fennimore Teague. He'd read every word. Some of it, he'd even memorized.

"Control protocol," he said to Ted, looking now at some indistinct space above his commander's head like a schoolboy reciting, like a bad actor squinting at distant cue cards. " 'When engaged in combat operations, the designated wing commander or so-acting officer or pilot has ultimate discretion over tactical orders when a rapidly developing situation in-theater requires his orders to supersede those of any command and control elements operating outside the area of combat operations. Said acting officer or pilot will, when the situation requires it, then assume the duties and responsibilities of the command-level officer or controller until such a time as the situation permits a return of command to out-of-theater command and control.' "

Fenn knew that passage. Fenn loved that passage. It was like poetry to him. Bread and meat. He smiled when it was done, savoring the ridiculous, rolling repetitions of the last line.

Ted was ruffled. More than he had been a few moments ago. "Yeah, well, this wasn't—"

"No. It was. I'm sorry, Ted. It was."

"Say that all to me again."

And Fenn would, word for word. Giving it life this time. Speaking it directly into Ted's eyes. It truly was a miraculous passage. It formed, in a way, the backbone of all the very little that Flyboy Inc. actually stood for, enumerating the difference between it and an actual military outfit. Armies fought to win. Mercenaries fought to get paid. Armies fought because they were told to. Mercenaries fought because they chose to. A soldier or marine might be told to go stand on a rock and die there rather than leave it. A mercenary might be told to go stand on the same rock and then, when his position appeared to become untenable, step off it and live (maybe) to stand on some other rock, some other day. When things on the rock got hairy, the mercenary might become, even if just for a moment, his own commander and the author of his very immediate fate. He could step the fuck off the stupid rock and go home.

After this second recitation, Ted would push back, half a step, twisting his head on his neck as though to get a better angle on Fenn, appraising him like somehow he'd become dangerous because he'd read a book once. Pulling down sharply at the hips of his jumpsuit to straighten its hopelessly muddled lines and then running a thumb distractedly down one of its wrinkled seams, he would ask, "What was it you said to me right before?"

"Before what?"

"Before Lefty went in."

"I don't recall."

"Before you decided to start giving orders."

Fenn said nothing.

"Don't be coy now, Fenn."

"I said, 'Fuck you, Ted.' Just before."

"Right."

"Fuck you, Ted."

"Anger. Spite, maybe."

"Frustration, call it."

"That'll look bad for you, don't you think? When this comes under investigation?"

Fenn would smile then. Gently. Not patronizingly, but still. "It's not like you or I will ever see that investigation, Commander."

"You might be right."

"You know what's coming in?"

"I know."

"It's not like any of us will ever see an investigation."

Out of some pile of himself, Ted somehow found the pieces necessary to straighten up. He stuck out his chin. For a minute, he regained the air of command that Fenn had seen broken out of him by the death of Morris Ross and that bitter instant of surprise when Ted Prinzi's war had gone all to hell.

"You don't know everything yet, Captain. Don't let ten minutes of command go to your head."

And then Ted turned smartly on his heel and stalked back out onto the field. Fenn made a bet with himself: ten dollars that he'd look back, unable to resist some last rejoinder. But he didn't, and Fenn never bothered paying up because it was a sucker's bet anyhow. Ted was a man who either would not, or could not, stop fighting. Missing some vital chromosome or neural connection, he didn't know how to quit. That was what Fenn thought, anyway. And it was something he liked about Ted, but did not envy.

| | | | | | | | | | | | |

Fenn watched the last of the planes coming in as night fell on Iaxo. He saw Carter fall from his plane and wondered if he was wounded— feeling the electric shock in the pit of his stomach telling him to run. To go see his friend. He tamped it down, swallowed the fire, and walked. Carter was okay. He was standing by the time Fenn made it to him.

"Fenn!" he said.

"Kev. Charming dismount you made there. You're going to start a new fashion if you're not careful."

"Fenn . . ."

Fenn laid a hand on Carter's shoulder and shook him a little. Carter leaned his head down and touched his cold cheek to Fenn's cold hand.

"I heard you went down," he said.

"Did." Fenn took his hand away. "Then I got back up again."

"But you're okay."

No. No, I am not.

"I appear to be, yes. Right as rain."

"You're okay."

"You appear to be as well."

"Not everyone else."

Fenn shook his head. "No. Not everyone else."

"But you're okay." Carter reached out for him, touched him, ate at him with his eyes.

"Yes."

"What happened?"

Fenn told him, more or less. He left out the more sticky personal details but transmitted the facts. Bullets, oil pressure, compression, crash. "I'll tell you," he said. "I don't know if I waited five minutes or an hour for Billy. I don't even recall the actual landing."

"Crashing."

"Crashing, yes. I don't remember it. All I remember is the smell."

"Dead indig."

"Dead everything."

Together, they went to their tent. They had a drink. They closed the door and banked the stove and then had another drink. There were deep, bruised circles beneath Carter's eyes. His hands shook for a long time. Neither of them would look out the window. They did not tell war stories.

"I can still smell it, you know?"

"I can smell it, too. It's on you. In your clothes, I think."

"There were brains on my tires, Kev. There was no ground to land on that wasn't full of them."

Carter was tired. He smoked an entire pack of cigarettes, one after another. Outside, they heard shouts. At least one gunshot, possibly two. Occasionally, faces appeared in the tent's window, fingertips parting the canvas flaps. They could never agree on whose face it was because no one looked like themselves anymore and neither of them knew for sure who was dead and who was not, and neither wanted to admit to the visitation of ghosts. When their door was knocked on, neither man rose to open it.

"You should get cleaned up," Carter said. "We both should."

Fenn was taking off his gear, stripping down to his jumpsuit, putting his belt back on. His sidearm. He paused when Carter spoke, then started stripping out of the jumpsuit as well. His skin beneath was pasty and pale, puckered and lined with dirt like spiderwebs wherever his flesh wrinkled. His windburned cheeks, his neck, hands, were all a different shade. Beneath his armor, he was pink like a baby. Fenn stood, naked for a moment, and then went into his footlocker for a sweater. He put on his knickers and his boots. He put his gun belt back on. He kicked the jumpsuit with his toe, then kicked it again until it lay in a pile of spidersilk near the blazing stove.

"I'm not cleaning it. Burn it. Burn the whole fucking thing."

He left the tent and made for the longhouse. On his way, he saw Vic. She asked him about Carter.

"Is he okay?"

"He is. Alive and whole. Walking and talking and dancing around like a real boy."

Vic gave him a look. Fenn didn't much like it.

"I'm not his mother, Victoria," Fenn continued. "Go see him for yourself. Ask how he is."

She dug her hands into the pockets of her oxblood leathers and stood, blocking Fenn's path. Fenn felt his lack of armor, his essential nakedness, in the gun sights of her gaze—cool and clear and unwavering. "Never liked me much, have you?" she asked.

"Never had much of an opinion one way or the other," he said, jinking clear of her, guns-D, and rolling, briefly, out of her field of fire.

"Because I'm taking your boy away from you? Because when I'm around, you've got no one to play soldier with?"

"Take him wherever you like. I don't see as it's any of my business where the boy chooses to put his dick."

"The *boy*," she said, yo-yoing the word, coming down hard on Fenn, and from a high, blind angle.

"Kevin."

"And that's all I am? Someplace for your boy to warm his dick?"

He could taste her on his six, feel the gentle brushes of her viciousness screaming past his undercarriage. "You'd have to ask him that, I think."

Vic seemed to consider this a moment, to hang back and prime her guns. She never took her eyes off Fenn. There were maneuvers going on in her gaze that Fenn could not understand or predict, a deft, probing wildness. "I'm sorry about Lefty," she said.

Fenn just shrugged.

"Charlie, too. Ernie. He was your friend, wasn't he? And George. They took his leg off. Did you hear?"

"It happens," Fenn said, keeping to his line, giving himself a little lag, and waiting for the moment he'd need to displace and roll. "It's a war. Anyway, he's got another."

"What happened to Jackrabbit, Captain?"

He'd missed his moment. She'd been toying with him, waiting to pounce and, in a panic as he felt her rounds strike true, Fenn went into a hysterical split S, desperate, suddenly, to disengage. "She died on me," he said, his chin sinking to his chest, eyes finding pebbles and snowflakes and the gray, indistinct horizon suddenly fascinating. "Very sad."

She was on him still, harrying him to the ground.

"Seems like you're running out of friends," she said.

"All of us are."

The earth rose to eat them both. One last lethal dive.

But then Vic's eyes softened. Suddenly breaking off the pursuit, she broke clear, closed her eyes a moment, then opened them again to clear blue sky. She bit at her chapped lips, white teeth raking over plum. "He loves you, you know. Kevin. You and that fucking rat of his."

"But not you?"

She laughed, sharply, explosively, but just once, carrying her over the perihelion of one of those sweet arcs that, to a pilot, seemed like reaching up to stroke the fringes of the sun. "Not what I've ever asked him for. I'm there for him for something else. The one thing you can't give him."

"I'll say. Seems to be fond of it, too. At least this week."

"No, dummy. He'd fuck you, too, I'm sure. If he was wired that way. His brother was. Did you know that? That something you ever talk about, the two of you? Something before . . . this?"

Fenn said nothing. He lay close to the earth, belly down, and prayed for cloud.

"He just can't talk to you. You can't talk to him. *That* is what I'm there for. And as for the fucking, that's only what he is to me. Gets cold here, you know? I'm warm when I'm with him."

"Well," Fenn said.

Vic watched him. From a great height. There was mercy in her altitude, her god-like view, and in her choosing not to fall.

"Well. There's a nice fire going at the homestead. Very warm. Kev's waiting for you, I'm sure."

Fenn stepped aside and swept a regal arm out to wave her past, the irony of his arrogance a shell around him, thin as a dream. Vic hesitated a moment, still watching him, considering, then shook her head, hunched it down into her shoulders, and rolled past, disengaging, walking on. Fenn went to the longhouse where the survivors of the day were counting bullet holes in the returned planes, making bets on the number. The whole thing had turned into a drinking game. When full dark came on, they put all the lights out from fear. Mostly, by shooting at them until Max reminded everyone about all the aviation fuel, bullets, bombs, acetylene, and other blow-uppable things that were around and how most of them were taking ten or twelve shots to hit an electric light ten feet away.

"Killing yourselves don't seem wise when they's so many other things out there wants to kill you right now."

It'd been Ted who'd started the shooting. Ted, sober and red-faced, sweating, who'd barged into the longhouse, shouted, "All lights out!" and then just started banging away. It was also Ted who'd stopped it.

"Okay," he said. "That was dumb. Fun, though. Everyone stay inside. No idea what's out there in the dark right now. Stay put. That's an order." Then he'd walked out.

| | | | | | | | | | | |

When all was said and done, the planes would all be pulled in, the blackout curtains hung. No lights would be lit but under cover, no fires, for even the smoke, in this terrible, wasting moment, might've been enough—the giveaway that would bring down the bombs, the shells. If the clocks could've been stopped, they would've stopped them. Every whisper came muffled. There was the thought that not even breath could come to any good.

In the night, there was a terror of artillery. Of cannon arranging themselves in the darkness, the green oculi of off-world range-finders registering their precise positions by the glow of cigarette ends or some fingernail sliver of light revealed in the gap of a curtain.

This was ridiculous, of course. Range finders, spotting scopes, night vision apparatus—it could all see just as well in perfect darkness as any-one could in the day and needed no special clues. No giveaways. But the fear of showing light was primal. It was the animal's fear of giving itself away to the unseen predator. And anyway, it was thought that con-cealment certainly couldn't hurt, so some men had run around, extin-guishing all the lights and wetting all the fires and hanging the heavy curtains. Doing something felt better than doing nothing, and in the sudden fear of the dark was something preternatural that none of them had felt for a long time.

In the night there was also the fear of gas—completely unfounded, as it turned out. In the rich, full dark, Carter would be woken briefly by the sound of someone running through the camp shouting it: "Gas! Gas! Gas!" And then this other sound, unmistakable, of a body hitting a body with force, the solid, dull smack and grunt of a well-executed tackle, then quiet.

Carter would turn to Vic at that moment as though to make some small joke or reassuring touch. He would never remember whether she'd been there or not.

This was the night after the day. The sun would set as though it'd been taken to pieces and stowed, and the Flyboy camp was a well of darkness in a place where, come the night, darkness still ruled.

28

VIC WAS THE ONE WHO'D HELPED POOR RAOUL OFF THE FLIGHT LINE when the flames had whipped him and lashed at the delicate skin of his face. She'd been the one who'd put him out—who'd hit him with her shoulder at a dead sprint to knock him down when he went off like a chicken, flapping his burning arm and doing nothing but spreading the fire, then smothered the flames first with her jacket and then an engine blanket when one was handed to her. She'd been the one who, once the flames were gone, had dragged Raoul to his feet and walked him blindly to the mess tent before the shock set in, because she knew that, once it did, she wouldn't have the strength to carry him to the place he'd probably die.

Vic was the one who'd hosed out Billy's fighter. Who'd scraped pieces of George Stork off the throttle handle and seat and flight electronics—wondering at the power of the bullets that'd caught him to be able to spread the bits of him so far and so wide. When they'd all started counting bullet holes in the longhouse, Vic had been there. She'd been the one with the idea to turn it into a drinking game, and then had left, headed back toward the tent line under cover of perfect darkness, had the misfortune of crossing paths with Fenn, then found Carter limping around outside in the cold like some sick, broken thing; cursing at mud puddles and damning tent stakes.

"What are you doing, Kevin?" she asked.

He answered without looking at her, his words soft and slurred. "Cat," he said. "Looking for Cat. I think it ran away and I can't find the poor thing."

"Cat?"

"I promised the stupid thing we could go home, but now I can't find it."

There was, she knew, this fallacy of men at war as being these hard, cold, impenetrable animals, unwilling or unable to feel or to give voice to the agonies that come of making a life of ending lives. And she knew it was untrue. Killing and death didn't make them hard or coarse. They were that way when they arrived—each of them, to a greater or lesser degree. What killing did was turn them into boys again: mindless, cruel, joyous, and insane. They were creatures now without compasses. Without wisdom. Each life they took extracted something from them—a draw of minutes or years which, in the end, offered them a perpetual, terrible youth of pain and confusion that all of them were too exhausted to bother hiding anymore.

Vic hadn't heard Lefty Berthold die. She'd been spared that peculiar window onto death. She'd seen the fireball of him going down. The brief, bright comet of his passing. But that was distant. She'd loaded planes with death, but that was remote, too.

She'd walked Raoul to the mess tent, though. Had half carried him as he shuffled and swore and began to shake; had borne his weight until her leathers smelled of his meat and blood and bits of his flaking, wet, charred skin clung to her hands and her face. That was close. Intimate. She'd held dying close to her. She'd carried it. And when, after setting Raoul down on a bench and backing away from him, she'd absently dragged the back of her hand across her mouth and tasted the salty, smoky, oily wounds of the fire and flesh on her lips? Well, that was close, too. She'd walked purposefully back to the longhouse. She'd vomited in the short grass. With a hand pump and water, she'd sluiced the worst of Raoul off herself. And then she'd gone back to work—patching planes, throwing herself at wounded machines to stop their leaks and mend their tears and get them up and fighting once more.

Now, later, she could still smell Raoul on her. In the darkness, she seemed to move in a cloud of it. And when she came close to Carter, she found that he, too, stank of fuel and oil and cordite and sweat and smoke and fear, so she took him by the hand and led him down to the shower tent. She turned on the blast heaters that she'd designed and built out of spare parts, and helped Carter out of his clothes while the water warmed. When there was enough heat, she stripped off her own gear and pulled Carter to her under the dribbling water, letting it run down over them and wash away the day, the bloody, awful day.

Carter did not speak much. He seemed not entirely sure where he was. When Vic reached up to rub a bar of soap into the tangles of his hair, he tilted his head up into the falling water and let it run in rivers across his face. When she bent, then kneeled, to wash his feet, he at first shuffled away, grunting from somewhere in the back of his throat.

"Shut up," she said. "Let me." And he acquiesced, standing still as stone and staring out at nothing as though embarassed by the intimacy of it, which was ridiculous. The boy had learned nothing, Vic thought. There was no kindness, no acceptance in him. Until she looked up and saw that he was crying.

Vic dried Carter. She dried herself. She helped him to dress and, by the hand, led him back to his tent. Together, they lay in his bed, fully dressed, clinging to each other like survivors to wreckage bobbing in a dark sea. Carter lost his mind for a time, then found it again, then lost it. The fear and the sadness seemed to come over him in waves. The rage. He cursed Lefty and he cursed the company and he cursed Iaxo over and over and over again. He lay, curled up, and held on to her legs, crashing his head into her in frustration until it started to hurt and she'd driven hard, knuckled punches into his neck and back that he seemed not to feel at all. He grew calm and she stroked his head. He talked like she wasn't there, and she listened in silence.

Eventually, Carter faded into sleep. Vic wormed her way free of him. She covered him with a blanket and walked away. Outside the door, she saw Cat sitting, watching her from the dark with its big eyes.

"He was looking for you," she said to the little monster. "Just thought you should know." And then she went back to her tent to mourn her own friend, Raoul, who'd died while she was washing the memory of him off her skin, tracing her fingertips over Carter's hot, wet flesh. He'd breathed in too much fire when the flames had climbed him, thrashing around his face. In panic and shouting, he'd sucked the licking tongues into his own body and, later, he'd strangled in a white bed with his blind eyes bandaged and Doc Edison sitting beside him, waiting to record the precise time of death.

Vic added Raoul to the long list of known dead in her head, but she crossed Carter's name off. She'd thought for sure she was going to lose him today, but she had brought him back somehow. Rationally, she knew it had nothing to do with her. She'd done nothing to allow him to survive this. But she knew what the men called her, how they thought of her. She was the Angel of Death. To gain her attentions was to wear an invisible bull's-eye forever and to have one's forever reduced to a short, finite, but unknowable number of hours. None of that was true. She knew that. She repaired machines. That was all she did. She gave her tenderest affections to those most in need. And if those who were already damaged almost to the point of death failed while under her care? Well, again, that was just math. It was bound to happen. But she gave them time, didn't take it away. Sometimes, rarely, she was even able to make them new again.

In her mind, Raoul felt almost like a sacrifice.

| | | | | | | | | | | |

Hours later, Fenn almost killed Willy McElroy when Willy tried to stop him from leaving the longhouse, catching him just outside one of the small doors as Fenn had tried to slink away into the dark.

"Orders," Willy said. "Ted said no one leaves."

And then, suddenly, Fenn was standing, legs spread, still in most of his gear, holding Willy McElroy off the ground, his hands bunched in the fabric of Willy's filthy jumpsuit, his face nose to nose with Willy's. Willy's head was craning back, pressed against the wood and corrugated ribs of the outside of the longhouse as he twisted to get away from

Fenn's face like he feared being bitten. Fenn was shouting in Willy's face, breathing the fumes of liquor and gun oil onto him. He was going to kill Willy, but he was stymied by the question of how to. With both hands twisted into Willy's armpits, how could he get to his sidearm?

If he'd had a third arm, Willy would've been dead. He didn't, so Willy remained alive. Strange, the vicissitudes of fate. Fenn dropped him instead, turned his back, and walked off.

After that, it'd been Fenn who'd tackled Ted as he ran through the camp, shouting, "Gas! Gas! Gas!" He'd hit him without knowing it was Ted. When he rolled off, Ted had said, "Told him that's what we needed. Gas."

"Told who?"

"Get the fuck off me, Captain. I'm still in charge here."

Fenn had slept in the mess, amid the mess. The bodies and pieces of bodies had all been moved out. The wounded were convalescing elsewhere. He'd tried the field house first, but it was locked. No one was inside. From outside the door, he could hear the radios hissing static. No one to listen through the long reaches of the night.

He'd tried to make coffee, but all the generators were off. The pantry was well-stocked, but there was nowhere to cook anything. He wondered how long it'd been since he'd eaten, and it was long enough that the very thought of food made his stomach turn. There were crackers. Survival biscuits of compressed meal, vitamins, protein powder. He gnawed one of those like it was a bone, and he sat with his head down, cradled in the crook of one arm, waiting for dawn.

It is a terrible thing to know, well in advance of it, how your story is going to end. To harbor no illusions. To have no faith in the miraculous or trust in your own essential cosmic goodness and importance to see you through. Most men, Fenn had decided, believed in something right up until the end. And he'd seen enough endings to have worked up what he felt was a fairly robust sample.

They believed in fate, some of them, or, at least, fatality. They believed in God or some higher organizing principle. Failing that, they believed in the mission or the men or *their* men or the nobility of their exercise. But in almost all of them, buried deeply near the core of whatever *else* it was they believed, was the belief that they were somehow special. That the universe had plans for them that predicated any mean or pointless death before they'd done what it was that they, in their specialness, were meant to do.

And while most men could be merely talked out of their larger faiths, be betrayed by them, broken of them by mere age or experience or hard eureka moments, it would often take some massive shock to the system to jar that one little last nugget of belief loose. To shatter it and show it for the nakedly ridiculous conceit it truly was. Death, Fenn knew, leveled all men. Death removed all illusions.

We are none of us special. We are not loved or looked after. There are no grand designs.

In the primal dark of a primal world, Fenn slept and dreamed alone of nothing.

29

MORNING. The last one.

Carter woke at dawn. There was no siren, but the sun coming back seemed an abomination that needed settling. The first instinct was to kill, as though the stars could be put out just by hating them.

In his tent, Vic was gone. Fenn had never come home. Carter had an instant's fear that everyone had died but him. Worse, that they'd all gone off and left him. That Eddie or Ted had come through with some late Christmas miracle and he'd missed the last ride there was ever going to be. The fear deepened until it became terror. A fist squeezing his heart so that he had to get up and find another human face or die right there in his bed.

So he rose, pulled his jacket on, stepped to the door, and was stunned by the diamond beauty of the breaking light over ice-frosted grass and glittering canvas gone stiff with faintly ammoniac ice. It was beautiful, fragile, gleaming, and terribly quiet. Almost hallucinatory, as though he'd been dosed by something in his sleep that brought out the hard angles and soft interior of everything on which his eyes fell. Head muzzy and full of cotton, he was afraid to step out and leave his dirty boot prints on this strange display of nature's alien perfection.

Looking down the tent line, he didn't see another living soul. He crouched down and ran a palm across a tuft of silvered grass, its gilding of frost melting under his hand. It seemed to him that he'd woken to a world made of glass and had been given the power to destroy it with his touch. The silence was narcotic. The sound of his breath, his heartbeat, the squelch of his pulse were the only sounds in the universe, and he was as alone as anyone had ever been until Lambert, the mechanic, came around the edge of his tent in a filthy jumpsuit and face blackened with oil.

"God, I thought everyone else had died," Lambert said. He had an accent that made him sound like a news commentator. Every word was a pronouncement. From his squat, Carter looked up at him and marveled, slack-jawed, as he grunted out a huff of steam. And even after Lambert had passed on in the direction of the field and the longhouse, Carter wasn't sure that he hadn't just imagined him.

He'd left boot prints in the frost rime.

Carter thought he might be imagining those as well, so he touched one—fitting his hand into the smear in the glaze of ice and considering it for a moment, feeling the odd sizzle of the sublimating ice against his palm.

He stood. He fished a cigarette out of the pack in his pocket, and the sound of the crinkling foil was like a peal of thunder. Squinting down the line, he felt something bump against his ankles and looked to see Cat butting its head against the leather of his boots, scales gone a dirty gray-brown, nails scrabbling at the dirt inside the door.

"Cat," Carter said.

Cat didn't respond. The thing never had, its name meaningless to it like the names of everything else here were meaningless to Carter.

"I was looking for you last night, you know."

Carter reached down and touched the little animal, bumping the tips of suddenly terribly sensitive fingers down the soft fuzz of its scales. Crouching in the doorway, Carter smoked and he stared—watching for movement, feeling for life beyond.

"How long did I sleep, Cat?" he asked, the words so close in the cold dawn that it sounded to him like he was whispering into his own ear. "Forever, I think."

Under his hand, Cat's body was warm like a gun. Carter's cigarette burned down to the filter, and the smell of it was like burning aircraft dope, chemical and sharp and sour, which he didn't like at all. It reminded him of Lefty. Carter looked at the smoldering ember and wrinkled his nose at the stink. He flicked it disdainfully out into the perfect snow.

Under his hand, he felt Cat tense—ready to bound off after it, to play its game with Carter. But then, Cat didn't run. It relaxed instead, opened its little mouth, hissed and spit a couple of times around its bright, needle fangs, then lowered its head, turned, and slunk back to its bed of tattered rags by the door and started tearing at it with a fury.

Carter watched. He felt there was some kind of lesson there. Some indictment or vital message that Cat was trying to get across, but he couldn't figure out what it might be. It was just the day, he decided. Everything felt portentous. He ran a hand through his clean hair, sniffed at the stinging, astringent air, and stepped out into the beautiful, empty world alone.

| | | | | | | | | | | |

Fenn woke before dawn to a quiet like death, like he was the last man alive. He was half-frozen, sore all over from sleeping with his head on a table, his back arched like a cat ready for a fight. There was no coffee. In the night and darkness, someone had come and thrown a musty blanket over his shoulders, but it'd slipped off to puddle around his feet on the cold ground.

He stood and stretched and, for a minute, saw lights sparking behind his closed eyelids like the blooming flares of antiaircraft fire. He had to sit down again. Without his armor on, the cold was even more ferocious and seemed to have leaked inside him as though through a thousand pinhole wounds.

There was just enough light to make out the frayed selvage between land and sky through windows turned into portholes by frost rime— closing apertures of ghostly diffusion, looking out upon a snow-globe world made marvelous by brief peace and the snow's disdain for detail. His breath steamed like a soul continually fighting for escape. In his head, he imagined the smell of eggs scrambling and toast burning and ham in a pan. A pine fire. The blanket joy of comforts, dimly recalled.

The worst of the mess tables was stained permanently with blood that had been scrubbed and bleached from the wood but still showed in dark smears. In the galley, he found a cleaver but felt it inadequate to the task he had in mind. He rooted around until, near an old potbellied stove, rarely used (though, had he known about it, one that would've made his night considerably more comfortable), he found an axe. He applied the axe to the table with some vigor. He tore up cardboard cases once used to hold bags of powdered egg. He pulled splinters from the rough wood posts used to hold up the tent canvas. By the time he was done, he'd worked up a sweat that froze against his skin every time he paused for breath, but had the makings of a decent fire. He piled his fuel, his tinder, his shredded cardboard, in the middle of a space he'd cleared on the floor and lit it with his lighter in ten places. He blew carefully on the guttering flames, coaxing them to spread, then squatted on his haunches, humming distractedly to himself, and waited to see if they would take.

They did. He tried to lift a tin coffee urn from one of the tables at the end of the mess and, when it resisted, tore it free of the wood to which it'd been bolted. His teeth were bared, his muscles full of blood.

He set the urn as close to the fire as he could get it. Inside, it was full of frozen coffee. No telling how many days old. Two, at least. With a stick of broken table, he pushed the fire up around the back of the urn and piled on more wood. When he saw that the smoke was not escaping, he climbed up atop another table and, with a knife from the kitchen, stabbed at the canvas until a tattered hole was born.

"Chimney," he said to no one in particular, then lifted the top of the urn off with his sleeve and saw that the coffee was beginning to melt. Just a few minutes more now.

He went to find a clean mug, powdered creamer, sugar. In one of Johnny All-Around's ice boxes, he found some native ham steaks, already cut. He stabbed one onto the end of a long barbecue fork and charred it over the flames while he waited. He ate it off the fork, pulling bites off with his teeth, burning his cheeks and his tongue. It was the best thing he'd ever tasted, and he grunted with pleasure at nearly every bite.

With a rag wrapped around his hand, he pulled the spigot on the cof-feepot. Coffee poured forth. This made Fenn smile, and he jammed his mug beneath the stream. It was terrible, tasting like smoke and burning plastic and only vaguely like coffee at all. He doctored it with powdered cream and rock sugar that he'd crushed to powder with the heel of a pan, and it was the best coffee he'd ever had. He had two cups. Then he poured a third. Then, with more rags on his hands, he wiggled the urn away from the fire, lifted it, and dumped the contents onto the flames to douse them. There were still embers remaining, however. These, he pissed on—standing at attention, with his back arched and his dick in his hand, staring out one of the windows at the slowly brightening horizon.

This was how he was when he saw the first shooting star arcing across the morning sky. Then the second and the third. He put his penis away, zipped up, and stepped to the door with a warm coffee mug cradled between his palms.

"Well," he said. "Well."

He stepped outside into the snow, leaving virgin tracks in the oblivi-ous whiteness. He walked a ways off across what had been the stubble field, toward the falling stars. Boots crunching the shrouded grasses, he felt the difference when he crossed onto the clipped apron of a runway, and he stopped. He sipped his coffee. He watched in silent reverence the miracles happening above and beyond him.

Silently, men gathered around him. Tommy Hill. Davey Rice, brought back from the dead. Albert Wolfe helped Porter Vaughn hobble over, one foot in a boot of plaster. Billy Stitches, walking as though every-thing were a dream, asked Fenn where he'd gotten that coffee. Fenn handed the cup to him and told him to drink. Max and Johnny and Emile and Lambert. Radio operators. Controllers. Mechanics. Vic drifted in from the longhouse, her glide path still having a hunting edge to it, a stiff breeze making wings of the blue quilted engine blanket she had wrapped around herself like a cape.

Kevin. He came from the tent line to stand beside Fenn and amid the coterie, the huddled remains of the Flyboy Inc. Carpenter 7 Epsilon mission. To stand and watch the gleaming traceries of fire in the sky; to watch with the same mute amalgam of horror, fascination, dread, and sickly, fatalist joy that their arrival had likely inspired in so many lesser creatures before them; to watch as the dropships spiraled down, standing on tongues of flame, and as the cargo containers, like bombs, fell and left their comet trails of smoke and brilliant friction across the bluing bowl of sky that once had been their sole preserve. No need to hide now, to muffle their shining arrival in the sun's cloaking radiance. No fear. No shame. No time left for pussyfooting around.

They watched the bold fireworks of their impending future coming to Earth, and not a man among them wasn't overawed by the display. Not a man didn't shudder and cower slightly—cringing closer to the man beside or behind him—when the sky was split and the dignified silence was shattered by the shriek of jet engines overhead, a wing of aircraft flying in close formation, howling directly past them.

"CB-30 transports," Carter said when it was possible to speak again. "Hundred men or ten thousand pounds. VTOL engines. Good application here. Smart."

Fenn turned to look at his friend. "Kev," he said, "what did you do before you joined the company?"

"I flew those," he said without hesitation, without looking away—shading his eyes and turning to watch the transports recede, to drop their men and machinery somewhere behind the Flyboy encampment. "For NRI. You?"

"I buried my wife and son," Fenn said.

Carter nodded. He said nothing in reply. One of the CB-30s was altering its flight path, executing a long, screaming hook a hundred feet above tree level, skittering across the brightening sky, then standing in the air, reorienting. Carter turned full around to watch it, setting his jaw and staring daggers at it as its blunt, black nose seemed to search for him, sniffing for his scent on the frozen air.

"Fuck you," he said under his breath. "Come get me."

The scramble siren started to blow. The men standing, watching, tensed at the sound, but they did not run. They'd lost the want, but not the reflex. Behind them, in among the tents, there was some action. Bodies moving. Sounds of activity. The camp waking to a new reality.

Ted appeared around the corner of the mess tent, stalking toward the knot of men in his perfectly pressed uniform blues, cleanly shaved, his eyes hard as flint. After finally getting around to some long-overdue business last night, he'd slept like a baby—not long, but deeply and with peace like a stone. His dreams had not been haunted. He'd done the things he needed to do. And when he'd woken, the entire world had taken on the cold, pure aspect of his imaginary white room. That was his gift. When he shouted, his voice carried the entire length of the field.

"You all gone deaf? That's the fucking siren."

No one moved. As Ted drew closer, they could see that he was smiling. Among certain of the men, this inspired more panic than anything else on that strange morning.

"Into the longhouse. Everyone. Now."

No one moved. The lingering CB-30 began to make a slow approach toward the infield of the Flyboy camp. Prowling. In the distance, booming could be heard. Followed shortly by whistling that became shrieking. Followed shortly by the beautiful, perfect, frozen ground some distance from the standing men and their ramshackle tents and misery erupting as though being vomited upward explosively.

"Longhouse!"

Now, the men moved. The CB-30 dropped its nose and laid on speed. The pilots, the mechanics, the controllers, and Ted all ran. Fenn ran. Carter ran. It became a race between them. By the end of it, they were laughing, and together they both slapped hands to the corrugated skin of the longhouse.

"We're bugging out," Ted shouted. "We're going home."

The transport was bucking up, its nose rising, engines howling, its assault ramps dropping even before it began to settle to the earth. More explosions shook the ground. They were closer, but still not close.

"Those guns are ranging," Ted said.

"Whose guns?" someone asked.

"Does it matter? Everyone pick a friend. No one gets forgotten. No one gets left behind. The minute that bird touches ground, we get on."

Carter grabbed Ted's sleeve. "That's an NRI transport," he shouted.

Ted pushed Carter away. He stumbled back but did not fall. "No, idiot. That's a mercenary transport that just happens to be under contract to NRI. I offered him a better deal."

"What deal?"

"Money. Gold. Whatever he wanted. Mostly a chance at seeing to-morrow. The marines are inbound, and this guy didn't feel like spending ten years in a colonial prison."

Carter turned back to watch the ship. "I know the feeling."

Fenn crossed his arms and looked at Ted. "What about the other two transports?"

"Going to pick up Garcia, Connelly, and his men. That crazy fucker doesn't need to die here either." He smiled back. It was all fake teeth and power. "Read that handbook you mentioned last night, Captain. Lots of interesting stuff in there."

Outside, the massive transport deployed landing skids and thumped to the ground. Out of the swirling snow, shapes of men began to emerge, running from every direction. The longhouse was empty in an instant.

Carter ran beside Fenn, the two of them pounding their feet on the frozen ground, feeling their hearts already lifted, already under the press of gravities of acceleration. A long time ago, Carter had said that when their ride finally came, he would be the first man aboard, bulkhead seat, and he pushed himself to make that come true—stretching for it with Fenn just over his shoulder, matching him stride for stride until Carter felt like he was airborne already, skimming the icy earth, flying without a plane. He understood that none of them were going home. That was ridiculous. But they were leaving this world, moving on to some next one, and that, on this morning, was enough. There was nothing left here for them on this rock. Their war was over.

The gaping, black maw of the transport yawned before him—dark metals, hard angles, steaming with the furious transitions from the cold nothing of space to the inferno of atmospheric translation to this frozen dawn on Iaxo. A wall of steel and molybdenum and ceramic, ticking and groaning like a groggy animal, an assault ramp for a tongue, its mouth open and waiting to swallow them whole. Somewhere high above them, hanging like a mote in the sky, there would be a guild carrier or freighter—two hundred million tons, under delivery contract to NRI through a series of increasingly esoteric shell companies, its belly full of supplies, ships, and faithful all being pushed out into space, birthed into darkness for the long fall to the surface. Carter wondered what they'd been told this time. What inspiring words they'd been offered as they'd loaded into their transports while some man like the one Carter had once been went through the formalities of drop prep and protocol. He wondered who would be scrubbing the blood and piss and stink of fear and dying out of the cargo bay now, in his place. He thought about Oizys, Vega, where he'd dropped NRI volunteers to fight the loggers. He thought about Frogtown, where NRI had tried to throw its protestors against the Colonial Marines and Carter had been shot down, beaten, arrested, becoming an unwilling martyr for millions of little frog-baby aliens—more valuable then to his masters than he'd ever been at the stick of an aircraft.

He wondered about the pilot of this transport. Some idiot kid like he'd been, veteran of Luna, Bloemfontein, and the battle camps of Washington Free State, now having been offered the best deal he was ever going to get by Ted Prinzi: one small betrayal in exchange for gold enough to effect an escape. It was the deal Carter'd never been offered—the one he would've jumped and danced and killed for. One lucky break and things might've all turned out so differently for him.

Eddie had told them—him and Fenn—that this was their only chance. That night when they'd gotten him drunk and watched him cry. He'd said there were emergency orders, a stock of hard currency set aside for just such an unlikely eventuality. No chutes for pilots, but one big golden one for management. He'd said all they could hope for was one pilot willing to pull their asses out of the fire when it all went wrong. And then Ted had gone and found three.

Eddie and Ted were supposed to be the only ones who'd known about this fail-safe. And now there was only Ted. When Carter'd left his tent this morning, in mortal fear already that he'd been abandoned, he'd gone to the field house because the field house was where the comms equipment was and the comms equipment was supposed to be manned continuously. He'd found the door locked. Inside, he'd heard only the whistle and static of equipment—no voices, no signs of human occupation or industry.

He'd kicked the door in. Convinced now that something had gone terribly wrong while he'd slept, Carter had barged through the door, meaning to get on the gear himself and call home, call for help, call someone.

He'd found Eddie's body in a heap on the ground near the FTL relay, shot twice—once in the chest and once straight through the lovely, thousand-watt smile. Carter'd gagged, turned away, then walked out onto the field and seen the men gathering. When he'd spied the first entry flares skittering across the sky, he'd understood. He knew what was coming. He knew that his fear of being abandoned, buried here, left behind, had merely been premonition. He knew that they were all leaving together. All who were left, anyway.

Another shrieking barrage of artillery shells tore up the ground, plowing up the far cross where B and C strips touched and marching near enough that their concussion wave twisted the walls of the machine shop and blew hot, black grit rattling along the skin of the dropship with a sound like stones shaken in a tin can.

Carter slowed. His boot touched the steel tongue of the ramp. He could smell warm plastic and lubricating oil rolling out from the cargo compartment. He stopped. Fenn burst past him, boots ringing on steel, then stopped. He turned around. Shouted Carter's name.

Carter thought of Frogtown. He thought of that sweet moment, lifting free of gravity.

Fenn darted back down the ramp to where Carter stood, one foot on steel, one in the mud. Emile pushed past him. Diane. Some mechanic he didn't know. Fenn was shouting.

"Kevin!"

Carter looked up. "I've got to go back," he said.

"No. We're going home, Kev. Now."

"Cat," Carter said. "I forgot Cat."

Fenn grabbed him by the shoulder.

"I promised Cat."

Carter ducked the punch he knew was coming. Twisting free, he turned and ran for the tent line.

Fenn did not follow him.

Fenn had run, keeping pace behind Carter the whole way by stamping his own boots down into the prints Carter left in the melting frost. As the black bay of the transport loomed large before them, he felt the runnels of hot water—snow melt and condensing atmospheric moisture boiling on the black skin of the ship—splashing his head and shoulders. Suddenly the frost was gone and Fenn found himself running alone.

He stopped, looked back, saw Carter slowing and, doubtless, thinking of something stupid. He got this face on him when his brain was working, Carter did. This face like he was chewing the fat of a steak he was no longer interested in eating. Fenn knew this face too well. This was the face Carter was wearing now.

Fenn darted back down the ramp to the martial tune of crumping explosions that made his ears ring and the castanet rattle of tortured earth being blown against the hot skin of the ship. Carter's foot was touching the ramp, but he was looking back over his shoulder at something. Fenn reached for him.

"None of that now, soldier," he yelled, forcing a tone of lightness into his voice, a jocularity he did not feel. Carter appeared not to hear him. Or not to care. Bodies pushed past them. Fenn didn't register the faces. He slapped at Carter's shoulder and tried again. "There's nothing out there for you!"

Nothing.

"Kevin!"

Carter looked up. "I've got to go back."

"No. We're going home, Kev. Now."

"Cat," Carter said. "I forgot Cat."

Fenn grabbed him by the shoulder.

"I promised Cat," Carter said.

In their two years of living together, Fenn and Carter had fought only once. Actually come to blows just one time. A lot of this, Fenn knew, was forbearance on his part. Kevin Carter was a difficult man *not* to punch most of the time.

But only once had Fenn lost control of himself. They'd been throwing a party in their tent—a half-dozen pilots off the roster for the night,

Ted, Vic. It'd been a booming good time, but Carter had gotten very drunk and very loud about his feelings about the aliens. Iaxo's natives. Any aliens, really.

"Aliens," he'd been saying. "Indigs, abos, anything that isn't us. Why should I care? We kill them. It's our *business* to kill them and their mothers and their babies. Like bugs. They're a nuisance. We kill them because they're in the way."

Billy had argued. Ted had said no. That wasn't it at all, and maybe Carter ought to put the bottle down and just shut up for a while.

And Carter had wheeled on him. Carter had asked what he knew about it, flying his desk in and out of combat all the time, and how long it'd been since he'd thought about how much killing they'd done since arriving here. "However many, it's not enough!" he'd yelled, and then turning to Fenn for support, had said, "Tell him, Fenn."

Nonchalantly—meaning only to cool things down—Fenn had stretched out in his chair, rolled his head on his neck, and said, "Well, I don't know about the mothers and the babies necessarily, Kev."

And Carter'd said, "I've seen you fly, you liar. You'd kill a hundred alien babies if they were in your sights. You're just like me!"

Fenn had hit him then, uncoiling out of his chair like a spring and slamming a fist into Carter's ear. Carter had gotten his hands up, but it didn't matter. Fenn was strong. His punches were like thrown hammers. And he wasn't ever sure what'd set him off, exactly. The dead babies, or that Carter thought the two of them had anything in common at all. It hadn't mattered. Fenn had beat him down to the ground, mounted him and beat him unconscious, then beat him some more until, finally, Ted and Vic and Billy and George Stork and some others had pulled him off, pinioned his arms, held him against the horrible weight of his rage. And Fenn had wondered as he stood, gasping for breath, wanting only to kill Carter because Carter had mentioned babies to him and Fenn had already buried one baby and never wanted to think about it again, whether or not, in that moment, Carter had been right. Maybe they did have something in common after all.

Fenn swung at Carter on the ramp. He was still strong. His punches were still solid. All he wanted now was to save Carter—to knock him down, drag him aboard, belt him in. But Carter wasn't drunk this morning. He was quick and determined. He ducked the punch and ran.

Fenn did not follow him.

| | | | | | | | | | | |

Carter ran. In the smoke and haze of gray and white, he made for the tent line by dead reckoning—working off an internal compass that he hoped was still functioning.

He'd seen Cat this morning. He'd talked to Cat. He'd watched Cat tear into its bed of rags by the door and, he hoped, that was where he would still find it. Loud noises never spooked the thing. Gunshots, airplane engines—it was accustomed to furious action and loud sounds. Carter told himself that Cat would still be there. That it *had* to still be there. He'd made a promise, and he wasn't leaving this place without the one thing on it that he'd never had any urge to kill. The one thing worth saving.

One thousand yards. He ran blindly through the smoke and, with artillery shells bursting behind him, saw the dark outline of tents rising up before him.

| | | | | | | | | | | |

"Counting off!" Ted bellowed over the clamor of voices and rasping of belts and crying of the wounded.

Fenn hung by the door, one foot still on the ramp.

"George!" someone yelled.

"He's here. Carried him," someone else answered.

"Raoul?"

"Didn't make it."

"Who's missing?"

"Eddie."

"Jack? Has anyone seen Hawker?"

"Carter," Fenn said, not loudly enough for anyone to hear.

"Captain?"

Fenn turned and saw Ted standing close to him.

"Carter's still out there," he said.

"Then he'd better hurry," said Ted.

"What about Eddie? I didn't see him come aboard."

"He died valiantly defending the FTL relay from the enemy," Ted said with a shrug. "Brave man."

"I'm sure he was," said Fenn.

Vic pushed her way to the open door and shouted, "Pilot is getting nervous. There's infantry headed this way. Where's Kevin?"

"Coming," said Fenn. "He had to do something."

"Do what?" Vic still wore an engine blanket around her shoulders. She looked haunted by something worse than dying.

"I'm not sure if he knew."

When she tried to bolt, Fenn caught her. When she screamed, he just pretended he couldn't hear.

| | | | | | | | | | | |

Carter came through the door of the tent like a spy—quietly and carefully, not wanting to spook Cat with sudden movement. He had a plan, if he could find the little monster. He snapped a blanket from his bed and kicked through Cat's nest. He found a sock balled up on the floor, threw it into a corner, and shouted, "Get it, Cat! Kill it!"

Cat had been hiding under the cold potbelly stove. Carter saw only the streak of movement headed for the corner, but he leaped after it, holding the blanket out like a net. When he hit the dirt, he heard Cat howl and felt the thing scrambling in sudden blindness.

Carter scooped Cat into his arms, wadding up blankets around it, trying to protect it and himself at the same time. He tried to speak comfortingly but found that everything came out as a scream. Explosions made the earth move beneath him and made the tent's poles bow above him. He existed now in a bubble of violence—the sweet candy center of a world going entirely to shit. He struggled to his feet, gathering up folds of blanket like trying to scoop water with his hands. Cat's head popped out the top of the bundle and snapped at Carter's throat.

"You're coming home with me," he said. "We're going now."

And then he ran—out of the tent, off in the direction of the infield where the transport had been. Over the ringing in his ears and the thudding of walking artillery shells, he heard big, vectored thrust engines roaring up a scale that seemed to have no crescendo. The pilot, he knew, was warming for lift, cycling up those massive alcohol-fueled engines, anticipating takeoff. He wondered if everyone else was aboard yet. It did not occur to him that they would not wait.

With Cat clutched tight to him like a baby, arms folded protectively around it as it squirmed, Carter retraced his steps. The smoke and dust swirled around him, seemed to acquire some organizing principle, then were suddenly sucked to tatters as Carter heard the gearshift thunk of engines being locked into place.

He ran faster, in a panic now. The engine noise plateaued in a scream like the world ending, and as the fog was torn from the ground, he saw the wreck that things had become.

The airstrips had been obliterated. The longhouse was twisted, burst in the middle, and it spilled broken, burning planes like toys left scattered by an inattentive giant's child. One of the shipping containers that had been left in the infield was upended, stuck into the dirt like a dart and curled like a broken finger. The field house, final resting place of Eden Lucas, was burning. The mess—the Flyboy O Club—had been blown over, and the tables and gear now sat naked and tumbled in the grass. And above it all hung the sleek body of the dropship—like a black eagle sitting on the columns of its jet wash, a huge, dark god come to settle the messy affairs of its mischievous offspring.

"There!" Vic shouted. "He's right there! Tell him to bring it down!"

Billy, still half in a daze of painkillers, jerked for the radio switch and slurred at the pilot to bring it around and down. Their last man had been spotted. In the open door, Fenn held on to Vic with one arm wrapped around her, his other hand holding the safety bar. Ted stood like an officiant behind them. Inside the compartment, the lights went red. The pilot had just enough time to say, "Hold on!" over the PA.

| | | | | | | | | | | |

Carter didn't hear the explosion that flattened him. It was that close. One instant he was looking up, raising one hand to Vic and Fenn and Ted standing by the still-open loading door and hanging ramp. The next, his vision had acquired an entirely new angle and a red haze of blood.

The transport was yawing. The shell hadn't hit it, but it had impacted on the ground beside Carter and close enough that there was now something wrong with the starboard engine. It was blowing black smoke, having sucked too much shrapnel and dirt and fire into the intake. From his back, he watched it twisting in the sky—wounded but still airborne. He watched it bow to him, dipping a stubby wing, and rotate so that he could see Vic standing in the doorway, an engine blanket around her shoulders, whipped in the wash from the engines until it looked like wings spreading above and behind her. She reached out a hand for him as the pilot frantically tried to recover his craft and put on altitude.

And Carter, still clutching Cat to him inside the blanket, opened his mouth to say something—to say, *Stay,* to say, *Go,* to say, *Come back, please. Don't leave me. I'm sorry.*

All that came out was blood.

EPILOGUE

AFTER ACTION REPORT:
TAG 14-447
Report Key: **FINAL**744B4RC3-AA001-C7EP3365
Tracking Number: 33-447aaa
Attack Code: None
Originator Group: FBLE-NODISPERSE
Updated by Group: FALSE
SigAct: **PRIVATE AND CONFIDENTIAL**, EYES ONLY, MGMT.
DO NOT COPY. DO NOT DISPERSE.

NAME/STATUS:

Acevedo, Simon P.	Missing, Presumed Dead
Anquiano, Edison M.	Missing, Presumed Dead
Ballinger, Patrice M.	Missing, Presumed Dead
Berthold, Louis H.	KIA 14-447 C7ep
Bishop, Lori R.	Missing, Presumed Dead
Carter, Kevin H.	KIA 14-447 C7ep **(see note 3)**
Czerwinska, Alicja	Missing, Presumed Dead
Derosiers, Bryce L.*	ExFil 90/365
Diaz, Daniel C.	KIA 14-447 C7ep
Forsyth, Noemi R.*	ExFil 90/365
Galambos, Soma	Missing, Presumed Dead
Gottlieb, Roger R.*	ExFil (Medical) 42/365
Habib, Emanuel A.	Missing, Presumed Dead
Halstrom, William J.	Missing, Presumed Dead
Hardman, Emile H.	Missing, Presumed Dead
Harper, Shun L.	KIA 14-447 C7ep

Hawker, Jackson M.	Missing, Presumed Dead
Hill, Thomas J.	Missing, Presumed Dead
Jordaan, Deviser S.*	ExFil 90/365
Khoury, Stephen A.*	ExFil 90/365
Komatsu, Miu L.*	ExFil 90/365
Lambert, Rudolph W.	Missing, Presumed Dead
Lucas, Eden H.	KIA 14-447 C7ep
Marsh, Chloe D.*	ExFil 90/365
McCudden, James L.	IN CUSTODY (see note 2)
McElroy, William R.	Missing, Presumed Dead
McRae, Juan R.*	ExFil 90/365
Meleuire, Stavros F.	Missing, Presumed Dead
Moller, Eric A.*	ExFil 90/365
O'Day, Ernst R.	KIA 14-447 C7ep
Pan, Sheng W.	Missing, Presumed Dead
Petty, Maxwell B.	Missing, Presumed Dead
Prinzi, Theodore R.	IN CUSTODY (see note 2)
Rice, David M.	IN CUSTODY (see note 2)
Riviera, Raoul M.	KIA 14-447 C7ep
Roberts, John C.	Missing, Presumed Dead
Rockwell, Castor S.	Missing, Presumed Dead
Ross, Morris V.	KIA 14-447 C7ep
Serdikov, Victoria G.	IN CUSTODY (see note 2)
Solvay, Mikke B.*	ExFil (Medical) 329/365
Stork, George R.	Missing, Presumed Dead
Tanner, Yoshi P.	Missing, Presumed Dead
Teague, Fennimore A.	Missing, Presumed Dead
Vaughn, Porter M.	Missing, Presumed Dead
Voss, Charles A.	KIA 14-447 C7ep
Williams, John S.*	ExFil (Medical) 404/730
Willis, Diane R.	Missing, Presumed Dead
Wolfe, Albert X.	Missing, Presumed Dead

*Engineer team (Derosiers, Forsyth, Jordaan, Khoury, Komatsu, Marsh, McRae, Moller) all **ExFil** at 90/365 Zulu, via Cavalier, as ordered. 3 Medical ExFil (Gottlieb, Solvay, Williams) as previously recorded.*

NOTE 1: *Due to the evolving situation on the ground at Carpenter 7 Epsilon, all personnel lost during the attempted exfiltration of operation Carpenter &c will be listed as Missing, Presumed Dead until such time as our legal department makes a decision as to the most advantageous or nonliable permanent classification. To the best of our knowledge, all contractors (excepting those separately named: see notes below) not given prior, official KIA status (see attached certs., Eden Lucas, dec.) were aboard a single CB-30 ATGV ("Newkirk") under OOC license (see attached invoice, ref: Theodore Prinzi, Cmndr) when said vehicle was damaged during takeoff by non-impacting ground fire. This fire disrupted ATGV Newkirk's flight characteristics, causing flare and rotary damage to the right lifting engine. ATGV Newkirk was able to lift but suffered a catastrophic right-engine failure after approx. 30 seconds of low-altitude flight and experienced a high-velocity ground interaction. Point of impact was 4.2 miles WNW of base area and extraction point. All aboard (excepting those named separately, as above) were killed on impact or received fatal injuries, with remains either recovered or identified on-site. Witness statements are currently coded SHRED, CONFIDENTIAL. Remains disposed of IAC.* **No formal notices are to be made at this time.**

NOTE 2: *4 members of operation Carpenter &c (McCudden, James L., Prinzi, Theodore R., Rice, David M., Serdikov, Victoria G.) were recovered alive at or near ATGV Newkirk's point of impact. All 4 are currently in custody of the Colonial Marine Third Expeditionary Unit and being held as unlawful combatants, location unknown. The seizure of personnel has been confirmed by statements from Third MEU, legal affairs, and private contacts.* **It is the company's current position that operation Carpenter &c was acting in conflict with stated company regulations, and without executive orders.** *We are claiming no formal knowledge of any actions taken by McCudden, Prinzi, Rice, and Serdikov. Final status of the 4 persons named above will be decided by oversight panel.* **No action is being taken at this time.**

NOTE 3: *Carter, Kevin H. was not aboard ATGV Newkirk. Witness statements (see Serdikov, CLASSIFIED attached) place him on the ground at the time that ATGV Newkirk received fire, being wounded in the face,* *neck, and upper-right quadrant by the same fire. While it is highly likely that these wounds were fatal, no body was recovered from the base area or exfiltration point. No remains were found during subsequent searches of the area.* **Carter, Kevin H. will be classified KIA 14–447 C7ep, pending recovery or new information.**

ABOUT THE AUTHOR

2009, LAURA SHEEHAN

Jason Sheehan is a former dishwasher, fry cook, saucier, chef, restaurant critic, food editor, reporter, and porn store employee. He was born and raised in Rochester, New York, and though he has since fled the Rust Belt repeatedly, he still harbors an intense fondness for brutal winters, Friday fish fries, Irish bars, and urban decay. As a young nerd, he fell hard for *Star Wars, Doctor Who,* William Gibson, Roger Zelazny, and the spaceship-and-raygun novels his father would leave on his bedside table. He dreamed of someday befriending a robot, stealing a spaceship, and wandering off across the stars in search of alien ladies and high adventure. Since that hasn't happened (yet . . .), he now writes about it instead—which is almost as good. And yet despite all this, his mother still kinda thinks he should've been an orthodontist.